LIKE NORMAL PEOPLE

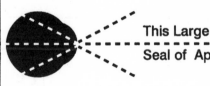

This Large Print Book carries the
Seal of Approval of N.A.V.H.

LIKE NORMAL PEOPLE

Karen E. Bender

G.K. Hall & Co. • Thorndike, Maine

Published in 2000 by arrangement with Houghton Mifflin Company.

G.K. Hall Large Print Core Series.

The text of this Large Print edition is unabridged.
Other aspects of the book may vary from the original edition.

Set in 16 pt. Plantin by Anne Bradeen.

Printed in the United States on permanent paper.

Library of Congress Cataloging-in-Publication Data

Bender, Karen E.
   Like normal people / Karen E. Bender.
     p. cm.
   ISBN 0-7838-9301-9 (lg. print : hc : alk. paper)
   1. Mothers and daughters — Fiction. 2. Mentally handicapped
women — Fiction. 3. California, Southern — Fiction. 4. Missing
persons — Fiction. 5. Large type books. I. Title.
PS3552.E53849 L55 2000b
  813'.54—dc21   00-046112

*This book is dedicated to my mother and father,
to Ardie, and, of course, to Robert*

Acknowledgments

Many people have helped me in my journey writing this novel, and I would like to acknowledge some of them here.

I want to thank my parents, Meri and David Bender, for believing in my work absolutely from the first moment, and for deeply valuing creativity in our home; my grandmother Ardie, for being a model of elegance and strength; my tender yet mighty sisters, Suzanne and Aimee, for their stalwart support; and my cousins Michelle Plachte-Zuieback and Natalie Plachte White for their encouragement and warmth. I want to thank my exuberant in-laws: Frances, Stanley, David, Perrin, and Sean Siegel, for their enthusiasm about my work. And thanks to Jonah for simply being an incredible baby.

I am enormously grateful to Ursula Doyle, who took a chance on an unknown writer; my agent, Eric Simonoff, for his patience and kindness and faith in my work; and my editor, Janet Silver, whose visionary edits helped me see this book in a new way. Heidi Pitlor and Frances Apt provided stellar editorial assistance. The Rona Jaffe Foundation gave me financial support at a crucial juncture, and the following people provided invaluable encouragement at various times: Eric Wilson, Marlene Marks, Meg Wolitzer, Bill Henderson, Lois Rosenthal, Rose Marie Morse, Katrina Kenison, Kathy Minton, Meghan O'Rourke, Kathleen Warnock, and everyone at the Writer's Voice.

My deepest thank you to Myrtle Mandiberg, for understanding who I wanted to be.

Many thanks to the following friends and readers who saw drafts of this novel at various stages and offered clear, useful insight: Cynthia Bosley, Hope Edelman, Alyssa Haywoode, Elizabeth McCracken, Martha McPhee, Max Phillips, Mark Svenveld, and Holly Wiseman.

And much appreciation to the following friends for listening: Julie Rose, Lucy Rector, Tim Bush, Jenny Shaffer, Evan Elliot, Katherine Wessling, Elisa Williams, Elizabeth Cohen, Norma Varsos, Randi Glatzer, Anne Sikora, Amy Feldman, and Susan Lasher.

Three people, especially, have been crucial in helping me write this book: Margaret Mittelbach, whose thoughtful advice and humor were a constant comfort; Jennie Litt, whose passion for the project pushed me forward and whose high standards were continually inspiring; and, most of all, my husband, Robert Siegel, who read every word of every draft with great insight, whose presence is in every one of these pages, and who understands all of me. His love is my great piece of luck.

One

It was seven-thirty in the morning when Ella Rose, clad in her pink satin bathrobe, walked across her Culver City apartment, turned on the pert voices of KNX Newsradio, and sat down at her kitchen table, ready to write her morning list.

Ella's wooden table was dwarfed by her bulky kitchen appliances. Her table was now always set, elegantly, for one: a single lace napkin, a straw placemat, her favorite crystal glass. Ella put her pad and pencil on the placemat; she began her list with the date.

On her refrigerator, her daily calendar was turned to the page: September 23, 1978. LENA ANNIVERSARY was written very neatly in red ink.

Ella did not remember when she'd last changed the day on her calendar; she wasn't sure that today was, in fact, September 23. She reached over to her black phone on the kitchen counter. Picking up the receiver, she looked into it and then hung up. She lifted her thick Los Angeles Yellow Pages beside the phone; the book fell open as though exhausted. Placing her finger on an ad, Ella took a deep breath and carefully dialed the number. "Santa Glen Hardware," a girlish voice said, and yawned.

Ella sat very still. In a quiet, polite voice, she

9

asked, "What day is it?"

Silence. "Santa Glen Hardware," the girl announced, a bit more forcefully.

"September twenty-third?" asked Ella, her voice sharpening. "Miss? Is it September twenty-third?"

"Who — Brett, what day is it!" the girl yelled. "Some — what! Twenty-*what?* Okay. Twenty-third. Hello? It's the twenty-third. Can I help —"

"Thank you," Ella said, and hung up.

Ella wrote SEPTEMBER 23, 1978 across the top of the page. She could hear the sounds of morning lifting off Pico Boulevard: produce trucks roaring like huge bison and birds cawing, sad, repetitive, from the trees.

On the pad, Ella wrote:

1. WISH LENA HAPPY ANNIVERSARY. Or perhaps, since Lena's husband was dead, this was not a good idea; she erased it and started again.
1. SEE IF LENA REMEMBERS ANNIVERSARY.

2. TELL MRS. LOWENSTEIN — What. Mrs. Lowenstein, the director of Panorama Village for the past two years, had called several times this week, each time describing Lena's latest misdemeanors with perhaps unnecessary detail. For twelve years, Lena and Bob had occupied Room 129. Ella had moved them into the residence when Lena was thirty-six and Bob forty-four. She had watched the two of them wander in, the babies of the place, her daughter's red hair shining like a poppy among the silver hairdos. Lena and Bob had always been on good be-

havior; Ella believed they had many friends.

Ella remembered why Lena was supposed to stop smoking and wrote this down: SMOKING IS NOW LIMITED TO CERTAIN ROOMS AT PANORAMA VILLAGE.

Why did they have to limit it anyway? What small joys did Lena have?

3. BUY LENA GUM.

No — her teeth were almost gone. 3. BUY LENA HARD CANDY.

4. BUY L NEW SLIPPERS. SIZE SMALL.
5. BUY L CHAPSTICK.
6. CHECK L TOENAILS. CUT.
7. CHECK BATHMAT IN LENA'S TUB.
8. CHECK FOR GLASS IN RUG.
9. CHECK FOR FOOD SPILLED IN ROOM.
10. CHECK LENA HAS SOAP. DOVE.
11. CHECK FOR ANTS.
12. CHECK FOR RUG STAINS. COVER THEM.
13. CHECK LOCK ON DOOR.
14. CHECK THAT WINDOWS CLOSE AND OPEN.
15. CHECK FOR

She tried to think of other points of danger in her daughter's room. With no further ideas, Ella amended number 15 to

15. CHECK ROOM.
16. VON'S.

Number 16 was a reminder for herself. Her hand was trembling slightly, and she put her pencil down.

She stood up, opened the refrigerator, and peered inside. Ella had lived alone here for three years, since Lou's death, and she was still not accustomed to a refrigerator that held only items that she liked to eat. At the moment, her refrigerator held two cans of V-8, half a roast chicken, a carton of Mocha Mix, a pint of low-fat cottage cheese, most of a box of See's candy — some of the pieces with one bite taken out of them — an ancient container of Parkay, a large bag of Oreos, and a plastic container of matzo ball soup. She kept a package of beef jerky, one of Lou's favorite foods, in the butter compartment. It comforted her to leave the jerky there, and she harbored a secret hope that she might open the compartment to find that the package had disappeared. She had vowed not to eat it herself, but last night she had missed Lou terribly and had tried a few of the dry, salty strips while she watched television. When she went to bed, her mouth tasted like his.

Ella picked up her pad and wrote on a second page:

17. JERKY.
18. BANANAS.
19. BALONEY.
20. BREAD.

What should number 21 be on her list? She closed her eyes, trying to remember, but her mind was dark. The content of number 21 was just another bit of information she had lost. And two weeks ago she had found in her closet a scallop-sleeved, eggplant-purple polyester dress that she was certain she had never seen before. The dress hung, limp and arrogant; it seemed to have blown in, of its own volition, to join her other dresses in the middle of the night. Ella tried very hard to remember when she had purchased it. She took the dress from the closet and placed it on her bed, wondering where it had come from and wishing it would go away.

22. TALK TO VIVIEN ABOUT LENA.

Her younger daughter's name had floated on and off Ella's lists for the last year or so. She often wrote it with the best of intentions but then crossed it out.

This was what Mrs. Lowenstein had told her in their conversations over the last six months: Lena had left her room at midnight and tried to get on an RTD bus. Lena had been caught in the 7-Eleven down the street, her pockets heavy with stolen cigarettes. Lena had demanded to use the office phone and had dialed a strange number; she had ended up calling Singapore.

The phone rang. Ella set down her pencil and picked up the phone on the fourth ring. "Hello?" she asked. She was very still. "Yes, this is Lena's mother."

Ella's brown Buick floated in front of Vivien's house. The broad ranch-style homes were similar, built on a tract; her daughter's lawn was the only one aglow with red roses, and to Ella it looked as though the flowers were being readied

13

for some exciting event. She didn't know exactly why she had come to Vivien's first, except that she needed company; Mrs. Lowenstein claimed that Lena had set fire to her room at Panorama Village, and Ella did not know how to handle this.

Her granddaughter Shelley was on the front lawn. Shelley was twelve years old and was sitting so quietly that Ella almost missed her; Shelley was staring at the empty street with a fierce expression.

Ella parked the car and got out. Shelley stood up and rushed to her eagerly, as though she were running downhill.

"Honey, where's your mother?"

"Out."

"Your father?"

"Out."

"You're all alone?"

This must have been the wrong question. The girl looked lost on the patch of lawn, as if she'd just dropped there from the sky. She shrugged violently and nodded. Then she examined Ella. "Why are you all dressed up?"

Ella had spent a half-hour selecting the right dress for her conference with Mrs. Lowenstein. After much deliberation, she had settled on a deep green silk dress with shoulder pads, her most recent acquisition from Bullock's. She had paired this with faux diamond earrings, which matched a star-shaped brooch. On her feet were her bone pumps in Italian leather. Lou had developed a theory that important people wore light-colored shoes, because this showed that they did not care if their shoes attracted dirt. "You buy shoes that show stains," he told Ella, his eyes large and philosophical. "You can afford to get them cleaned."

"There was a fire at Panorama Village," Ella said. She tried to say this in a calm voice. "The director said Lena set it."

Shelley's face woke up. "A real fire?" she asked. "How big?"

"It was in her room." Ella tried to remember what else Mrs. Lowenstein had said. "Lena's fine." Mrs. Lowenstein had sounded saddened by that fact. "They only needed two fire extinguishers, and the fire affected only one corner of her room. The wall. Maybe the rug. There was some water damage to the floor." Her voice surged on, trembling; perhaps it would be better to stop. "Now. I just wanted to see if Vivien would like to come —"

"I will."

"You'll what?"

"I'll come!" Shelley ran toward the Buick, pulled open the door, and slipped into the front seat.

Ella remembered that there was a rule about Shelley's going to Panorama Village, but she couldn't remember what it was. Her grand-daughter had visited Lena and Bob every Saturday for the past year or so. During her nightly calls, Lena had told Ella mysterious facts about

15

these visits. "Shelley thought it would be fun to swim in a pool filled with lemonade," Lena reported happily. Or, "She came at twelve-thirty and left at four-eighteen. She wore a blue leather cap." Lena's voice was breathless when she described the visits, and had a boastful edge.

Ella did not know what to make of her twelve-year-old granddaughter's choosing to spend so much time with her retarded aunt and uncle. Neither did Vivien. "You should see what she wears to visit them," Vivien had told her in a wondering voice. Shelley never told anyone what she, Lena, and Bob did together. A puzzled aide, who had helpfully spied on them for Ella, told her that the three of them wandered around the same two blocks; occasionally they visited Sav-on. Lena, Bob, and Shelley looked forward to the visits. "Have a nice time, Lena," Ella would say. "Make sure you take good care of her."

Shelley had stopped visiting Lena after the accident several months ago.

Ella walked over to the car; Shelley was already belted in. "She's waiting for us," she said. "Let's go."

Ella did not want to drive down to Panorama Village by herself. She got in and they rode through the hills, furred and golden with chaparral, to the San Fernando Valley. It was the beginning of the day. The light seemed brighter, older, as they passed into the valley; the gauzy gray mist separated to reveal the sky burning hard and white overhead.

16

When they arrived, Ella and Shelley sat on orange plastic seats in the lobby, their faces set in similar, alert expressions, as if they were entertaining versions of the same thought. The sun fell in pale, dusty strips on the gritty linoleum. They waited for Mrs. Lowenstein to bring Lena to them.

Usually at nine on Saturday, there were few human sounds in the lobby; most of the residents were still sealed in their dreams. But this morning they had been awakened, and most of them clustered, buzzing, in the hall.

Ella observed the residents wandering through the lobby. One woman turned to her with a weird, frothy smile; Ella realized she had toothpaste in her mouth that she'd forgotten to spit out. One lady was sitting with her legs apart, in a nightshirt; her hairless vagina resembled a large pecan. There was also a dapper-looking gentleman who sometimes emitted a deep bark.

Ella was glad to have her granddaughter sitting beside her, but she deeply wished Lou were here. Not that he had come with her often when he was alive — Lou had mastered the art of leaving Lena's problems to her. But now, in her mind, he became extraordinarily helpful. She closed her eyes and imagined him sitting beside her in his navy linen suit, his aftershave smelling sweet and aquatic. He would be brimming with schemes to bribe Mrs. Lowenstein. "Let's give her a lifetime store discount," he'd murmur. "Any shoes she desires, fifty percent off. Or just cash. Three

17

hundred, plus damages, no questions." He would be so enamored of his plans, the fire would seem a bad joke, another crooked dream.

Ella had also considered ways to prevent Mrs. Lowenstein from realizing that her daughter might be a budding arsonist. Right now, Ella had a strategic box of See's candy on her lap. She kept a few boxes in her apartment for such emergencies. She looked at the box with longing, wondering whether she could steal a candy without Mrs. Lowenstein's missing it.

Shelley was tapping her hand against the chair, as though she were secretly playing music to accompany the residents' slow movements. When she noticed her grandmother looking at her, she immediately stopped tapping and folded her hands firmly in her lap. "Let me ask you," Ella whispered. "How do we know any of *them* didn't do it?" She scrutinized the crowd aimlessly milling around. "That man. With shaky hands. Now wouldn't he drop a match, more than Lena would?"

Shelley looked at the man. "It could be him," she offered. "They could be framing her."

"Lena's too nice a person," said Ella. "They know they can get away with it." The two of them observed the residents, most of whom looked too worn out to plot a conspiracy.

"They can't kick her out," Ella said. "She needs her routine. She likes the red Jell-O." She sat up straighter. "They've all done bad things. It doesn't matter if they're a hundred. Some of

18

them get away with it." She gripped the box of candy. "Do you think she'll like nougat?"

"Who?"

"Mrs. Lowenstein. She likes candy."

Ella noticed Shelley's puzzled expression and quickly covered the candy box with her purse. "People like to be appreciated," she said. "They regard you in a more respectful way."

She adjusted her shoulder pads, hoping she looked a little like a general. She wished she had asked Shelley to change her outfit before coming here. The girl's arms were skinny as a child's in her tank top, and her denim shorts were frayed. But she did not seem concerned about her appearance. She gripped the bottom of her chair as though trying to keep herself from shooting through this place; Shelley also seemed grimly attached to the chair, as though afraid of what, let loose, she might find.

"You know," said Ella, "appearance is the first thing people see about you. Then they get to know the real you."

"I look fine," said Shelley, brushing some lint off her tank top.

Ella removed a small brush from her purse. "Fine for sitting on the lawn," she said, "but not for a fire." Gently, Ella began to brush Shelley's hair. The girl arched up, like a cat, into the brush strokes. The aides, glistening in their white nylon uniforms, were clearing the residents. They did this tenderly, like angels separating clouds. Shelley and Ella sat and waited for someone to claim them.

Mrs. Lowenstein was coming toward them with Lena. They were walking arm in arm, like a celebrity with her escort, down the fuzzy, fluorescent hall.

Shelley jumped up. Ella had hoped that Shelley would walk beside her, in a dignified fashion, but the girl shot ahead. Ella fumbled with her dress and then rose and followed Shelley, her heels clicking on the linoleum.

And here was her daughter, coming toward her with such breathless force that she broke free of Mrs. Lowenstein; it was Lena all alone, hurrying toward Shelley. She was wearing a new peach-colored cotton housecoat, covered with daisies, that came from Lane Bryant. Ella could see the price tag poking out of a sleeve. Her cherry-red sneakers didn't quite match the housecoat. Her fine short hair, glinting with rusty gold, looked pretty in the light. She was running her fingers down her hair, a gesture Ella recognized as an attempt to brush it.

Mrs. Lowenstein stepped into a doorway and began talking in Spanish to an aide. When Ella reached Shelley and Lena, she saw how happy they looked; they were touching fingertips and talking excitedly.

"I made a fire!" Lena exclaimed. "It smelled bad." Her arms were powdery with ash.

"Shhh!" said Ella, glancing at Mrs. Lowenstein. "Don't say that." Lena's palms were grimy, and she was making a mess out of Shelley, too. Ella dug a Kleenex out of her purse and began to wipe Lena's palms; getting her cleaned up was the first order of business. Lena reeked of fire and Thrifty's Intimate perfume.

"It was an accident," whispered Ella, hoping. "It was an accident, and thank God you're all right." She carefully wiped her daughter's fingers. They did not appear to grow old with the rest of her; they were chubby and pink and seemed to promise a great future. "Now, what happened? Tell me —"

With her free hand, Lena brought one of Shelley's palms to her face and kissed it noisily. "You don't come to see me anymore."

"I wanted to," Shelley began. "But they —"

"You're here," Lena said. She patted Shelley's hair as though it were a towel she was using to dry wet hands. "Today is a special day."

"Fine," said Ella. "Now what —"

"You can't say it's not!" Lena shrieked.

"All right!" said Ella. She tucked the dirty tissue into her purse. "Honey, you can't go around saying you set a fire. It's not going to make you lots of friends —"

Shelley stepped up to her grandmother with the demeanor of an irate lawyer. "I would like to take my aunt out for coffee," she announced.

"Coffee?" asked Ella. "Twelve-year-olds don't drink coffee."

Shelley tried to stand taller, as though that would help. "Doughnuts," she amended.

"Just down the block."

It was a ridiculous request, but Lena and Shelley were urgent in their desire to be taken seriously. Ella noticed Mrs. Lowenstein turn toward her. "All right," she said quickly, "Go. Whatever. But come right back." They ran down the hallway, urgent as two salesmen on an important mission. They went around a corner and were gone.

Mrs. Lowenstein, a heavy woman in her forties, seemed to have been born in a boxy navy suit; Ella thought her appearance too official for her role in Panorama Village. Every time Ella saw Mrs. Lowenstein, she wondered whether the woman had some secret job — perhaps selling insurance. This thought helped Ella maintain a healthy skepticism toward anything the director said about Lena, especially anything she didn't want to hear.

"Mrs. Lowenstein," said Ella, standing up and holding out the candy box, "I've brought you a present. I was surprised to hear what you said this morning and —"

"Ella, you didn't need to do that," Mrs. Lowenstein said, somewhat sharply.

Ella continued to offer the box. "I know you like nougat. I asked them to put extra in."

"Okay, okay," said Mrs. Lowenstein. "Thank you." She took the box and led Ella into a small room, where she seated herself on a couch and indicated that Ella do the same.

"Now," said Mrs. Lowenstein, "we need to talk."

"Yes," said Ella. "Certainly."

"I just called Vivien. Let's wait to discuss everything when she arrives."

Ella was startled. "Vivien? I'm sure she has plenty of other things to do." She tried to laugh. "I would be happy to talk about it now."

Ella knew exactly how to fix Lena's life; it was what she had done for forty-eight years. Vivien was busy with her husband, her children, her work. She would be included in the discussion about Lena when Ella found it necessary. Mrs. Lowenstein, apparently, had broken that unspoken rule.

Mrs. Lowenstein glanced at her fingernails, which were polished a clear flesh color. It seemed to Ella that if Mrs. Lowenstein wanted to polish her fingernails that plain color, she should not polish them at all.

"Why don't we wait?" said Mrs. Lowenstein. "Why don't you take a look at Lena's room?"

She got up and walked quickly into the lobby. Ella remained on the couch. What had she done wrong? Why didn't Mrs. Lowenstein want to speak to her alone? Ella wanted to make clear that Vivien was to be called only at her request. The sun flushed fiery against the windows. Outside, in the garden, the pink gardenias and birds of paradise looked brutally healthy, reaching up into the morning light.

Ella watched as the director placed her hand on a resident's shoulder. It was a gesture of sickening delicacy. Clearly, Mrs. Lowenstein had a grudge against Lena or against the retarded; perhaps she had had bad experiences with fire. Ella wanted to rush up and accuse her of prejudice. Instead, she headed down the long hall to Lena's room.

The hallway was so familiar to her she felt as though she were not walking down it of her own accord but was being carried down its length. The doors on either side were marked with large gold numbers. Some of the doors were ajar, and Ella saw rooms filled with shadows. Each one had a TV turned up high, with a game show host shouting into the room. Ella caught glimpses of faded flower arrangements, stuffed animals with wide grins, a bouquet of metallic red balloons lilting in the air conditioner's low whir. The rooms were festive in a shabby, hopeful way.

Ella paused before Room 129, where Lena and Bob had lived. She had been here hundreds of times over the past twelve years, bringing Kleenex, Q-tips, Chap Sticks, Hershey bars, new bedspreads, posters, plastic bowls, aftershave, toilet paper, various brands of shampoo. She'd brought combs, plastic sunglasses, toothpaste, toothbrushes, Nivea, Tic Tacs, Sucrets, Band-Aids, suntan lotion, and sunburn cream. For twelve years, Ella had walked down the hallway carrying her white plastic bags from Thrifty's and Sav-on. Each time she approached this door, she could feel herself become a useful person. Each time, she could feel them waiting for her.

Two

A side door opened at Panorama Village, and Lena and Shelley gingerly stepped outside. They soared through the alley, which was gray with the morning's shadows; raw tendrils were about to unfurl themselves from the moist brick wall.

Shelley had never run this way before — with all of herself and toward nowhere. Her legs stretched out, loose, before her. Lena ran with the fury of a toddler, flat-footed, straight-kneed. She followed Shelley in crooked arcs from one side of the road to the other, her arms ape-loose, her palms slapping parked cars.

The stores flashed by in a blur: the stern plaster genie atop Carpeteria, arms folded, surveying the boulevard; the Toyota dealership with its rows of glittering cars. To Shelley, streaking by, it was all jeweled, magnificent.

They slowed, and Shelley listened to the gentle, curving sound of their breath. Lena was gasping, hands on her hips. "Where are we going?"

Shelley had no idea. "Farther than one block."

"I want to play the game," said Lena. "Start now."

A large, beaten-up RTD bus turned the corner. The air rose raw and cool in Shelley's throat. The bus stopped, and the doors opened. A merry expression flickered across Lena's face.

"I dare you," Lena said, and hopped on the bus.

In all the times Shelley had played the game with Bob and Lena, they had never reached another place. They had walked a couple of blocks one way or the other, but they'd never gone far. Now, Shelley watched her aunt get on the bus and give the driver her fare. It was an action both startling and natural, as though Shelley were observing someone else's curious dream. She'd never in her life seen her aunt get on a bus. It occurred to her that Lena should not ride the bus alone.

She leaped on to the stair, dropped some coins in the fare box. The bus grunted and roared down the street. Lena hurried to the back, and Shelley sat beside her. The seats were a dull silver vinyl, patched with rubbery black tape.

Lena surveyed the passengers. There were seven of them. She sat very straight, looking around proudly. Then her face melted with concern.

"Where are we going?" she whispered.

"You're the one who got on."

"Oh." Lena picked at her lip. "I think I left something in my room." She scrubbed her dress back and forth over her knees and glanced around the bus, her scrubbing becoming more frenzied. "Shelley!"

The bus rolled up the ramp toward the freeway.

Lena bit her lip. "I forgot something," she said, and gently touched the seat.

Shelley had fallen in love with Lena and Bob when she was ten years old. It began in her parents' garage. That was where, every night, she sat on the concrete floor by the silent cars and jugs of detergent, holding the phone on her lap and listening to the voices leap toward her, hushed, eager in the dim light.

Apparently there wasn't much to do in Panorama Village after dinner, so Lena and Bob would call Shelley's parents two or three times a night. Her mother always took the first call, carrying the phone under one arm as she set the table or made scrambled meat on the stove. Shelley wondered what Lena said to her mother, for Vivien listened to Lena's day fully, with all of herself. It was different from the way her mother listened to anyone else.

Half an hour later, the phone would ring again. "Hi, Lena. What's new?" her mother would ask. This time, she might set the receiver in the fruit bowl while she fumbled in the refrigerator, letting Lena talk for a few minutes to the apples and pears.

Lena's third call often followed by less than a minute. Now Shelley's aunt was picking up steam. Her mother's goodbyes became peppy, enthusiastic. "Hi, honey! Got to make dinner now! Bye!"

One night, there was a fourth call and then a fifth, and that was when her mother decided to hand the phone to Shelley. "Here, Aunt Lena wants to speak to you," she said.

"Me?"

"She asked especially for you."

Shelley was flattered that Lena had asked for her. She wanted to talk in private, so she carefully took the phone into the garage. It was just off the kitchen, but the watery brown light made it seem far from everyone else. Sitting, chin to knees, on the cool floor, she looked into the receiver.

"Hello?" Shelley said.

A confused silence crackled between them. She knew, instantly, that Lena and Bob had not asked for her. Their breath, thick, anxious, floated over the line.

"Hello. I had a good dinner," said Lena. "Meatloaf, mashed potatoes, green beans."

"I had the same," said Bob.

"We had to sit by the window. That man, Harvey, took Bob's favorite seat," said Lena.

"I wanted to punch him," said Bob, "but he's ninety-five."

"You always want to punch people," Lena said, "but they're always too old to punch."

Their voices were a little quick, tumbling over each other, as though they wanted to impress Shelley, even if they had not asked for her. This made Shelley lean into the phone, trying to give them something in return. "I had lunch with

Wendy today," she offered, "but she switched to sit with Marjorie halfway through."

"Why?" Lena asked.

"She didn't say why." Shelley had tried not to look at the girls all through the lunch period, but when she did glance up, she saw them sweetly conversing, their foreheads almost touching. It was awful to see.

"Well, I hate her," Lena said decisively.

"Me, too," said Bob.

"She should sit with you. You're the best lunch person!" Lena proclaimed.

Shelley was surprised. "Why?" she asked.

"You just are," Lena said.

Shelley opened and closed her mouth, unable to think of an answer. Her heart felt like a pitcher of cream, brimming, all the cream about to pour out.

"Thank you," she said.

From then on, she regularly took Lena and Bob's second call. Sitting on the cool cement floor of the garage she would listen to them talk.

They had many complaints that they wanted to air. Sometimes Harvey took Bob's favorite seat, or Warren did; sometimes Jessica, a neighbor, wanted to borrow too many cigarettes. Sometimes the vending machine was out of Lifesavers, or the bingo game looked rigged. Other times, they reported their accomplishments. "I won a purple soap shaped like a rose because I was a good trash picker-upper," said

29

Lena. "It smells very nice."

It took a while for Shelley to learn how to listen to them. Both Bob and Lena spoke quickly, and their voices swerved, unsteady with excitement. Occasionally, she offered solutions to their problems, which they seemed to appreciate. "What about just giving Jessica two cigarettes and telling her no more?"

"Oh," Lena said solemnly. "Okay."

The calls took only ten, fifteen minutes. Each moment was like a raindrop, glittering and full. Shelley tried to picture Lena and Bob sitting in their bedroom as they talked. Her mother had brought them souvenir snowdomes from the family vacations to Lake Tahoe, the Grand Canyon, places Lena and Bob would never go. The snowdomes were arranged on Lena's dresser in a carefully prescribed order: snow scenes in back, beach scenes in front. As they talked, the twenty snowdomes would be luminous; the unmade bed would be sinking under Bob's and Lena's weight. Their three voices floated, strong, disembodied, through the darkness. Every night, Lena and Bob asked for her.

Shelley's voice grew larger when she talked to them, as though the words that revealed her true self were unfurling in an enormous place. When she hung up, she would sit in the garage for a moment, feeling a hard strength in herself. It was not what she experienced in her regular life.

This was the year she had stopped. She had

done so with great suddenness and mystery, and she did not understand why. Around this time, her mother and father had begun to speak to her in a sort of code. Sometimes their discussions felt unfinished, their words half-breath and unformed.

Her father was the rabbi at Temple Beth-Em, a Reform synagogue. He was a tall man, always bursting with energy out of his faded suede jackets as he walked around the temple grounds, saying hello to people. He had an eye for troubled people, new perspectives on God, and clever ways to raise money. The synagogue always needed money. Her father would walk with her through the building, pointing out the places that needed repairs: the worn carpet on the *bima,* a security system for the windows after a burglar broke in. He was always full of plans to fix everything that was wrong. There were fairs and talent shows, and debates with other rabbis and pastors from neighboring churches. Her father would ask Shelley to help at the fund-raising events. "You're the first child of the temple," he said. "You're going to help bring in the dough."

She loved it when he called her the first child; it set off a tiny explosion of light in her chest. As they walked around, talking of ways to improve the place, she would slow down, forcing her father to set his loping pace to hers, so that she could make the moment last a long time.

She had jobs at the temple fairs. One involved selling tickets. Each time she sold a ticket, she would tell a joke to the customer, hoping that would make people buy more tickets. She believed she was successful when they laughed, though it could not be a fake laugh. After the fair was over, she would sit with her father, adding the receipts. "Four hundred and sixty-seven dollars!" he might announce; she would see the pleasure in his face and wonder whether her jokes had helped.

But that year, at the Purim Fair, she did something new and reckless. She and a couple of boys from Hebrew school had come up with a secret deal for their tickets. The boys were named Jason and Danny, and their lips were so red, it seemed as if they were wearing lipstick. They had strong brown hands, and their T-shirts smelled of detergent and sweat. Sometimes they played tag during a break, and she loved the thrill of the air between them as they ran after each other.

Their plan was simple: each boy would buy a ticket and she would slip in a third for free. Stooping by the box to tear off a couple of the salmon-pink slips, she realized that the tickets were worth whatever she deemed them to be. It was a thought that made the sky seem ready to burst open. When the boys leaned forward and took the tickets, the three of them giggled. "Thanks," Jason and Danny said, but she did not look at them, for her action bound her to them in a private new world.

When she had finished selling tickets, she wanted to get away from the table; her hands felt tingly, as if she'd been holding fire in her palms. Jason and Danny had disappeared, which was all right. She had given away a free ticket, and she wanted to run and run. She banged into a group of kids from the after-school program. Often she entertained them by doing a series of flips on the steel gymnastic bars. Today, she was so pumped up, she said she'd do fifty for them. "Everybody count," she told them, and their sweet young voices rose in the air.

Usually, she wore pants when she did the flips, but that day she was wearing a dress. Whenever she turned over, the dress cascaded over her head, and she felt the cool afternoon on her legs. Her underwear flashed by during each flip, but it was a good, free feeling. The little kids were counting. She was at forty flips when her father walked by.

He came over and put his hand on her arm. She froze. "I want to talk to you for a second," he said.

He walked with her to the far side of the field, cleared his throat, and gazed over her head. "Sweetheart," he said, "you shouldn't do that anymore."

Her heart picked up. "Do what?"

"In a dress. Do flips." He touched his hand to her shoulder.

She waited for another accusation; there was none. "Why not?"

He laughed, a short, confusing sound. His dark eyes were strangely sad. "Just trust me." His jacket sleeves looked too short on his arms. He shoved his hands in his pockets and walked away.

She felt broken off, alone, watching her father leave; she wanted to confess to a million things all at once. The kids were calling "Fifty! Fifty!" When she returned to them, they looked up at her, waiting, but she was silent. She didn't know what to say.

Her mother had her own kingdom; she taught classes at Waltz with Vivien, a ballroom dance studio in Culver City. One of Shelley's favorite activities was to help her mother in the practice sessions, when the students got ready for competitions around the state. These students were big, grand girls with golden dyed hair and oily bosoms. Their partners were thin-armed boys with silken mustaches and hair parted down the center. Shelley, in sneakers and old jeans, stood in, at the rehearsal, as a place marker for anyone who was absent; that was her job.

One day, after the session, Vivien rummaged through her costume bag, found a tunic studded with rhinestones, and slipped it over her daughter's head. Shelley looked down at herself, sparkling. Her mother circled her, examining. "You want to show off this cute body," she said. "Let me show you some steps."

Her mother was the man. Holding Shelley around the waist with one arm, she clasped her hand with the other, and began to move, as though through syrup. She tilted Shelley's chin with her hand so that the girl lifted her throat to the air. "I'll lead," her mother whispered. "You're stepping on diamonds. Let your shoulders make music. Glow."

Her mother's words were hushed, but they were brimming with something enormous. Vivien led her across the floor in a step-two-three, arms steely, full of purpose, and Shelley realized that she had been waiting a long time for her mother to ask her to dance. "Imagine you're dancing with Donny Osmond," Vivien said. "Or you're dancing with Andy Gibb . . ." This idea seemed especially odd. Shelley did not know how to describe the glitter in the air when she ran between the boys at Hebrew school. The sureness of her mother's body made Shelley's heart a little hard with fear; she was sure she would never be as beautiful.

"Now," said her mother, and suddenly swung her down into a dip. Shelley was staring up at the auditorium ceiling the way the big girls did, the way her mother did when she demonstrated a step. Whenever she'd seen the students dip, their faces seemed to ache, as though they were tasting caramel. She could imagine them all doing flips on the jungle gym, over and over, slowly, naked, for everyone to see.

"Drip rubies from your fingers," Vivien whispered now. "Go."

Shelley's arms felt stiff as a puppet's, and finally her mother raised her up. She squeezed

Shelley's shoulders and peered at her as though she were blurry. "Almost," her mother said.

They kept trying. Her mother held her gently, but her grip became looser, as though she did not quite know how to hold her now. At last, they stopped. "Next time," her mother said, but she did not make the offer again.

Later, when her mother drove them home, Shelley stared at her pale hands on the steering wheel. It was astonishing that her mother and the other women could live in such private versions of themselves. Suddenly, the streets seemed infinitely dangerous and full.

Shelley had stopped. And this became worst of all when she was left behind by her friends and they became her former friends. They moved on to their new selves in junior high school, and she was left watching them as though through a pane of glass.

Her former friends were a gang of girls with whom she had hung out in elementary school. They were named Denise, Wendy, Tracy, Lisa, and Tami. She could count on them to get together every Sunday afternoon to ride their bikes or play elephant tag. But once they moved to junior high, everything suddenly changed.

On the first day of junior high, Shelley spent half an hour looking for her friends. The school was large, fed from elementary schools all over Los Angeles; it was like being in a brand-new city. Finally, she found them sitting around a cafeteria table, but she did not recognize them at first. Each girl had drawn lines of blue on her eyelids, and each was wearing a camisole top and a thin cotton skirt. No one had told her that they had planned these outfits.

She sat beside them, but it was clear that she was not part of them anymore. They spoke in darting, urgent whispers, erupting into laughter that sounded like shrieks of pain. Their old selves had been discarded, forgotten. Some new and magical truth seemed sealed within them, remote and inaccessible to her.

It became a true loss when she called them and they had become busy. If she called on a Friday afternoon at four o'clock, they'd already made plans, and these plans excluded her. They seemed to know of a crucial calling time, and she had missed it and would never learn what it was. "Sorry," they'd say, their voices airy. "We have plans." She tried calling at different times — three o'clock on Thursday, eight on Wednesday, but it was always the same.

She began to hate Sundays, the long hot stretch of time when she sat alone in the dull glare of her front yard. Sometimes she'd walk quickly around the block as though she, too, had exciting plans and was off somewhere; she'd try not to stare at her friends' houses to see what was going on inside. But she had no plans. That was when she decided to visit Lena and Bob.

Lena had come up with the same idea. "I think

you should come see us," Lena said during a phone call one evening. "We can get a cup of Coca-Cola from the 7-Eleven. It has little square pieces of ice."

For Shelley to get to Panorama Village by herself would involve a forty-five-minute bus ride over the San Diego Freeway. It would be like going to another state. She got hold of an RTD bus schedule and studied the complicated document. Each arrival and departure time seemed to have been selected for some important and mysterious reason: 10:21, 9:54, 5:16. After many phone calls, Lena and Bob and Shelley decided that she should take the 11:23 bus.

She didn't confess that she was afraid of the trip. But she liked listening to Lena persuade her. "I'll give you three Lifesavers," said Lena. "Four if you're really nice."

"Soon," Shelley said.

And she had to tell her parents. When Shelley handed the bus schedule to her mother and told her of her plans to visit Lena and Bob, her mother examined the bus schedule critically, as though it were a passport to an unfamiliar place.

"You really want to go all the way out there?" she asked.

"I think so," Shelley said.

"Well," said her mother, "you'll have to call us when you get there. You'll have to bring lots of spare change." Then she smiled. "But they'll be so thrilled to see you." And it was that last part that convinced Shelley, that unburdened sound in her mother's voice.

One day she got up and did it. She went out the front door of her house, walked across the lawn, and waited at the bus stop for the 11:23 to the Valley. When the bus pulled up, she got on and asked the driver whether he stopped at Mango Boulevard; magically, he said yes.

She was eleven years old. The greasy, clattering RTD bus took her to this new place. She was proud of being the youngest unaccompanied traveler on the bus; she did not count the children and toddlers because they were with their mothers. The whole ride, she sat up straight, her eyes open, alert. For forty-five minutes, every person was a stranger — the tan blond boys clutching skateboards, the maids in white uniforms, the elderly, bluish men. Not one of them knew anything about her, and as the bus rolled down into the San Fernando Valley, she felt released from a pain she did not know she had held.

The bus turned down Mango Boulevard, and she saw Lena and Bob pacing the sidewalk in front of Panorama Village. They walked close to the curb, as far from the home as possible — far enough so that they could feel the rush of air from passing cars, but close enough so that an aide could keep them in view. Bob wore a lime-green T-shirt that glowed in the bone-white sun. As he walked, he held his arms, like Marlon Brando, away from his sides. Bob and Lena seemed not to notice each other and to notice each other absolutely; when they passed each other, they brushed hands lovingly, and they stubbed out their cigarettes at the same time.

The bus windows were tinted gray, but Shelley imagined that Lena and Bob, staring at the bus, saw her sitting there like a little god, and she felt their gladness leap up in her own heart.

As she stepped onto the street, her aunt and uncle embraced her; their soft arms gathered her in. They had dressed up for her visit. Lena wore her pink plastic cow barrette, which dangled from her rusty gold hair. Bob had splashed on some aftershave lotion, and the air around him shimmered with the scent. The three of them stood on the bleached and empty street, feeling like the most important people in the world.

Lena bent toward Shelley and whispered, "I have something important to tell you."

"What?"

"I lost another tooth."

Shelley wasn't sure how to react to this. "Let me see."

"You don't really want to see."

But she did want to see, absolutely; she nodded.

Lena bent her knees slightly and opened her mouth. It was shimmery blue and red like an oyster and was almost empty. Shelley looked longer than necessary; it was as good a place to look as anywhere else.

"You're supposed to brush your teeth," she said.

"I forget," Lena said.

"You need to try," said Shelley. She liked the authority in her voice. "Twice a day."

"I like the tooth," said Bob. "I want it."

Shelley laughed. "What for?"

He shrugged. "I want a piece of her," said Bob. He had gorgeous, pale blue eyes that, had he been a fish, would have allowed him to see through lightless water. "Why?" asked Shelley.

He dug into his pocket and brought out a handful of tiny gray chips. "I like to carry her around with me," he said.

They walked down the sidewalk, under the valley's barren, hazy sky.

"What do we do?" asked Lena.

"What do you usually do?"

"I don't know. Walk around."

They all seemed deflated by this.

"Let's play a game," Shelley said.

She was thinking of one she'd watched at school. Ten boys and girls sat in a circle under a lilac tree and whispered urgently to one another as petals fell on their hair.

"Dare," said one boy and whispered something to her old friend Wendy. Wendy got up, walked across the circle to another boy, bent over, and kissed him. The boy lifted his face to hers as though he had been waiting all his life for this moment. Their cheeks hollowed as they kissed. The others watched in a silence that was almost holy. Then Wendy stepped back and returned to her place.

Each person responded to a different dare. One girl stood up and lifted her shirt, revealing, for a second, her pale, soft breasts. One boy applied lipstick to his mouth and then rubbed it off. The others observed in silence, then burst into laughter at the end. When lunch hour was over and the group dispersed, Shelley lingered in the area, the site of so many brave acts.

She outlined the game to Lena and Bob without describing the specific content of the dares. "You do something you're afraid to do," she said. "Everyone else has to go along. You can't make fun of anyone. You can dare anything you want."

They stood on the sidewalk like three little birds perched on a branch. "I'm first," said Bob.

He smacked his open palms against his hips, feet together, thinking. "Grab the chairs," he ordered.

"Which chairs?" Lena squealed.

"I dare you," he murmured. "The patio ones. Grab them. Put them under this tree."

There were six nylon-web folding chairs on the home's patio facing Mango Boulevard, each marked, in black, DO NOT REMOVE. Bob bounded onto the patio, Shelley and Lena behind him. Holding a folded chair over his head, Bob dashed toward the magnolia tree, and Lena and Shelley followed and set their chairs under the tree.

They were breathing hard; they had done something very brave. A sparrow's song pierced the air. They looked up into the thick, vanilla-scented spread of leaves, the white diamond cracks of sunlight. Bob spread his legs as though he were sitting on a velvet recliner.

"Why did we do that?" asked Lena. Shelley was grateful for the question.

"Here," he said. "It's a special spot. No one can take our seats."

"What now?" asked Lena.

"Your turn," said Bob.

"I have to think." Lena closed her eyes and concentrated, biting her lip. Then she reached into her pocket and brought out a Reese's peanut butter cup.

"I dare you to eat this pie I made," she said.

Shelley and Bob looked at the candy. "Eat it with good manners," said Lena.

This was a more difficult dare. They had to believe the candy was a pie and that Lena had baked it. Bob removed a plastic comb from his pocket and sliced the candy into three pieces. "It took a long time to cook," bragged Lena. "I had to put it in a teeny pan."

They balanced the pieces on their palms and looked at Lena. "I dare you to be a lady and gentleman," Lena said. "Watch your manners. Chew with your mouth shut."

Shelley closed her eyes and tried to believe she was eating a piece of pie. She did not understand why Lena wanted this to be a pie she had made, or why she wanted them to be polite as they ate it. But she followed Lena's instructions. When

43

she was done, she opened her eyes. Bob had been neat, too; the only chocolate smears were on their hands. Lena wiped these with a Kleenex. "You see? You did it," Lena said. Her eyes were proud. "You ate it all up."

Now it was Shelley's turn. Walking back and forth on the pale ribbon of sidewalk, she tried to think what she could ask of them.

Here were the stucco apartment buildings, the dry lawns, the parking lot that spread out before Sav-on. Because she had come here by herself, everything looked beautiful and new. The pastel apartment buildings seemed to be delicately frosted with peach icing; the dried-out lawns were gray as ice; the asphalt parking lot sparkled like a frozen black sea.

Shelley drew a sharp breath, because she wanted to be as magnificent as everything around her. She turned toward Lena and Bob reclining on the plastic chairs. Lena was delicately licking the Reese's wrapper, and Bob had spread his legs wide, as though trying to fill every inch of the seat.

"I dare you," said Shelley, slowly. "I dare you to give me a name."

They stared at her. "What kind of name?"

"A name for a great person." She almost laughed, listening to herself, but she meant it. "A name for someone you'd admire. A name you wouldn't give to anyone else."

They whispered to each other while Shelley paced the sidewalk.

"We have one," Lena said.

She walked over to them. The sun was hot on her hair.

"Sequina," said Lena.

"Sequina?" she asked.

"It's shiny," said Lena. "Like you."

Sequina. It was a beautiful name.

"I dare you to call me this name," she said. "Only you two are allowed to say it."

They stood up, delighted, and poured toward her, their arms outstretched. Sequina. Your name is like your barrette. Sequina. We named you. Sequina. You are here.

Every Sunday, they played the game. Each generally focused on a different kind of dare. Bob often dared them to find special places. He once made them sit in an empty fire escape on the first floor of a nearby apartment building, Sunset Towers. Even though they had to crouch, knee to knee, in the cramped space, they had a good view of someone's white-carpeted living room and an intriguing pair of clear acrylic spike-heeled shoes. Another time, he took them to the Toyota lot across the street and made them sit in an unlocked 1977 model; Bob took the driver's seat, Lena the place beside him, and Shelley stretched out in the back. They spent a couple of hours here, humming songs they imagined they'd hear if they could turn on the radio. Finally, a mean salesman said, "If you're not buying, you'll have to get out of the car."

Lena dared them to learn some of her many skills. One day she showed Shelley how to put on perfume. Lena stood in front of her bedroom mirror, held out her sixteen-ounce economy-size bottle, and sprayed her Intimate perfume on her hands, her hair, and — delicately — her shoes.

"Now you," she said to Shelley. She arranged Shelley's hand around the bottle, and, together, they did a practice squirt. Shelley squirted perfume on her wrists and throat, and then Bob applied some to himself. Lena dared them to walk through Sav-on with their bold new perfume smell. The three of them walked up and down the aisles, absurdly fragrant, while passersby watched them and sometimes coughed.

Lena also knew how to — as she said — borrow things. They once strolled by the big apartment buildings lining Mango Boulevard, and Lena showed them how to pick up sunglasses or sandals left on empty patio tables. She had mastered the art of borrowing these items and then quietly returning them after a few hours. She walked around one table, careful not to look too hungrily at the sunglasses sitting there. She plucked them up and trotted back to the sidewalk, wearing some stranger's Yves St. Laurent sunglasses on her nose.

(Lena had a theory about all her borrowing. "It's just sitting there," she said. "No one's using it." After wearing the borrowed item for a couple of hours, she'd make sure the table was still unoccupied, and put it back.)

Then Shelley and Bob walked around the apartment buildings, looking for objects to take. Bob borrowed a pair of nail clippers, and Shelley found an old copy of *Field and Stream*. It was not clear what they were supposed to do with these items, except to make Lena happy for having taught them how to borrow. At the end of the day, Shelley and Bob replaced the nail clippers and magazine.

To Shelley, every excursion to Panorama Village was a dare. She was daring herself to be someone fabulous; each time she visited Bob and Lena, she dressed in a new way. Her standard for choosing an outfit was her fear of wearing it. She tried this first with a miniskirt, a silver satin skirt she had discovered at the temple in a box labeled FOR THE NEEDY AND POOR. She matched it with a tank top and a pair of sandals studded with rhinestones. She'd never worn anything like this before, nor could she imagine wearing it to school or around her family, so she tried it out on Lena and Bob.

She watched their faces carefully when she dropped off the bus. Giddy, she did a little leap.

"You're dressed up," said Lena.

Shelley twirled around. "What do you think?"

Bob gazed at the sky and bounced on his feet. Lena clapped her hand over her mouth. "I think you look like a silvery grownup," she said, and she seemed to mean it.

With Lena and Bob, she dreamed up strange and wonderful futures. At the end of each visit, they dared her to invent a new job for herself.

She came to them, on different Sundays, as a budding ballerina, photographer, fashion model, actress, or senator. They listened to her campaign speech on her policies concerning the Mideast oil crisis. They allowed her to take portraits of them with her Kodak Instamatic. She brought them carefully typed invoices when the pictures were developed, and they paid her for her services: thirty-five cents.

One day, she decided that she wanted to write a message on a dollar bill — and then spend the dollar. The three of them spent most of the afternoon figuring out a good message, and finally settled on SEQUINA KNOWS EVERYTHING ABOUT YOU. Using a green ballpoint pen, Shelley wrote this message on the back of the bill. Then they went to Sav-on and spent the bill on two cans of 7-Up. During the bus ride home that day, Shelley was excited, imagining the people who would read her special message: A San Francisco businessman. A New York concert pianist. A gym teacher in Texas. And then they would all want to know more about her.

The three of them imagined, one day, living together in their own new house. Their voices became rapid, excited when they discussed this. The details of this house changed over time. At one point, it was made of logs, like Abraham Lincoln's cabin; later, it was a clear cube of glass. After they had all watched an episode of *Fantasy Island*, the house changed into a marble palace, with a swimming pool. Lena wanted the pool to stretch endlessly into the distance so that they'd always have a new area to explore. Shelley's pool was to surround a grand fountain, with creamy sprays of water shooting up around a glass pedestal; when people stood there, they would appear as gods through the mist. Bob's pool was to resemble a huge bathtub ringed by servants who would rush toward you with soft towels when you emerged.

Bob said the house would be open to all visitors, so it would not require a key. Lena wanted the house to be on a hill so that people would look up and envy it; it would be ample enough for big, noisy gatherings, and she would be the perfect hostess, offering her guests many hors d'oeuvres. Shelley wanted the house to be set in a remote region, a place where she was unknown. The three of them sat on the hot curb outside Panorama Village, and their bright, hopeful voices overlapped and combined like streams of water. Sometimes it was hard to know whose fantasy belonged to whom.

While they sat on the curb, sucking the Lifesavers Lena had got from the vending machine, Shelley told them what had happened to her that week. Lena and Bob did not offer advice, but they listened attentively, making concerned noises. When Shelley was finished, she felt filled with sweet air. Every Sunday, as they walked down the street together, it was as though the world had opened up, like a brilliant flower; it seemed that they were free.

Now the bus was heading west. The view from the window was utterly different, now that she and Lena were alone. Los Angeles flew by with an astonishing clarity, as though it had been cleansed by a sudden rain. Shelley stared out the window at the tall, skinny palms, all leaning to one side against the white sky. The empty boulevards were lined with fast-food emporiums — Burger King and Jack in the Box and Arby's. The city looked dry and silent, through the thick window; it all seemed to have been created right then, for her. Shelley rested her forehead against the window, feeling the speed tremble against her face. She had not expected to move again this way in her life. For the six months since the accident, she had not been allowed to visit Panorama Village. Now she wanted to run outside and touch everything, to taste the chaparral and eucalyptus and even the warm tar in the street.

Only an hour before, Shelley had been doing what she did now every Sunday — sitting on her front lawn. The sweet songs of the sparrows curved through the honeyed air. Outside, ranch homes sat on their browning lawns. The neighborhood was perfectly still, but she was aware that, inside the houses, people were changing at remarkable speed, becoming teenagers or college students or old people. Some were becoming dead people; two of these were Uncle Bob and her grandfather Lou. All over Los Angeles, the world, people were changing.

Except for her. Her former friends had moved on; so had her family. That morning, she'd listened to them wake up and go about their activities while she lay in bed. The sounds they made were soft and ordinary, as if they knew they had a right to be part of the day. Her mother was getting ready for a dance rehearsal. Her father was going to the temple, where people sometimes waited on hard metal chairs to talk to him. She did not get out of bed to join them, because she wanted to spare them her strangeness; she had become unfamiliar even to herself.

Since the accident, Shelley had begun to wake at night with a puzzling desire. She would jump out of bed and rush across her shag rug to her collection of glass animals. Shelley would touch the animals, their heads and tails and bodies, three times, or she would allow herself to touch them in multiples of three — nine, twenty-seven — as her breath came in soft sobs. She didn't know why she touched them; she knew only that she could not stop. When she returned to bed, she would lie with her arms and legs rigid, panic flowering in her throat, trying to remember whether she had touched the bear nine times or seven, the group of cows only twice. Then she would fling off the covers and fumble back through the darkness, trying to touch the animals the right number of times.

Lately, she had needed to do her threes more often; they were keeping her up many hours of the night. Last night, her mother had caught her in the living room, furiously tapping a geode rock ashtray, trying to remember whether she was at number twenty-eight or twenty-nine. Her hand tapped fiercely, like a bird claw. She looked up and saw her mother in the doorway. She couldn't quite see her mother's face but imagined it was full of fear. "Sweetheart," her mother said, coming toward her, "what are you *doing?*" Shelley stood frozen for a moment; then she ran. That was the smartest answer. She ran to bed and hid under the sheets, and when her mother knocked on the door in the morning, she pretended to be asleep so that she wouldn't have to talk to her.

And now she was sitting in the bus with Lena. For months, she'd tried to imagine what she'd do or say when she again saw her aunt. She was perfectly still, waiting to die, for that seemed what she owed to Lena, and she was afraid that it would hurt. Bob had abandoned them to their lives, left the two of them torn and blinking on the overpass. It was as though Lena and Shelley had become the same species, in a way they had not been before.

Lena kept twisting around, observing how the other passengers sat. She tried out their positions: the curved slouch of a boy with a skateboard, the prim, upright posture of a lady Ella's age. She settled on a pose like a tourist, staring out the window, her lips almost touching the glass. The neighborhoods melted into each other, gray boxy buildings blanched from the sun.

Lena looked at Shelley. "I didn't think you'd come."

"Why not?"

She shrugged. "I thought you didn't like me anymore."

"No, no," Shelley whispered. "Since, you know . . ." She did not know how to refer to the day. "My parents didn't let me . . ." She stopped. Since Bob's accident, her parents had not allowed her to visit Panorama Village. She was here now only because Ella, her grandmother, hadn't remembered that rule. "I wanted to come."

"Well," said Lena. She sat up proudly. "I made a fire. Me!"

"No, you didn't," said Shelley, not knowing which answer she herself wanted to hear.

"I woke up." Lena smiled. "I smoked my first cigarette. I waited." She pressed her forehead to the window so firmly that the glass shuddered. She stared hard at the view for a moment, then lifted her head. "He was *late*. Today is a special day. I took this." She brought her cigarette lighter out of her pocket and began to flick it on and off.

"Careful," Shelley said, and Lena stopped.

"I put the fire on the curtain, and there was more. I thought it was pretty." Lena's face softened. "I put the lighter on the carpet. There was a fire down there, too. There was a lot of fire. And smoke!" Her voice was growing louder; the passengers looked at her. "So I ran out."

"You wanted to burn up your room?" Shelley wasn't sure whether she wanted a yes or a no.

Lena heard the discomfort in her voice; she sat up straighter. "I didn't want to be in my room by myself."

Shelley could understand this. She was grateful for the tall signs of McDonald's, Jack in the Box, Arby's, sticking up out of the colorless streets.

"I know what I want to do for the game today," Lena said. "I want to talk more about our future house."

"The house," Shelley said.

"Remember. The big one. With the pool," Lena said. "There will be so many rooms. You can have one overlooking the pool." She beamed. Shelley looked away, for it was confusing to hear Lena describe their old fantasy. It seemed to bound, like a cartoon, into the air.

"What else?" Shelley asked, softly.

"We'll live there," Lena said, a little shyly. "It'll be nice. We can listen to the pool when we go to sleep." Lena considered. "Maybe we'll have a dinner party there. You say one."

"I can't."

Lena looked impatient. "We both have to do it."

Shelley hadn't allowed herself for months to imagine anything so beautiful. She looked around at the people on the bus, and they seemed dim, not like people but like stuffed dummies; with the correct threes tapped out, she could bring them back to life. She sharply drummed out nine on the seat. A woman a few seats away glanced up at her. Shelley put her hands in her lap and tried to force them to be still.

Lena sighed sharply, waiting.

"Well," Shelley said, "people will want to visit us. They'll hear that we are wonderful hosts."

"That's good."

Lena was watching her, expectantly; Shelley tried to come up with more. "We will hand out numbers." She imagined her former friends, the entire city, waiting anxiously, numbers in hand. "We will have to be extremely careful to let in only the best."

"Who are the best?"

"People will have to bear gifts for us. They may write poems admiring our great qualities, or make sculptures of us to set on the freeway, in crowded spots. At our parties, people will talk about their secrets. What they're afraid of, who they love. They won't hold anything back from us, because we'll make them want to talk and talk."

Lena was sitting forward, rapt.

"Boys will have to pay a thousand dollars to kiss me. Two thousand if they want to do it that very day." She hadn't been kissed by a boy, and she wondered what it would be like. "If they do not appreciate the kiss fully, they will leave, and they'll never be able to kiss another girl in their life."

"Never," said Lena.

Now Shelley wanted to go on and on. She could even picture the house, its walls sparkling and sugary; she remembered some of the hopes they had shared. She saw Lena in a silk apron, holding out a plate of hot dog hors d'oeuvres, and she saw herself swimming gently through their grand fountain, arcs of water sending rainbows into the pool.

Suddenly, she was on the verge of tears, exhausted. The heat hitting the bus seats made them bright as metal, poor and dingy in the stark light.

"Are these okay?" she asked Lena. "Do you like them?"

"I think they're all good," Lena said.

"I can add more," Shelley said, "if you want me to."

"We can both add more today," Lena said.

Three

Ella could smell Lena's room before she saw it. The hallway was filled with a wet and sour odor, heavy with burned rubber. Before entering the room, Ella touched the ends of her silver hair, straightened the hem of her dress. Her face was composed, as though for an interview. Then she went in.

She stepped over the huge beige panties and housecoats that Lena had strewn all over the carpet; such a sight usually annoyed her, but now it cheered her. The window was open, letting in a square of glaring light, and the avocado curtains fluttered slowly, like creatures at the bottom of the sea. The rest of the room was deep in shadow. It took her a moment to see that the fire damage was confined to one corner. There, the walls were cloudy with gray ash, the curtains only skeletal remains. The shag rug was blackened, sopping and flecked with pink chemical foam. Patches of red melted rubber flashed like muscle beneath the burned rug. Ella made herself look at the damage for a minute before she turned away.

During all the years before Lena moved to Panorama Village, Ella had begun her day the same way: she made Lena's bed. This was, right now, all she could think to do.

She stretched the elastic ends of the bottom sheet under the corners of the mattress. Then she flapped the top sheet over, tucked it in, smoothed the ribbed blanket on top, and covered everything with the bedspread. She puffed up each pillow and set it neatly at the head of the bed.

But she wanted to do more, so she went to the dresser. In the top drawer were Lena's socks and panties. In the second drawer, Lena's sweaters, tops. She gently patted the sleeves, which seemed to need comforting. When she tried the bottom drawer, it stuck; she pulled hard, and it jerked open.

An assortment of items lay jumbled in the drawer. Ella recognized her 1976 datebook, Lou's favorite screwdriver, with its chipped yellow handle. He'd used it around his store and had been trying to locate it for years. There was a cosmetic puff, dusty with powder, from her vanity table, and one of Shelley's sparkling eye masks from her Gypsy costume one Halloween. There was a magnet of the letter Q from Vivien's refrigerator and three of Vivien's teaspoons, one coated with a curious white substance, perhaps milk.

Ella stared, helpless, at the contents of the drawer. How beautiful each thing seemed, carefully selected and hidden. Each item seemed holy, infused with a desperate love.

A band of sunlight fell, darkly, onto the carpet,

as though some brightness had been stolen from it. Ella quickly shut the drawer and sank down on Lena's bed. For a moment she sat quietly, her hands clasped. Then she stood up and continued cleaning her daughter's room.

When Ella was growing up in her family's apartment, there was one corner that belonged to her. It was the slim, dusty space between the stove and the window, where no one else could fit. The floor was dirty and rutted, and her spot was not very comfortable; she had to squeeze her arms to her sides and brace herself against the window's chill air. But from there she could watch the laundry hanging in the narrow alley between the tenements. Wednesdays were the prettiest days. She loved the sight of large families of laundry floating along the clotheslines, long, bodiless dresses, men's pants; the pant legs filled with air, kicking, and some of the shirts were holding hands. The clothes were weightless, full of odd grace. She imagined them filled with people who would like her; she believed they would be kind to her.

Ella had grown up in the Dorchester neighborhood in Boston. In four rooms on the fifth floor of a tenement, she lived with her parents and her three older sisters. The ceiling was tin, and the air in the room seemed always to be the color of dusk. The hallway smelled of unclean breath and sour urine from the toilet they shared with their neighbors. The apartment itself held the less definable sound of six personalities trying to assert themselves in a small space.

Ella was the only child who had been born in America. Her father had emigrated from Russia alone, and it had taken him six years to make enough money to bring the others over to Boston. Ella was the product of her parents' re-union. At the dinner table, Ella sometimes went hungry, because in Russia her sisters had learned early how to grab. Sometimes she suspected that her sisters secretly wanted to starve her. They were big, anxious girls with thick accents; Deborah was six years older than Ella, Ruth eight, Esther ten, and they seemed less like sisters than a force of weather.

Her father loved Ella best because she had been born here. Often, during dinner, she sat on his lap while he read to her, slowly, from the *Boston Globe* while her mother talked to her sisters in Yiddish. Her father had learned English during his six years alone here. He was embarrassed by his family's ragged pronunciation of English; he wanted to make sure that Ella learned to speak more correctly than the others. She would sit in his lap with her back against his chest as though she were on a throne. The vibrations of the words as he read thrummed lovingly through her back. Those words, and the feeling inside them, made her into a person. Her father's pale blue eyes became fierce, adoring, when she began to speak in a way that was different from all of them.

What had her parents been like before their lives here? The rest of the family knew this history, and this inhabited a world of feelings that was forever denied to her. It was hard to believe that her parents could have been different from who they were. Her mother was shy, tousled, smelled of boiled meat; she poured herself so completely into her tasks that, at times, she seemed to disappear. Ella's father, too tall for the apartment, was restless, eager to get away. Sometimes Ella came upon them in a kiss that appeared stronger than love; in its rage, it reached toward an innocence. To Ella, those were the only times they seemed married.

Ella had the greatest sense of belonging when she and her sisters headed out, away from home, into the world. Her sisters delighted in teaching her games on the sidewalk, and they were kindest to her then; away from her parents' favor, she was a toy they prized.

In winter, the streets were often black with dirty snow, and white steam billowed up, like furious breath, from grates. On their street was a saloon and a butcher shop. She loved running with her sisters, a pack. The girls were supposed to avoid the drunks, but they liked to tiptoe right up to an unconscious man and pretend to jump on him or kick him. Sometimes they would pull down the man's pants and roll him over; his penis would be limp and pinkish, a tiny elephant trunk resting in matted hair. Deborah liked to leap over a sleeping man, one smooth arc over his skull; she liked the idea that he'd open his tired eyes to see a flutter, one big, braided girl soaring over him. She liked the idea that someone would believe, for a moment, that she could fly.

In 1910, when Ella was seven years old, Deborah, then thirteen, took her into the dark crowded bedroom and shut the door. In the closet she groped around, searching for something. Ella's thin arms were lit by a platinum line of light. Deborah's breath was quick, excited. Her calves twitched slightly under her stockings. She opened old boxes and found what she had been looking for.

It was a small white box, which she handed to Ella. "Look," she said, and took off the lid. Inside was a tiny, fanglike child's tooth.

"Whose is it?" Ella asked.

"Don't you know?" asked Deborah.

Ella could barely make out Deborah's face, but she could feel a superiority rising, like heat, from her sister.

"This is Eva's," said Deborah.

"Who's Eva?"

"Our sister."

The tooth lay in the box, pale and sharp.

"We don't have a sister named Eva."

"We did."

Deborah picked up the tooth and, tightly gripping Ella's wrist with her other hand, began to trace slow circles with the tooth in Ella's palm.

"Mama didn't want you," she said.

The darkness deepened. Ella's heart began to march, but she stood up straighter, trying to look her sister in the eye.

"If Eva hadn't died," whispered Deborah, "they wouldn't have had you."

Deborah began to prick Ella's palm with the sharp end of the tooth. "Can you feel it?" she whispered. "She's biting you."

Ella stood in the doorway of the kitchen, watching her mother bend over the counter, slicing raw meat. It took a long time for Ella to ask the question.

"Who's Eva?" Ella asked.

The odor of blood from the meat filled the kitchen. Her mother wiped one hand on her apron, then the other. "Who?" she asked.

"Eva," said Ella, and began chanting, "Eva, Eva, Eva . . ."

Her mother resumed slicing; Ella kept murmuring the name. Finally, her mother turned around and said, sharply, "Eva was your sister." Then she told a story, in a rush. Eva was the youngest daughter in Russia. One day when she was seven years old, she ran into the street and was kicked by a Cossack's horse.

"They killed her," her mother said. Her face was empty of all feeling; it was not familiar.

The floor under Ella's feet became fragile; her mother abruptly turned away.

Later, Deborah took her into that closet again

and whispered, "She lied. Eva wasn't killed by a horse. She died on the boat when we were coming over. She coughed to death. They had to throw her overboard. This was all they let us keep."

"Liar," said Ella.

"You don't know," Deborah said. Her face was arrogant; she belonged to the family in a way that Ella could not.

Deborah pushed open the door and stormed out of the room. Ella remained, wondering whether she would ever feel she was part of something, or whether she would always be Ella, alone.

One day when Ella was eight, Mrs. O'Connell, a neighbor, asked her mother to take her place cleaning for a woman who lived on Beacon Hill. Her mother agreed, and since Ella was home from school with a slight fever, her mother took her along.

When they got off the streetcar at Beacon Hill, Ella was amazed. The buildings looked like beautiful gifts made of bright red brick. The people walked slowly as though through fluid. The air was clean, fragrant with lavender. Ella walked solemnly beside her mother, trying to show off the one bit of beauty she had: a lemon-colored hair bow Deborah had stolen off a pile of laundry. Her mother trudged along, staring at the sidewalk, her shoulders hunched around her ears. Ella touched her bow and turned her head so that passersby would see it. She wanted to send a message of worthiness strong enough for both of them.

They found the house. The woman who opened the door was tall and slim, like an elegant tree. Ella felt shy, and she was proud when her mother spoke. "I'm Golda Oscowitz. I'm here to clean the house." Mrs. Jones introduced herself and led them inside.

The house seemed fat; the walls were a foot thick and covered with purple velvet wallpaper, fancy enough for a woman's fine dress. Ella squinted, for the hallway gleamed with many types of lights. Yellow gas lamps flickered on the walls. A fixture, shaped like an upside-down cake made of diamonds, flushed white and brilliant from the ceiling. Suddenly, her clothing was too heavy; the air in the house was warm. Mrs. Jones showed her mother which rooms needed cleaning; she was to do only the first floor today.

Mrs. Jones went up the stairs, and Ella realized that the upper floors, too, were part of her house; one family owned the whole house. Ella and her mother were left in the living room. Ella sat on the carpet, wary of the furniture. Then her mother became a maid.

Her mother was a bad maid; even at eight, Ella could tell this was so. Jewish women rarely heard about cleaning jobs; that was Irish work. And her mother didn't know how to act like a maid. She worked slowly, carefully running her rag around each of the crystal vases and decanters that flushed in the light. Then she put them in the wrong places. Ella saw her mother withdraw into a quiet place within herself as she cleaned; her anxiety made her very slow.

Ella could feel her heart drum in her throat as a sense of protectiveness and sorrow rose in her like a pair of wings. This was her mother, and she did not want to become like her. It was a thought she had never understood so clearly.

She wandered into the hallway just as Mrs. Jones was coming downstairs. The woman smiled. "You may wait in the kitchen," she said. Stiffly, Ella followed the woman. Mrs. Jones gave Ella some bread and jam, and also a fork and knife, which puzzled her.

"Are you hungry?" Mrs. Jones asked.

"No."

"Your name is Ella?"

Ella nodded.

"What grade are you in?"

"Third."

"You have lovely hair," said Mrs. Jones. Her tone was tender. "Do you know that?"

Ella didn't know whether to agree or not. She shrugged.

"You're a pretty girl," said Mrs. Jones. "You're lucky."

Ella crossed her arms and squeezed them tight. She stared at the bread.

"It's difficult to run a house like this," said Mrs. Jones. "I try to take good care of it." Her skin bore the slight scent of orange. She seemed to be pleading for some acknowledgment, recognition. "I've been through seven maids. One maid, I'm sorry to say, stole a silver candlestick."

Ella could not look directly at Mrs. Jones. Her mother was far away. All of a sudden, she wished her mother would steal one of the crystal vases in the living room, even though it would look incongruous, ridiculous, on a shelf in their flat.

But she enjoyed the way this stranger was looking at her. Easily, Mrs. Jones liked her.

"My mother is a very good maid," said Ella.

"I see."

"Yes," said Ella. She felt suspended, belonging neither to her mother nor to this stranger. It was a terrifying sensation, but one that also made her free. This airy feeling was replaced by a harder one. She was better than both of them. She smiled at Mrs. Jones with a joyous insincerity and said, "I think your house is very nice."

Girls were supposed to stay chaste until they were married, but few did. Ruth and Esther roared into the apartment, shouting out names of girls they suspected were pregnant; the others' decline proved their own worth. "Nobody's seen Ruby for weeks. She was sent to her aunt in Washington." Or, "Minnie's parents won't let her go to school. You know what that means." Girls disappeared for months and came back with babies and sad, elaborate stories; their husbands had been sent to France, were killed on the front. When Ella's sisters hit twelve, thirteen, boys were everywhere — pressing them against stairwells, following them and calling their names. Her sisters wore the bitter, grassy smell of boys, the places they'd been with them, as they whisked in late at night.

Her mother said two things: "If you keep your mouth shut, no man will know if you're smart or dumb. If you're spoiled, no man will want you."

It started before Ella was ready. Boys hissed as she walked down the street: "Hey, look at me, doll. Smile for me." She thought they were joking. A conspiracy of other men joined in: the paper boy, the butcher's helper, a street drunk. She was a young woman; somehow, they all believed this.

From the time she was young, Ella had wanted to be loved, and she needed that love to be immense, ferocious. After her sisters married and moved away, she often sat alone in the bedroom she had shared with them, wondering whom she would love. And who would love her? The streets outside her window at night were empty, silvered by the moon. She longed to be able to walk down them joined wholly with someone else.

A job led you to the man you would marry, but in 1920 only a few jobs were available to unmarried girls in Boston. Ella watched her sisters to see what they chose. Their jobs shaped them in basic ways. Every day, Esther, the oldest, limped home after ten hours of shouldering huge plates of food at Bloom's Kosher Restaurant, barely able to make it up the stairs. She got married first, to one of her customers, a large, moon-faced man who frequently ordered omelettes; they met when he let her sit in his booth to rest her feet. Ruth worked the graveyard operator shift at New England Telephone and turned into a pale, ghostly person who rarely spoke. She married late, in part because she spent her time packed in a room with fifty other female operators, and few people bothered to flirt with a voice on the telephone.

Deborah had the best job. She worked at the women's hat counter at Filene's, and Ella often visited Filene's just to observe her sister. It was a beautiful place: the mirrors at the jewelry counters shone silver; the aisles were radiant with sweet fragrance. Ella was proud to know a famous person — her sister, the Filene's hat girl. She could never get enough of listening to Deborah talk to a well-dressed customer, a woman who would not even nod to her on the street, telling this woman — smoothly, knowingly — "I know this hat will be perfect for you." Ella watched the rich women remove their hats, revealing flat, dry hair, and tip their heads obediently, like children, for her sister to crown.

The Salesmanship class was composed of seventeen girls and three boys. They were all immigrants or the children of immigrants, and they were all sixteen years old. On the first day of school, the teacher, Mr. Reilly, asked them all to

69

come back the following morning in their best clothes — or, rather, their best selling clothes — so that he could examine them. He was going to tell them whether they had the skills to become salespeople; he was going to tell them who they were.

On the second day of Salesmanship, Mr. Reilly moved around the classroom, examining the students as they stood by their desks in their best clothes. He told them that not only had he been born in this country but his parents had been, too — and he, therefore, knew what was what. "Look at this jacket," he said to Jacob Katzman. "It's *red*. You look like a clown. From a circus. Do you want the world to laugh at you? Do you want a red nose to go with it?" Trish O'Donnell, a slight girl, stood shivering in a mealy black sweater. "You," he said, "are a scaredy-cat. Why would anyone want to buy anything from you?" To Rosie Delano, done up in wrinkly, baby-pink chiffon, he said, "You think you're a princess? You're coming out of the castle for us?"

Mr. Reilly complimented only three students, and not on what they were wearing. He praised John Delaney for his impressive height — six feet one — "like an oak tree." He approved of Pearl Johnson's melodious voice and told her to say "Pleasure to meet you" several times; and then he admired Ella's smile. "Look at this," he said, turning her head, like a doll's, for the other students to see. "Is this a smile you would buy a hat from? A dress? A vase?"

He paused and answered, "Yes!"

He gave them rules, and Ella wrote down every one. When a woman walks into the store, watch her closely to see which piece of her clothing she wears most proudly, then compliment it. Make sure your hands are perfectly clean. Nod one full second after someone asks you a question, not before. When a customer walks in, count to ten before you say, "May I help you?"

The students practiced looking into each other's eyes with confidence. "Pretend you see a flower inside your customer's head," said Mr. Reilly. Ella tried to see roses, lilies, marigolds, blooming behind her nervous eyes. "This time, look *interested*," said Mr. Reilly. "The flower is shrinking. Keep watching it until it goes away." Rosie Delano was better at looking interested than anyone, but John Delaney had the most confident look. When the others asked him what flower he saw, he answered, "A very big blue rose."

"There's no such flower as a blue rose!" they shouted, and he shrugged.

"That's what I saw," he said.

During the semester, they had to sell numerous absurd items that Mr. Reilly brought to class: an ugly rag doll, a satin shoe without a heel, a cracked marble, a banana peel. At first, almost everyone stuttered and spoke in a wispy voice. Mr. Reilly stood at the back of the room and yelled, "What! I can't hear you! Americans speak loud." He pounded his chest. "Loud! Are you an American? Or do you want to go back?"

Some of the items were impossible to sell. It took three students to get rid of the banana peel (by that time, it had dried up). Of course, no one actually bought anything, but Mr. Reilly knew when a customer might relent, and Ella learned to detect a subtle change in the room. When a student successfully sold an item, it was as though he had planted a new longing in you. One day, Anna Stragowski held up the black, dry banana peel and said, "You need this peel. You must buy. Why? Because it is a duster!" and she whirled around the room, whisking the stiff peel against desks and windows. The students were quiet with amazement, breathing softly; there really was one more thing they could want.

Mr. Reilly was hard on Ella for the whole term. She did not live up to the unintended promise of that first smile, so she wanted desperately to do well when he handed her the final object to sell — a tiny, broken child's tooth.

Ella cupped the tooth in her hand. The tooth seemed to be jumping around in her hand, and she was afraid, for a moment, to look closely at it.

"Hello," she whispered. "I am Ella and I have something —"

"Louder!" yelled Mr. Reilly. "Who's talking? I can't hear you!"

"I am Ella —" Mr. Reilly was shaking his head.

She felt as though she were yelling. "Do you have trouble chewing?" she asked. "This is what you need!"

The field of faces blinked and yawned. A few of the students laughed. "With this extra tooth, you can have a better smile!"

"They have teeth," said Mr. Reilly.

The panic was rising again, and Ella popped the tooth in her mouth and swallowed it. She and the other students looked stunned.

"Where'd it go?"

"She ate it!"

Ella placed her hand on her stomach. She had swallowed a stranger's tooth. Whose mouth had it come from? Why had she swallowed it? Would it harm her insides? Would Mr. Reilly want it back?

The class was in an uproar.

"Mr. Reilly! Now we can't buy the tooth!"

"Ella, where is the tooth?" asked Mr. Reilly. Ella gently patted her stomach. "Is that your sales technique?"

"Yes," she said.

"Tell me, class. Do you want that tooth?"

Nineteen pairs of eyes were fixed on her. "Yes!" the students said.

"Then I have to say that you pass," said Mr. Reilly.

Ella remained in front of the class for one more moment before she sat down, feeling those rapt, hungry eyes on her. She knew the others wanted the tooth only because it could not be had.

Ella's tooth-swallowing trick so impressed Mr. Reilly that when she was about to graduate from high school, he referred her to his friend Marvin, a floor walker at Johnson Massey's Treasure Trove. It was a plum job, even more prestigious than being a hat girl at Filene's.

The Treasure Trove was situated on the fifth floor of the elegant department store. On the elevator directory, the Treasure Trove was indicated by a scrolled gold plaque. It was where the wealthy bought objects with which to decorate their homes —vases and light fixtures and china figurines that were imported from all over the world.

But the moment Ella walked into the Treasure Trove, she felt she did not belong. The door was flanked by two black Grecian columns, and inside was a vast array of extravagant objects that she had never before seen. Porcelain vases, painted with delicate, gilt-leaved roses, stood atop lit stands. There were jade dogs and horses and rabbits and domed chests encrusted with purple stones. There were gentlemen with bowlers and ladies in silk dresses and flowered hats. Above, a huge teardrop chandelier sparkled like frozen raindrops. Ella kept her hands out of her pockets, to show everyone that she was not a thief.

"Reilly sent you?" asked Marvin. He had a strange accent, almost British but not quite. His thin face with fine cheekbones made him appear knowledgeable in matters of taste. Ella nodded.

"Let's get a look at you," he said.

She turned around, arms held out, and tried to smile. He looked her over. "What do you think of all this?" he asked her, gesturing to the room.

"It's *beautiful,*" she said. Her voice was thick with feeling.

"Fine," he said. His accent slid a little; it sounded almost like hers. "We'll fit you up in a uniform. Be here tomorrow at nine."

And just like that, he trusted her to come in every morning and dust off the figures made of jade or ivory or gold; he trusted her to sell the precious objects to the customers. She wore a uniform, a forest-green, cap-sleeved blouse and a calf-length skirt. On one side of her collar was a nametag, on the other, a sparkling rhinestone pin with the initials JM for Johnson Massey. Ella did not think the pin's jewels were real, but she also did not want anyone to tell her they were not.

She memorized everything Marvin told her about the objects; the information seemed culled from the encyclopedia: *Jade is much prized in the Orient. Different methods for carving jade are used in China and Japan.* When she was tired, she sometimes made up her own facts. "This fine chest stored dishes in the castle of King Howard the Fourth," she said. She loved how the customers nodded, listening, how vulnerable they seemed, examining the treasures in their careful hands.

Lou said that he knew almost the minute he saw her that he wanted to marry her, but it took her a year to decide. By then she was twenty-one, and her mother was pressing her for a decision. "Better do it quick," she told Ella, "or you'll be left on the shelf."

Lou had wandered into the Treasure Trove by accident. She came up behind him and asked, "May I help you?" He turned around and saw her. He removed his hat. "I'm just a salesgirl," she said. "You can put your hat —"

"You're Ella," he said, reading her nametag. "A pleasure to meet you. I'm Lou." He gazed at her. "I'm searching for a gift from" — he looked around — "the Fourth Prussian Dynasty."

"Yes," she said.

"From 1834 to 1857. A great era in history. A time of great riches. Beautiful queens." His voice echoed strangely. She could not recall anything about the Fourth Prussian Dynasty. "Ella," Lou said, "show me what you have."

They strolled past the delicate, glimmering objects. There were no other customers or salesgirls in the store just then. He walked close to her, his shoulders, hunched, assuming a posture of protectiveness.

"Prussia," she said, hoping for more help from him.

"I'd say the year 1852."

She gazed around the room, and a feeling of boldness came over her. "This," she said, pointing to a gold grandfather clock. "This is from that time."

He smiled, stepped up to the clock, and tapped the surface with his knuckles. His face went soft with approval. "It is," he said. Ella stepped back, surprised. The clock was certainly not from the Fourth Prussian Dynasty, whenever that was. Each understood that the other was lying. The light in the room seemed to brighten. "It chimed to call them to dinner," he said.

"I think so," she said. A puff of glee burst in her chest.

They walked around the room, deciding that almost all the objects must be from the Fourth Prussian Dynasty. "This," announced Lou, gripping a vase dangerously by its neck, "held the bracelets that belonged to Edwina, the Prussian princess."

"No," Ella said, "that was for her earrings. Her bracelets" —she tapped a carved ivory tusk — "hung on this."

Now Ella began to feel a little dizzy. He walked close to her, as though they were already intimate, and when she took her place behind the counter, he seemed lost. He bought the least expensive item in the room — a tiny jade rabbit — and appeared stunned to have purchased anything. "Thank you very much, Ella," he said, in a puzzled way, clutching the store's box. "Thank you for helping me today —" And then, as though afraid of what he might say next, he dashed out of the store.

A few days later, as she came through the glass doors of Johnson Massey, she noticed Lou standing by the store windows. He was moving his hat restlessly from hand to hand; when he saw her, he quickly put it on. "Ella," he said. His face was stern with purpose. "I'm Lou."

It was a fall day, and the sky was pale with cold. His hands looked clumsy and large in brown mittens. "Hello," he said. His breath curled in the chill air. "What a lovely pin," he said, looking at the sparkling JM pin on her collar.

"I think they're diamonds," she burst out, and then stopped, embarrassed.

He smiled, so she knew that he knew the stones could not be diamonds. They began to walk together, toward nowhere. The air between them brimmed with a feeling that was not yet love, but a stubborn, reckless sense that they were bound by something larger than themselves. Around them, the city's cold was savage. The afternoon seemed to part before them. "If you're still looking for presents," she said, knowing that he wasn't, "Sophia can help —"

"I have something for you," he blurted. They stopped. Crowds melted around them. He held out a package, badly wrapped.

It was easy to accept the present; she was curious. She unwound the tissue and found the jade rabbit she had sold him. She stared at him, confused.

"There was no Fourth Prussian Dynasty," she said. She'd looked it up in Marvin's encyclopedia.

"No?" He tried to laugh. His face was as open as a child's. "But you were so . . . helpful. I wanted to give it to you."

She touched the rabbit's ears. She had never owned anything from the Treasure Trove.

"Have dinner with me," he said. The words blossomed from a tender place inside him. He stepped back a little. There was a brisk gust of wind, and his coat flapped around him.

There was no one else who wanted her then, and she began to look forward to seeing Lou walk through the Grecian columns of the Treasure Trove. Soon he was visiting her several times a week. She was cautious, but she liked him, partly because the other girls did. They hovered around him, laughing at his jokes, the way he made fun of the gaudiest, most grotesque objects. "What fool would buy this?" he said, lifting a huge, gilt ashtray with cupids balanced on the edge. The girls shrieked with laughter. Ella watched the salesgirls change lipstick, looking for the one color that would make him love them. They acted like men when they flirted, slapping him playfully, calling him "mister" or "kid," as though that gave them new rights to him. They smiled coldly at Ella. She did not understand her claim on him. She began to love him almost to appease her colleagues.

Ella and Lou started to take walks when her shift ended. He was full of opinions, and he seemed so happy to be with her that she wanted to listen. He told her about the classes he'd taken in college; how he helped manage his mother's suit store; how he'd read a great deal about California and wanted to live in a place that was always warm. Lou was full of jokes at the Treasure Trove, but when they were alone he had an earnest quality that told her he took her seriously. His admiration seemed to be part of him, like bone.

He had money. That gave him confidence; he entered restaurants, stores, with none of her trepidation. She began to love the careful, greased slickness of his hair, gleaming like black licorice, or the way he shook his coat on, commanding and sharp. He was educated; he read all the sections of a newspaper. He walked through the world as though he knew that he belonged in it.

She remembered the moment she passed from lonely to loved. She was having dinner with Lou in a bright red booth at a diner in Brookline. She sat, anxious, straightening the fork on her napkin. The waitress brought her a piece of brisket. It wasn't a fancy place, and the meat was too tough to cut. Her knife skidded from her hand to the floor.

"They should take it back," said Lou. "It should be more tender."

Ella felt embarrassed, responsible, somehow.

"No, I like it this way," Ella said.

He looked at her. "Then let me try," he said.

Lou slid her plate over, pressed his fork deep into the meat, and carefully cut off a small piece. He held it up as though it were a jewel.

"How's this?" he asked.

She stared at him. "Fine," she said.

He cut the rest of the meat into bite-sized pieces and set the plate back in front of her. "That should be better," he said.

It was wonderful, the way he'd cut the brisket for her. It was, somehow, the gesture she had been waiting for her whole life. Lou chewed his green beans. Ella stopped eating her brisket.

Perhaps this was how life was supposed to be. At that moment Ella was so certain of her future, she did not feel she needed to do anything — to pick up her fork, drink her water. An odd happiness slowly filled her, and she knew that life would carry her to the next good place. She understood what love was.

Ella remembered little about her wedding: the rabbi's gray, acne-marked face, her ivory satin dress, paid for by Lou's family, and the juicy red roast beef that they had also provided. At one point, she was held up in a small wooden chair, dozens of hands reaching for her, as though she were floating on a wild sea. She barely saw Lou during the party, until, bending through a flurry of rice as they left, she clasped his hand.

A taxi took them to their hotel. They sat quietly in the back seat. She was married. Her heart had become a trumpet, trying to play a great new sound. The car stopped at the Hotel Essex, where Lou registered them as Mr. and Mrs. Lou Rose. It was that easy; that was who she was.

She had so many questions, but they seemed too dangerous to ask. Why had he chosen her? And why had she chosen him? What made a person decide to marry another? Did a small thing push you over — the beautiful curve of a lip, or the startle of hair in the sun — and if you lost this thing, was the love forever gone?

She had never been inside a hotel. The room had creamy walls and a ruby-red carpet. The room was like a regular bedroom, but one that had somehow never been occupied. It had dark blue linen draperies, an enormous, tidy bed. A bottle of champagne sat in a silver bucket. The room smelled clean, antiseptic. Ella wanted to touch everything. She moved all around, examining the night table, opening and closing the drawers. Lou followed her. "Let me introduce my wife to the dresser," he said. His voice was hoarse. "Let me introduce my wife to the lamp . . ."

The word *wife* startled her; it was as though an intruder had entered the room. When she found fragrant squares of wrapped soap in the bathroom, Ella opened one. "It's our first soap," she said. "Hold out your hands." He did; his palms were pale pink and delicate. Gently, in the scented lather, she washed their hands together.

He dried his with the plush hotel towel. They went back to the bedroom, and Lou kissed her.

It was all very fast. She wanted to be a good bride, to be still as Lou unzipped her dress and pushed it down her shoulders, but she also wanted to kiss back. She stepped out of her dress in one quick, determined motion. He unhooked her bra and took her breasts into his hands. No man had ever touched her breasts. It was an astounding sight, her breasts, pale and soft, in his hands. It seemed too easy, too calm.

"You're beautiful," he murmured.

She stood in her slip, wanting more words. She heard only his breath, shallow, quickening. He snapped off the light and gently guided her onto the bed. The gold bands on their fingers gleamed, ghostly, in the darkness, as though to show they belonged to the same club. His fingertips traced her skin from her hair down the curve of her back, over the inside of her thigh. She felt utterly naked and she wanted him to touch her more. She was surprised at the rubbery quality of his fingers, surprised that she could feel the edge of his fingernail inside her. There was a loneliness that she had not expected. She smoothed her hands over his warm, silky skin, wanting to touch far more than his body.

"Ella," he whispered. Their breath was like a hushed conversation. She wrapped her arms around him. She was aware of the cotton sheet below her and the clock ticking on the wall and his breath, so fast, doglike. She pressed her forehead to his shoulder, waiting for whatever love this act created.

Then he stopped.

Lou rolled off her and pushed his face into the pillow. Ella looked at his dark hair, his ear. His ear was so close to her lips, she wanted to shout and shout into it, but she did not know what she would say.

He reached down and touched her private place with his finger. She flinched. His finger was bloody.

"Are you all right?"

He dabbed her with the blanket. There wasn't much blood. He tucked the blankets around their shoulders and they were face to face in bed, like cold children.

"Well, my love," Lou said, "we're married."

They blinked into the brackish, honeyed smell of each other's breath.

Lou fell asleep. Ella watched him as he slept soundly. She was married; this was a thought she held alone.

Suddenly, she understood how no one completely owned anyone else in the world. Every person wanted an exclusive hand on the beloved. A wife owned her husband differently from the way his mother did, or his daughter. Ella had hoped that her love would be more selfish — a love that would locate herself and Lou completely in this dark together, alone.

That was the wife's claim to ownership: the

privilege of being touched. Its secret nature bothered her; she wished she could describe it to the world. But neither his mother, nor hers, would choose to hear about it. And Lou belonged, truly, to neither of them. If he died, he would separate into two different people in their dreams.

Her heart burned with enormous love and grief. She was married. As her eyes adjusted to the darkness, she saw her wedding dress, stiff and opalescent in the deep blue light. The dress had been left in such a way that it looked as if it had fallen and was trying, very delicately, to stand up.

It took nothing to send them to California: a cramped attic apartment; the fact that she could not help Lou open a shoe store, as she had said; a newspaper article that said homes in Los Angeles were cheap.

It was Lou who suggested the idea, and it seemed immediately right to Ella. It was a way finally to become a true member of her family — to leave them the way they had left their country, two decades before.

It was 1926. They moved west, a new bride and groom, in a used Ford. Gripping hands, Ella and Lou watched as each state fell away behind them, revealing the vast country, alternately brown or verdant beneath the springtime sun.

Four

A dusty red palisade descended from the highway, and on the other side of it was Lahambra Beach. The bus slid down the off ramp, approaching the beach. A faint, rose-colored glow hovered above the Pacific Ocean. Shelley could see a swarm of half-naked people gathered by the water. They were lying on towels or zooming down the bike path on roller skates or jumping up and down by a volleyball net. The surf began at the north end of the beach and extended south like a long, white zipper undoing the sea.

They had been on the bus for forty minutes. Lena pressed her face to the window. She had done this so frequently and fiercely during the ride that her forehead bore a red mark. All during the ride, she had been quietly giggling, but she did not tell Shelley of her stream of thoughts. But now, as they passed a large Sav-on on the street across from the beach, Lena sat up. "Look," she exclaimed, pointing to the store. "It's the same sign."

Lena had been watching other passengers reach up and pull the wire running above the window when they wanted to get off the bus. Her own fingertips had crept along the wire, but never hard enough to make a sound. Now, Lena reached up and firmly yanked it. "Dare!" she said to Shelley. "Get off!" She scrambled up to the front, and Shelley followed. The driver brought the bus to a stop; he, too, seemed to believe that they had reached their destination. The two of them jumped off.

The air was new here, coated with gasoline and salt. The light shimmered in great, pale sheets, filled with sheer cascades of green and blue. Cars formed a slow, endless caravan down the highway. They were dusty with sunlight and sand, as though they had been driven through a desert. The loud voices of Donna Summer and the Bee Gees and the Eagles made their way out the different car windows, engaged in their own important discussion. Some of the drivers had pickup trucks, and bare-chested boys and bikini'd girls lounged in the open backs. They tipped back beers or lifted their faces to the sun; there was a lazy, languorous look to them, like that of seals basking on rocks.

Shelley and Lena were in a new and unknown land. Shelley's breath was coming quickly, almost in sobs; the sound of her emotion surprised her. She held her breath for a second to stop that sound. There was a penetrating quiet here, under the noise of the singers, under the roar of the sea.

Shelley had known Lena only in four places. She had seen Lena and Bob at her parents' house, at her grandmother's house, at Panorama

Village, and at the International House of Pancakes, where her parents sometimes took them for lunch. She had never seen Lena by herself in the world. Lena was clasping her arms against her chest; the wind of the cars from the highway fluttered her housecoat. Her eyes were shut and her face scrunched up in concentration; it was as if she was imagining herself as a beach person, as someone who could exist here.

Shelley turned away, trying to imagine herself the same way. The Pacific was a flat plain of silver.

"That's where we'll have it," said Lena, gesturing toward the ocean. "Our vacation house with a pool."

"That's the pool?" Shelley asked.

"It's big," said Lena. "I wanted it to be big."

"It's the ocean," said Shelley.

"I want to make it our pool."

"You can't just own the ocean," Shelley said, feeling bossy.

"Why not?"

She wasn't sure. "There are legal rules," she tried. "It belongs to the countries around it." That didn't sound quite right. "Or to the Sea Authority." She stopped.

Lena looked suspicious. Shelley clicked her wrists together several times.

"Well, I want it," said Lena. "You can't say I don't." The mica in the asphalt made the air appear lavender. Lena knelt and scooped up some sand and examined it, patting it gently. She looked at Shelley. "You're scared," she said.

"I am not."

Lena giggled. "You are! You know I can tell."

Shelley was not scared. Only a child would be scared. She was not sitting, like a stuck person, on her front lawn anymore; she had begun to move the moment she ran out of Panorama Village. But now she did not know how to stop. She kept shifting her feet, step-tap, step-tap, in a bizarre little dance. She needed to keep going, to run like a normal person into this new place.

Her aunt seemed to understand. Lena got up and put her hands on Shelley's shoulders; Shelley was still. Lena squeezed her shoulders, and her grasp was a little too tight. "Sequina," she said, seriously, "don't worry. I'm here. I'll take care of you."

Shelley let Lena take her hand and lead her on a walk beside the oily highway. The heat was as thick as cream. They both watched everything around them; there was so much to see. Girls in bikinis tried out roller skates in the beach rental store's parking lot. The girls were so bright with tanning oil, they looked glazed. They swooped from car to car, grabbing roofs and door handles, until they rolled, screeching, to the boardwalk across the street. Boys in OP shorts marched down the highway. Their surfboards resembled large, flat fish that had been captured with great heroics, and were now tucked proudly under their captors' arms.

Down the road was Sav-on, and they headed

toward it. They passed a woman carrying a large plastic bag with the store logo.

"What did she buy?" Lena asked.

"I have no idea."

"Did she buy spoons?"

"Doubtfully."

"I need spoons," said Lena. She held up her fingers and counted off items: "I need spoons and a present and maybe a plate."

She was surprised by the specificity of Lena's list. "How much money do you have?" she asked.

Lena dug into her pockets and brought out some coins. Shelley counted them: forty-seven cents. She herself had a dollar. The two of them looked unenthusiastically at their combined loot.

"This isn't very much money," said Shelley. "What are you planning to buy?"

"I don't need any money," Lena whispered.

"What do you mean?"

"I don't need money," Lena said, and winked, alarmingly. "I get things myself."

They entered the huge cavern of the drugstore. The fluorescent lights ribbing the ceiling emitted a low buzz, and there was a sharp, antiseptic odor in the air.

Lena pulled out a shopping cart and lovingly gripped the red handle. "Mother only lets me get two things," she said, "but I really get lots of things." She gave the cart a little shove and stood in front of it with authority.

"We need toothpaste. We need Alka-Seltzer. We need Pine-Sol." She was obviously determined to put something — anything — in the basket. Wandering down Aisle 1 (*Gardening and Gifts*), she dropped in a pair of pliers, a packet of geranium seeds, and a wicker plate of apricots wrapped in red cellophane. She turned down Aisle 2 (*Cereal and Deodorant*) and tossed in two boxes of Captain Crunch, three bottles of Aqua Velva, and a cylinder of Quaker Oats. Shelley could see the two of them in the curved mirrors bulging in the ceiling corners; their reflections had gigantic heads and tiny, useless arms.

"When Bob and I had our apartment," Lena murmured, "we had many things."

"When did you have an apartment?"

Lena stopped by a table with a coffee machine. A Dixie cup contained several white plastic spoons, and Lena plucked out three and neatly deposited them in her pocket. "Once. A long time ago."

Shelley couldn't picture her aunt living in her own apartment. "Did you like it?"

Lena nodded. "Mother has a house. Vivien has a house. They have furniture and lawns."

Shelley noticed a shadow of envy pass over Lena's face. It was a feeling she understood.

The store offered a reassuring wealth of choices, everything you'd need to live in the world. There was a surprising variety of laxatives, and an entire aisle devoted to hair-coloring products; the models on the boxes had hair the color of burgundy or wheat. Lena and Shelley passed a pyramid of mouthwash bottles, a cardboard tree whose branches were composed of round hairbrushes. The sheer number of items made them both itchy and grandiose. "I'll take that," Lena said, "and that and that." She spoke the words as if they were a song. Shelley knelt by the Halloween costumes and picked through a box of fabric scraps: pieces of beautiful cheap velvet and a big swatch of satiny gold material with sequins. Selecting this satiny piece, she felt it and then replaced it. Lena watched.

Shelley remembered Lena's expression when she borrowed the sunglasses from the patio tables; then, her aunt appeared slightly irate and superior, as though annoyed with the owners of the sunglasses for not taking better care of their belongings. Now her face seemed entirely too peaceful. It was a calm that seemed to conceal unsavory thoughts. Shelley did not want to ask her aunt what she was going to do, afraid of microphones hidden behind the bottles of mouthwash, of cameras tucked inside boxes of Saltines. She walked a few steps behind Lena, enough to pretend not to know her if she had to, but close enough to watch what she did.

They both stopped when they reached the back of the drugstore — *Cosmetics* — and looked up at the huge faces smiling down at them: Jaclyn Smith and Cheryl Tiegs.

"I want to put some on you," said Lena. "I

want to make us fancy today."

"On me?"

"I like putting lipstick on people," Lena said. "I'm very good. I put it on Mrs. Delaney. She has shaky hands. And Mrs. Johnson. Her thumb got mushed. I put it on Mr. Harrison, but he doesn't know. Most of them like when I do it. I'm in demand."

Shelley touched her hands to her face. "You go first."

She had never seen her aunt put on makeup. Lena picked through several lipsticks until she found one the color of Hawaiian Punch. She stood, feet apart, like a football player, and evaluated herself in the mirror; swiftly, she outlined her mouth. Then, with a tiny brush, she touched pale green eyeshadow to her lids. When she was finished, she turned her face to Shelley, waiting for a response.

"I think you look sophisticated," Shelley said, not knowing what other adjective Lena would appreciate.

"Mother doesn't like me to do this. She thinks I look cheap!" Lena said with some pride.

This fact made Lena's face seem even better. "Well, maybe you can be both."

"Now let me try you," Lena said.

"I don't want any."

"But I want to put it on you. What does Sequina look like?" asked Lena.

Again, Shelley touched her cheeks. Softly, she said, "I don't know."

"That's dumb," said Lena. "I want us to both be fancy. Stand still."

Lena smoothed back her hair and cupped Shelley's face in her hands. Her hands were chapped, but she moved them slowly, knowingly. She brought the lipstick to Shelley's mouth and delicately rubbed it along her lips. Then she picked out a brush and swept color along Shelley's cheeks. At one point, she touched a lipstick to Shelley's eyebrows. Another time, she admired the lip gloss she had just applied and took a moment to put some on herself.

Shelley held still, hardly caring how she looked. Lena's touch was exquisitely gentle.

"Look," Lena said.

Tenderly, Shelley once more touched her cheeks. In the mirror that was part of the Revlon display, she examined herself. Though little had been done, she appeared remarkably different. Her lips looked pink and buttery, her cheeks were a velvety bronze, and her eyebrows were those of a fairy, they were so lovely and glittery.

Lena was wiping her rouge-tipped fingers on her housecoat. She looked at Shelley eagerly. "Do you like it?"

"I do."

"Now I have to go buy a present," said Lena. "Watch."

They abandoned the cart and headed down the aisle with their new faces. Now Lena did not just look at the products; she picked them up, examined them. She fondled staplers, vinyl address books, Liquid Paper. Her examination was complete and involved smelling items in a generous and unbiased way. Shelley hung behind, rubbing her palms against her hips, watching the salespeople. The salespeople wandered around the aisles like blue-uniformed, heavy gulls. Shelley made sure to look away from them so that they wouldn't see any suspicious desire in her eyes.

She knew when Lena found what she wanted. Her aunt stood in front of a pile of plastic snowdomes, silver flecks floating inside. Each snowdome said Lahambra Beach Pier and featured a tiny surfer posed on a frozen sea.

Lena squatted, her knees jutting out, large and shiny, and she rocked back on her feet. Humming, she picked through the domes. They made a soft, clattering sound. Eventually, she selected one and balanced it on her palm. She looked like a small jungle animal who had come upon something delicious. She slid her hand into her pocket and kept it there for a moment, her brown eyes sleepy. Then out came her hand, graceful, fingers fluttering. There was nothing in it now.

She looked at Shelley demurely, her eyes flirtatious; she was proud. Shelley stood, frozen, at the other end of the aisle, by stacks of Chips Ahoy and Oreos. Making a shooing gesture, Lena walked to the opposite end of the aisle and found the box of fabrics that Shelley had looked through earlier. She fished out the gold piece, wound it around her hand like a bandage, and slipped it into her pocket.

"Ready?" she asked.

They walked through the store, Lena stealing the items that took her fancy, and Shelley trying to help. The languid faces on the boxes of hair dye seemed alert now, accusing. Shelley tried to direct Lena, like a silent traffic cop, to empty aisles. Lena ignored her and went right for the aisles full of salespeople; she was almost taunting them now. There was a stock boy on his knees, wearily sliding bottles of Wella Balsam into shelves. He was skinny, and his straight red hair fell over his face like a sheer curtain. Lena slowed down; Shelley stopped a few feet away.

"Hi!" Lena said.

The boy looked up. Lena was friendly, expectant. He examined her. "Hi," he said, and turned back to his shampoo.

And then Shelley understood how Lena did it. She knew that people wanted to look away from her. No one could believe that she might be holding something wonderful in her housecoat. So she was in no hurry. Her hands thrust deep in her pockets, she strolled through the glaring aisles of Sav-on, past the boxes of Clairol, the bottles of Listerine. Shelley followed, copying Lena's posture, her gliding step across the linoleum. A voice that could be male or female echoed from a loudspeaker: "Cashier." Beyond the open mouth of the store was the beach, the sound of roaring. Lena went toward it, and Shelley walked with her until they were out of the store.

Five

Ella learned what was wrong with Lena on August 5, 1934. Ella knew the exact date because the pediatrician had written his diagnosis of Lena on a prescription form. Ella told him to write it on this form, because that was the only way, she thought, that Lou would believe it. After the exam, the doctor gave Lena a red lollipop, and it glowed, wet and glossy, in the day's scorching heat. Mother and daughter stepped out of the doctor's office and walked to the car. The day was blue and dry; it seemed powdery, as though one could blow it away with a single breath. Ella clutched Lena's hand. Lena's diagnosis, written in the doctor's formal handwriting, said:

Lena is mildly mentally retarded. This is probably due to an accident at birth. Her intelligence is lower than normal. This does not mean that she cannot lead a happy life.

Ella lay beside her husband in bed. Their breath rose, soft, almost frail, as if they were ashamed of making any sound. Outside, the night moved, thick and dark, and the air was heavy on her arms.

At first, Ella had swiftly and gratefully sunk into sleep, for she felt that she had awakened to the wrong world. For two months after they learned what was wrong with Lena, she and Lou slept, side by side, on their backs. Their arms were cool, like dead people's. They did not kiss; they did not touch.

She and Lou had come to California in 1926, a year after their wedding. Ella had expected a moment of crossing — a line between, perhaps, Utah and Nevada, a place where her life in Boston ended and her life in California would begin. But both she and Lou missed the state sign; the flat, scrubby desert that was Nevada became California with an almost mocking calm.

They had driven together across the country. She and Lou were really just getting to know each other. She woke at night in motels, tiny outposts in Nebraska, Texas, Kansas, the black sky expansive and flooded with stars. All across the country, she watched her husband sleep. It was an astounding thing to sleep with him; it was like entering a realm of great privilege, in which she could touch his skin and watch him dream. She liked to stay awake and hold him in different positions — to wrap her arms around his back and press her lips to his smooth shoulder, or turn her back to him, pulling his arms around her like a belt. They could lie side by side on their backs or their stomachs, or they could face each other, and he would drape a leg over her hip. Their breath rose and fell together. The hushed sound had a terrible sweetness, because they were thousands of miles from anyone they knew.

She was learning new and surprising things about him. When he woke, his breath smelled like cottage cheese. At times of boredom, he engaged in a ritual: he ran his fingertips across tender places in himself — his lips, his wrist bones — as though trying to prize them. When he was in a jaunty mood, he tossed trash out the car and seemed to think this was a daring move.

He told her that he had a theory that when they got to California, they would feel different, grander — the true versions of Mr. and Mrs. Lou Rose. "I'd like to be a flashy dresser," he said wistfully.

"Flashy how?" she asked.

He considered. "I'd like to own an assortment of red shirts." He grew excited and tossed the apple he was eating out the window.

She had her own ideas. "I'd like to learn to make whipped cream desserts," she said. She had read about them in a cookbook one of the girls had brought to the Treasure Trove; she thought them beautiful. She wanted to learn to make desserts with French names. She had a fond picture in her mind of Lou and her eating in a kitchen filled with California flowers; they'd be sharing a whipped cream dessert, and Lou would be wearing a red shirt.

She realized they were in California when they were filling up at a gas station; the glass souvenirs by the cash register had changed to little green palms, with the words *California: The Golden State* wound around each brown trunk. A tiny fear jumped inside her. She tapped Lou's shoulder.

"We're here," she said.

He gripped her hand. "I'd like this, too," he said to the man at the register. "And a chocolate bar."

Lou walked to the back of the station, delicately removed his shoes, and stepped gently into the sand. Ella removed her flats and felt the sand slip beneath her stockings. She broke a white blossom off a cactus and fixed it in a buttonhole on Lou's shirt.

"Flashy," she said.

The desert shimmered with silvery heat. Lou broke the chocolate bar in two. It was already melting. Ella ate hers in one bite.

She looked at Lou. The flower drooped like a crumpled trumpet. "Welcome to California," said Lou. Ella kissed her husband. They tasted exactly alike.

They began armed with a crooked, raw arrogance. Unpracticed, Ella copied Lou. It made them sleepless, talkative. She, too, threw trash out the car window, and the rhythm of her speech began to match his. They began to speak more quickly, in a rush to become the new version of themselves. The streets of Los Angeles were vast and gleaming. Their car crept along the wide boulevards as they looked at everything, trying to absorb it all. Many of the streets were empty, the blue sky clear of clouds.

They had a small sum of money for a down payment. They visited homes for sale in unattainable neighborhoods — Hancock Park, Beverly Hills — she wearing fancy hats with veils, Lou sporting one of his red shirts. The homeowners regarded them with puzzled expressions. "Mr. and Mrs. Lou Rose," announced Lou, offering an eager hand. They strode into gorgeous homes with bemused, challenging expressions, as though the owners should be the grateful ones. "*That* puddle? That's the swimming pool?" asked Lou. Ella inspected the closets, vetoed them all.

These homes were completely beyond their reach. They left, exhausted, throats dry with greed. They took pastrami sandwiches to Rancho Park or the La Brea Tar Pits, sat on the grass, and gloriously mocked everyone. "That last man was a ghoul," said Lou. "Did you hear the way he breathed?"

Her bare arms were too pale. "I did not care for those bushes," she said with disdain; for at that last house the bushes had been trimmed in the shape of bears.

She deferred to Lou. She wanted to believe in his authority; she did not want them both to be children. They ate their sandwiches under silver-green eucalyptus trees and watched small lizards dart across the sidewalk. She had never seen such creatures; they were tiny, prehistoric, their tongues shooting out and deliciously licking the air.

The houses they could afford were in the San Fernando Valley. They had known all along they'd have had to settle for that. It was hotter there, a quiet heat that magnified sounds. The house where she would start her family was not what she had hoped to own. It was a two-bedroom, burnt-orange stucco house, with slightly warped hardwood floors and a garden that was mostly dirt. The street was filled with these houses. Laundry lines were strung between avocado and lemon trees; fans whirred, guttural as airplane engines. Their neighbors had come from the Midwest or from farms that had failed upstate in the Central Valley.

Ella and Lou had their suitcases and a used bed purchased from Salvation Army. They bought some canned food and bread and coffee. They had an address.

The first night they spent in the house was before the electricity had been turned on, so they ate their first dinner in darkness. They bought some flashlights and set them in the empty rooms. Each white beam shot up through the darkness like an eerie plant with a single transparent stalk. They walked through the dim, chalk-smelling rooms, closing doors, turning on faucets. They were inside their lives now, not outside, suspended in their newness, peering into a ring filled with vague images that were dazzling and bright.

Lou had a surprise for her. He told her about it in their future living room, the flashlight beam turning filaments of his hair incandescent in the dark. "You have to find it," he said. She walked around the empty house, feeling her way along the walls. He followed, enjoying her pure and delicate blindness.

She found his surprise in the bathroom as she ran her hands along the bottom of the pink porcelain bathtub. There was a slender spike at the bottom; it swelled into a heel. She lifted it out — an elegant, silk high-heeled shoe. She ran her hand in the tub again; there was another shoe, too. Ella, puzzled, slipped her hands into them.

"Put them on," said Lou.

She stepped into the shoes. She had never worn such high heels.

"Look at you," he said.

Ella undid her blouse, her skirt. She let everything fall. "Look at me," she said.

She walked through every room in their new house naked, except for those shoes. The sharp heels made a sound of grand and audacious authority. Of course, Lou followed her. She picked up a flashlight and turned it toward him, herself, her bare body. He unbuttoned his shirt, and she turned the flashlight away until he, too, was completely naked. They took turns holding the flashlight on each other; they both looked glorious. But they did not immediately go to each other, for they merely wanted to look — here, breathless, unashamed.

Before they tried to start a business, they had to get real jobs. Lou worked as an assistant to a fur salesman. Ella worked in the A. E. Little department store's equivalent of the Treasure Trove; she found it far less glamorous, because there was no uniform or fake diamond pin to wear.

By 1930, Lou wanted to open his own store; the question was what to sell. At night, he threw himself into planning advertising campaigns. His experience in Los Angeles had made him good at selling products people did not really need. He considered, briefly, men's accessories, because he was proud of his slogan: *Lou's accessories are successories!* Then he switched to pants: *No need to lose precious doubloons. Buy Lou's pantaloons!* His mouth hung open with concentration. His hands were quick, almost frantic. With a set of colored pencils, he sketched signs for his future store deep into the night.

Ella paged through movie magazines, searching for names for their child. They were trying to have a baby; it was the next step. She sent letters to movie stars she admired, awaiting glossy photos with their signature. The star who wrote the nicest reply on the photo would win; their baby would bear that star's name. One of those stars would sense her special qualities, thought Ella; one of them would know. Polite letters went out to Marlene Dietrich, Carole Lombard, Lillian Gish, and others. Every afternoon, Ella eagerly checked the mailbox, and she kept each publicity photo in a drawer. But the replies made her restless, not quite understood.

Marlene Dietrich was the only one who used her name when she answered: *Good luck, Ella. Thanks, Marlene.* Marlene shimmered, her hair and her lips were suffused with light. She was so beautiful that she seemed not a citizen of this earth. Yet the reply was personal; that was why she won.

Ella did not know when she became pregnant. There was no immediate shift in her body; the beginning of life was mundane. In the deepest, quietest part of her, love was turning to flesh.

Lou decided on shoes. *Lou's Shoes. I'll Help You Step Into Your Future.* They painted the sign together on a large sheet of metal, several times, until the letters were absolutely straight.

They set up the store on a brilliant September day. Ella was six months pregnant. There was one large, sunny room, for sales, and a back room for stock. Lou stacked the boxes and installed a cash register, unrolling cylinders of quarters, pennies. He hung a large banner that said: *We're not God, but we do save soles.*

During that fall, the unborn child was kicking; it was as if clear, heavy bubbles were bursting inside Ella. The child moved toward its life. The sky was flustered with gray-bottomed clouds; the light fell through them darkly, different; Ella

105

watched the world with solemn joy. This was the last September she and Lou would be alone together, the last October before the child was born. She bought baby furniture at second-hand stores and arranged it in the empty room. Sometimes she stood in the doorway and surveyed the silent room, the faded yellow crib, the smiling toy bears. The room's emptiness was pure. She tried to imagine the sound of the baby's cry, the way the child would crawl or walk across the room. She would have to wait.

The birth of her first daughter came and went quickly. Ella was in labor for twenty-five hours, and Dr. Brown, the resident substituting for Dr. Morton, was younger than she was. He drew the baby out of her with a long steel instrument. There was a large bump on one side of the baby's head. Later, Ella remembered mostly the color and shape of the doctor's hands. His fingers were extraordinarily delicate, and his hands had the tenderness of an infant's, frail and shell-pink.

They did not want to look at the bump. It disappeared slowly, turning black and blue, then fading away. It was as though someone had stepped on Marlene, some other baby had stamped on her in her hurry to get out. Then Marlene was just a baby, that pink, blameless fact, a surge of fat and silk hair that evoked a pure, reflexive love. They called her Lena; Ella expected her daughter to grow into the name Marlene. Neighbors she barely knew brought oranges, lemons, walnuts from their backyard, gave her clothes that their children had outgrown. They stroked her baby the way they stroked all babies — reverently, running a finger along Lena's soft arms.

Ella had not known how she would love her child. Later, Ella wondered whether she had loved Lena differently before she understood that anything was wrong. It was as though she and the baby had broken off from Lou, into their own secret world. He was busy. He had to work during the day as the fur assistant to ensure a paycheck; he kept his shoe store open only on weekends and at night.

She was alone with Lena all day. Who was this person? What did she want? No one had ever been so dependent on her. Ella did her motherly duties — she nursed Lena, changed her, took her along to the market. But these activities simply made her resemble other mothers; they didn't account for the change within her. Her heart was assuming a new shape; it was becoming a great, curving sky.

She tried to tell Lou what Lena had done during the day, but each act she described sounded less important than it had been. "She enjoyed her bananas," said Ella. "She ate five spoonfuls."

"Five?" asked Lou. "All five?" He looked at Lena, making a comic face. He seemed oddly shy; self-conscious. He wanted mostly to be liked. Lena stared back at him with every baby's serene expression of self-regard and haughty dis-approval.

A baby was bound to its future. It was as though Lena were mysteriously joined with all the people she could become. To Ella, alone with her daughter, the house was filled with these un-known people, and Ella began to make plans. One day, she wanted Lena to be a glamorous ac-tress. Another day, she wanted Lena to be fluent in French. Or perhaps proficient in preparing the fine foods of several European countries. Ella, excited by these prospects, imagined their discussions about various issues. "No, Lena," she would say, "I do not think you should take that size suitcase to Paris." She imagined the tone of voice she'd use, ranging from patient to rather shrill. The kitchen was silent; the discus-sion was all in her head. And it absorbed her completely.

Lena had beautiful, gleaming brown eyes. Mother and daughter gazed at each other in the small kitchen, and they waited.

Lou wanted Ella to help him at the store. Be-sides, he was lonely without her. People wan-dered in at night, touched the shoes, looked sheepish, and went out. Ella made up wax-paper bags of her chocolate chip cookies and sold them at the register, twenty-five cents a bag. A gas sta-tion opened down the block, and a diner. More people came by; a few stayed.

It was a stranger, armed with her three-year-old, who first suggested that something was wrong with Lena. Ella forever remembered that woman; she became engraved in Ella's mind. The woman had curly black hair that was almost navy, and she was examining a sleek white bridal pump. Lena, propped on one of the metal chairs, was staring at her feet, as though deciding whether to eat them. Her mouth hung open, and a clear thread of drool dropped to her lap. Ella asked the woman whether she needed help.

The woman was looking at Lena. "I remember her," she said. "I dropped in a couple of years ago. Lena. How you doing, cutie?"

Lena smiled. The woman suddenly looked intent. Lena's smile was the shape of an orange slice. Perhaps that was what made it not quite right; it was like the smile of a baby seal. Ella had never looked at Lena's smile this way. Lena twisted down from the chair to the floor and walked around the room with her peculiar walk; it was like a drunken hop.

"Is her leg all right?" the woman asked.

"Oh, sure," said Ella. "Probably asleep."

When Lena drew closer, Ella put her hand on her hair and gently fingered it.

"Harvey, this is Lena," said the woman to her son.

"Hello," said the tiny boy gripping his mother's leg.

Lena's face swerved into an expression of glee. "Tal!" she shrieked. It was an odd sound, almost a bleat. Her breath rose and fell, like a giggle, like a tiny vampire. The boy was still.

"How old is Harvey?" asked Ella, and then realized it was not what she should have asked.

"Three," said his mother.

"Oh? So's my Lena," blurted Ella.

The world broke apart — softly and too fast. Sorrow blew across the woman's face; her child had won some unannounced contest, and she had been handed some unnecessary guilt. She became extremely polite. "You do have such nice bridal shoes!" she exclaimed. She wandered about, looking at more shoes, listlessly; then she and the little boy walked out into the hazy light. Ella stood in the empty store while Lena rolled silently on the floor. The white sun fell on the carpet, grotesque and watery bright.

Ella began to watch other children. Trying to control the anxiety in her voice, she would ask customers, neighbors, the ages of their children. Standing behind the register, she carefully observed children in the store. She watched them wrestle with each other, try on shoes, and she heard them speak — clear sentences, words.

Would Lena be worth more if other children didn't exist? In such a world, Lena would be perfect. Ella began to wish the other children would disappear — all of them, the nice as well as the poorly behaved ones. She wished so powerfully for their disappearance that when she crouched to fit shoes on them, she was afraid to touch their tiny, outstretched feet.

She had to tell Lou, partly because she was jealous of his ignorance; she could not live alone in her confusion.

They were in the kitchen, eating chicken salad on lettuce leaves. Lou had recently purchased a four-foot-tall blue neon boot that said LOU! on the heel. It was to be placed in front of the store. He was simultaneously proud of it and concerned. "My name is on the heel," he said, soberly. "I don't know if I want customers to see that."

"Why not?"

He cleared his throat. "Perhaps they may think I am a heel."

"I doubt that customers think so much."

He was eager to argue. "No, sweetheart," he said, "you can't underestimate the customers. They're smart —"

"I don't care," Ella said, in a tone harsher than she herself had expected. He looked hurt.

"Ella," he said, "decisions like this can make or break a —"

"I'm worried about Lena."

The air hardened. Lena looked from one to the other and began to cry.

Lou put a hand on the girl's arm and stroked it, trying to comfort her. "Shhh," he said, kissing her tiny hand. "Don't listen to her. Shh."

"Lou. She doesn't talk like the other children; look how she walks."

He pulled Lena into his lap. "Look here," he said, his voice husky with fatigue. "Look. You're a smart girl, so stop trying to hide it!"

Lou would not meet Ella's eyes; that proved her right. "You have to wake up," she said.

"Ella!" He wrapped his arms around their daughter. "How is she going to feel when she hears you saying that?"

For two months after they had learned about Lena, Ella rose every morning without kissing Lou. She woke up first and went into the bathroom, taking a shower and filling the room with white steam. She liked the warm mist clinging to her as she applied her lipstick, set her hair; it was as if, during the night, something unclean had happened to her and Lou, their chaste sleep a little obscene. Mold began to grow in the corners of the floor. The carnation-patterned Royledge paper lining the shelves started to curl. When she came out of the room, Lou was always up and completely dressed.

He wasn't exactly like Lou now; he was bigger, like a cartoon Lou, coated with a shiny cheeriness. He called her an assortment of pet names he'd heard in movies. "What's for breakfast, Pumpkin?" he'd ask.

"What do you want?"

Everything she said sounded vaguely leering, flirtatious. By this time, Lena was hurtling around the house, a thin, off-key song trailing through the halls.

He answered, "What do *you* want?"

Their shock had given way to a horrid politeness. "Anything," she said. "Waffles, pancakes, Cream of Wheat."

"Well," he said, hesitating. The sun poured through the curtains into the bedroom. His features were gilded by the light.

How young he looked. He was already thirty-eight, but his skin was as creamy as a girl's. Part of Ella ached for him to know everything. She wished he were six feet tall or had a lush beard or a fancy car — anything that would convey authority and command.

His eyes, as he looked at her, were hot with tenderness; it was as though she could see through them into his thoughts. She turned away. She didn't want to know what he was thinking for fear that his thoughts were as dark as her own.

"We'll have Cream of Wheat," she decided. Lena banged on the door, and Ella opened it. Lou scooped up his daughter, and Lena squealed, her legs kicking, as he swung her into the air.

She had to learn to understand Lena, but she didn't know where to begin. She decided to start at the local library, where she found a book: *God's Special Children*. It featured descriptions and photos of children who had been born wrong. Ella read it secretly at night, for instruction, and also to conjure up some feelings of superiority and comfort. There were children with huge heads, children with cleft palates, children

113

with fins for arms. As she stared at the pictures of deformed children, an evil feeling of gratitude came over her; at least Lena was a pretty girl.

She looked at pictures of mongoloid children, at photos of retarded adults engaged in various activities. They hunched over plates at picnics or sat on porches or leaned against cars. Often their faces looked hopeful. Ella tried to make friends with the men and women in these photos. She gave them names. Here was Alfred; here was Lorraine. Ella kept the book under the bed, ashamed to be reading it. Yet it was all she could think to do. Ella forced herself to study the pictures until her eyes burned, until these people appeared understandable.

She had no idea what Lena was going to be. She sent away for information from any organization that seemed relevant. There was a Committee to Aid the Feeble-Minded, the Jewish Children's Fund, the Council for the Mentally Impaired. She crossed theology lines and received the Baptist League pamphlet, which said, *You must reform. This child has been cast upon you because of your many sins.*

She opened the envelopes with trembling hands. She would read the enclosures methodically, completely. With each new pamphlet, she would pour herself a glass of orange juice and read. Much of the information was vague and cheerful, and all the organizations requested money. One brochure had a chart linking IQ levels with abilities to do certain tasks. She sat with this chart for a long time, waiting for it to reveal the future. A person with an IQ from 55 to 69 could learn to read to the sixth-grade level. A person with an IQ from 40 to 54 could learn to sweep a floor and count change. A person with an IQ of 39 or lower would have to live in an institution. *These people cannot be trained. It is best for them to live in a safe and controlled environment.*

Once, she sent away for information from an institution, the California Home for the Mentally Handicapped. There was a photo of a large, barren dormitory filled with a dozen beds. The citizens of the home wore uniforms; they looked like large children wearing pajamas. And they had sorrowful, wondering eyes. Ella calmly held this brochure over the gas flame on her stove.

From her reading, Ella had estimated Lena's IQ at around 56. There was no basis for her choosing this number, but it struck her as high enough to approach a normal intelligence without being too obviously ambitious. Soon, Lena would have to begin kindergarten, which Ella hoped to postpone as long as possible. There were so many things Lena needed to learn. She was four years old and not yet toilet-trained; Ella bought dresses that were oversized so that the diapers wouldn't show. Lena spoke words now, with great enthusiasm, but didn't always create sentences. Ella lay beside Lou in bed, and her mind spun with plans. She was possessed with an energetic sense of purpose that went nowhere. One night, she arrived at a small but important decision. She would teach Lena to give up her bottle and learn to drink her milk from a cup.

The next morning, she set a cup of milk next to a plate of waffles glistening with maple syrup. Lena dunked her fingers into the cup and sucked the milk from her thumb.

"More," she said. She gestured elegantly, like a small emperor.

"Lena," said Ella, cheerfully, "I want you to learn to drink your milk from a cup."

Lena rubbed her fist against her open mouth with the vigor of a teething baby. Lou looked up from his newspaper. "What are you talking about?" asked Lou.

"She's capable of learning this," said Ella, trying not to sound too much like the Miracle Worker.

"Mmm," he said. They sat in silence for a moment. Lena patiently stirred her milk with her fingers, and Ella put her hand on Lena's. "Honey, no," she said. Lena looked at her, annoyed, shook off her hand, and continued stirring the milk.

Lou's expression was unformed. Then it flickered, like a little boy's, into amusement. "Lena," he asked, "how do you do that?" Lena smiled broadly. He dunked his thumb into the creamer and licked off some drops.

"Lou!" Ella said.

Lena watched him and laughed; then she

wiped her milky hand on the tablecloth.

"Tastes pretty good," said Lou. When he saw Ella's expression, his face turned sheepish and he jumped up.

"Lou," she said, "I want your help in —"

"Goodbye!" he said, brightly, backing toward the door. "Have a good day!" The door opened and fell shut.

She and Lena spent their regular day. At the market, they bought bananas, Ajax, a chicken, onions, and pears. Ella had short, strange conversations with Lena in which Ella heard herself speak in an adult's voice and heard Lena blurt exuberant words. The sky was clouding over; the leaves glittered in the clear air.

They went to the local park, and Ella spread a blanket on the dry grass. She tickled her daughter, which Lena loved. The girl had a businessman's deep laugh.

Lena was made of her. That fact made Ella hot and fragile with love. She kept looking for pieces of herself in her daughter. She did not know how this knowledge would reassure her, but she searched for small, external markers. Lena had her caramel-brown eyes, her delicate eyebrows, her petal-like ears. How could Lena not understand the simple task of drinking from a cup?

Ella poured apple juice into two paper cups and arranged Lena's hands around one of them. "Now just like this," she said, raising her own cup. "Watch."

Lena held the cup, but it seemed to have

fallen into her hands; she was not, in any real way, holding the cup.

Ella showed Lena how she enjoyed lifting her cup and drinking from it. "Delicious," she said. "Like this. Do you want to try?"

Lena watched and chortled, but she wasn't interested in imitating her mother. For the entire afternoon, Ella tried. The air became cool and the clouds grew thicker. Ella tried apple juice, orange juice, lemonade; impatience curled into her voice. "Lena, just try!" she snapped at last, and she and the child stared at each other, aghast.

At the end of the afternoon, they went to help Lou at the store. Before they left the park, Ella tied an orange ribbon around Lena's hair. She knew that customers could see that something was wrong with her daughter. Small things told them — the way her mouth hung open, her blank expression, the way she blinked with great emphasis, as though the action required deep thought. She tied the ribbon around Lena's hair so that people would find something positive to say about her; she sensed they would be grateful for that.

Lou was king of Lou's Shoes. A Woolworth's had opened near his store, and other shops; the blue neon heel glowed even during the day. Lou had a couple of seats reserved for people who wanted to keep him company and make humorous remarks.

It was a relief to enter the store; gratefully, Ella

breathed the scent of shoe polish and fresh leather. Fred Epstein was sitting on a metal folding chair. He was a small, sarcastic janitor at Woolworth's who came to Lou on his coffee break; he pretended to be sales help so that he could flirt with the customers. He was watching a woman judge herself in a pair of pumps before the square shoe mirror. "Higher heel," he suggested.

The woman looked at him. "Do you think so?" she asked.

"Better for the leg," said Fred, his face awash with false innocence. "Makes them shapelier."

The woman rubbed her leg. "Could always use that," she said.

"Don't listen to that guy," Lou said. "Comfort. That's all that counts."

Lou was leaning against the counter, his arms crossed. "Hello," he said, his face lighting up when he saw Ella. "You two have a good day?"

The windows were white with dust from the Santa Ana. Ella took a rag from under the counter and began to clean them. Lena picked up a ball of socks and began to suck them.

The customer decided to buy the shoes. When she stepped past Lena, the girl looked up with a hungry expression. "Hi!" she screeched and, with violent appreciation, grabbed the woman's leg. Ella stopped wiping the windows. The woman jerked away "Ow," she said.

"Don't mind her," said Lou. "You want me to wrap that up?"

Ella didn't recognize Lou's voice. There was a cheerful, detached quality to it that made her shiver. The customer paid and left. Lou looked at Fred merrily. "She bought them!" he said.

Fred was chortling; he shook his head.

"You hike up the price, and look what happens," said Lou.

Slowly, Ella put down the rag and walked across the store to him. "I need to talk to you," she said.

She went to the one private place, the stockroom, and Lou followed. She shut the door. The room smelled of old merchandise, a licorice, factory smell. The air between them was stifling.

"You're an idiot," she said quietly.

He looked hurt; then his face changed to an ugly, fake innocence. "Why?"

"You know why."

"She grabbed a customer's leg," he said, plaintively.

"So?"

He began lining up boxes on shelves. His shoulders tensed; she could see the muscles shift under his cotton shirt. "Ella!" he said, turning around. "What if she embarrasses me!" The words fell between them like chunks of ice. "I'm trying to sell things."

"She won't embarrass you."

"How do you know?"

"I just do."

He rubbed his face. "We don't know anything. I don't know who she is . . ."

His eyes had a needy wetness. Ella felt searing

hate shoot through her. "Well," she shouted, "you embarrass me!"

She ran out of the stockroom. Fred was pretending to read a magazine; Lena was rolling merrily on the floor. Ella grabbed Lena's hand, pulled her to her feet, and rushed out to the street.

It was raining. In her hatred, the world seemed sharper, more beautiful. The sky was swollen like a whale's underbelly, a soft gray, and the smell of dry grass rarely touched by rain rose into the air. Looking down, she could see herself and Lena reflected in the shiny pavement, the soles of their feet clapping against pale versions of themselves. Cool pearls of water clung to their hair.

Ella ducked into Woolworth's and waited for the rain to stop. She was aware that she had suffered some perverse, invisible damage; touching her throat, lips, she could find no external change. The injury was deep in some place she could not detect.

She dried Lena's hair with a Kleenex. Whimpering, the girl pressed hard against her mother; swiftly, like a robber, she grabbed her mother's wrist. "Shh," Ella murmured, her voice trembling. She shivered, as if ice were forming around them, preserving them as they now were.

Outside was the urgent click of women's heels on the wet pavement. Anger drained from Ella, leaving her hollow. Lena's hair was neatly combed. The rain stopped and the street sparkled.

By the time they got home, Lena was in a surly mood. She didn't want to try to drink milk from a cup. "Bottle," she demanded, her eyes glittering; exhausted, Ella gave in. Lena marched around, sucking the bottle of milk triumphantly. She looked like a trumpeter announcing the imminent arrival of a regal being.

Ella had no idea how to fill the emptiness within her. She decided to make borscht. The kitchen was quiet except for Lena's sucking, a ravenous, squeaky sound. The evening evolved, dark and wet, through the sheer curtains. Ella felt good and useful as she grated the beets. The juice stained her palms pink and the counter a beautiful purple. She and Lena were at the kitchen table eating the soup when she heard Lou. Ella hadn't yet cleaned up; purple borscht violently splattered the white sink. The door slammed, and Lou came in.

"Hello," he called. He sounded like himself, but tentative. He hung up his hat and took off his wet shoes. Lena began to pound a spoon on the table, a thin, repetitive clink.

The air between Ella and her husband was bruised. She looked at her soup, not knowing what to say.

Then she heard him gasp.

The sound was as insistent and horrified as a baby's cry. She looked up; Lou was staring at the purple stain in the sink. Quickly, Lou turned and reached the table in two large steps. He studied his wife and daughter. The silence between them was brimming. Then something wilted in him, and he was ashamed.

He joined them at the table and reached over to smooth Lena's hair. Ella spooned out some borscht and sour cream for him. The shock had comforted her, made her believe that the feelings they had were somehow the same.

He stirred the sour cream until his borscht turned a creamy pink. "This looks delicious," he said.

She watched him; there was struggle in his face.

"I'd like to ask you something," he said.

"Yes?"

He swallowed a spoonful. "Do you remember when we met?"

"Of course."

"What do you remember?"

She thought. "You said my name. Immediately. I liked that."

He smiled and looked into his bowl. She wondered what he was getting at.

"Do you wish you'd married someone else?" he asked.

She was startled. "What do you mean?"

"I don't know." He set down his spoon. When he spoke, he had pale lavender teeth; they both did. There was a question in his expression, of his own worth — a feeling she fully understood.

"I can't sleep. I watch you. You're so beautiful."

"Lou," she whispered.

"I think, wouldn't this beautiful woman's life be easier if she'd just said, 'Wait. Someone else will help you'?"

Ella put her hand on his. Her heart expanded as though it were filled with sweet air. They were married to each other. His fingers were solid and warm. She rubbed her fingertips lightly over his. She did not know what she and he were becoming, but surely they were being formed anew, with all their strange emotions. His hand squeezed hers and she felt, with a deeper love, the muscular heartbeat in his palm.

Lena again was clinking her spoon against the table. Suddenly, the thin sound stopped. She looked at her parents, and a happy expression suffused her face. She dipped her fingers into the milk and held them out to her mother. She laughed, a delighted caw, and gently touched her fingers to her mother's lips.

Six

Shelley and Lena moved together, like soldiers, out of the drugstore. The sunlight was bone-white and made the world look speckled. The beach revealed itself in its hard brightness — the line of cars moving slowly down the highway, the palms leaning like lonely giraffes into the wind. On the other side of the highway, the sand spread out, dirty with violet hollows.

"Are we safe yet?" Shelley whispered to Lena.

"Shh," said Lena, "we're making our getaway."

Lena crossed the parking lot primly, then tried to burst onto the busy highway while the light was still red. It was this transgression that made Shelley understand, clearly, what they had done. "Hey!" she yelled, grabbing her aunt around the waist. She held Lena tight, feeling her heart pulse through her broad back. Together, they stood at the edge of the parking lot, and Shelley waited, almost calmly, for someone to come after them. But, easily, the light turned green, and they hurried across the highway to Lahambra Beach.

They'd made it! Shelley was dizzy with triumph. Potato chip bags floated slowly, majestically, through the air; fat seagulls made their wistful calls. Shelley slipped off her sandals and untied Lena's sneakers. They pushed their bare feet into the sand, which pooled around their feet like warm caramel.

They looked at each other with the delight of two people who had just learned something brand new about each other. Then they fell on the sand and laughed with glee. "How did you learn how to do that?" Shelley asked.

"Jessica. My friend. She showed me," Lena said, with pride. "I know how to steal cigarettes, bobby pins, Reese's peanut butter cups, Mallomars, Chap Sticks, and Juicy Fruit gum."

"But how?"

"Number one, you have to have big pockets. Number two, you have to keep your hands in them. You have to have big hands." She held up her hands, the fingers splayed. "Mother gives me five dollars a week, but sometimes I want more things."

"Does anyone ever catch you?"

"No," said Lena. "They just let me go by. Do you think you know how now?" She studied Shelley's face.

"Why?"

"I want to teach you something." Lena looked away and plunged her feet deep into the sand.

The borrowing they'd done was different; Lena had somehow convinced Shelley that they were helping out the sunglasses or nail clippers by giving them a job. But now they were just helping themselves to the world. Shelley tried to accept the idea. They were robbers on an unknown beach, and Shelley looked smugly at the other beachgoers, hoping they were afraid. "I think I do," she said.

"Jessica showed me," said Lena. "She's nice. But sometimes she pinches me if I turn on a bad show." She held out her wrist. "She likes *Love Boat*," said Lena, "but I like game shows —"

Shelley took Lena's wrist and stroked it tenderly, as though it were made of glass. "Honey, friends shouldn't pinch," said Shelley. "They're supposed to be nice to you."

Lena began to pull things from her pockets. Out came the snowdome, the spoons. And out came the gold material. She was eager to present it to her niece. A couple of the sequins fluttered to the sand. "It's for you," said Lena. She held it toward Shelley. "I bought it for you."

Shelley stood up and wrapped the material, with a flourish, over her shoulders and twirled around. It made a good shawl. The material had the antiseptic smell of Sav-on. Because it was not supposed to be theirs, it was all the more valuable. Lena had bought the shawl for her, but Lena had no beautiful thing of her own to wear. Shelley found a small run at a seam, and started to tear the cloth in half.

Lena shrieked, "Don't!"

"Wait," Shelley said, taking apart the fabric until it was two scarves.

"That was my present," said Lena.

Shelley draped one half around Lena's shoulders, the other around herself. "Now it fits both of us."

Lena tugged at the scarf suspiciously. "Why?"

"Because," Shelley said, "we have to have something to wear to our party. We're fancy. We're dressed up."

"Oh. I'm fancy," Lena repeated softly. "I'm dressed up."

Shelley stroked the flimsy gold material. She tried to remember what she had worn the last time she had visited Bob and Lena. She remembered little except that her outfit had been quite complicated. Lena and Bob had been so eager to see her, they were almost hovering above the sidewalk. That day, they'd been bursting with their dares. The three of them had headed down the street with a brutal enthusiasm, as though trying to leave new imprints of themselves in the air.

Now Shelley sat down beside Lena; it was too quiet. She wanted them to keep talking. The two of them swirled the warm sand with their hands.

"Have you been brushing your teeth?" she asked Lena.

Lena shook her head.

"Honey, remember. It's important." She kept saying *honey* because it made her feel old.

"I hate it," said Lena.

"Let me look in your mouth."

"No."

"Why not?"

"It's ugly."

"Come on. Just open."

Lena opened her mouth reluctantly, like an infant awaiting unwanted food. She had only five teeth left. One, a front incisor, was an eerie moonlike white. The act of looking into Lena's mouth made Shelley feel more like herself.

"You're not brushing anymore."

"I have no one to give my teeth." Lena dug into her top pocket and pulled out a handful of broken chips. "He used to keep these in his right pocket. This one came out when I was eating salad. This one came out when I was eating a banana." She held out her palm as though offering her niece hors d'oeuvres.

"Give them to me," said Shelley.

"Why?"

"I'll keep them for you."

"But you're not him."

"Let me try."

She cupped her hands, and Lena poured the little shards into them and watched as Shelley slipped them into her shorts pocket. "Are they safe?" she asked anxiously.

"Yes," Shelley said. "I'll keep them safe."

She was glad to be holding Lena's teeth, to touch the pebbly lumps in her pocket.

"Thank you," said Lena, and pressed her fingers against her mouth, trying to push the gratitude back into her lips.

Lena stood up and brushed off the sand. "Let's go," she said, putting her new possessions back into her pockets. Suddenly, she was in a great rush. A boardwalk, like a fat silver road along the sand, was crowded with people both rich and shabby, smug and desperate. There was the smell of fried foods, the sweetness of coconut oil on hot skin, the sourness of salt water and urine. Shelley and Lena were not invited, but they joined the crowd.

Everyone was looking at everyone. It was as if each person had a wish that could not be spoken, that was so obscene or private that it would be shameful to speak it aloud. Rows of older teenagers rested against a stucco wall covered with graffiti, huge purple and pink letters. The teens were white and black, their hair water-stiff or curled high in combs. They all wore the same bored expression. An enormously fat woman roller-skating around in a black vinyl bathing suit and bobby socks passed out leaflets that said *Learn about your life. Palm reading $5.* She rolled toward Shelley and Lena and said, "Come on, ladies! Two for one, seven bucks. Don't pass this one up."

"No, thank you," said Shelley.

The woman's face dropped. "We'll tell you whatever the fuck you want," she said. "Seven bucks is all —"

Shelley meant to explain that they didn't have seven bucks, but the woman had skated away.

Roller skaters came at them at violent speeds, their thighs buttery in neon blue or yellow or pink Spandex. Just before colliding with them, the skaters parted around them like a sea.

Lena and Shelley passed a booth with posters of almost naked ladies, including three leaning over a motorcycle with the caption *Nothing butt fun.* Some people seemed to find this funny. They walked by others crouched on faded movie towels, *Jaws* and *Star Wars* and *Saturday Night Fever.* They looked as though they were bowing to the others who passed them on the boardwalk, their heads bent, shoulders burning. Everyone was selling things: incense curling off long sticks, four-minute massages, unflattering oil paintings of Farrah Fawcett, toe rings. One woman sat on a concrete wall behind random food items arranged carefully on her towel: a bottle of Heinz ketchup, a bottle of A-1 sauce, a package of Cheerios.

This was the first time Shelley had been outside in her tank top. It was pale blue cotton with little lace straps and ended right below her belly button. She felt almost naked; she was aware of the watery motion of her new breasts inside.

Sometimes, when she was alone in her house, she would walk around with her hands under her shift, feeling her breasts. It was daring to touch her breasts in the kitchen, the backyard, the living room; the action marked these places in a way no one would ever know. She cupped her breasts with her whole hand or pressed her fingers on the nipples to create a doughnut shape.

Now something new was happening around her as she walked. She could feel men staring at her in a way no one had done. Their gaze was un-blinking, and their faces were both severe and babyish. It was as though they were involved in a silent conversation with her. She thought it was because she was doing threes against her hips, and her hands froze, briefly, as she walked. But they were looking at her with an altogether new expression, one she had often seen on the faces of boys looking at other girls. One man sent out a whistle, a low, sultry sound.

Shelley found the world separating itself into two streams. She was walking down one stream, and Lena down the other. Hers was brighter, for she was illuminated in this new and unexpected way. She had not allowed herself to hope that others could look at her in this flattering manner. She also noticed how people regarded Lena. Their eyes settled on her, stopped, moved on.

She looked at Lena, trying to see what made others want to look away. Lena's green eyelids were a little faded, and she had licked her lipstick off; now she looked as if she'd been drinking red juice. Her housecoat was faded in the sunlight, and Shelley saw an orange stain on the back. Her thin hair riffled back from her scalp like little flames. But she gazed at the crowds in a direct, open way. Though few people looked at her, Lena stared intently at everyone else.

She brushed up beside Shelley. "Where are they going?" She gestured to the crowd.

"I don't know. Different places. Some are probably just walking along."

Lena slowed down. "They like being almost naked," she said. This seemed to stir her up. She stormed forward, watching the girls in thong bikinis, the fathers in their swimming trunks, pale, with forearms pink to their elbows, like gloves. She carefully opened the top button of her housecoat. "Why?"

This seemed a complicated question. "Because they want to get tan," Shelley tried.

Lena nodded and undid another button; she was pleased to join in. They walked together down the boardwalk. Sometimes Lena stopped, closed her eyes, and lifted her face, letting the warm salt wind blow through her hair.

A large group was assembled around a wire fence, watching what was going on inside. Shelley and Lena pushed to the front, and Lena clapped a hand over her mouth as a man, packed tight into pink Speedos, walked into the pit.

"He's wearing panties!" She giggled. "Outside!"

The man was walking royally, past the other bodybuilders. His hairless bronze arms were swollen with muscles; he held them out, like wings, by his sides. His behind looked like two grapefruits stuffed into a plastic bag.

"Let's watch," Lena said. Bleachers surrounded the fence. Shelley and Lena found space on the bottom rung.

There were seven men in the pit, and they were walking around the rubber mat, lifting steel weights. Someone had turned a portable radio to a Donna Summer song, and her high voice threaded delicately through the pit.

Shelley had never seen men with bodies like this; she was mesmerized. One man, in a red bandanna and zebra-striped tank top, was lifting a barbell. He grunted, a sound like *huh,* and muscles popped out of his arms like oranges or walnuts. His face was burning red and his jaw was clenched and his eyes were white and murderous. The people in the bleachers were silent. He clutched the barbell, arms trembling, for a few seconds, and then set it down with a little scream. Some spectators applauded. Another man bent his arms behind his head, girlish, exposing hairless, cavernous armpits. He stood that way for a moment, admiring his reflection in a blurry sheet of steel.

They stood in their trunks of fire red and lemon yellow and lime green, and their bodies swelled up around them like weird, hopeful dreams. Their thighs were hammy hunks, and their chests had hard, womany breasts. Their bodies were covered with veins. Some had blurry tattoos on their arms. They were shiny with oil and sweat, and they kept glancing at their bodies in the steel sheet. The rubber mat smelled rich and sour in the beach heat. A woman in the bleachers burst out in an appreciative whoop.

Shelley thought of the couples in her school. Once, she'd passed a boy rolling on top of a girl; he was kissing her and pressing his hips into her.

The girl, limp underneath him, was looking into his face with deep understanding. Students walked by, whistling at them or staring. Shelley's throat felt cool as she wondered what it would be like to be that girl. It made her hurry away, brought up a dark taste in her mouth.

She had seen her parents do this, too. Recently, she had been up one night, trying to stop her threes, and she'd spotted them in the dark living room. They were completely unaware of her. Her mother, in a thin peach nightgown, was curled up in her father's lap. Her father had wound her mother's long hair in one hand. His other hand ran up the back of her nightgown, as though he understood everything about her, and her mother held his head in her hands, with an urgency, as though she were pulling herself to a new place. Her father rolled down her mother's nightgown to reveal her pale breasts, and her mother's hair fell back and her back arched. They had become something to each other that she did not understand.

Her own desire seemed potent but formless. It was an incredible feeling, to touch her breasts under her shirt — it was cool and stormy and as though she were breaking many rules. She wondered whether the feeling would be different if it was an actual hand of a real boy, and the thought was almost unbearably thrilling.

She had her own ideas about what would happen when she kissed a boy. She could imagine the strange pressure of his lips on hers, and she hoped that, as their lips touched, his thoughts would come pouring into her head. His thoughts and feelings would pour into her head, as hers would into his, and they would both be so full of their brilliance that they would not care about anything else at all. She had never asked anyone about this theory, because she secretly hoped she was a genius and had figured it all out by herself. She wanted to chase this feeling, to capture it in her hands. Now the feeling flew about, big-winged in her chest, uncontrollable. What would it be like to be loved in this way? Did she deserve it? What would she become?

The men were like lonely monsters, their huge shoulders turning pink under the dry blue sky.

"I think you should like *him*," Lena said. Her aunt pointed to the biggest man, the one with the delicate, fawn-like face. "You do this. You wait for them to be alone and you go up and say hi. At Goodwill, I told Bob, 'You're a good parker.' He was. No one else told him that."

"I can't say hi to him."

"You have to. That's what I did." Lena crossed her arms. "He has blue eyes. I like blue eyes."

"You have brown eyes."

"I know. Bob has blue eyes. I like something different from me." Lena was breathless, trying to tell Shelley everything she knew. "The best thing is when he runs to you, when you're walking to your room alone and knock on the door. When you hear the feet running." Her hands squeezed into balls and her face seemed to broaden with thought. "And then he comes and kisses me. Smack! He waits for me."

One of the body builders was moving slightly to the music. He was maybe in his thirties, with a haggard, boyish face and wispy brown hair. He was wearing a short turquoise unitard that fit like a sausage casing, worn Puma sneakers, and a Dodgers cap. He was listening intently to the disco playing on his boom box; he looked up at Shelley and winked.

She felt that wink land in her like a cold weight. He looked at her as though he understood something marvelous about her. He winked again. And then he walked toward them. It was a slow, casual walk. He shook his arms out once, though they did not appear to be wet. She and Lena watched, alert.

He smelled of sand, of the beach. He grabbed the wire fence with one hand and leaned away from it, pretending to stretch.

"Hey," he said, "what's going on?"

Shelley and Lena looked at him. It was as though he was continuing a conversation they'd been having for a while.

"Fast songs," he said. "Sometimes I'm just not in the lifting mood unless there are fast songs."

He closed his eyes, nodding to the beat coming from the boom box.

"Music gives me that edge," he said. "It gets my blood going, you know? It gives me thoughts. You think a lot of these guys think when they're lifting? No way. My mind opens up."

His eyes flicked from Shelley's face to her tank top. "Some of these guys," he said, leaning in toward her, "they make this their whole life. They eat, sleep, and do bodybuilding. They don't stop to smell the roses." He was trying to convince her of an important fact. "I'm not like that. Listen. The rest of the day, I'm a human being."

She wasn't sure what he was talking about. His eyes were surprisingly radiant, as though reflecting a tiny sun in his mind. She believed the radiance was directed at her. This was astonishing and unreasonable. She had no idea what she thought of him, but she sensed a vague direction to her restlessness, a discernible current; it was flowing toward him.

Lena gripped her hand.

"What's your name?" the man asked Shelley.

She did not know what to answer. It was as though he were asking her to be born.

"You can tell me," he said.

She would tell him her name was Sequina. He would be the first person in the world she would tell.

Lena stood up. "We have to go!" she announced.

The man swung away from the fence.

"Come *on!*" said Lena. She yanked Shelley up, and before she could tell him her name, Lena was hurrying her across the beach.

The sunbathers luxuriated on their towels, prone and open to the rays. What had just happened? The man had asked for her name. Shelley kept glancing back at the body-building pit, but the man was gone.

For a couple of minutes, Lena would not speak to Shelley. "You didn't like the one I picked," she finally said.

"I didn't tell him to come up to us."

Lena bit her lip. "When I met my husband at Goodwill, *I* went up and said, Good parker. That's what you should do."

"Why not the other way?" asked Shelley.

"I know how."

"I think he liked me."

Lena released her hand. "I know."

"But why?" It was a reasonable question. "How could he like me?"

"Maybe he thought you'd like him?"

"But how would he know?"

Shelley looked at the people lying on the beach. Invisible strands of longing connected them to each other, like spiderwebs. She had an urge to run through them to feel what they were like.

"You're Sequina!" said Lena, plowing through the sand in giant steps. "That's why."

"It was based on nothing," said Shelley. She was now convinced that he was in love with her. The next moment she thought he was a crazy bum. Then she was certain that he'd been making fun of her. She was full of conflicting theories. "He just wanted money for more music tapes," she tried. Or, "I saw him looking at my top."

Lena rushed ahead. "Stop talking about him."

"Why?"

Lena stopped. "You're not supposed to say why."

Shelley stepped back; she had never heard this sharpness in Lena's voice. "I can say why if I want to."

Lena's whole body seemed to be straining toward a vague and hopeful authority. Her brown eyes were large, staring at Shelley. "I say you can't," Lena said.

Now there was some distance between them as they moved down the shore. The foam bubbled up around their ankles, luscious as cream. Lena eyed Shelley suspiciously. Every so often Lena plucked a potentially useful item off the sand. "We can use a nice rope," she announced, picking up a strand of seaweed, "and an ashtray." She peered into a curved pink shell. She carried these discoveries for a few yards, then dropped them back on the sand.

About a mile down the beach, they reached the Lahambra Beach pier. It was old and rickety and stretched out into the glittering water. It contained what looked like a small, happy city; Shelley saw game booths, a merry-go-round, a Ferris wheel.

Lena took a great interest in the underside of the pier. The pier rose up on the sand; its pillars surrounded by gray boulders. Lena walked over and placed her palms on them, as though she were thinking about climbing up. There was a space where a few were missing, and she crouched down and wriggled inside.

Shelley followed. The space beneath the pier was the coolest part of the beach. Lena settled herself delicately on the hard-packed sand. The wood above her head was velvety and moist, speckled with mollusks. The pier smelled like the salty inside of an oyster. There were thin cracks between the pier's slats, and the light fell through them in translucent bars. Though she and Shelley could hear the footsteps of people traipsing across the pier, the other people seemed very far away.

"Let's sit here for a while," Lena said. "We don't have to talk to anyone *else*."

Shelley found herself sitting like a child, cross-legged, hands in her lap. She did not want to admit that she, too, was relieved to be hidden, in this private place. Lena took a pack of cigarettes from her pocket, slid out two, and handed one to Shelley. "You may have one before dinner," Lena said. She flicked a Bic lighter, and the two began to smoke.

Shelley held the burning cigarette for a little while before she tasted it; the last time they had done this they had been three. Bob and Lena had taught her how to smoke. Lena had dared Shelley to do it. Six months ago, Lena had taken a cigarette from the pocket of her house-coat, handed it to Shelley, and lit it with her Bic.

"Just relax," she'd said. "Breathe in a little, then out."

Shelley, Lena, and Bob then took a walk along Mango Boulevard with their cigarettes. Bob smoked in short, authoritative puffs while massaging the soft muscle in his upper arm. He blew smoke briskly out one side of his mouth, like a gangster, and his blue eyes squinted. He looked manly, and was aware of that.

When Lena smoked, her right shoulder drooped; she moved back from her cigarette as she exhaled. Her eyes were half-shut, as though she were overwhelmed by the beauty of her action. The three of them blew long streams of smoke into the air. They were like a great factory, creating some essential product.

Now there were just two of them smoking. It was shocking, impossible, that the two worlds could live side by side: one in which three of them smoked and one in which only two of them did.

Shelley no longer wanted to smoke. Grinding her cigarette into the sand, she did threes, grabbing larger and larger clumps of sand in a series, until her hands felt as if they were going to split.

"You didn't even start it," said Lena.

"I don't feel like it right now." She kept grabbing handfuls for a while; then stopped.

"When we find a house," said Lena, "we can have dinner. I can show you to anyone who comes to see us. I'll say, This is Sequin. You have to meet her. She is special. I can tell them about your day."

Lena looked at Shelley slyly, like a child who has just been caught holding a fragile object.

"What else?" Shelley asked.

"We'll say please come over and have some dinner with us. Then we can go for a swim in our swimming pool. Then you can lie down, and I can put you to sleep. We'll need pillows. We'll all be together and have a little life."

She kneaded the sand with her fingers. Her voice echoed in the small space. "I have many thoughts. I didn't stop thinking, even when you didn't come. I thought things for both of you. Bob wants a nice shag rug that he can run his feet through. He also wants windows on all sides so he can look out and see other people and what they do."

"What do I want?" asked Shelley.

"You want a really big lunch table where all your friends will eat lunch with you."

A warmth spread in the girl's chest. The wooden slats of the pier creaked above them, with the heartbeat thud of many feet. "How do you know that?" she asked.

"I know lots of things," said Lena. "I can tell you if the friends are good."

"Okay." Shelley's hands were strangely still. She did some threes to remind herself of what she usually did.

"We can have a grand party in our house," she said, getting to her feet. "Let's plan."

Lena's face slowly filled with light. "Me?"

Shelley ran down to the sea. The dusty light from the pier's cracks illuminated squares of the black water, and she stood in one of these bright, watery squares. She faced the land and opened her arms.

"Greetings!" she cried. "Welcome to our party. Allow me to introduce myself. I am Sequina!"

She picked up a handful of silvery foam and flung it dramatically back into the water. "We can only invite nice people," she said. "No one who would stop calling once they were solid friends."

"Yes," Lena said.

"Who would you invite?"

Lena considered. "Someone who will let me watch my show. Someone who will not pinch."

"Good," said Shelley. "They will have to tell a secret. That is how we will start up conversations."

"What kind?" asked Lena.

"They will have to say why they decided to dress all alike one day, if that ever happens. Or why they think it's a good idea to put blue on their eyes. Or! Why they want to know your name without knowing you." She was pumped up now. "I'm going to practice now. Sir. Hello. What do you feel like right now? Describe exactly."

"Um," said Lena. "Happy and sad."

Shelley nodded hard, unsatisfied. She wanted

144

to wrap her palm around Lena's heart and squeeze the exact emotion out of it and compare it with her own.

"Is that good?" asked Lena.

"What do you feel like, inside, here!" She slapped her chest.

Lena took a deep breath. "I feel my top." She touched her chest. "It feels nice."

"What does it feel like to be in love?"

"Oh," Lena said. She sighed. "Soft."

"Did you know it the first second you met him, or did you not know at first?"

"I knew when he kissed me on the lips."

Shelley watched her aunt's face carefully. "How?"

Lena considered this. "Because of the way he pressed. Hard."

Now Lena was rubbing her gold scarf along her lip.

"What did it feel like to have sex?" Shelley asked.

"Heavy." Lena examined her foot. "He kissed me lots of places." Her hand brushed her breast, her thighs, her crotch. "He always kissed me hard."

"Was it like" — Shelley wanted to describe what she felt when she touched herself — "pepper?"

"Okay."

"When you had sex," Shelley asked, "did you know his thoughts?"

"No."

"You didn't know *anything?*"

Lena shook her head.

This made Shelley restless. She walked through the water, allegedly to toss a beer can out of their little space, but really to peek through a space in the boulders. She wondered whether that muscle man was in the area, perhaps thinking about her.

But she did not see him anywhere. Abruptly, she turned back and said, "We need music." She critically surveyed the available trash, picked up a dented Coke can, tapped it, tossed it away. Next, she picked up a green 7-Up bottle, circled the glass rim with her finger, and blew across it. It made a low, owlish sound: *hoooooo.* She found this incredibly beautiful. *Hooooooooo.*

"Now. Let me fix you. Stand up." Shelley undid yet another button on Lena's housecoat and folded back the cotton. Lena held out her arms, obediently, like a large paper doll; her fingers quivered. "Be proud of yourself," Shelley told her. "Pretend you're walking through water; like this." She stepped through the foam, slowly, regally "Now go," she said.

Lena moved forward stiffly. As she walked, Shelley blew across the bottle opening. *Hoooo. Hooo. Hoooo.*

"I don't want anyone to watch me," said Lena.

"Oh," said Shelley, "but —"

"You. Do a fast song."

Shelley lifted the bottle to her lips again and did a series of *hoos: Hoohoohoohoohoohoohooooooooo.*

Lena listened. The tide was sucked back into the ocean.

"You can do everything," said Lena softly.

"Oh, come on," said Shelley.

Lena clearly recognized emotion in Shelley's face. "Stop," she said.

She led Shelley up to the sand and had her sit down. Then she sat in front of her and fiercely took hold of Shelley's feet.

"What are you doing!" asked Shelley, giggling.

Lena lifted one foot and kissed a toe. It was such a gentle, ticklish gesture; Shelley felt something tall and stiff topple within her. She made no attempt to move away.

"It's just us," said Lena. "We have a roof. We have a little sea." She touched the sand lovingly and then began to toss it, in big handfuls, on Shelley's legs.

"Wait," said Shelley, annoyed now. Lena held the girl's feet down hard with one hand, scooped up more sand, and spread it across Shelley's legs. Finally, Shelley's legs were covered to the knees.

"Shh," said Lena. She rested one hand on the sand covering Shelley's legs. The wooden slats of the pier creaked. Shelley was strangely comforted by Lena's sand blanket.

"Think happy thoughts," said Lena.

"Like what?"

"You want to spend the day with me," said Lena. She seemed peaceful, sitting here under the pier. "Look," she said, in a soft, proud voice as she gestured to a sodden clump of seaweed glistening green on the shore, at the light pouring through the wooden slats. "We have water to put our feet in and lights and sand! We have this and this and this!"

She looked radiant. Shelley's heart opened and opened like a rose. The underside of the pier was suddenly alive and crazy, with its footbeats and dark, milky light.

"Go on," she told Lena.

Lena proclaimed, "Soon we'll be all together. In our home."

"All together?"

"You, me, and Bob."

"Bob?"

"Together," Lena whispered. "All three of us. It will be so nice. We can smoke together. Eat hot dogs. It'll be warm. We can see the sky."

She was looking up, watching the light fall through the cracks.

"We can be dressed up. All three of us." Lena blushed when she said that. "You can be my daughter. We'll eat a little dinner together, all dressed up."

"But he's not here," Shelley said.

"He has to come," Lena said. "It's my anniversary today."

Shelley took a sharp breath. "What do you mean? Bob? Where's he coming from?"

"I don't know. Walking around."

"But why?"

"He knows I'll be mad."

The silence between them was filled with pain.

Lena hummed an awful song.

"Lena," Shelley asked softly, "do you think about that day?"

"I don't know," Lena said.

"I think about his face," said Shelley. "When he didn't know anything bad was going to happen." She thought about many things. About what he must have seen when he watched her standing on the overpass. About how ordinary the world was as she and Lena watched him run forward. Then she imagined leaping toward him, grabbing him around his waist, and wrestling him to the ground. All these thoughts made her heart race wildly, as though trying to understand how it could beat in this world.

"I cry," Lena said.

There was a cool, horrid silence between them.

"He hurt himself," said Lena. "I wanted to help him; he hurt himself!" She rose on her knees as though to stand, then rocked back. "He is my husband!" It was a soft scream. "I want to have a good anniversary for him. I want to kiss his lips. I want to put a Band-Aid on him —"

Shelley's parents had driven her back from the hospital, where she and Lena had gone to wait for news about Bob. Their response had surprised her; they had been so grateful that nothing happened to her. She sat in the back seat, stunned, watching the world back away from her. The other drivers glided forward on the freeway, convinced of their right to live.

She'd never thought the day would turn out like this. But her parents, of course, had known Lena and Bob far longer than she had, and it was as though they had long been expecting a moment like this for years. Now that it had happened, they were glad it had not been Lena or Shelley. She had never understood that they feared she could disappear as well.

Her parents said odd things. Once, her father burst out angrily, "Why the hell did he walk on there, anyway? He knew better than that."

"Was he showing off for Lena?" her mother asked.

Suddenly, she believed that they did not know Bob at all. "No," she answered.

They wanted her to tell them, in detail, what had happened. In a flat voice, she said that he had not listened when she and Lena shouted at him. As she spoke, she saw again the nimble beauty of his leap. She waited for her parents to be angry, but then she understood that they did not want to believe she could have stopped it. They merely wanted her to be alive.

From that time on, when she couldn't sleep, she crept to her bedroom window. There was a hard pressure, a beating in her head; she wanted to grab hold of the night and stop it, keep it from moving into the cruel dawn. But the night rushed away from her. There was the deepening to midnight, and then the pink swell of the new day.

"He can apologize," said Lena, "but he'll have to be *very* nice."

The sea lapped the boulders. They were dark and wet and looked like large heads. The sea sounded dry, like thousands of crackling leaves. She could not quite understand what Lena was saying.

Through the crack in the boulder, they peered out at the beach. She did then what she'd sometimes done on her visits to Panorama Village after she'd had a bad week. She sat in front of Lena and leaned gently back in her aunt's large lap. Lena loved it when she did this. Now Lena leaned forward and whispered, "Don't worry. We can have a fun time. It's my anniversary, and Bob is going to come."

Seven

Five afternoons a week, Ella and Vivien picked up Lena from her special class at La Rosita Elementary School. The class was held in a small bungalow, isolated from the other buildings. The school itself was new, an assortment of drab, plywood bungalows that had the stern look of army barracks. Ella and Vivien, a toddler, sat on one of the steps outside Lena's classroom. A stand of eucalyptus grew around them; their trunks were peeling, like a strange sunburn. The whole area was lacy with purple shade.

While she and Vivien waited for Lena's class to end, Ella allowed herself to fantasize about Vivien's future. It was like learning to think for the first time. Her fantasies began slowly and daringly, as though they were sexual — for they seemed forbidden in that way. A janitor was raking up dry leaves nearby, and they could hear the sound of a radio leaking from his pocket, the faint strains of a big band.

The fantasy entered Ella's mind before she could stop it. It was the most ordinary idea. Ella looked at Vivien, just beginning to walk, and summoned up an image of Vivien's high school graduation. There was Vivien, in a graduation gown, walking up to the stage and shaking the principal's hand. Her classmates applauded. The picture made Ella warm with gratitude. She gripped Vivien's tiny hands and tried to stop these thoughts, but the fantasies flooded in, merry, colorful, illicit: Vivien going to a prom; packing for college. They created in Ella a vast and apprehensive joy.

Lena's instructor was Miss Clay, and because she had chosen to work with the handicapped, Ella was suspicious of her. When Ella walked up the three wooden stairs to the classroom, she found Miss Clay sitting close to Lena, giving her some odd instruction. One day Ella saw the teacher holding out her palm with a scrap of Kleenex on it. "Now, honey," she said, "I'm going to blow this paper off my hand. Can you do that?" She pursed her lips and said *p,* and the paper flew to the floor. Lena pressed her lips together tightly and tried to say *p.*

The room always smelled of spilled fruit juice. A poster on the wall said: *Our Three R's: Repetition, Routine, Relaxation.* Today, three other students sat on chairs on the beige carpet: Jane, who was deaf; William, a retarded boy with iridescent red hair; and a dazed girl, known as Sweetheart, who rocked back and forth holding her ankles, her long blond hair falling into her mouth. As they did every day, when they saw Ella, all the students erupted into welcoming, wounding sounds.

Lena, from the very first day, was not shy. She shot away from Ella and Vivien as though she

153

was sure the world wanted her. Ella watched her run from them into the morning. The air was honeyed, aromatic, and the sharp sound of her shoes on the pavement made Ella hopeful and a little sick. Sometimes, after Lena had gone through the gray-green doors, Ella would wait until she was the only mother on the sidewalk, until the bells shrilled to mark the start of the students' day. She would listen to those bells, their peculiar insistence. Then she'd leave.

When Ella picked Lena up after class, she often found the child sitting by herself on the front steps. Lena was like a tiny, forlorn god, sucking her fist and looking at the other children. Occasionally, Ella found Lena bullying William. Lena would chase him, shrieking, and he'd run away, in little feminine steps. Lena's laughter was raucous. William's mother, a stern, boatlike woman, would scoop him up into her car and speed off. Lena would watch him go; she'd look let down. She didn't want to make friends with William, as Ella suggested; she wanted to run after him and make him scream.

Then Lena, with great speed, would run toward her mother, head down, hands balled into fists. The other children drifted away from her like wind-swept leaves. The way she ran to Ella said everything about her day. It was nearly impossible to believe that the day had divided itself between them, that it was large enough to hold the different experiences of their lives. Ella brought treats — lollipops, candy corn. "Hello, my love," she would say, kneeling, while Lena ferociously ate the candy, and Lena's kisses smelled unnaturally sweet.

Ella had two daughters, two comets, each producing her own fierce light. Ella felt herself become a planet both grand and dim, living in their gauzy play of shadow and bright.

At home, they practiced simple things. This is a stop sign. This is how you tie your shoe. Lena was nine, sitting in the kitchen, holding out her leg and waiting for Ella to tie her shoe. "One lace meets the other lace," said Ella. "Like this. You try." Lena lolled back like a queen, allowing Ella to tie the shoe. She did try once or twice, but she soon got bored and would cry and kick the shoe off her foot.

Lena and Vivien, in the same room, seemed to breathe different air. Ella was sharply aware of the imbalance between them — the fact that she fantasized about Vivien's future while Lena's was wholly unknown. Moving between them, Ella thought of herself as a mean spy, gathering information for no known purpose — noticing that Vivien started to walk at ten months, a year before Lena did, and that when Vivien spoke, Ella could understand her words. Ella felt guilty as she carried these facts around with her, as if it was wrong to think about them or acknowledge them. She tried not to be too excited about Vivien. And her children did not know what she thought. Lena was never jealous of Vivien; it was as if she understood that a baby would not judge her.

Lena asked to hold her sister the day the baby was born, but Ella waited six months before she let her do so. The first time Lena held Vivien, Ella had Lena sit on the carpet by the couch, and she arranged the girl's arms in a secure position. When Lena looked up at Ella, her arms empty and waiting, Ella knelt and pressed Vivien into Lena's arms as though planting her there. Lena's breathing was anxious. "Don't move," Ella said. "Gentle. Good."

When she finished positioning Lena's arms and slowly stood up, Lena looked at the baby, and her breathing became more subdued. Her body seemed to take naturally to this position of gentleness. And her gaze was at once blank and as wise as a king's. Vivien's infant eyes looked into the air, open, believing.

"Good girl," said Ella, and Lena smiled.

They lived in a neighborhood full of children, and Lena wanted to join them. The children poured into the street at twilight, a charge of excitement in the clear air. The games mainly involved running after one another, and these games were known by many names: Chase, Cowboy, Crook.

Lena never understood how to play. She'd watch and sometimes run along with the children, laughing when they did, as though to hear the sound of her glee. But the children didn't know how to act with her, so she would give up and watch them. She always sat in a particular spot, the massive root of a magnolia tree. The root had cracked through the sidewalk like a gigantic vein. Because Lena occupied it, the root became the place where rejected children went. No one who wanted to compete ever sat there. Once in a while a child joined Lena, a child who was feeling sick or worn out or bored. Ella noticed that Lena beamed when someone sat with her, even though the child did not usually speak to her — as though the presence of the child made the root turn silver, cast a wonderful light onto the street.

When she was too young to play, Vivien sat on the root with Lena. Sometimes Lena chose a child or team and cheered at sporadic moments; Vivien wanted to join in, so she cheered, too. Lena cheered with great exuberance, which confused the other children. They'd slow down, trying to figure out what was going on. But Lena and Vivien enjoyed hearing the joyous sound of their own cheering.

One day, when Vivien was four, she decided to play. She slid off the root and walked over to the group, as though she knew that she belonged. The children were playing tag, their faces damp and flushed. Lena watched her sister and yelped, "Viv!"

Ella was watering the lawn; she lay down the hose when she heard Lena. The girl had got up from the root and was standing beside it, staring

157

at her sister. She looked as if she had been pressed into the air like a butterfly into glass. Everyone had stopped running.

"I want to be a cowboy," Vivien announced in a deep voice, like a radio announcer. She expected everyone to listen to her. The older children — seven, nine, ten, thirteen — swung above her like sunflowers. Vivien was wearing a little pink cotton dress. Looking serious and determined, she fingered the sash and said, "Now."

Laughter swept through the group.

"She's too small."

"Just put her on Fred's team."

"You, Vivien," called one of the girls, "just run with them. Everyone, try not to step on her."

Vivien looked around, flushed, and clapped her hands. Then she saw Lena standing by the root, staring at her.

The street was quiet; Lena walked toward the group. Ella felt a warning within her. She pretended to water the fuchsia bush, but she was watching; she had to watch. Lena lurched forward with the same determination Vivien had shown; she was trying to copy her sister. When she reached Vivien, she gripped her hand and said, "I want to play too!"

The other children began negotiating.

"Lena can't play. It's too hard."

"She gets in the way."

"Tell her to go sit on that tree again."

Vivien jumped up and down. "She can hold the It place," she said. "She can hold It."

Lena was assigned the task of holding a branch that would serve as the It place. If a child touched the branch, he was safe.

Her hands trembled as she took the branch. They told her to stand on the curb by a tree, and there she stood. In the course of the game, children ran to her, touched the branch, ran away. She grew excited whenever they ran toward her. "Go!" she exclaimed. "Go!" Vivien circled away from her team to bubble around Lena, jumping to touch the branch just to touch it.

The sky grew dark. Lena sat on the curb, and the branch reached up as though it were growing from her hands. When it was time for dinner, she ran into the house still holding it aloft.

"Did you have a nice time?" Ella asked, hopefully.

Lena was ten years old. Her eyes were filled with tears. "I held It today!" she screeched with joy.

From that day on, Lena and Vivien joined the children in the street. They went together, as though lifted there by the same sudden wind. Lena would hold a branch or a shoe or rope for the others to reach or grab. She still burst into cheers, and occasionally Vivien joined her. Vivien sometimes cheered for a member of the other team just so that Lena wasn't cheering all by herself.

Ella watched Vivien run. She ran with the ferocity of a younger sister, as though trying very hard to imprint herself on the world. She was

159

competitive in a way that astonished Ella. If someone caught her just before she crossed the finish line, she would erupt in a violent scream. Sometimes the other children stepped back and let her run, her untied sash winging behind her. Her desire for mastery was immense.

Yet Vivien was linked by an invisible rope to her sister. Ella could see that they were attuned to each other, like a couple that had been married for a long time. Vivien might be engaged in a game, but she always flew back to Lena the moment before Lena would begin to complain or cry. She went to Lena in one clean movement and stood beside her, stroking her hip with a comforting motion. Lena would calm down.

Ella noticed, too, that Lena might decide at odd moments to stop playing. "Bye!" she'd announce, turning and heading toward the house. Vivien followed close behind, as though she did not want to be left alone.

When Vivien began school, Lena swooped down on her like wind. The first day, Lena gripped her sister's hand and pretended to walk her to school. She was twelve, and Vivien was six, and Lena was bursting with pride. The walk took twice as long as it should have, because Lena had to show Vivien the many landmarks along the way. "This is my purple school tree," Lena said, as they passed a jacaranda on La Rancha Street. The tree stretched up, aglow with purple blossoms. Vivien nodded, drinking in the tree's new title, even though she'd seen it hundreds of times. Ella walked two steps behind them, supervising, but they pretended they were walking alone, like big girls.

When they reached the school, they first took Vivien to the primary-grade bungalow. She stood, a little anxious, before her mother and sister. She was wearing a pink check dress and neatly buckled black patent leather shoes; she had buckled them herself. She looked like a tiny, worried pink general.

Lena understood that she was to continue her day by herself. She backed away and began to hum while sucking on her hand. Ella felt as though their different futures divided her into two separate people. It made her feel confused, for she was afraid she would say the wrong thing to each. "We'll pick you up at three," she said, bending to quickly kiss Vivien. Vivien turned and ran into the first-grade yard.

At the end of each school day, Lena no longer had to wait alone for her mother. Vivien was always sitting right beside her on the steps. Lena would drape an arm around Vivien's small shoulders, and they would sit very still, like rulers of an invisible kingdom.

"How was your day?" Ella asked, as soon as she arrived.

"Viv helped me find my quarter," Lena announced.

"I looked inside her shoe," Vivien explained.

"Good for you," said Ella. "Lena, did you buy

161

your lunch with your quarter?"

"Yes."

"Was it good?"

"Yes!"

"Vivien, let's see your lovely drawing —"

"It was lost and she found it!" Lena burst in.

Ella once visited school during recess to drop something off with Vivien's teacher. She saw Lena gripping the wire fence that separated the lower grade area from upper grades; she was watching her sister play with the girls in her class. Vivien was jumping rope, and the other girls were counting, their voices chiming together like seagulls' cries. Lena's hands clutched the wire fence, and she shook it slowly, a big, silent motion; it shimmered. Her face was dark.

Lena became more aggressive. One day, Ella found her robbing Vivien from her classmates during recess; she was tugging Vivien to an empty area of the playground. As Ella watched, Vivien knelt before Lena and tied her shoe. On another day, Ella found Lena roaming the long metal tables in the cafeteria at lunchtime, looking for her sister. When she found her, she sat beside her and organized the food in a little row. The red Jell-O went behind the milk container, the milk behind the hamburger on its bun. When Ella came up to them, she heard Lena saying, "First, bite your burger. Then, sip your milk. Then Jell-O."

Vivien was six years old. She listened to Lena's instructions as though her sister was describing the true rules of the world. But she was not merely listening. The intensity of her desire to obey Lena made her seem physically smaller.

Ella sat beside them. "What are you two doing?" she asked.

Shock passed over both girls like a shadow. They looked at her as though she were an intruder.

"Hi!" Lena said.

"I've brought your sweater, Lena. You forgot it."

"Thank you," said Lena. But it was clear that they wanted her to go. They were embarrassed, as if their mother had caught them in a private act.

Ella began to see Vivien disappear. The change was slow, barely perceptible. Her work at school, which had placed her at the top of the class, became careless. Her handwriting began to shift —from the cursive she had earnestly tried to master to a loose scrawl. Teachers wrote sad evaluations: *Vivien does not complete her homework. Vivien does not speak in class.* Soon, she started to walk like Lena, her shoulders hunched as though against a constant chill. While Lena struggled to create light in herself, Vivien was willing her own light to grow dim.

Ella saw it clearly on her visit to Vivien's second-grade class on Parents' Day. When the teacher handed a folder of Vivien's work to Ella, she did not smile, as the first-grade teacher had.

Nor did Ella recognize her daughter. She had to scan the room before she saw the small auburn-haired girl slumped in her seat. Her hair had the brilliant sheen of Vivien's, and her dress was the yellow one Vivien had worn to school that day. But this girl's arms were wrapped around her body, as though to protect it from violent weather. Her face was slack with sadness. She did not speak during the entire period. Her head remained bowed.

When Ella and Vivien walked home at the end of the day, Ella was afraid to look too closely at the world. It seemed brighter, magnified, as though seen through the goggle eyes of a giant. The roses and magnolias blooming in neighbors' gardens looked stiff, as if cut from red and orange construction paper in someone's childish dream. The world was sharp, and her fantasies had no place in it. Vivien in the classroom was not the girl Ella knew. But who could she be? Ella walked quickly, afraid to let herself think.

Ella looked at her daughter, and her love flowed and flowed out toward her. When Vivien glanced up, her face looked apologetic. It was as if they both understood some unspoken deal had been broken, and neither knew what to say.

"Why didn't you speak in class?" asked Ella.

"I don't know."

"The teacher likes you —"

"I have nothing to say."

Vivien walked fast, like a small soldier, her eyes on the pavement. Ella stopped her and knelt and held Vivien's delicate face in her hands.

"You are so wonderful," she said. "So smart. You must use it. You have so much to say."

The words sounded flat as she spoke them, but Ella believed them fully and intensely.

Helene's School of Dance had opened in the space above Lou's Shoes, and the blue neon boot outside Lou's Shoes was joined by a pink neon tutu with a single, shapely leg and pointed foot. Helen's sign seemed to Ella rather eerie, as Ella felt it would be more enticing to have a sign that featured a whole person. However, she grew used to it. The new sign made Lou feel competitive, as he enjoyed having the only neon display on the street. But Ella convinced him that it might bring in more customers. "They see the leg, then they see the boot. Maybe they'll think the boot will make their leg look good." Lou gave her a skeptical look, but he had no choice in the matter. He did stock a few pairs of tap and ballet shoes for any dancers who might wander in.

Helene's School of Dance did not seem to specialize in any particular dance form. Ella thought that many of the students heading up to the studio looked surprisingly heavy, and she started to categorize them. The large-hipped ones were belly dancers, because they needed to lose weight in that area. The small ones were ballet dancers, because they could be believable fairies on stage. The overfriendly ones, who shouted "Hi!" to her, were tap dancers, because they liked to make a lot of noise. During classes there was the sound of thunder on the ceiling of Lou's shop, and a few times Ella went up to look in at a class. The sight of ten or fifteen girls moving in unison was so strange and surprisingly beautiful, Ella did not know what to feel.

Ella and Lou decided to separate Vivien and Lena for a while. Ella kept thinking about Vivien's sad face as Lena told her what food to eat in the cafeteria. That was not the expression of the girl who ran so eagerly across the finish line that the other children stepped back, awed. So one day she told Vivien that her father had some exciting tasks for her in the store. "He thinks you'd do a great job as a salesgirl," she said.

Vivien was seven years old. Her first reaction was dismay. Shifting from one leg to the other, she asked, "Why do I need a job?"

Ella did not want to tell her the actual reason. "You can make many valuable contributions," she said.

Ella took her to the store on the afternoon that Lena would be at a birthday party with her special class. She and Lou had bought a pair of blue patent leather shoes for Vivien, and Lou handed them to her as she walked in. "If these shoes fit," said Lou, grandly, "you're hired." Vivien sat down, and Lou knelt before her and lovingly slid her feet into the shoes, as though he were a prince.

"What do you know? You're hired!" said Lou,

beaming. He shook her hand.

They decided that it was important to have a child in the store for two hours, a couple days after school. Vivien was to organize the shoelaces by color, say hello to the people who came in, and carry out any other duties that she, as Store Child, found necessary.

Ella meanwhile tried to keep Lena away from the store. But Lena was developing a keen ability to detect the opportunities denied her. She immediately learned that Tuesdays and Thursdays were Vivien's job days, and on those days she would burst out of her after-school class and demand to know where her sister was.

First, Ella tried lying. "She has a doctor's appointment."

"No!" Lena jumped up and down. The wooden step rattled under her anger.

"Fine," said Ella. Her own anger began to unfurl. "She's at her job."

"I want a job."

"We'll go home," said Ella, "and you can help me wash the vegetables . . ."

"No!" Lena ran down the stairs and refused to speak to her mother as they walked home.

The afternoons when Lena was alone were awful. Lena angrily roamed around the yard. She headed back and forth, toward nobody, and her hands were open, waiting to grab. She broke off magnolia blossoms and left a trail of torn flowers behind her, a fragrant, zigzag trail across the yard.

Away from Lena, Vivien became restless. After she finished her tasks, she wandered around the store, humming listlessly. To Ella, this churning was better than sadness; she waited.

One day, Vivien disappeared. She did this swiftly, skillfully, as though she had long been nurturing the talent to escape from her parents' world. Neither Lou nor Ella saw her go. Vivien was suddenly gone.

Ella searched the back room, the parking lot; she walked the length of the block in front of the store. Finally, she climbed the stairs to the dance studio. There was Vivien, sitting cross-legged in a corner, watching the class. Students ran and leaped in a swift rhythm across the floor. The teacher shouted, "One, two, *three!*" The room reeked of sweat. Vivien was sitting absolutely still; the quick rise and fall of her chest was her only movement.

Ella went over and touched her shoulder. "I've been looking everywhere for you," said Ella.

Vivien glanced up, upset at having been interrupted. Her face held an expression of certainty that was almost too large for her.

"I'm here," she said.

Taking dance classes became Vivien's job. Her schedule was arranged around children's dance classes; she took whatever was offered that day — ballet, tap, belly-dancing. For each class, she needed different shoes and costumes, and Lou

168

was able to get them at cost. Vivien would slip into the studio to join the skinny little girls posing sexily in black high-heeled tap shoes or solemnly in flesh-colored tights. Each group followed the teacher's movements like a hopeful tribe.

One day, Ella visited tap class when the girls were skipping in a diagonal line across the room. The air was ragged with arrhythmic clattering. Because all the girls were dressed alike, it took her a moment to find Vivien. And it was the way Vivien moved that told Ella who she was. The other girls held back in their movements, but Vivien threw herself into them as though trying to eat the air. The teacher and students recognized her talent; reverently, they gave her room. She danced the way she had played tag, but with even more fervor. It was as though she were hurling herself forward into her special place in the world. She moved to the corner, where she did a little turn of her own creation. Her eyes were set on the image of herself in the mirror, on the adept little stranger there.

Lena, in her loneliness, was slowly tearing apart the magnolias in the backyard, and Ella decided it was time to bring her to the store.

On the first visit, Lena gripped Ella's hand tightly as they walked in. She stepped with caution, as though the floor were made of ice. Vivien had just finished a tap class, and was sitting there, her face flushed, in her regular clothes.

Lena stopped short and studied Vivien's rosy face as though she had not been introduced to her before.

"Are you busy?" Lena asked Vivien.

Vivien looked at her. "No."

Lena moved closer, until she stood over Vivien. "I want a job," she said. "Viv. Give me a job."

Vivien got up, whispered in Lena's ear, and led her out of the main room.

After a few minutes, Ella was curious; she checked all over and finally heard the girls' voices coming from the stockroom. The door was locked. Bending down, Ella looked through the keyhole and saw Lena standing and Vivien sitting on a chair.

She knocked. The girls shrieked.

"We're busy!" cried Vivien.

"It's secret!" added Lena. "It's called Dress!" She paused. "Go away," she said to the door; there was a great, melting pleasure in her voice.

It was that tone in Lena's voice which kept Ella at the keyhole. Dress appeared to be a sort of game. Scattered around Lena and Vivien, Ella saw, lay an assortment of merchandise from the store. There were shiny galoshes, silk-covered high heels, fluffy bedroom slippers, black office shoes. There were heavy dark shoelaces for men, sparkly ones for children. There were women's silk stockings in pink, blue, and metallic colors. Brightly colored cloths for shoe polishing. Accessories for bridal shoes: white satin bows, silver buckles, white sequin clips. The girls had never taken such an interest in the merchandise. Ella crouched down to be more comfortable. She was perfectly still.

Vivien whispered to Lena; her words, though unintelligible to Ella, were obviously serious. The girls nodded to each other solemnly, as if to acknowledge the absolute necessity of each to the other, the way each girl needed the other to carve her own distinctive place.

Vivien sat in the chair while Lena, giggling, dressed her. She picked through the pile, selecting the yellow polishing cloths to drape over Vivien, perhaps to make her so bright that it would be impossible not to see her.

Next, Vivien held out her arms, and Lena slipped blue fluffy slippers on her hands and another pair on Vivien's feet. Vivien slowly moved her tiny blue bear paws. Lena walked around and around the chair, and then stopped and assessed her creation.

When Lena seemed unsure, Vivien helped her. She pointed out the most brilliant items on the floor and coaxed Lena to put a sequin bridal clip in her hair, to drape a pair of silver-flecked pantyhose around her neck as a scarf. Vivien was both sharply aware and supremely unaware of Lena even as her gaze was set on a far, romantic place. Lena did whatever Vivien suggested. She tossed a creamy white piece of velvet over Vivien's shoulders as a cape and clipped barrettes with clusters of fake white and red diamonds to the cape's edge. They worked together quietly, and Lena did not mock any request that Vivien made.

Finally, Vivien stood up and held out her arms. She seemed utterly convinced of her magnificence. After turning around to show herself to Lena, she circled the chair as Lena watched, entranced.

"Your turn," Vivien said.

Lena sat down and Vivien removed the blue paws so that her hands were free. She did not ask Lena for help; she had many ideas of her own.

Vivien made Lena look like a much larger person. She put Lena's small feet into a pair of huge, dark men's shoes and encircled her waist with a long belt made of many stockings. Over Lena's shoulders she hung a big blue jacket from the store's lost and found closet.

Lena, sitting in silence, was Vivien's first true audience. In the enormous shoes and large jacket, she watched Vivien perform a proud and languorous dance. Lena had a solemn demeanor, like a member of the clergy.

Vivien had not yet learned formal dance steps. With her arms raised, she whirled in wild circles, her movements almost frenetic. Lena watched in awe.

Ella, still crouched by the door, could not make herself leave. It was as if her daughters' game would tell her what was to become of them. She was not ready to let herself fantasize again about Vivien's future. But if she had, she would have seen her on stage in the high school auditorium, at ballroom contests in the Los Angeles Forum, where men and women glided together, their costumes scintillating in the light. She would have seen Vivien rushing proudly into space, her legs flying and her long red hair falling back in the air. She would have seen Vivien as herself.

Eight

Ella was cleaning Lena's room in Panorama Village. She had pushed open the windows and sprayed Lena's perfume into the air, plucked up the underwear that Lena had abandoned to the floor, and spread one of Lena's bathroom towels over the burned rug. The square pink towel wasn't wide enough, and Ella spent some time trying to make it right. When she stepped back and examined her efforts, she had to admit that the towel looked ridiculous and hid nothing — perhaps she could pretend that Lena had left it there.

She had a sudden urge to turn to Lou and ask him to estimate the damage. She could imagine him walking around Lena's room and saying, lightly, "Well, why did she do this? Why? She wanted to upgrade. It's Lena's way of redecorating." He'd rub his hands together. "I, personally, would have started with the bedspread, not the rug."

But he was not here to help her. Ella did not feel less married to Lou because he was gone. She would look at something he had touched — a check made out in his handwriting, the Aqua Velva she kept in the medicine cabinet — and his absence seemed unreal. She still looked up when she heard footsteps on the stairs to her apartment; she still waited to hear his keys in the door. She remembered with great clarity what she loved — the commanding way he gestured when he talked, the dark grace of his eyebrows, the rooster crow of his laugh (which he had, frankly, stolen from her). Now, with his death, their marriage had taken another step; their love was simply different — for it had not disappeared.

Her love for him had become simpler in his absence. She couldn't get angry at him for leaving his shoes in the den, for laughing with her but not listening, for escaping to the TV. In death, he did whatever she wanted; he was entirely good. At other, moments, she longed for him so fiercely that she wondered whether she had become something other than human — a costume of a woman, containing nothing but pure need. This feeling came over her now, as she tried to decide what to do; it rushed out of her, into the morning's blue haze. She wanted to chase the feeling, but there was nowhere to go.

Sometimes, when she missed him most, she tried to think about another subject. She would think about Lou's extramarital affair. Ella had no reason to believe that Lou had ever had one, but the idea made her miss him less, so she tried to believe it was true. She would spend a great deal of time conjuring up suspicious moments — the few times Lou came home late with no explanation other than bad traffic; the times when it had taken him several rings to pick up the phone.

It was, admittedly, not much evidence, but sometimes she clung to it with a rumbling, righteous anger. His lady friend, she decided, was named Lorraine. She had frosted blond hair and long legs the color of ivory. Lorraine had indulged in some ill-advised plastic surgery, which made her face resemble that of a wax doll. Ella could spend hours imagining Lorraine's complaints about her plastic surgery and her compliments to Ella on her beautiful face, just as it was.

She also imagined telling Lou about the handymen, for a small, mean reason she didn't quite understand. There were four or five meaty men whom she called when something in her apartment broke down. The plumber was named Saul, she thought, and the electrician Ned. Each had a particular fragrance — Ned was a little smoky, Saul smelled sharply of Certs. Ella enjoyed having them come to fix things, because they were company. Yet she was sure that each one was making a move on her.

The more vividly she imagined Lorraine, the more she wanted to tell Lou about Saul: how his large hand lingered on her shoulder; how he glanced, longingly, into her eyes. Whenever Saul came over, Ella busied herself with small tasks — balancing her checkbook, cleaning the stove — but the apartment seemed to light up with the man's suppressed feelings toward her. When he was finished, he would saunter up to her and boom, "Well, Ella, everything looks good now. Got to go." He'd stand there with his toolbox, his worn face lonely. The air between them twinkled with a curious promise as a thrilled indignation came over her. She handed him his check. "Thank you and goodbye," she said, smiling brightly, and showed him the door.

Ella missed Lou the most keenly in the morning. When she woke to the clear sunlight in her bedroom, she began the day by touching herself. She started lightly, almost casually, though this action was important to her. She thought of Lou, or sometimes the handymen or other strangers, though she did not know how other men would make love to her, since she had made love only with Lou. She touched herself in ways that she wished he had touched her. She tried to remember the act of sex, but without much clarity, so that she would not long for it; she conjured up Lou in a variety of ways. She saw him standing in a navy suit beside her bed, as though he were about to go to work, watching her; she saw him naked beside her at thirty, forty, fifty, sixty seventy years old. In her memory, she contained all of the versions of him. All the Lous were there, a quiet, shifting crowd. As her desire built, she felt herself grow larger than the room. Sometimes she wanted to shout in a deep and frightening voice, or to swear, but she did not want to start her day until she had finished. She refused to die until she had finished. There was a shudder, a moment of absolute yearning. Then there was the sensation of having fallen into a pool of damp air.

She knew when she had climaxed. It was never very large. She had never asked anyone, so she was never sure when it was quite time to stop. She looked at her room, her window, the desk, the carpet, and she thought: I am here.

Vivien was standing in the doorway of Lena's room, watching her mother. She had a slightly lost pose, the way she sometimes stood when she thought no one was looking at her. It was the posture of someone unwilling to make a decisive movement, someone who preferred to remain in shadow. She was accustomed to watching the world quietly, in a strategic way. Her hands were open, aimless, as if they wanted to fit into a pocket. Ella saw this person for only a moment. Then there was the Vivien Ella was accustomed to seeing.

She thought Vivien looked like a movie star, even now, when she was not really dressed up. Vivien had a shy streak, but Ella believed her intrinsically glamorous. That was how her daughter looked now, sleeveless in a navy leotard top, long Danskin pants, and silver platform sandals. Her large sparkling sunglasses were pushed up on her head; her cascading red hair was in a ponytail. It was not just Ella who thought Vivien looked like a movie star; others did, too. This was proven in the photo captions in the local newspapers, where her success in contests was recorded; Vivien was "skillful," or "notable." Ella underlined the words with her ballpoint pen. Her favorite caption was from the *Santa Monica Evening Outlook*. It read: "Vivien Rose is an orchid of grace. When she moves across the floor, the stage is in bloom." The statement had been made by a judge named Andrea Unger. From the moment she read this statement, Ella believed the name Andrea to be one of the most beautiful she had ever heard. Whatever Andrea meant by her words, Ella had no doubt that she was absolutely correct. To see her own feelings about Vivien corroborated in print made Ella feel that she truly understood something of great importance. The article had appeared in 1971, and Ella carried it in her wallet, until it had become unreadable.

Now, Ella said, eagerly, "Darling, come in. Turn around and let me look at you."

"Oh, please, I'm not wearing *anything* —"

"Humor me."

Vivien shrugged and turned around. Ella experienced the same proud thrill she had when Vivien was seven years old.

"Well, darling," said Ella, "that is a very distinguished outfit. Though I am not in love with the silver shoes."

Vivien instantly stopped twirling and gave her mother a once-over. "Well, I don't understand why women near eighty insist on wearing high heeled pumps."

Ella stuck out her foot and scrutinized her green pump. "It's not so high."

"I worry that you might trip."

"Well, I enjoy being fashionable," said Ella, "and I'm not going to trip."

"All right," said Vivien and quickly kissed her. Ella's gratitude for this daughter filled her like clear water.

Vivien walked around, scanning Lena's room. She was clutching a brown paper bag. Abruptly, she sat down beside Ella. "I brought you a muffin," Vivien said, taking it from the bag. "Carob bran. It's delicious."

Ella looked at the dense, tough-looking muffin and then, longingly at the bag, hoping a paler and more sugary muffin would emerge. No such treat was forthcoming. "Thank you," Ella said, without enthusiasm. Vivien set the bran muffin beside Ella on a paper napkin, and there it sat, untouched.

"It's like a brothel in here," said Vivien. "A brothel from Kmart."

"That's Lena's perfume," said Ella. "I thought it might hide the fire smell."

"Good God," said Vivien, fanning her hand.

"Better this than the other," said Ella, though the burned odor was still perceptible, dark beneath the cloying sweetness.

"Well," said Vivien. She picked up Ella's muffin and took a bite. "It's not so bad. I thought the roof might be gone."

She stood up and went to the window and tried to push it up more, but it was open to its widest point. Setting her hands on the windowsill, she leaned out into the warm air, tilting up her face as though waiting for someone to pluck her. She stood there for a moment, the sun white on her face, then ducked back inside.

"Shelley was up at three this morning," Vivien said, "doing God knows what."

"Excuse me?"

"She was in the living room. It looked as if she was cleaning, maybe, picking up things and putting them down. She was just touching things like a crazy person, and she was crying." Vivien's voice had become hoarse; she sounded like a teenager.

"What did you do?" asked Ella.

"When she saw me, she froze and then ran to her room and wouldn't talk to me."

"It's a boy" said Ella, firmly. The authority in her voice soothed her, and she continued, just to hear it fill Lena's smoky room. "She's twelve years old," said Ella, "That's what you should talk to her about. She must be in love with someone. Or someone must be in love with her."

Vivien wasn't listening; she seemed to be caught between the vision of her unhappy daughter and the bareness of Lena's room. After a moment, she shook herself and surveyed the burned room once again, as though she, too, belonged in it. It was the random chance of six years that had granted Vivien an independent life.

"She's going crazy," said Vivien. "I did something and raised a crazy daughter."

"Why do you want to say that about her?" asked Ella.

"I don't *want* to," she said. "But I'm afraid. She's been like this since the accident. She won't talk about it."

"What could she say?" asked Ella.

The room was hushed.

"She wishes she'd saved him," said Vivien.

"What do you mean?"

"I know my daughter," said Vivien, passionately. "She was right there. How could she not wish that?"

Ella suddenly wondered where Lena and her granddaughter were at this moment. Before she could ask, Vivien took another bite of the muffin and said, "All right. Enough. Let's clean up."

Ella, watching her daughter walk around the room, remembered how argumentative Vivien had been when the two of them were searching for a residence for Lena and Bob. That was twelve years ago. She had sent the coordinators scurrying on their knees with her questions: *And where exactly do you take residents on your "creative and stimulating field trips"? Is this really someone's underwear lying on the floor? What is that strange smell coming out of the kitchen?* She had been unrelenting and wonderful.

Now, Vivien was tracing her fingers along the wooden dresser, picking up and setting down some of the snowdomes she'd given Lena after her family's trips. She shook each one and placed them all in the row, and she and Ella watched the snow swirl inside each tiny dome.

"She's kept every one you gave her," said Ella. "Every single one."

She hoped Vivien would be comforted by this; instead, it made her sad.

"I never thought she would actually keep them," said Vivien, softly.

"I think it makes her feel like she's been on trips," Ella suggested.

"She *should* be able to go on many trips," said Vivien, her voice urgent. "She should be able to go to Hawaii." She quickly turned away from the snowdomes.

"I gave Mrs. Lowenstein a box of See's candy, and she was very appreciative," said Ella, brightly.

Vivien looked at her. "Oh, you did?" she said.

"Nougat, mostly," said Ella, "though I took a chance and included some soft centers."

"Well," said Vivien, "if that doesn't convince her, she is a hard woman indeed." She bent down, gingerly lifted up the pink towel, and touched the burned carpet. She and Ella quietly looked at the damage Lena had done.

"What do you think?" Ella asked, anxiously.

Vivien rubbed her forehead with one hand, slowly. "Well, it was kind of an ugly carpet."

"Right," said Ella. "I wish I'd burned it up myself. Years ago."

Vivien lay the towel down.

Ella, to reassure her, quickly said, "It was an

accident. Lena's a peaceful person; she's not interested in making fires."

"*I* know that," Vivien replied.

"An accident that could happen to any of us," said Ella.

"Sure," said Vivien, absently. She rubbed her long arms as though trying to warm herself. "All right. All right. We'll get this all cleaned up and march Lena over to Mrs. Lowenstein. We teach Lena a little speech. Something like: 'I am so sorry. It was an accident. I enjoy my room. I won't smoke in here anymore.' " Vivien paused. "Something easy but heartfelt," she added.

"*We* could give the speech," Ella suggested.

"We'll practice," said Vivien, pacing. "So. Mrs. Lowenstein. Hello! I am so, so sorry. It was an accident. I've lived here a long time —" She smiled at her mother. "Okay! Let's practice. Where is she?"

All at once, Ella remembered — and she was horrified. She'd been wondering where Lena and Shelley were, and now she knew: they were not in Panorama Village. They had left for someplace else.

"I think they just went down the hall," she said, trying to sound cheerful. "They'll be back in a moment."

"They?"

"Lena and Shelley. You know. Wherever young people go." Ella tried to laugh. That was the wrong thing to do.

Vivien said, "Shelley? She's supposed to be

home." She leaned toward Ella. Her eyes were too bright.

"I brought her," said Ella. "I wanted company." The words sounded pathetic; she stopped herself. The sound of sparrows, obstreperous and joyful, sparkled through the window.

"Wait here a sec. I'll be right back," said Vivien. Her voice was crisp now, official.

"I'll go with you," said Ella.

"No," said Vivien.

"Why not?"

"Because," said Vivien. "I'll be right back." She dashed out of the room.

Ella started to follow her, but Vivien had already disappeared by the time she reached the doorway. Ella stood there, alone.

Vivien was trying to be a good daughter to her in ways that Ella did not quite approve of or understand. Sometimes, Ella would open the door to her apartment and there was Vivien, with a roast chicken from Junior's or a box of Kleenex. "I was just in the neighborhood," she'd say, as though she always toted around a roast chicken in her station wagon. Sometimes she brought a supermarket bouquet of roses, swathed in cellophane and dripping water, which made her visit seem even more precisely planned. She'd move through the living room, peppering her conversation with pointed questions. "I love your hairdo! Did you call the electrician? The hall light's still out."

"Feed your own family with it," Ella might say, indicating the chicken that Vivien was trying, with some obviousness, to slip into the refrigerator. "What? With what?" Vivien said, rushing into the living room, swiping a mint from the crystal dish. When Ella did eat the chicken — she could never bring herself to throw it out — she did so as though not to admit its presence. She would pull off a leg and eat it over the kitchen sink. She made a point not to slice it properly or put it on a plate.

She could buy her own chicken, her own Kleenex. It was simply a waste of Vivien's time to bring these items to her now.

The hallway leading from Lena's room was hazy with fluorescence, and some of the doors were slightly open. There were cheap, sentimental oil paintings on the walls — of fruit baskets and Parisian streets and noble St. Bernard dogs gazing into a snowy sky. Ella thought she heard the sounds of whisperings in the air. There were no words that she could identify — they were simply hushed and intense and perhaps saying things about her.

Ella tried to follow the sounds, until she realized that she was hearing the whir of a plastic fan at the end of the hall.

She had no idea where Lena was. She was aware now of a dampness in her armpits, a sobbing sound in her breath. She wanted to walk throughout the entire building, looking into all the rooms, but the hallway suddenly seemed unsafe.

Heading back to Lena's room, she sat down in a sunny spot on the bed. It was as though she existed only in this room, in its warm sun and softness. She watched the tiny bits of snow still floating, slow and aimless, inside the snowdomes, falling onto the miniature skiers and hotels and pine trees; she waited for Vivien to return.

Vivien came through the door about twenty minutes later. She lurched into the room, jangling her car keys. Her expression of frustration shut off as she entered the bedroom, like a light quickly dimming.

"I've looked everywhere; they're not here."

"Well, where are they?" Ella asked, glad to accuse someone.

"You tell me."

Ella remembered Shelley and Lena hurrying down the hallway together, moving toward an unknown place.

"They went on an errand."

"What kind of errand?"

"To buy soda. Toothpaste. Soap."

Ella slowly smoothed the cuffs of her blouse. She hated the pleading quality of her voice.

"Why did you let them go?"

Ella turned away and looked out at the light-spangled garden. A long row of pink pansies stretched across the yard like a bright, fragile seam stitched across the earth. Ella waited for a good answer to reveal itself to her. But she had done something wrong. She looked up at

Vivien with large eyes.

"I don't know," she said.

Vivien took a sharp, deep breath. "You know that we told Shelley not to come here after what happened. You know that."

"I don't think you told me."

"I did." Vivien picked Ella's sweater from a chair.

Ella's shoulders curved forward in the posture of someone who had been scolded. She remembered holding the phone, the kitchen curtains fluttering, as Vivien told her the rule about Shelley's visits. She did not remember Vivien's exact words.

Vivien held out Ella's sweater. "Put this on," she said. Ella thrust her arms into the sleeves and Vivien smoothed the sweater on her shoulders.

"Where are we going?" asked Ella.

"We have to look for them."

Ella folded her hands and held them, trembling, in front of her chest.

Vivien had her purse over her shoulder. "Ready?" she asked, in a softer voice.

"Your leotard's dirty," Ella said, reaching forward and rubbing a spot. "You need a better detergent."

Vivien looked at her mother's face. "Okay," she said. She put her hand gently on Ella's shoulder, and they walked out, Vivien closing the door of Lena's room. The two of them headed down the sidewalk toward the station wagon. Butterflies and silver moths curved happy, crooked paths in the air.

Nine

When Lena was fifteen, Ella decided to tell her the Rules of Being a Woman. She could not ignore Lena's adolescence anymore. It had taken the seven-year-old girls in the Van Nuys Community Pool locker room to tell Ella that Lena had breasts now. Lena had joined the beginner swim class, and on the first Wednesday afternoon, she stood in the locker room, a fifteen-year-old looming over several seven-year-olds. The first time she peeled off her wet swimsuit, they stared at her body with a new respect. Their giggles, clear as bells, quieted, and they gave her room.

Ella, holding Lena's towel for her, looked at Lena more critically. Lena's breasts were beautiful, like small tulips, but Ella understood that they had no clear purpose. They would never, she thought, be kissed by a man; they would never be suckled by an infant. Lena's skin shone in the locker room, innocent not like a woman's skin, but like a child's — available in a way that adult skin was not.

That was the first event. Then Lena tried to figure herself out. She sauntered through the house bare-chested, examining her new breasts, pulling at her nipples. Sometimes when she sat at

189

the kitchen table, she would pluck pubic hairs and hold them up, curiously, to the kitchen light. One day Ella came on her in the backyard with a neighborhood child. The girl was sitting beside Lena, whose small breast was in the child's mouth. The two of them looked peaceful. "What are you doing!" shrieked Ella, and the girls popped apart, both looking with interest at the place where the child's mouth had been. Ella wanted to slap them, especially when Lena said, wistfully, "I just wanted to see what it was like."

That evening, Ella sat beside Lena at the kitchen table. She had a yellow tablet with a list of carefully considered rules. She had written them with a black ballpoint pen to make them seem official. "Here," said Ella, "are some Rules of Being a Woman. You must follow every one, all the time."

"Why?"

Ella thought. "Otherwise, you won't be a woman."

"What would I be?"

Ella hesitated. "I don't know."

Vivien was at the table, too, doing her homework and listening.

"One," Ella said, "you can't walk through the house bare-chested."

Lena sat perfectly still.

"Two, don't put your breast in anyone's mouth. Three, don't put your hands in your pants."

"Even when I go peepee?"

"Only then. Four, don't talk to boys. Smile nicely but walk away. Five, don't get into a car with strangers."

"I talk to boys," Vivien said.

"This is between me and Lena."

"I go peepee without my hands," Lena said, urgently. "Sometimes I do!"

Vivien got up and read over the list. "I don't always wash my hands before I pick up fruit," she said. "I don't always brush my hair at eight-thirty in the morning."

"All right, all right!" said Ella, shielding the list with her hands. "Sit."

"I forget everything," Lena grumbled.

"You are not going to forget," said Ella.

The sisters looked at her. They were like flowers in a desert, ready to drink whatever she said.

"I want a list, too," said Vivien.

"You can have some of mine," Lena offered. She grabbed a sheet and began to tear it in half.

"Hey!" said Ella, standing up and grabbing back the paper. "Both of you. Calm down."

"What's *six!*" Lena wailed.

"I have a rule," said Vivien, excited, "No sleep before ten!"

"No asparagus!" said Lena.

Now they were hysterical; Ella left the room.

There were issues for which Ella had not even imagined rules. Lena did not understand about menstruation, so each month presented a new problem. Once, she forgot to strap on a Kotex, and left streaks of blood on a neighbor's couch. Another time, Ella found her sitting at the kitchen table, her hands cupping her genital area; she was trying to catch the blood. She thought she'd been injured and she wanted a Band-Aid.

At least she did get her period. Ella marked Lena's cycle on a calendar and checked each month to make sure it occurred. She flipped through fashion magazines with a secret ambition — to find clothes that would make Lena pretty enough to be treated well by other people, but not so pretty that boys would be drawn to her. She decided that Lena would wear loose, flowered dresses that ended right below her knee. Her auburn hair could be decorated with rayon headbands or, on occasion, hats decorated with small, delicious-looking fruits. Her bras would be simple, but would have complicated hooks that only Ella could manage. When they whisked through May Company together, Lena slowed down by the makeup counter, delighted by the glossy, oyster-shaped compacts, the seductive, silver mirrors.

"You don't need those," Ella said.

Lena hung by the counter, unconvinced.

"Honey, you're so beautiful in your natural state, you don't want any cosmetics interfering," said Ella, and, to her relief, Lena seemed to accept this as fact.

In the ladies' clothing department, Ella

marched through the racks and picked out dresses. Lena followed her in a haze of shyness; she didn't know what was all right to want. When Ella saw a dress that fit her specifications, she held it out to Lena with happy enthusiasm. "This!" she said. "I know. This is you." They went into a dressing room, and Ella brought salesgirls over to tell Lena how wonderful she looked. The dresses had the unusual effect of making Lena appear ageless. As she turned around in the dressing room, she looked both older and younger than she was.

One day, Lena picked out a dress by herself. The May Company had reduced a rack of orange dresses that had not sold during the summer, and Lena was enchanted by the color. She fingered the cotton sleeves and gave Ella a beseeching look. "I want this," she said.

Ella looked it over. "It's the same color Henrietta wears," she said. "You'll look just like her." Henrietta was the crossing guard at the intersection near the school.

The idea of wearing a uniform thrilled Lena. She wore that dress only on Thursdays, and each Thursday was a special day.

Vivien walked home with Lena every afternoon. When Vivien started her dance classes, taking a bus to the studio, Ella went to fetch Lena. Lena always waited in the shadow of a large eucalyptus tree, its silver-leafed branches stretching upward like celebratory arms. The other students were socializing on the lawn, their voices frenetic. Lena sat on a wall, clasping her lunch pail in her lap, and watched the kindergarten children playing next door.

One afternoon when Ella arrived to pick her up, Lena was not sitting in her usual spot. Ella stood by the empty wall and waited — twenty minutes, then thirty — and her heart grew chilled.

She looked for Lena in the crowd of teenagers. The circles of young men and women formed soft, interlinking rings of desire. Many of them had attended Lena's elementary school and middle school, but they had become unrecognizable with age. The boys sported hair slick with pomade; the girls lifted hands flirtatiously to adjust the collars of the boys' shirts. Ella touched the arm of a blond girl she remembered; her name was Marjorie. Now Marjorie was about sixteen, elegantly dragging on a cigarette. She looked at Ella warily.

"Marjorie. Have you seen her?" Ella said.

She was startled. "Who?"

"Lena. Lena Rose."

"The slow girl?"

Ella winced. "She wore a bright orange dress today."

The girl shrugged. "No."

"Oh, yes, Lena," said a boy, smirking. "She went on a date."

"With who?"

"A whole bunch of them. They went out on the town."

"What are you talking about? Where?"

"Can't say."

He wore a smile the way the girls wore their hair clips: lightly, easily, on and off. A deadly feeling poured through Ella's heart. "What do you mean?" she asked. "A date?"

His eyes had settled appreciatively on Marjorie's shapely calf.

Ella stepped up to him. "What did you do to her?"

His eyes snapped back, stupid. "Nothing!"

"If anyone bothers her," Ella said, "I'll kill you. Do you hear me? I will shoot you with a gun."

The two teenagers froze. They stepped back, their hands raised. "Hey, lady," said the boy. "Why don't you cool it?"

Ella rushed through the crowd. She felt crazy, searching. Lena was nowhere to be found.

And then she spotted the bright orange figure heading with determination down the street, a group of children swirling around her. Ella ran. Just at that moment, Lena stopped in front of a house and pointed to the door.

"I'll watch you," Lena said. "Go."

A girl of about six trotted up to the door and rang the bell. She waved to the rest of them and went inside.

Ella had caught up with them. "What are you doing?" she asked Lena.

"I'm walking them home."

"Why?" asked Ella.

"I'm wearing orange," said Lena proudly.

The children observed Ella. "My brother walks us usually," said a little girl, "but he was sick today."

The children looked obediently at Lena. "Everybody," said Lena, "make a line. Quick!" They shuffled into formation, and Lena looked them over. "That's good."

Lena faced them. "Daniel," she said, "say where."

"Turn at this street, please," said Daniel.

Lena led the line down the sidewalk, and Ella trailed behind. Lena was pleased with herself. She walked each child to his front yard and said goodbye. After Lena had delivered all the children to their homes, she walked to her own, occasionally glancing back at Ella; on Lena's face was a cool expression of pride.

The next day, Lena heard from the teenage boy that her mother had threatened to shoot him. When she got home, she wanted to know why.

"No reason," said Ella, lightly. "Just stay away from him."

"But they like me."

"Don't go near them, honey. They're bad boys."

"He let me feel his muscle."

Ella immediately said, "That's rule number seventeen of Being a Woman. You don't feel a boy's muscle."

"It was round," Lena said.

"Rule eighteen. Don't feel round ones."

"Other girls feel muscles," said Lena irritably.

"You're not like other girls."

The words just flew out of her. Lena wrapped her arms protectively around herself and stepped back. "Am I a boy?"

Her daughter stood before her.

"No," Ella said, ashamed, "you're not a boy. You're Lena. You're my darling."

"I like to walk them home."

"Okay," said Ella, wondering how she could trail Lena each day so that her daughter could continue doing this. "And you were very good at it."

She went to her daughter and grasped her hands. They were limp, unresponsive. She shook off Ella's hands and slid away from her.

"What, darling?"

"Nothing."

Lena backed off farther.

"Tell me."

Lena rubbed her fist against her mouth. "Are you going to shoot me?" Lena asked.

Lena graduated from high school on a hot day. The wind blew in the sweet, ancient fragrance of the desert; the grass was dry and brown. Lena stood with 219 other black-capped graduates of her high school on the faded baseball diamond. Their gowns rippled in the pure heat of the Santa Ana, making them look like a battalion of superheroes, and their hats flew into the air with the sound of hundreds of wings. It was 1948, and their futures spread out, sparkling, before them.

With the passing years, Ella had watched Lena's classmates evolve into adults. Some changed into waitresses, and Ella spotted them at local restaurants, smartly writing down orders on their pads. Some got jobs building highways or planes. Others married and moved to new neighborhoods — Santa Monica, Redondo Beach. Some enrolled at Valley College or UCLA.

The look of the neighborhood shifted; the younger brothers and sisters became the older ones, and the older ones went off to live their own lives. They all assumed one thing, with absolute confidence: motion. But Lena was still. Every morning, after Vivien left for school, Lena got dressed and walked to the kitchen. Slowly, she ate a bowl of Wheaties — then another. Her spoon clinked against the bowl with an earnest sound, like a small animal trying to dig to a new place.

After breakfast, Lena would move from the kitchen to a chaise longue in the backyard. She kept a pair of heart-shaped sunglasses in the dirt of the potted geranium, and she would lie outside all morning wearing those sunglasses, even on cloudy days. An edgy, demanding quality crept into her voice. "I want my lunch now," she'd call in the middle of the morning. "On a plate." She glared at Ella as though her mother were a servant, became picky about the presentation of her food. She refused to eat a mound of cottage cheese that Ella had arranged nicely on a lettuce leaf. She wandered through the house, leaving half-eaten fruit on end tables. Her high school figure softened, swelled.

When the cloud of neighborhood children appeared at the end of the block at three-thirty every day, she walked them home. She would sling their school bags on her shoulders and walk each child ceremoniously to the front walk. "Here is your bag," she would say.

"That's not my bag," the child sometimes said.

Lena was peeved by this reaction; she seemed to think the child was to be grateful to get anything. "Yes, it is."

Clearly, Lena had to have some scheduled activity out of the house. Though Lou couldn't think of anything for her to do at the store, Ella bribed him with a chocolate pecan coffee ring, and he agreed to devise some job for her. The first day, Ella dropped by and found Lena sitting by Lou, a pile of loose socks on the floor.

"I'm the sock roller!" she announced. She picked up a cup of Coke and took a long, noisy sip. "Now I'm tired."

"She did seventeen socks," observed Lou.

"And —" prompted Lena, beaming.

"And she did an excellent job of picking lint off shoes," he added.

Lou agreed to take Lena three days a week;

Ella would take her the other days. On the days when she was to work at the store, Lena woke before anyone was up. Ella would find her in the kitchen, pacing. She changed breakfasts midway through the meal — decided she wanted Oat-i-os instead of Wheaties, or some type of egg. Lou would buy her a soda at Woolworth's each day, and before they left the house, Lena had to decide on that day's flavor: cherry or cola or lime. Some days, she was so restless that she skipped breakfast and waited outside on the front step. She stared at the night-damp lawn, the concrete walkway glistening with silver snail tracks, and she waited for her usefulness to begin.

Vivien was in high school, and her energy was focused, designed to loft her to a higher place in the world. She had moved from Helene's Dance School to the World Dance Academy in Hollywood. She proudly announced to Ella the names of her teacher and of the professional students in the class; her voice trembled as though the names constituted a kind of argument. "That's wonderful," Ella said, wanting to stand with her daughter in this bubble of excitement, even if she didn't recognize any of the names. Vivien apparently had a talent for ballroom dancing, for coordinating her steps with a partner's; she was very sensitive to the movements of another.

At fifteen, Vivien was lovely; when she walked through the house in a bathing suit, oblivious of the new shapeliness of her body, Ella was dizzied by her beauty, and Lou felt the need to spout elaborate theories about Eisenhower. And the world opened up to her. She shared gossip with her high school friends but concealed it from Ella; she received numerous calls from eager young men. Sometimes, to Ella's delight and confusion, she came to her for advice.

"Harry," Vivien said, "calls me all the time, and he's nice, but he has a laugh like a horse and he's not all that bright. I don't know whether to date him again or stop."

"He laughs like a horse, forget it. You're a wonderful prize, sweetheart; you can get better than that —"

"But Genevieve thinks he's going places." Pause. "I like it when he calls."

Ella felt a million answers rise up in her. She burst out, "Just do whatever you want."

Ella sometimes found herself trying to ignore Vivien's adolescence, for fear that she might ruin it. Afraid of giving the wrong advice, she said nothing; instead, she bought Vivien expensive, absurdly sexy dresses she thought her daughter would like. They were on sale at May Company or Bullock's and Ella snapped them up for no particular occasion; they were wild creations, with beaded bustiers or sequined waistlines, and held the promise of glorious events. Vivien accepted them and then changed them in her own particular way. When she wore them, she never looked quite as Ella had imagined she would, and this incongruity made her daughter a shimmery, unreal person — like a movie star on a screen. Ella did not know how to talk to this person, so sometimes there was a wariness, a silence between herself and Vivien. She did not know how to help Vivien grow up.

When Vivien entered high school, Lena was twenty-one and had never been on a date. One morning, sitting in the kitchen, shaking salt on a scrambled egg, Lena made an announcement.

"I think I would like a husband."

Ella sat still.

"Is that all right?" asked Lena.

"Well," said Ella. She gripped her coffee cup so that Lena couldn't see her hands tremble. "Why?"

"I'd like someone to hold hands with," Lena said in a serious voice. "I want someone who can walk with me around the block."

"What kind of husband would you like?"

Lena smiled. "A nice one. With blue eyes. Someone who likes TV and coffee shops." She leaned toward her mother. "I want someone who loves me very much."

Ella could barely wait for Lou to get home and hear about this new development. He shut the door to their bedroom, sank onto the bed, and removed his shoes; then she let it out.

"Lena wants a husband," said Ella.

His feet dangled in their purple socks.

"She does; she's thought about it. She wants to get married, Lou. She wants someone with blue eyes."

"Who would marry her?" asked Lou.

He did not say it unkindly.

"Perhaps some man," tried Ella.

"She needs someone to take care of her. Not to have a romantic affair with," he said.

"She wants a husband," said Ella.

"She's my daughter, she's sweet, but, honey, I can't think of anyone who would marry her. I have to admit that if I was a young man again, I wouldn't marry her."

"You don't think that Mr. Weiss down at Van Nuys Flowers?"

"The floral assistant? You mean the lush?"

She sighed. "That Jake Steiner always compliments Lena's hair —"

"Lena's and every lady's on the block!"

She felt barren, a bad mother, unable to produce a man who could love her daughter.

"So what does she do her whole life?" asked Ella. "Stay here with us? Sit in the living room, watching TV?"

"Well," said Lou, "at least it's a nice living room. Ella, Ella." He caught her arm. "We can't force anyone to marry her. We can't" — he laughed — "pay anyone off."

An enormous engine spun inside her, but it couldn't move her to the place she wished to be. She paced around the room as he changed his clothes.

"Would you marry Vivien?" Ella asked, suddenly.

"Vivien? What?" he said.

"If you weren't married. If you met her. Would you marry her now?"

Lou pulled a ratty sweater over his head. "Vivien," he said. "She's certainly pretty. Just like her mother. She's a little bossy when she wants to be. That would drive me crazy. No, I don't think Vivien would be the right wife for me." He winked at Ella.

Ella tried, unsuccessfully, to smile.

Ella had seen the ad for the matchmaker posted in a deli on the West Side. The matchmaker, named Ilana Golden, had an office on Fairfax Boulevard. Over the phone, she told Ella to bring two 3-by-5–inch color photos: a recent close-up, with makeup, and a full-body shot of Lena, preferably in a dress.

Ilana Golden's office was on the second floor, above an insurance office. A silver *mezuzah* hung on one side of the doorway. The walls were filled with wedding photos, dozens of smiling brides and grooms. Some clutched each other; some jointly lifted pieces of cake. They were short and tall, handsome and plain; they wore many types of tuxedos and veils. Yet they all had a curious similarity, as though they had all become related on their wedding day.

"Ella?" said a petite woman with frosted blond hair sitting at the desk.

"Hello," said Ella.

This was not a matchmaker. The matchmaker she'd once seen in Boston was a bludgeon-like woman who knew enough not to dress better than her clients. Ilana Golden wore a blue silk dress with shoulder pads and held a clipboard; she looked as if she was checking inventory.

"You have the daughter named Lena," said Ilana Golden, consulting her clipboard.

"Yes," said Ella.

Ilana handed Ella a questionnaire. "This is what we use nowadays. You answer a few questions; we set them up. It's almost scientific. Now let's take a look at her."

Ella gave her the two photos. Ilana held them to the light. "Nice hair, nice hair," she said. "What is she? Eighteen?"

"Twenty-one," said Ella.

"We'll say eighteen," said Ilana. "Bigger pool. Now, hobbies? Interests? Does she play the piano?"

"You probably can't tell from the picture," said Ella, "but she's slightly retarded."

"Oh, now stop," said Ilana lightly. "I'm sure she's a nice girl. Now, violin?"

Ella sat forward, alarmed. "No," she said, "she's retarded. I don't — I don't know what to do."

Ilana patted Ella's arm blithely. "Darling, darling. Don't you worry. So she's a little slow. We're all a little slow. Me, I can't for the life of me understand how airplanes fly. It makes no sense! My sister, she can't balance her checkbook. It's a task that's beyond her grasp."

The questionnaire was two pages long and included such questions as: *Do you prefer outdoor or indoor recreational activities? Do you regularly celebrate Shabbat? How loud do you play music in your home? What time do you usually go to bed?*

"She — finished high school," said Ella, "but she's not normal. She needs a man who's like her."

"I see," said Ilana, winking.

"They — can't go . . . they have to stay at the house for the first — the second date."

"Well, relax, Ella. We'll find a man for her." Ilana waved at all the frozen smiles lining the walls.

Ella referred back to the questionnaire, searching for one question she knew she wanted to answer. Failing to find it, she handed back the paper. "She would like someone with blue eyes," she said.

He was not slightly wrong. He was deeply wrong, the kind of person you watch and wonder — because of the falseness of his smile, the aggressiveness of his stride — how you can both claim membership in the same human race. His name was Edward. He was tall, in an easy way; he'd shot up into the world knowing it would welcome him. Loneliness clung to him like a scarf, easily discarded; he was not like Lena, who'd never really had a friend.

"You're here for Lena?" Ella asked.

"Yep. Lena Rose," Edward said. "Great name."

Ella rushed upstairs to Lena, who was sitting

on her bed. Lena had never waited for a date; she didn't know how to do it. She didn't know how to seem uninterested, the way Vivien was before a date. Lena had plunked herself on her bed and was simply waiting.

"Honey, we need to talk —"

"Mother," said Lena, "my date's here."

He lasted two hours. They sat on the patio, and Ella brought them her homemade chopped liver, which she referred to as her liver pâté, and a plate of Ritz crackers. Lena and Edward sat in the milky beams of the patio lights, and their faces glowed. He talked. Ella spied on them through the kitchen windows. It was apparent why he'd had to consult a matchmaker. His over-confidence was the saddest thing in the world. He spread himself out on the chaise longue and told idiotic jokes. When Lena didn't laugh — because she never laughed at jokes — he sat up and leaned toward her; he was one of those grabby types, desperate to yank out happiness, no matter how false. "Come on, sweetheart," he said. "Don't you get it? Smile for me."

Lena rubbed a strand of hair across her mouth. Edward rarely looked at Lena; he told his jokes to the darkness of the yard. All of a sudden, as though it were time, he turned toward her and took her face in his hands.

It was not clear what he meant by this action. Puzzled, Lena began to laugh. Her hands reached up to his, and she lifted them off her face. She began to giggle, little explosive sounds, and then jerked back, laughing, almost a kind of shrieking.

Edward stood up, shook Lena's hand, and walked off the patio to the front door. Ella followed, several feet behind, craving answers to questions he would not be able to answer. He walked through the hallway, now not a date but a stranger, took his coat from the closet, slapped on his hat, and headed back into his life.

Lena was standing in front of the refrigerator, taking out whatever she could find: Bing cherry Jell-O mold, more chopped liver, cold stew.

"He told bad jokes," said Ella. "You don't want him. Thank God he's gone." She pushed open the screen door and began to wave out the air. "Come on, help me get him out of the house."

Lena stayed in front of the open refrigerator and began to cry.

Perhaps Ella could buy Lena a husband. Or hypnotize one of the matchmaker's desperate clients. Ella had made this daughter, finger and bone inside her body, and was offering her up to a life alone.

"Wait," Ella said. It was such a dumb bit of advice; it meant one thing when she gave it to Vivien, another when she told it to Lena. Wait, you may stop wanting this. Wait, you may begin to love flowers or dogs. Wait until I can find someone to love you.

One day, Lou handed Ella a flier a customer

208

had given him. It said: *Wilshire Charm School for Young Ladies and Gentlemen Who Are Mentally Retarded. Now forming. Anyone interested call 229-1640.*

She looked at it, alarmed. "What do I do with this?" she asked him.

"I thought Lena might want to go," he said.

"You think Lena needs to be more charming?" she asked.

"Maybe she'd have fun," he said.

She signed Lena up. The class was to be held every Thursday at four o'clock. Ella could not imagine what it would be like. She tried to picture Lena possessed of charming attributes: well-groomed fingernails, a little pillbox hat.

The class was held in an empty elementary school building near Wilshire Boulevard. The room was a little dark, and the windows were tall white rectangles of glare. The desks were arranged in a large circle. There were seven young women and two men, and their mothers sat in chairs right outside the circle; the students looked like planets closely surrounded by moons.

Two instructors stood in the center of the circle — Mrs. Latham and Mr. Hughes. "We are here to teach social graces to our students," said Mrs. Latham. "To present themselves well to others, and even to date." She wore a mustard-yellow cashmere sweater and a strand of pearls. Her daughter, Camelia, was a member of the class. Camelia was a heavy girl who sat, hands clasped, at a child's desk and looked at her mother with wondering pride. "I was visiting a clinic for the mentally handicapped in Philadelphia, where they offered these classes for adults, and decided to start one here. From now on in this class, we are not girls and boys, but ladies and gentlemen."

A couple of the girls squealed at this. Then everyone settled into a puzzled silence.

The mothers introduced themselves and their children, who ranged in age from eighteen to thirty-six. Ella stood up, her hand on Lena's shoulder. "My name is Ella," she said, "and this is my daughter Marlene. We call her Lena." Lena looked up, surprised; Ella had never called her Marlene in public. The ladies were Camelia, Lottie, Jane, Evelyn, Sophia, Marta, and Lena; the gentlemen were Ronald and Larry. Ella was pleased to see that Lena was the best-looking of them all. While the daughters were clothed in plain, almost dowdy outfits, the mothers had all dressed competitively; some wore silk hats, and the air was thick with the sharpness of perfume.

"Today we will cover grooming," said Mrs. Latham.

The two gentlemen went off with their mothers and Mr. Hughes, who held a can of shaving cream and a razor. The ladies' mothers were instructed to sit quietly in the back.

"Your appearance is important," said Mrs. Latham. "When we wash our hair and put on makeup, we present ourselves well to everyone else." The room was hushed; the ladies shifted around, scratching their arms, chewing on their hair. But they were listening. Mrs. Latham handed each one a lipstick. "We're all going to put on lipstick by ourselves," she said. "I'll show you how."

The ladies removed the caps from the lipsticks. Camelia stood up as a volunteer. "Do one lip at a time," said Mrs. Latham. "See? Follow the line of your lips. Pretend you're using a crayon, and fill it in." Camelia proudly walked in front of the others, turning her face regally so that they could see her red lips.

Then all the ladies made attempts with lipstick. There was a sudden camaraderie among the mothers as they all tried to see as much as they could. Mrs. Lawrence, mother of Evelyn, whispered, hoarsely, "Peach is *not* her shade." Their daughters leaned intently over small square mirrors. Jane drew a lipstick heart on the back of her hand. Sophia licked her lipstick as though it were a tiny Popsicle. Their mothers tensed.

When their faces were fully made up, the teacher had them parade past their mothers. "And we present the well-groomed ladies of the Wilshire Charm School," said Mrs. Latham.

The ladies glanced at each other, not knowing what to do next. A couple of the mothers applauded weakly. Jane began to giggle. Sophia coolly examined her fingernails; then, without warning, she squealed, dropped to the floor on all fours, and began scuttling across the room, making chirping sounds like a mouse. One by one, the other students dropped to the floor and began to chase her, squealing in an exuberant game of Cat and Mouse.

The mothers rushed forward. Ella went to Lena. "Up we go," she said, grasping her daughter's hands. And Lena and then the others sprang up like immense flowers in a garden. Their hands were gray with dust.

Lena immediately began to practice her new skills at home. She wore a full face of makeup to every meal. Her manners became impeccable, authoritarian. "Say thank you, Daddy," she told Lou after she passed the margarine.

"May I ask why?" he asked, suspicious.

"Because you have to," she told him, blinking her deep blue eyelids. "Please put your napkin on your lap."

Every Thursday for three months, Ella brought Lena to the class. The ladies put on fancy gloves; they walked across the room balancing thin books on their heads. Even when they dropped the books, there was a strange, silent grace to their movements. One day, the gentlemen learned how to hold doors open for the ladies, and they spent the afternoon escorting them in and out of the classroom.

Ella stood watching, rapt, and allowed herself to imagine events that were unbearably vivid: Lena drinking tea with a friend, Lena walking down the street with good posture, smartly attired in a hat and gloves. The other mothers stood with her. They did not share their fear that all this effort would lead to nothing.

When Ella came to pick Lena up from the eighth class, Mrs. Brown, Sophia's mother, hurried toward her, a concerned expression on her face.

"She's teaching them how to date!" Mrs. Brown announced. The two of them rushed to the classroom, their heels ringing brightly against the polished corridor floor.

The gentlemen and ladies were separated into two groups, sitting on opposite sides of the room. Everyone was giggling. Ronald, a dainty man whose mother dressed him in crisp shirts and bow ties and who was often obsessed with finding out the correct time, sat at a desk, gripping the handpiece of a pink toy phone. "Would you like to have dinner, Jane?" he murmured in a flat voice.

Jane, sitting at a desk in front of him, pressed an identical plastic phone to her ear. She looked perturbed, as though wondering why she did not hear his voice through it. Quickly, she set down the receiver and began dialing. After she had dialed a number, she said, quizzically, "Mother?"

"Honey, it's a toy," said Mrs. Latham. "You'll see your mother later. Now, what do you say to Ronald? Yes, no, or I have to check my calendar. This is a practice."

Jane looked aghast. "I don't want to go!" she blurted.

"Now *that's* a proper response," murmured one of the mothers. Hurt, Ronald slammed down the phone.

Ella felt the back of her neck go cold when it was Lena's turn. Lena was acting cocky, whispering to the other students how she had already been on a date. It did not seem to matter that the date arranged through the matchmaker had been a disaster.

"Go," she said, when she had settled facing her phone.

As Ronald diligently dialed, Lena sat straight, a half-smile drifting across her face. She closed her eyes briefly and shuddered. When she answered, her voice was honeyed, mature. "Yes, I will go to dinner," she said.

Lena brought home an invitation printed on a gold-trimmed card: *The Wilshire Charm School Invites You to a Summer Party.* Under that it said: *Our students would like to show you what they have learned.*

All the parents were invited. The party was to be held on a Saturday evening in May, in the recreation room of the school.

Ella let herself become excited about the event, and it was a wonderful feeling, bubbly, like champagne. She and Lena visited several stores before they found a dress they agreed on. It was elegant — a sleeveless aqua sheath.

Ella and Lou dropped Lena off at five so that she could help set up, and they returned as guests at six-fifteen. Frank Sinatra was singing on the record player, his voice creaky and sweet. Many of the other parents were already there, flanking their children like generals guarding dictators of small, important lands.

The students had done their best to make the room look cheerful. There were streamers and red and blue balloons. A long metal table, covered with a white paper tablecloth, held a glass bowl of red punch and trays of canapés that Mrs. Latham had made: pigs-in-a-blanket, deviled eggs, sweet-and-sour meatballs, carrot sticks.

"The kids didn't cook the food, did they?" Lou whispered, eyeing it hungrily.

"I don't think so," Ella whispered back.

He looked relieved. He'd never met the students and their parents, and his hands fidgeted around his sleeves, his collar; he seemed surprisingly shy.

When Lena saw Ella and Lou, she headed toward them at a gallop.

"Lena!" said Mrs. Latham. "Posture!"

Lena stopped, straightened her dress, and tried to walk with grace toward her parents. But her excitement propelled her, and she almost fell into their arms.

"Honey," said Ella, hugging her, "isn't this a nice event? Doesn't it all look festive?"

"I helped with the eggs."

"You did? What did you do?"

"I put them on the plate." She squinted at Ella. "You need a deviled egg!"

Lena rushed off to select one especially for her. Some of the other students were bringing their parents food, gingerly, on white napkins.

Ella had never before seen the ladies and gentlemen dressed up. It was as though they had walked right out of their parents' suppressed dreams. Larry's mother had put him in a smart plaid coat with a green handkerchief in his pocket; he matched his father. Sophia was dressed as though for a fabulous prom, in a bright yellow dress; the straps, studded with rhinestones, clung to her powdered shoulders, and the skirt was a joyous wave of yellow net. Jane kept playing with the zipper on the side of her dress; she left it half-zipped, revealing a slim oval of pink skin. The fathers paled in contrast with the mothers, who had loaded on makeup and glitzy jewelry.

"Doesn't Lena look lovely!"

Mrs. Brown, Sophia's mother, glided over like a yacht.

"Doesn't Sophia," said Ella carefully.

"That's my prom dress," said Mrs. Brown. "Took it out of storage just for her." Her voice shook slightly. She was clutching a cup of red punch; gingerly, she took a sip. "You know, Mrs. Latham's going to expand the course next semester. Job training."

"Why?" asked Ella.

"So they can get jobs," said Mrs. Brown. She

tried to sound as if this was the most natural thing in the world. The punch stained her lips.

"Who would hire them?" asked Ella.

"Apparently, some people do. They can be messengers. Some work at Goodwill." Ella recognized a brute optimism in Mrs. Brown's voice; it had the quality of a small person pushing an impossible load up a hill. That optimism made Ella feel a sudden tenderness toward her, though she knew nothing about Mrs. Brown other than that she was Sophia's mother.

"Do you have plans for the summer?" Ella asked.

Mrs. Brown's face lit up — carefully. "Warren and I are hoping to go to Hawaii. Sophia could stay with my sister in Fresno." She paused. "It's been ages since we've been out of California."

"Us too."

"The pineapple." There was real excitement in her voice. "I've never tasted pineapple that fresh before."

"Neither have I," Ella said. "You know, this may sound terrible, but I've forgotten your name."

"Patricia."

"Patricia, I'm Ella."

They smiled at each other.

Mrs. Brown looked toward the center of the room and let out a low whistle. "Look at that."

Larry and Sophia were dancing. Larry pressed his hand to Sophia's back, firmly, and her right hand was lifted in his. They were not sure how to move together, but they were trying. Their feet shuffled from side to side, their mouths were slightly open, and their faces were sharp with concentration.

The other students began to follow their example. Ronald carefully put his arms around Camelia; his palms hovered just over her back, as though he was warming himself on her. Lena walked around the dance floor, looking at everyone. The gentlemen had been instructed not to dance too long with one lady, and Lena stood near Larry until he put his other arm on her shoulder. Now, she, Larry, and Camelia were swaying together. Soon, all the students flowed into the dance area, and, together, moved to the music. They danced in enthusiastic and unusual ways — running under raised arms, standing in one place and then lunging forward like skiers, gripping each other's waists. They made a formless community under the drooping streamers and shining balloons.

Mrs. Brown set down her punch cup; then picked it up; then set it down. "Sophia said she couldn't wait to dance," she murmured.

Ella stood and watched. She did not know the rules for hope.

1. *Allow yourself boundless hope.* Was that correct? Was hope a bright feeling to nurture within herself, to turn to for comfort or help? 2. *Do not let yourself be fooled by incorrect hope.* Was it this, a sly joke, able to fool and mislead her, a feeling that could only lead to disappointment, grief?

She did not know if it was best to keep this feeling, or relinquish it, if it would save her or do her harm. The world of hope was wild and lawless. She and Lou and Mrs. Brown and the others were standing in the rec room, a quiet audience while their children danced. Her hope was leaping out of her like a big and ravenous dog.

A balloon came loose and fell from the ceiling. The students screeched as it bounced on their heads. Without speaking, Ella and Mrs. Brown moved toward their children. That was what they knew to do. Ronald jumped up and ripped another balloon off the ceiling; then all the balloons came down, buoyant blue, floating to many different pairs of hands.

Ten

Shelley and Lena were starting their new life together in the dank, shadowed space beneath the pier. The space was both wonderful and poor — wonderful with the light pouring into the blue shadows, the frothy sea rushing up on the shore; poor because the area was strewn with straw wrappers and cans. Lena and Shelley crawled around, tossing the litter on the beach outside, but the sour beer and trash odors remained.

Shelley wasn't sure what time it was. By the rich gold of the sun on the water, she estimated that the day had slipped into afternoon. She was a little bit hungry, and this sensation alarmed her. Lena had generously given her five Life-savers, and Shelley had eaten them slowly, trying to ration them and savor the sweet cherry taste. She'd finished the last one a long time ago.

They sat here, beneath the wet brown bottom of the pier, trying to behave as though it were their shelter. But there was a restlessness in the air. Lena said that Bob was coming to see them today, and Shelley knew this could not be true. The girl moved from boulder to boulder, but none was better than the others; none soothed her. It was as though her heart wanted desperately to speak a word that it could not pronounce. She was afraid to look too closely at Lena, because Lena's comment had made her into a stranger from a bad dream.

Lena was restless, too. She removed the stolen items from her pocket, lined them up, admired them, put them back. She kept trying to catch Shelley's eye; she had so much to talk about. Lena was bursting with ideas for their new life.

"We'll buy groceries," she announced, "in big markets with lots of food. We can get many frozen dinners. They're easy to heat."

Shelley, watching the water, said, "Uh-huh."

"You can go to school," Lena said, "and I can pick you up. When I see you come out, I'll jump up and run to you so you'll know I'm there."

She looked at Shelley, eyebrows lifted, waiting for approval.

"What school would I go to?"

"I don't know. A school school."

"But where?"

Lena shrugged. "I can pick you up. I went with Vivien one time and I saw her do it." She paused. "Bob can come, too."

Shelley pictured Bob walking toward them, full of accusations, his clothes filthy and torn, his face a small walnut of fury. This image made her sick and her feet seem raw and icy; she wanted to run away. But she and Lena were already running away. She jumped off her boulder and stood in the water, hoping it would make her feet feel normal. Then she glanced at Lena. Her aunt was sitting cross-legged on the sand, her knees poking huge and horribly childish out of her housedress. Shelley could not look at her.

"Lena, what do you remember about his funeral?"

She remembered little of it herself, except for the absurd green of the cemetery grass, the cold gray of the sky. There had been a mist over them all. Her parents had both held her closely as though she were a sick person. She remembered that her grandmother had gripped Lena's arm the whole time; the two of them looked like a mismatched plastic pair on a wedding cake. Her aunt was confused, crying when the others did, tugging at her black dress. Mostly, Lena peered anxiously around her, at the pale fog flowing through the limbs of the trees.

"It was a chilly day," Lena said.

Shelley's heart wanted to explode into a million angry words. She kicked the water and walked up to Lena sternly, hands on her hips. "Let me ask you," she demanded. "How are you going to buy us groceries?"

"You know how," said Lena, haughtily. "I *showed* you."

"But you can't do that every day."

Lena ducked her head. "You're supposed to do what a daughter does," she said. "Live with me and Bob in our house. Say you'll go to school. I will buy groceries. You'll have a boyfriend come visit you sometimes. I can tell you what I think of him. You'll say I have good ideas."

They did not understand each other anymore.

This was a secret Shelley could not share. She shivered. It occurred to her that they were many miles from anyone they knew.

She stepped into the surf again, feeling it curl around her feet. Now she had another secret thought, and it was awful: she was the only grownup here. "Remember," Shelley said, snapping around, "this is a beach. You have to be careful. Don't — don't talk to strangers."

Lena looked at her curiously.

"Don't go off alone with anyone."

"Like who?" Lena asked.

"I don't know. Anyone who asks."

"I don't like all these don'ts."

"Okay, *okay,*" said Shelley. "Do breathe in the fresh beach air." She drew in a huge breath; Lena copied her.

"When I say something," Lena said, "listen! Don't say no."

Shelley said, "Mmm. Well, you also have to listen to me."

Lena folded her arms in her lap and regarded Shelley. "Everyone has different rules," she said.

"What do you mean?"

"I had a rule that I couldn't put my hands in my pants."

Shelley laughed. "When?"

"When I was a little girl. Vivien didn't have that rule. She had a rule that she had to be great at all times."

"She did?"

"But she was great every time anyway."

"What about Ella? Did she have any rules?"

Lena chortled. "Mother had the rule that she always had to be right." She rolled her eyes. "I had more rules than anybody. I think Mother was scared about me."

Lena rubbed her palms against her knees. "What do you mean?" Shelley asked.

"She was scared I couldn't do things," said Lena. "I know she was."

The thought seemed like an open hand, reaching to shake another in her own chest, for Shelley understood this completely; she believed her mother felt the same way about her. "Huh," she said, hoping to convey some sympathy. But her aunt was watching the waves wash up against the rocks.

"Did you have any rules that you broke?" asked Shelley.

Lena squinted, thinking, then sat up very straight. "I got married!" she said. "Everyone was surprised." She twisted her hand with her wedding finger lovingly around her cheek and kissed her thumb. "I dreamed about it many times, and then it happened to me."

Eleven

Bob had first called on an April day in 1963. Ella picked up the phone and heard a male voice whisper, almost plead, "Lena. Lena. Lena there?"

It was a question she rarely heard. "Who may I say is calling?" Ella asked.

"Bob. Goodwill. I drive trucks — Bob . . ."

She knocked on Lena's door. "Lena. There's a — Bob on the phone for you."

Lena burst out of her room with naked joy on her face. "Tell him to wait!" she exclaimed.

She was wearing a little rouge and perfume when, five minutes later, she deigned to pick up the phone. At first, Ella couldn't figure out why her daughter smelled familiar. Then she realized that Lena had put on some of her Chanel; Lena smelled like her.

Lena had been working at the Van Nuys Goodwill for some time. She sat at a long cafeteria table and sorted socks and blouses that no one else wanted to own. Ella called Dolores, the coordinator of Goodwill's disabled employees, to check out Bob.

"Bob. Bob," muttered Dolores. "Why?"

"A Bob called Lena on the phone."

225

"This is so nice!" said Dolores. "We have five Bobs. Bob Winters is considerate but a drooler. Bob Lanard you wouldn't let in your house, not if you care about your china surviving the night." She paused. "Are you sure it's not Rob? We have a Rob who's — well — a former convict, but I think he's very nice, too."

"It was Bob. He said he drove trucks."

"Trucks," muttered Dolores. "Oh, Bob Silver."

"Tell me about him."

"A sweetie. Short, quiet, gray hair, good driver."

Ella tried to feel relieved but didn't, honestly, know what she felt. Bob Silver. It was just a name, but it seemed ferocious as a comet hurtling toward her home to do some new damage.

Bob called again that night. "Is Lena there?"

"Lena who?" Ella asked.

She was sorry the moment she'd said it; she could actually hear the clutch of terror in his breath. "Lena Rose."

"Who may I say is calling?"

"Bob."

"Why?"

Now he was dying. She heard his breath, everything slow on his end as he struggled not to tell her why he was calling.

"I just want to talk to her," he said.

Bob was half an hour early for their first date.

226

He pulled up in an old, candy-apple red Ford that gleamed, dully, in the afternoon. While Lena sprayed her hair upstairs, Ella and Lou huddled in the sheer-curtained window by the door and watched him come toward them. Bob rushed up the walkway, his hands plunged deep in his pockets, head down as though he was walking against a wind.

Lou opened the door. "Glad to meet you," he boomed.

Bob kept his hands in his pockets. The part in his hair was crooked, like a road that needed to be fixed.

"Bob, Lena's not ready," Ella lied, touching his arm; she wanted to see how normal he felt. His shoulder was a little damp and surprisingly muscular. Quickly, she removed her hand.

Bob glided deftly past her into the den and plucked up *TV Guide*. He flipped wildly through the pages, stumbled across the room, and clicked the channels until he found *Gunsmoke*. Then he backed up to the couch, propped his feet on Lou's green vinyl footstool, slunk low into the couch, and thoughtfully eyed the action in *Gunsmoke*. He was about forty, with short gray hair, but his feet, in blue sneakers, bounced on the footstool with the blunt, coarse merriment of a boy. Ella was used to Lena's stubbiness, the way she seemed to bump up unsuccessfully against adulthood. But it seemed strange in Bob, and she could not help thinking that even though he was taller than Lena, he resembled an aging dwarf.

Lou sat on the couch and rubbed his palms rapidly against his knees. His face looked as though it had been sculpted hurriedly into an expression of calm — the cheeks were uneven, the smile was off. He surveyed Bob as he would any stranger, as though deciding whether to hire him. "You like *Gunsmoke?*"

Bob clasped his hands on his lap. "I like the man in the hat," he said.

Lou began to lean into another question, but Ella felt he would ask the wrong one. "How is the job?" Ella asked.

Bob arranged his hands around an invisible steering wheel and twisted it to the right until it came to an abrupt stop. "I drive," he said. "I like to drive."

"Do you like big trucks or small ones?" Ella asked.

"I just drive big ones," he said, as though insulted.

Cowboys galloped across a desert. Ella kept glancing at her aquamarine vase near his elbow, pretending not to stare at him. There had to be reasons to like him. His fingernails shone. His sneakers were neatly tied. He had blue eyes. And the main point — he wanted Lena.

"How long have you worked for Goodwill?" she asked.

"A while."

"And you live?"

"On a cot."

"Excuse me?"

"With the Ensons."

"And they are?"

"A man and a wife."

Before she could inquire more, Lena appeared in the doorway. Ella had helped her match her yellow rhinestone earrings and scarf with a yellow shift, the dress she'd worn when she applied for the Goodwill job. It seemed lucky. Bob lifted his eyes from the TV.

Ella had never tried to look at Lena the way a man would. Dressing her was like adorning a child — for a specific, decorative purpose, but not for men. Now, lavender eyeshadow gleamed, iridescent, on her eyelids, and her hair was expansive with spray. Bob gazed at her frankly, as though he had a right to her. Lena whisked past Ella, bumping her with her purse.

"I've been talking to your guest," Ella began, "and —"

"Hi, Bob," said Lena.

Bob smiled. "Finish your socks?"

"Shut up!" squealed Lena, clapping her hand over her mouth.

"Excuse me?" asked Ella.

"Learn to park!" Lena said.

"I'm the best parker," Bob said. "I'm the number one parker. And you know it."

Lena screeched with giggles. "Liar!" She rushed to the front door with exuberant haughtiness. Bob ran after her, as though afraid she would disappear.

"Where are you going?"

"House of Pancakes," said Lena.

"It's going to be crowded," said Ella, feeling vaguely hysterical. "There's going to be a long wait —"

"I'm hungry," said Bob, tugging Lena.

"Do you have enough money? Let me give you some —"

"Bob has money."

Bob's eyes, focused on Lena, were clear and intelligent with desire. He put his hand on her arm.

"Bye!" Lena said, waving tentatively.

Ella could not speak.

"Bye!" said Lena. "You — you look very pretty." And they left.

Ella watched them bound across the lawn. Lena's yellow dress fluttered too slowly as she ran, as though governed by new physical laws.

Lou sprang back from the window, like a child embarrassed by what he has just seen. He pushed his hand into his glossy gray hair. "Well," he said, "we're not losing a daughter — we're just gaining another mouth to feed."

Lou had never owned Lena the way Ella had. For thirty-three years, he had tried not to look too closely at their daughter, cultivating, instead, a relentless optimism that Ella found incomprehensible yet necessary. Now it made her feel alone.

"We're not gaining anything," said Ella. She

grabbed her sweater and followed the two figures walking down the street.

She walked briskly but casually, keeping a block between herself and her daughter. When they turned into a shopping center at the corner, Ella stopped beside a Buick that was parked at one end of the lot.

Lena and Bob walked through the empty, sparkling parking lot spread, like a dark lake, between the House of Pancakes and a Hallmark, an ice cream store, a laundromat, a pet store. It was Sunday and the stores were closed, but Bob and Lena stared hard at the windows as though willing them to open. The asphalt was torn in places, seemingly delicate as lace. Ella waited for something to go wrong. Bob went over to several cars, rubbed their dusty tops, nodded like an expert, returned to Lena. She put coins into a newspaper rack, removed a paper, and handed it to him; he rolled it up and tapped it against his leg.

Slowly, they ambled around the lot, once, twice, three times. The orange flanks of the House of Pancakes loomed, unreal, candied in the Valley's pale light. Some customers left the restaurant and headed toward their cars with casual confidence; Bob and Lena stood in the dark lot and watched them walk. As the two of them finally walked through the restaurant's door, Bob touched her daughter's back just for a moment; his small hand reached for the yellow fabric, trying, gently, to hold on.

Bob came to the house once a week. Lena was always dressed and ready an hour beforehand; she sat absolutely still on her bed, as though his imminent arrival was so fragile a circumstance that she had to take care not to disturb the air. Yet she always made him wait. One night, when Bob had installed himself in the den to wait for her, Ella swept into the den to quiz him about his life.

"Where is your cot?" she asked.

"Near the garage."

"Who are the Ensons?"

"A man and a wife."

She dragged out of him the following scintillating facts: he preferred lamb chops to chicken, peas to potatoes.

Ella ruled that Lena and Bob had to spend part of each date at the house. Sometimes they sat on the patio while Ella washed the dishes, observing them through the kitchen window. One night near nine o'clock, when the sky had turned dark, Ella heard a jump and rustle and the sound of running; she looked out a window onto the shining, moon-silver lawn. Lena and Bob were not kissing or touching but just chasing each other, endlessly, like large, slow bears. Their sound was of the purest joy, a soft, hushed giggling as they followed each other through the dark yard.

Dolores told Ella that the Ensons, a couple in Sherman Oaks, were paid Bob's rent by Hugh,

Bob's brother in Chicago. Ella got Hugh's number and called him.

When she told him that Bob was dating her daughter, there was a silence so hostile she wondered what she had actually said.

"I'm sending money," Hugh said irritably. "I'm sending money."

"I'm not asking —"

"It's not easy, lady. Do you think it's easy sending —"

"Sir," she said, "I'm not asking for money. I just want to know what he's like."

Another silence. "Well, you see what he's like."

"For the last few months. What about before?"

"What is there to know? He's forty-one. Three years older than me."

"Where did he live before?"

"The folks had him at an institution for a while. They didn't know what the hell to do with him. He's been at the Ensons' for six years, since the folks died. They're the ones who got him to Goodwill. He likes driving, I hear."

"What else?"

"You might want to know this. He had a vasectomy."

She pressed the phone more firmly to her ear.

"They did that early. When he was sixteen, seventeen. No little Bobs running around."

Ella did not know how to digest this fact, so she decided to move on. "Anything else? Health problems, disorders, anything?"

"No, he's just real slow."

"And you?" she asked, in spite of herself.

"Me?"

"You. What do you do?"

"I'm in insurance. Life and homes. I got married two years ago. I've got a son now," he said, his voice suddenly soft and eager to please.

"How nice," she said coolly.

"I hope he and your daughter get along real well," he said, his voice high-pitched with false sincerity. "I'll call back to see how he is." He hung up. She never heard from him again.

One night as Ella was putting on her sweater before going out for her usual reconnaissance mission, she felt Lou's hands on her shoulders. He turned her around.

"I have to go," she said.

"Have dinner with me."

"Dinner?" she asked. "But they're —"

"They're just going to the House of Pancakes." He looked away. "Who else is going to marry her?" he asked.

He was wearing an undershirt, and his shoulders were thinner now at sixty-seven, almost girlish. She followed him to the kitchen. Lena had discovered her own perfume — a chirpy, lavender scent from Sav-on — and the fragrance wafted through the hall.

Lou paced around the kitchen while she heated chicken with mushrooms. "What do you think they're doing?" she asked.

"Eating," he said.

"They'll forget to pay," she said.

"Then they'll get arrested," he said. He folded his arms. They were caramel-colored, dusted with silver hair. His gaze stopped on her, held her. "Let's fool around," he said, a soft huskiness in his voice.

She stopped; she wished she could feel interested. "If you want to," she said, "then come over here."

He gently wound her hair into his hands. His aftershave smelled drugstore-blue and sharp. His breath was a hot current against her neck. His hands slid down her arms and cupped her breasts, and Ella tried to let herself go against him, but couldn't.

Lou stopped, sensing her resistance. "She's fine," he said.

Delicately, Ella disentangled herself.

"I need you, too," Lou said. He lightly slapped her hip, as though she were a cow, and she heard him walk away from her.

Lena and Bob marched into the kitchen one evening, their fingers wound together, as though they'd been assigned to be buddies on a school trip. Lena held up their hands. A plastic yellow ring encircled her index finger.

"I'm married!" said Lena.

Bob swiped a bruised pear off the table and took a big bite.

"You're what?" Ella asked.

"He gave me a ring!"

"You're engaged," said Ella.

"I'm going to have a husband!" squealed Lena. She pulled Bob to her side, like a purse.

Ella put down her dishtowel. She lifted Lena's hand; the yellow ring was the kind that fell, encased in a plastic bubble, out of a machine in the supermarket. Bob's breath came hard, thick as a puppy's, and his bristly gray hair seemed a harder silver than before.

Lena giggled and said to Bob, "Say what I said to —"

"Do I have to?"

"Yes."

Bob slowly got to his knees in front of Ella, rubbed his hands on the sides of his pants, and looked at the floor.

"I forget," he said.

"You know," said Lena. She whispered, loudly, "I want to . . ."

"I want to propose a marriage," Bob said, looking directly at Ella's knees.

"Lena," Ella said, "honey, he's supposed to kneel in front of you, not me."

"But he's asking you."

Ella looked at Bob on his knees before her. She saw the rosy, bald circle on his scalp. He looked like a gardener sprawled onto a patch of lawn, pressing seeds into a plot of dirt. He was inevitable, and perhaps because of that, she felt an unexpected rush of love for him.

"Lou," Ella called, carefully. "Lou."

"I'm married!" Lena shrieked as her father

came in, and she rushed into his arms. It was something Lena did so rarely that Lou was unsure how to hold her, and his arms curved around her awkwardly. He stepped back and looked at her, blinking.

"Married," Lou said.

"Stand up," Ella said to Bob. He rocked back onto his feet and stood, grabbing Lena's hand for balance. He was standing up, one of them now.

"We have to have a toast," said Lou, slowly.

Ella took a pitcher of cranberry juice from the refrigerator and filled the glasses. Lou arranged Lena's and Bob's arms in the gesture of a toast. Lena and Bob clutched their glasses fiercely, as though expecting the glasses to rise toward the ceiling, pulling them, legs kicking, off the floor.

"*L'chayim,*" Lou said.

It was Lou's idea that they get married in Las Vegas. They had a nine P.M. appointment at the Chapel of Eternal Love, at the far end of South Fifth, but Bob played the slot machines so long that he almost made them late. Lena played right beside him, a little wobbly in her heels. Her veil was plopped, like an exhausted, translucent bat, on top of her slot machine.

Afterward, the four of them walked down the Strip to the chapel, past the Stardust and the Dunes and the Thunderbird and the Riviera. The streets glowed with the hotels' gaudy pink and orange and white lights. Lena wore a polyester puff-sleeved ivory dress that she and Ella

237

had purchased off a mannequin in the window of Treasureland, a discount emporium. The mannequin rose grimly out of a litter of golden ashtrays and inflatable palm trees. Lena had stopped by the window, pointed to the mannequin and said, with great assurance, "Her."

Ella was holding Lena's hand. With her other hand she touched Lou's arm. "Do they know we're coming?"

"Yes."

"What about flowers? Do they provide them?"

"Relax." He did not look at her. "It's going to be beautiful."

She wanted to ask him whether love was truly good, whether marriage made you safe, whether the right man or woman would make anyone happy. She wanted to ask whether she had, in fact, given birth to Lena — if her daughter truly lived outside her body.

When they reached the chapel, Ella took Lena to the far corner of the parking lot and drew a lipstick across her trembling lips.

"Ready?"

Lena nodded.

"Scared?"

Lena shrugged.

Ella took her hand. She wanted to tell her something. Marriage, she thought, was not simply choosing your mate, but the person you wanted to be for the rest of your life. She, Ella, had married a man whose feet made a ringing sound when he came home to her, his face startled with joy. He made her laugh with stories of peculiar fashions and foolish customers. But when she tried to speak to him about Lena, he would lean toward the TV set, brushing away her words as if they were pale moths.

Vivien had married Mel, a reform rabbi, a kind, exuberant man who stood on the *bima* in a navy blazer and talked about the ways that everyone could heal the world. Ella often noticed how gently he and Vivien held hands, as though each understood and wanted to protect the fragile parts of the other. He could be busy with the demands of many people, but he seemed most comfortable when he listened thoughtfully to his wife.

There were other wives Ella and Vivien could have been. Their marriages had shaped them, firmly and precisely, but Ella could not see the marks of her own evolution; she could not see how the love she gave and took had made her what she was.

And here was Lena with one suitor, one choice.

"Do you understand what this means, Lena?"

"It means that Bob and I will be together, and we will be happy."

Ella adjusted Lena's veil. "Where's your bobby pin?" she asked. "Don't let this fall off. Don't keep touching it."

Lena swatted her hand away. "I want to get married now."

The justice of the peace looked worn down by

all the eternal love he'd seen that day. His assistant, wearing a red sequined minidress and a sparkling nametag that said *Witness*, took the wedding fee of twenty dollars from Ella and flung open the door to a large refrigerator. In it, rows of cold bouquets were lined up like a silent, aloof audience inside. She shivered. "What color roses, hon? Red, pink, white, or silver?"

"I would like silver, please," Lena said.

Lena and Bob stood side by side, their elbows touching. She tugged her wedding dress straight and nodded obediently at the justice. Her hand gripped the refrigerated spray of silver roses, which were the color of a dull nickel. Her face had the alertness of true happiness.

Ella stood on the other side of Lena; Lou held his navy fedora as he stood beside Bob.

"By the power vested in me by the state of Nevada, I pronounce you man and wife," said the justice. He coughed, as if he just realized he was intruding on a family gathering.

Lena moved first. She raised her hand to Bob's face with a great tenderness, her fingers spread to capture as much of him as she could. Ella wondered where Lena had learned to touch like that.

The witness hauled over a large, blue-sequined sack of gifts for the newlyweds. "Something to start off your new home," she said. It was brimming with boxes of detergent, spatulas, colanders. The justice thrust his arm in the bag and brought out a box of Tide.

"Yuck," Lena said.

"This is your free gift," the assistant said.

"I don't want that one," Lena said, pouting.

"You don't want it?" asked the justice.

"Let them pick," Ella said.

The justice glared at Ella and checked his watch. "Lady, I'd like to stay here all day, but . . ."

"Let them pick," Ella hissed. She would not let them walk back into the streets of Las Vegas with a bad gift. Lena and Bob plunged their hands into the sack together. They brought out another box of Tide, pale detergent flowing through a crack in the top. Ella pushed in front of Bob and Lena and slapped the box back into the bag. She grabbed hold of a spatula and pushed it into Lena's trembling hand.

"Congratulations," Ella said.

After they all left the chapel, Ella told the married couple that new husbands and wives were not allowed to share a hotel bedroom. Newlyweds, she told her daughter, learned to be married slowly, in separate rooms. So for the first two days of the honeymoon, Ella shared her room at the El Tropicale with Lena, and Lou slept in the other room with Bob. The four of them would elbow their way to the Hacienda's $2.50, 97-item buffet table, piling their plates with magenta, fat-laced barbecued ribs; they lay, sun-doped, on a sparkling swath of concrete by a pale blue swimming pool. The sounds near the pool echoed, magnified by the water; even the children's shrieks were transformed into the caws of aroused, hysterical birds. Ella could pretend, then, that she didn't hear when Lena said, very softly, that she wanted to share a room with Bob.

That evening, Ella told Lena about sex as they sat in a quiet lounge off El Tropicale's main casino. The chandelier's cluster of near diamonds shed their earnest but subdued light. Her thirty-three-year-old daughter sat patiently, twirling a pink vinyl coin purse embossed *Las Vegas: City of Luck.*

"You're a wife," Ella began.

Her daughter smiled.

"There are certain things you can do."

"I'm called Mrs.!" squealed Lena.

A cocktail waitress holding an empty tray strode swiftly across the lounge, her nylon stockings an opalescent orange in the light of the chandelier.

"First," began Ella, then stopped. "Well, how do you feel when Bob kisses you?"

"My mouth feels wet."

"Do you like it?"

"I like it." Lena paused. "Sometimes he puts his tongue in too much. I don't like that."

A sign by the Canary Room said: *8 PM Tonite: Hilo Hattie and the Hawaiians.* Loud tourists flowed eagerly through the lounge toward the casino. "Married people — are naked in bed, Lena," Ella said.

"Naked!" Lena said, with a tiny shriek.

Ella felt something very tall collapse inside

242

her. "Don't be scared," she said, trying to fit her voice around the immense gentleness that surged within her. "It's just — skin."

"I liked when he touched here," Lena said, reaching up and squeezing her breast.

"Where did he do that?"

"In the bathroom. At the House of Pancakes." She giggled.

Ella said, "You don't do that in the House of Pancakes. You don't do that in any — public place. You do it in your bedroom. Nowhere else."

"In my bedroom," repeated Lena.

"After, you take a shower. You wash your hands with soap."

"It smelled like the ocean."

Ella let go of Lena's hand.

"When he put his hand in my panties, I liked that. He took his hand out and he smelled like me." She clapped her hand over her mouth and laughed with delight.

"Lena," said Ella. "When did Bob do that?"

"We came in through the backyard."

"You let him do that in my backyard?"

"I liked it."

"Soap," said Ella, a little desperately. "You use soap."

"Mother," said Lena. "What about when we're naked?"

Ella did not want to continue. Apparently Lena and Bob were doing well enough on their own.

"If he's ever not gentle with you, Lena, you tell me."

"Tell you what?"

Far away, Ella heard the clink of dishes being washed in the hotel coffee shop, the whir of a vacuum cleaner being pushed across the lobby, the sounds of maids and waiters cleaning the guests' messes of the day. "If he ever does something you don't like."

"Mother," said Lena, impatiently, "does everyone married sleep naked in a bedroom? Him?" She pointed to a porter leafing through a newspaper with the headline: WAR OF THE BOSOMS CONTINUES. "Him?" A man pushed a rack of pink and peach-feathered costumes toward the Lido de Paris show. "Her?" A tall showgirl, her hair in a rumpled bouffant, sipped a glass of orange juice and blinked awake. Her feet were swollen in silver sandals and her eyes were ringed with fatigue.

"They use soap," said Ella. She tried to think of one more crucial rule to tell her daughter, but her mind was filled with only this — in the deep green of her backyard, Bob had plunged his hand into Lena's panties. Now everyone moving through the lounge seemed profoundly tainted. Ella noticed the nubbiness of the bandleader's ruby velvet jacket, the too-proud grip of a tourist on his white-blond wife, the obsessive way a waitress counted her tips, turning all the green bills in the same direction, before she vanished into the dim, clockless casino again.

Out by the pool, the Las Vegas sun hammered their faces as though trying to melt their features into new elements. Ella watched her daughter spread herself on a plastic chaise longue. Lena's eyes were masked by her horn-rimmed sunglasses, and her nipples were visibly erect under her yellow bathing suit. She lay on the chaise in silence, as though she were spinning quiet, magnificent thoughts.

"Do you want some lotion?" Ella asked.

Lena didn't answer. She stood up regally and walked over to the undulating aqua of the pool. Standing a little unsteadily on its edge, she looked down at Bob in the water. He swam over, yanked her leg, and she crashed into the water.

Ella was not the only one who watched while Lena and Bob tumbled and splashed, cheerful, muffled bellows rising from their mouths. Their slick arms smacked the waves and swooped under the water, and their faces butted and kissed, but it was not exactly clear what they were doing to each other. The crowd around the pool was riveted. Ella felt the backs of her knees tense. She was just about to stand up when Lena swung herself out of the pool. She glittered, the water shining on her hair, and walked back to her chaise.

"I would like to share a room with Bob," Lena said.

That night, as the four of them stood in El

Tropicale's dim hallway, Bob circled Lena's shoulder with his arm.

"Honey, may I have your key?" Ella said.

Lena handed her mother the key. Lou was silent. Bob's fingers fluttered on Lena's shoulder, and Ella tasted fear, metallic, in her throat.

"Lena," Ella started, as her daughter took Bob's hand, "Lena, knock if you need anything." Lena whisked into her room and closed the door.

Lou had assumed a posture of odd, formal politeness. "Do we want to sit at the piano bar?" he asked.

"I don't feel like it."

"Do we want to play the slots?"

"No," she said, opening the door to their room, the next one.

They were as twitchy as a couple meeting illicitly. The walls were a glossy, wet-looking blue; it seemed the color could come off on their arms. With a sharp motion, Lou shrugged off his jacket. His white shirt was sticking to his shoulders in the heat.

"Have you noticed the footwear they sell here?" he asked.

"Footwear?"

He tossed his jacket over a chair. "People are on vacation; they lose their shopping sense." He took a deep breath. "Pink loafers. They take them home, and they ask themselves, Where the hell am I going to wear pink loafers?"

"They're going to have to live with us," said Ella.

"They probably don't want to."

"She can't cook or clean," said Ella.

"I don't think he'd notice."

She thought she heard the TV's muffled garble start in the other room. "I hear them," she said.

The two of them froze. "No," he said, "you don't hear them."

She put her hands on the wall adjoining Lena's room. It was strangely cool. She heard only a faint, staticky wave of audience laughter.

"Look!" said Lou. He knocked on the wall sharply, twice. "Hello!" he called. Breathless, they awaited an answer; there was none. "See?" he said. "They can't hear us." He turned and walked away from the wall. "Come away from there," he said. She wanted to accuse him of something; she wanted to see pain on Lou's face, a sorrow she could recognize.

"Leave her alone," he said, not sounding entirely convinced. He sank down on the sofa and rubbed his hands over his face. "Let's have a drink."

She couldn't. Instead, Ella pulled the ice tray from the freezer and, in a gesture that felt both normal and alien, dropped some ice cubes into a glass. She sat on the bed and chewed the ice cubes slowly and deliberately, trying to listen only to the hard clink they made as they fell back into the glass.

At about one in the morning, there was a sharp knock on the door. Ella opened it to Lena, who was shivering in her nightgown. Bob was right behind her, naked, holding a white towel across his waist with only middling success.

"What?" Ella demanded. "What's wrong?"

"I'm bleeding, Mother. Look, there's blood —"

Ella yanked Lena into the room, and Bob followed, wearing the frightened smile of a child unsure of what he had done. Lou got up. "What's —" he began, and Ella saw his face melt in alarm.

"I've got her," Ella announced. She pulled Lena into the bathroom. "Sit," she said. She wound a long ribbon of toilet paper around her hand. "Show me where."

Lena sat on the toilet and daintily flipped up her nightgown. Ella saw a smear of blood on Lena's beige panties; she reached up, grabbed the elastic and pulled the panties down to the floor. Ella dabbed Lena's vagina with the toilet paper; it came back pale red.

Ella knelt and peered critically between her daughter's legs. She had no idea what she was looking for; there was only a little blood. She held a towel under warm water and gently dabbed Lena's pubic hair.

"Am I okay, Mother?"

Ella didn't speak.

"Am I okay?"

"I don't know." Ella let Lena wonder a moment. "Answer me. Was he nice to you?"

"I think so."

"Does it hurt?"

248

"I started bleeding."

"Do you feel better now?"

Lena touched her vagina tenderly, then stood up.

Ella reached for her daughter's hands. She spoke carefully. "You've had intercourse, Lena."

Lena slapped Ella's hands away, impatient. "I have to go see my husband now."

Bob was waiting in a chair, the towel arranged, like a large napkin, across his lap. Lou was sitting on the other side of the room. Each had the alert demeanor of someone trying hard not to speak.

"I stopped bleeding," Lena said proudly to Bob.

Bob folded the towel around his waist, jumped up, and hurried out of the room. Lena bounded after him, and Ella followed into the hallway "The TV's still on," Bob called to Lena.

"Leave it on," said Lena.

As Lena followed him into their room, Ella saw her nightgown sticking over her hips; she reached forward to tug it down. But Lena pushed, grandly, past her mother. The door shut, and Ella was left standing in the corridor.

Back in the room, Lou looked at her. "Is she all right?"

She nodded.

He gingerly lifted Lena's beige panties off the floor. "She left these."

Ella remembered buying the panties for Lena; they were on sale at Henshey's, two pairs for the price of one. Lou folded them gently, barely touching the edges, and handed them to Ella. She was moved by the way he handled them. She went to the bathroom and threw them out.

Then she opened the refrigerator and took out a perfect, tiny bottle of Scotch, unscrewed the cap, swallowed half the contents, and handed the bottle to Lou.

There was only one thing she could think to do.

She went to Lou and kissed him.

They kissed in the strange room, surrounded by lampshades and bedspreads and dressers that were not their own. Ella let her husband kiss her neck, her breasts, her knees, hard enough to erase Lena. Ella had not expected to feel abandoned. She had not expected that Lena's closing the door would make her turn to Lou. The kindest thing he could do was make her forget. And because Lou had been, ever since Lena's birth, second place to her daughter, Ella sensed, in the muscular trembling of his fingers, how much he wanted to make her forget. She felt the nakedness of their lips in the deep, cooling dark.

Long after Lou had fallen asleep, she lay awake beside him. Then she went to the window and looked down at the street. It was the street Lena had walked down to her wedding, and it burned with the hotel's lights. She watched the messages — BINGO and POKER and WIN! — that flashed a brilliant display of pink and orange and yellow into the empty street. Ella believed, suddenly, absolutely, that Lena was also looking out her window. In her mind, she saw her daughter leaning, naked, toward the window, her hair fluttering over her bare shoulders, gazing at the bright casino lights and their strange, insistent attempts to illuminate the sky.

Twelve

It was a six-hour drive back to Los Angeles, and Ella and Lou sat silently as the Chevy moved through the desert. Ella watched Bob in the rearview mirror. His blue eyes were set on his wife as though she were delicious candy. His own family had relinquished him, through death and disinterest, and now he belonged to them.

He had walked into their lives with unbelievable ease. Now he was her daughter's husband; he was also her son. Ella was waiting to understand the emotion within her, for her heart was restless, trying hard to beat with a feeling that she did not yet understand.

What she did was watch Lena — for she had never seen her daughter so happy before. "We're ordering a davenport!" Lena burst out. "In tangerine."

"No, purple!" Bob crowed. He giggled.

"And where are you going to put this davenport?" asked Ella.

"In our house." Lena clapped her palms on the vinyl seat. "We're going to buy a house with children," she announced, then fell back against the seat.

The car rose over the highway into Los Angeles. First stop: the Ensons, who lived in a ranch home in Sherman Oaks. When the Chevy pulled up, the Ensons were watching TV with absorption; their expressions seemed like flowers stuck in half-bloom. Mrs. Enson shook Ella's hand. "Bob's a good boy," she said, simply, without love.

Bob's room was by the garage and was humid, windowless. His clothes were stuffed into a plastic supermarket bag from Von's — he scooped his pillow up under one arm and picked up his bag of clothes. He gazed at Ella with an expression of panic. "Where?" he said.

"You're coming to live with us," said Ella. "You're married now."

Bob hugged his pillow very tightly as he climbed into the car.

Everyone became increasingly tense as they approached the house. Bob sucked on his pillow; Lou whistled in a crazy way. When Lou parked the car in front of the house, and they all got out, Ella and Lou hung back while Lena took her personal house key from her pocketbook and rushed with Bob up the walk.

"Where are we going to put him?" Ella murmured, though they had already discussed this.

"In the garage." Lou had encouraged Lena and Bob's courtship more than she had, disregarding the consequences — this. "Under a large, unstable rake."

"Bob, please meet our orange bush," Lena said, politely.

"Hello," said Bob.

253

The screen door banged behind them. The lights went on, like an intake of breath. Ella headed inside. Lena and Bob were standing in the dim hallway, waiting to be told where to go.

"You'll be living in Lena's room," Ella said.

She painted the room a new color every few years, lifting the walls from yellow to salmon to blue, but the room always had a faded, bare look. It was not a child's room; it lacked that hope of transformation. Vivien had tried to help Lena decorate it. Vivien's souvenir goblet from her high school prom sat on Lena's dresser; blue ribbons that she had won at her dance competitions fluttered on the lampshades. All these items seemed adrift, without context. Some stuffed animals sat in a corner. On the wall were wooden plaques that Lena had won for being an exemplary employee at Goodwill.

"You're sleeping in here," Ella said. Her tone felt right: firm, a little condescending, yet also nice.

Bob's eyes flew, anxious, over Lena's stuffed animals; suddenly, he did not want to go inside the room. "There's no place for my pillow!" he cried, throwing it on the carpet.

"Bob," Ella said, tentatively, not knowing how to touch him. "Don't worry."

He bolted toward the open window. Gripping the sill, he leaned halfway out. The muscles in Bob's arms quivered; his feet kicked, as though he were paddling through water. He floated back down to the rug.

"Where are you going?" asked Ella.

Bob erupted in a short, piercing cry. His blue eyes were hazy with confusion. He looked at his wife, and Lena plunked to the floor, as though weighed down by her hurt feelings. "It's a *nice* room!" she said, and began to cry.

The three of them waited for the action that would bring them together. Finally, Bob sat down, cross-legged, beside Lena and put his arm around her, like a husband. The two of them turned to Ella with hope.

He belonged to them. Ella picked his pillow off the floor — it smelled sweetly of Johnson's baby shampoo. She placed it on Lena's bed. "Here," Ella said. "Welcome home."

The morning after Bob moved in, Ella woke early and went to the kitchen; she wanted to sit by herself in the soft dawn and feel the day begin. Half an hour later, Lou joined her. He had shaved too enthusiastically, and his skin, smelling of menthol, was raw. He had bedecked himself in his best suit; to this he had added his silk tie with green tigers. Once before he had worn this outfit, when, through a secret meeting with a Philadelphia distributor he became the sole vendor of pink Lucite heels in the San Fernando Valley. He looked dapper but sheepish.

"Why all fancied up?" Ella asked.

"Why not?" He eyed the door. "I bet you Fred used my spare key and smuggled in a girl while I was away. Probably got her up in a pair of those spiked heels. Watched her walk around in them and then *schtupped* her in the backroom. Don't look at me like that." He flapped out the *Los Angeles Times*, glanced at a headline, thwacked it down. "And the new linen socks. He gives a dozen pairs to her, free, free, *free*."

She made him a scrambled egg. He moved about the kitchen, making sure his favorite things were in their proper place: the orange juice squeezer shaped like a sombrero, the plastic snowdome from Reno filled with bikini'd ladies; when you shook it, their bikinis fell off.

"Should I lock up anything valuable?" she whispered.

"What else could he take?" Lou said.

Bob appeared in the doorway.

"Where's Lena?" they asked, as though he had killed her.

Bob seemed to instantly understand their accusation. "Dressing," he said.

Lou grabbed a bagel. "Gonna be hot out today," he growled and headed out.

Bob had been a visitor here many times before, but now, as a family member, he was unsure where he was to sit. "This is your chair," said Ella, pulling out Vivien's old seat at the table. She brought him a bowl of Froot Loops. There was a silence between them. She could feel him pulling, trying to yank some spare drops of love from her. "You should comb your hair," she said. Bob touched his scalp. It was the first motherly thing she had said to him, and the words startled both of them. The intimacy was a fresh, confusing heat in the kitchen.

"I'd like some juice," he said quietly.

Now Lena stood in the doorway. "I'll get it!"

Lena was dressed in the flowered nylon shift she'd last worn when she was named Most Congenial employee at Goodwill. She stepped daintily into the middle of the shining linoleum as though into a beautiful lake; she wanted them both to watch her. She took a bottle of juice from the refrigerator and set it in front of Bob. "Hello, darling," she said, kissing the top of his head.

"Bob," Ella said, "do you want peanut butter and jelly for your lunch?" He nodded so vigorously, she knew that he didn't. "Well then, what?"

"He likes tuna," Lena piped up.

"Tuna," Bob echoed.

Ella got the bowl of tuna salad from the refrigerator and made a sandwich. Lena chewed on her thumbnail and watched. The cool air of disapproval entered the room. Ella was wrapping the sandwich in wax paper when Lena picked up the knife and began to thwap tuna on another piece of bread. "I'm making Bob's sandwich!" she whispered to her mother. *"Me."*

Lena had never in her life made her own sandwich. Now she spread tuna so thickly that the bread tore, but she puzzled the slices together. "Here," she said to Bob, "I made it for you."

He looked at Lena's creation and then, longingly, at Ella, who quickly slipped her own sandwich into Bob's brown bag.

"I made you a sandwich," said Lena, proudly.

"Thank you," he said.

One afternoon when Ella returned from the market, she heard familiar voices floating down the hall. They came from her bedroom. Ella walked quickly down the hallway. She was afraid to open the bedroom door; instead, she crouched and peeked through a crack. The room seemed an aquarium of ruby, lustrous light.

Bob was standing still as Lena draped one of Ella's red rhinestone necklaces around his neck. The gold-brown hairs on his thick forearms glinted. The long necklace twinkled over his broad chest. Then Lena snapped a pair of plastic pearl earrings on his ears. He touched his hands to the earrings and laughed a hearty laugh.

The two of them opened Ella's closet and considered the clothes. First, Lena slipped Ella's bathrobe on Bob. The robe hung over his T-shirt, his worn jeans. Lena knelt and straightened the hem and looked up at him, gripping his small feet.

"Talk," she said.

"Lena," he said, his voice swooping and musical, "you have to clean your room."

"More," she said, giggling. "Say it."

He thought a moment. "I can help you button your shirt."

Lena turned him around in front of the mirror so that they could admire him from different angles. Bob struck a variety of poses: arms crossed on his chest, hands on his hips. The delicate lace bloomed around his wrists.

Ella turned and walked away with increasing urgency, until she was running out the front door. There was an unclean feeling as though someone had reached a dirty hand through her skin. She looked at the flowers, waiting for her breath to return to normal, but the garden seemed wild, filled with shouting silence. Then she went inside again. Lena and Bob were sitting in the den, watching TV and they were holding hands.

Ella did not tell Lou what she had seen. But she locked her bedroom door whenever she left it. She thoroughly washed all the clothes they had touched. When they were out of the house, she searched their room, but did not discover any of her belongings. Nor did she ask Lena about the episode in the bedroom, mostly because she was not sure what to ask. An unexpected shyness crept over her, and when she spoke, her voice sounded tinny, thin.

They lived together. Bob and Lena were the earliest risers, as though they couldn't wait to go forth into the day. They were in the kitchen by seven, drinking juice, waiting for Ella to come in and give them their bowls of Froot Loops. Some mornings, Lena insisted on making Bob his sandwich; on other days, she allowed Ella to make it and pretended that she had. They were off to Goodwill by eight-thirty, driving in Bob's ancient red Chevy.

At night, the four of them sat in the den, watching *The Wild Kingdom*. Lou had always liked to fool around recklessly, like a teenager, all the years Lena had lived with them. When Lena was asleep upstairs, he'd whisper, "Shh," untying Ella's apron, pressing himself hard against her buttocks. Ella needed that, his abandon. But Bob's presence had made him shy. Ella and Lou sat on the sofa next to each other, oddly sexless.

Lena and Bob sat on the floor; Lena leaned against him, her legs spread, her skirts rumpled above her knees. Ella pretended to be watching the show, though she was mostly watching Bob's chubby hand. It was as if she was waiting for it to do something bad. She tried to count to ten while his hand caressed Lena's thigh, her foot, her knee. One night, a sigh broke from Bob's throat and his hand darted up Lena's leg and inside her cotton shirt.

Ella looked at Bob's hand squeezing Lena's large breast; Lou coughed loudly and grabbed a box of green drops.

"Anyone," he said, "care for a mint?"

Bob withdrew his hand from Lena's blouse and tentatively took a mint. He munched it, looking at them innocently.

"Time to go to sleep!" Ella said.

"I'm not tired," said Lena.

"Now you are," Ella said. "Good night."

Lena and Bob reluctantly went to their bedroom. Lou grabbed Ella's hand. "Let's get out of here," he whispered.

The air of the valley was like warm bathtub water on their arms. Lou walked with great energy down the sidewalk.

"Let's go to Europe," he said.

"Paris," she agreed. "London."

At the end of the third block, they stopped. They bought Hershey bars at the drugstore and stood under a sycamore, eating the chocolate; it tasted wonderful, almost sour.

"I smell his aftershave everywhere," said Lou. "Sometimes I forget if it's his or mine."

She could not see Lou's face clearly in the dark. But he sounded as if he was about to cry. She had married him for this, though she did not know it when she had married him — she understood the feelings inside him, and she believed he would understand her. Putting her hands on his shoulders, she kissed him. She wanted to swallow everything around them — his chocolate lips, the velvet sky. Lena was a dream, and the orange stucco house was empty. She and Lou would live forever on this corner, under this tree.

It was quiet when they returned home. They brought the empty glasses from the den to the kitchen. On the way, they passed Lena's room.

The door was wide open, and Ella could see them making love. The lamps burned yellow, and Lena and Bob looked to her like monsters, large, naked beings, absurd and beautiful. They grabbed at each other with their hands, a brutal delicacy, as though trying to pick gold from sand. The bed squeaked. Lena's small feet kicked the air.

Ella turned to Lou. He reached over and shut the door.

Lena began carrying around one of her stuffed animals, a Dalmatian named Spot. She held him so that his plush head rested on her shoulder, and stroked him with a careful hand.

One morning, Lena brought Spot to the kitchen, seated him in the chair beside hers, and poured him a glass of juice. Then, with a vicious motion, she grabbed his juice and quickly drank it herself.

"Honey, do you want to talk about something?" Ella asked.

Lena said, "Where's my child?"

Ella's heart exploded, quietly. "Your what?"

"I'm married," Lena said. "Vivien wants to have one." Her brown eyes flashed, sorrowful, competitive. "Where's mine?"

Ella reached over and held Lena's hands. "You don't want a child."

"Why not?"

"You have Bob."

"He's my *husband*." Lena turned to Spot and smoothed his ears.

Ella said, "Honey, you can't have a child."

"Why not?"

When Bob's brother, Hugh, had told Ella about Bob's vasectomy, his infertility seemed like a gift, an excuse not to have to sterilize her daughter. "It's not you." Ella's voice felt thick and distant. "Bob can't have children."

She squeezed Lena's hands with a kind of remorse for Ella felt she had answered badly. She wondered what kind of mother Lena would have been. Lena let go and backed up her chair very fast; it screeched against the kitchen floor. "You're stupid!" Lena yelled. She jumped up and threw Spot on the floor. "*Stu*-pid!"

"You're a daughter," said Ella, leaning toward her. "You'll be a wonderful aunt."

"*We* can't have children," Lena said, as if trying to memorize a phrase in another language. Her eyes were focused on the ceiling. "*We* can't have children." She picked Spot off the floor, held him close, and slowly walked out of the room.

Two weeks later, Ella woke up in the middle of the night to sounds in the living room. The radio was turned on loud, and pop songs coursed down the hallway, as though the house itself were trying to speak. She threw on her bathrobe and went to investigate.

Lena and Bob were building a wall. Bob placed a pillow on a lawn chair as though he were setting down a piece of crystal. Lena, on her knees, was arranging Ella's silver candlesticks on the floor. It took a moment for Ella to believe that Lena and Bob were real; their faces were taut with concentration, and they worked silently, like slow, graceful ghosts. The wall was made from many items in the house. There were six lawn chairs lined up in a row; on them and around them were sofa pillows, plastic canisters, butter knives, forks, a stainless-steel stockpot, and lace doilies from end tables around the house. Oval platters from the kitchen were propped against the lawn chairs, and Ella's Lu-Ray dinnerware was strewn across the floor.

"What are you doing?" Ella asked.

They flinched and looked up. "Making a wall," said Lena. "This is your side" — she pointed to one half of the living room — "and this is ours."

"*Your* side?" asked Ella. Bob tried to conceal a soup bowl in his hand.

"Yes," said Lena. "Ours and Spot's. You have to stay on that side. You can come to this side if you pay us twenty-five cents."

Ella pushed away one of the sofa pillows and a lawn chair and walked to Lena's side. She switched off the radio. All her anger burst out at once.

"This is my house!" Ella said.

Lena's eyes met hers, defiant. "No. It's *mine,* too."

Ella sat on a metal chair in Dolores's office. Dolores, who had been the coordinator of Goodwill's disabled employees for years, wore the bemused expression of a person used to sorting out real disasters from imagined ones. Ella was never sure what Dolores actually thought about anything, and she was grateful for that.

"They were dividing up the house?" Dolores said. "Which rooms did you get?"

Ella gave her a look. "Not the good ones."

"Mrs. Johnson's son, Alfred, tied himself up with a garden hose. He wanted to be a bush that she watered," said Dolores. "That did not go over well."

Dolores had a fund of stories about parents who were worse off than she was. It did not always help. Ella said in an undertone, "Sometimes I want to crash the car right into the house."

Dolores shrugged. "You're not the first," she said, tapping her fingers on her desk. "You know," she said, "there's an apartment on La Casita Avenue, a couple of blocks from your house. Hedy Brownstein and Georgia Marsh lived there for five years, but Hedy died last month and Georgia moved to a group home. The landlord will rent to our employees if they're quiet. He may want a little extra for renting to Lena and Bob. If the apartment's still available, I can recommend them."

"For what?" Ella said.

"To live there," said Dolores.

Ella did not understand.

"I think they should try it," said Dolores. "They can live there all by themselves."

Ella met the landlord first, alone, at 237 La Casita. Al was a stout man, with purplish stubble and jeans that smelled of dirt. The building looked like a peach-colored motel.

"Seventeen units, heated pool," he said. Al unlocked the thin wooden door to the vacant apartment; the walls were painted pistachio green. The beige carpet was stained in several places. "Everything as is," said Al. "The idiot painters slapped on this color. Dolores's people don't care, and I don't have to repaint."

Ella walked around. "Is it safe?" she asked.

"Are they dangerous?"

She fiddled with her watch.

"The rent's seventy," said Al. "Then there's a one-time fee."

"A fee?"

Al glanced around the apartment, searching for something. "To fix the curtains," he said, gesturing toward the windows. "Make sure they have a nice place to live."

Ella fingered the aqua curtains; there was nothing wrong with them.

"Two hundred and fifty dollars," he said.

"Two hundred," she offered, her voice trembling. He nodded, and she wrote him a check.

When she told Lena and Bob they were going to have a home of their own, they looked puzzled, as though trying to understand a complicated joke. Then Ella walked them over, and they stood in front of 237 La Casita. "Number five is where you'll live," she said.

Bob grabbed Lena's hand. "Alone?"

"You can come see us any time," said Ella

quickly. "I'll drop by every day." She wasn't exactly sure how this would work. "We're just down the street."

Lena and Bob clung to each other. Huge pink clouds twisted up into the sky. "What do we do?" asked Lena.

"The same things," said Ella. "Eat, sleep. Watch TV. Brush your teeth."

Lena and Bob did not know what to make of this, whether the apartment was punishment or reward. Lena jumped up and down, and then stopped her celebration. Bob blew out a few long, stern breaths, as though checking that he was still alive. Lena was thirty-four years old, and Bob was forty-two, and neither had ever lived on their own.

To prepare them for the move, Ella held a conference on the subject of household jobs. She, Lena, and Bob sat at the kitchen table, Ella with a piece of paper in front of her. "In a household," said Ella, "everyone has a different job."

"I take out the trash!" exclaimed Lena.

Ella wrote *Lena* on the right side of the paper and *Bob* on the left. "Lena, you're the wife," said Ella, "so you cook." She wrote *Cook* on Lena's side. "You also sweep and make the bed. Bob, you're the husband, so you take out the trash."

"I take out trash!" said Lena. Grabbing the pen, she scrawled TRASH under her side. "Bob has no job," sang Lena, "no job, no job —"

"I drive trucks," said Bob angrily.

"Bob," said Ella, "you turn off the lights. You make sure the door is locked."

Bob nodded. "Okay."

"Let's try breakfast," Ella said. "Bob, bring over the cereal. Lena, get the spoons."

Lena and Bob stood in the middle of the kitchen and turned around like puzzled dogs. That morning, and on subsequent ones, they were bad students. They became frustrated very quickly; Lena threw her dishtowel across the room when she couldn't figure out how to fold it. Bob banged his head repeatedly against a door when he forgot, the third time in a row, to turn off the light. They began to treat each other not as spouses but as siblings, vying for Ella's praise, which she lavished on them for anything — on Lena for remembering to close the refrigerator; on Bob for throwing an empty milk container in the trash.

Bob and Lena each became enamored of one skill and wanted to repeat it in every room: Bob insisted on opening and closing all the windows, and Lena, clutching a dustcloth, repeatedly ran it over any surface she could find. Everything that Ella did — boiling water, sweeping the floor — was created at that moment, weighted with fresh beauty.

They moved out on April 26, 1965. Bob drove his Goodwill truck the two blocks to the apartment. And Ella and Lou walked on the pavement beside it, because Lena wanted to lean out the window and wave to them.

It was evening when they moved in, and the stocky palm trees flanking the entrance were lit, like celebrities, by a milky light. Things flowed into the apartment magically and found their places: an old TV, Vivien's chipped, amoeba-shaped coffee table, a green loveseat, a card table to eat on, plastic plates. Lena set Spot carefully on the sofa and made him a bed from a salad bowl lined with a blue washcloth.

Everyone moved around the apartment with care, as though they would all vanish if they stepped in the wrong place. At last, there was nothing more to do. "We have to go," Lou said.

The four of them stood in silence. Everyone looked confused.

"Where will you be?" asked Lena.

"At home," said Ella. "Just down the street."

"Okay," said Bob, his shoulders tensing, as if he were preparing for something awful. "Okay."

Lena rubbed her palm in circles over his bristly hair. "Bye," she said.

Ella could not speak.

"We'll talk to you later," said Lou. And he grasped Ella's hand.

Ella let him lead her down the stairs. They headed home. The sky washed around them, a hubbub of silver clouds and stars, and the other houses on the street, buildings of lime green and rose and yellow, looked like little frosted cakes, delicate and sweet. Ella felt in a great hurry to break free of her confusion; she was afraid that her own house had disappeared. Then she and

Lou stood on their lawn, sunk in shadows, and tentatively walked forward and opened the door. Ella trembled at the sight of the dark hallway. But the house was merely empty, and there was only the unfamiliar sound of peace.

Thirteen

Ella and Lou watched each other to learn how to live in the empty house. It was thirty-five years since they'd been alone here, and their voices rang through the rooms as though they belonged to giants. Lou took great delight in disagreeing with *Los Angeles Times* editorials. "Look at this jerk," he said eagerly. "Thinks we should charge money for walking on the beaches." She listened, understanding that he needed to protest something, but she heard a curious sweetness in his voice.

They felt compelled to become new and different. Ella developed an urge to redecorate. She began with a pair of ceramic salt and pepper shakers she found at a local yard sale. The shakers were blue cows wearing ballerina tutus, and she was captivated by them. When she placed them on a shelf above the oven, the room was completely changed. She bought more shakers, focusing on the animal theme, and built a special shelf for them. Soon she had shakers in the shapes of elephants, bears, cats, rhinos, and, for variety, Notre Dame.

Lou had long been interested in World War II generals; now he focused on how he would have escaped from Germany in 1939 if he had had to.

He gave Ella a gold chain from May Company that she was to pawn for escape money if the Nazis ever took over America. He developed a secret alphabet, coordinating letters with shoe sizes; his messages resembled complicated order forms for his store. Somehow, this pursuit increased his confidence in himself. At breakfast, he and Ella, filled with shy pride, would discuss their new interests.

Some nights they sat out on the chaises and speculated about Lena and Bob. "What do you think they're doing?" Ella asked Lou.

"At this moment," he said, "eating slices of bread."

"I'll bet they are getting crumbs all over the carpet."

"I'll bet," he said, generously, "they're trying to use plates."

Guesses, bits of longing, drifted into the night.

Lena called at her scheduled times. At first she was stilted, polite. "May I please speak to Mother," she'd say.

"Honey, it's me," Ella said. "Are you having a nice day?"

"Fine."

"Anything to report?"

"Fine. Bob wants to say hello." There was a rustling.

"Hello," Bob said and breathed heavily; he never knew what to say.

One day, Lena called with important news. An

orange cat had wandered into their apartment. "Mother," said Lena, excitedly, "it liked your lima bean soup!"

"Is that so," Ella said.

"Its name is Simone," Lena said. Her voice had become flutelike. "Ask me about her day."

"Um. Does she have fleas?"

"She made a meow that sounded like hello."

"Sweetie," Ella said, "are you out of milk? Look at the bottle. Shake it. I can pick some up."

"Ask something else."

"I don't know what." Ella sensed surprise at the other end. "Did you leave towels in the —"

There was a thudding, disappointed silence. "No!" said Lena. She had discovered the pleasure of hanging up.

Lena and Bob's independence had been carefully planned. Pamela, a post office retiree, was Lena's new next-door neighbor. Paid off with a weekly strudel from Ella, she promised to knock on Lena's door every morning to make sure she and Bob were awake. Lena would call Ella at eight-fifteen in the morning and three in the afternoon, and Ella would drop by after dinner to make sure they had locked their door.

Ella made other drop-in visits to Lena and Bob, on the theory that such visits would keep them alert. On one visit, she could hear the cheerless voice of a game show host as she climbed the stairs. Ella put her key in the door.

Lena and Bob were sitting on the couch, wearing only T-shirts, their big legs open and

273

their hands in each other's laps. Lena was ruffling Bob's pubic hair, and his hand was in Lena's rusty curls. Their faces were peaceful. They were smoking cigarettes and sitting in a cloud of smoke.

They looked at Ella and removed their hands from each other's lap. They seemed embarrassed for her, not for themselves.

"Mother, learn to knock," said Lena. She spoke quietly, but Ella stepped back as though Lena had shouted.

"I just stopped by," she said. Neither Bob nor Lena said anything. "I didn't know you smoked," she said.

"Now we do," Lena said, and lifted up a coffee mug filled with cigarette butts.

"When did you learn to do that?" asked Ella.

"Bob taught me. On our wedding night."

Bob blew an affectionate, furry stream of smoke in Lena's face.

"Like the movies," Lena said, with a giggle.

"What do you mean, like the movies?"

Lena released a long, thin line of smoke. Bob generously offered his half-smoked cigarette to Ella. "Here."

"This is not a good activity," said Ella. "I propose a new habit. How about chewing gum?"

They slumped back into the couch, sulking. "I *like* smoking," Lena said.

Ella went into the bedroom. "Time to get dressed!" After tossing shorts at them, she quickly inspected the apartment.

There was a pool of urine under the bathroom sink. She wiped it up and switched off the electric heat. She picked up slices of baloney from the hallway floor, the damp towels on the kitchen table, the open jar of peanut butter sitting on top of the TV set. Lena and Bob padded behind her, feet crackling along the plastic tile.

When Ella opened the refrigerator she was surprised to see a full bottle of milk. "How did this get here?" she asked.

"Bob bought it at Lucky's," said Lena. "The register man was named Harvey. It was thirty-five cents."

Ella smelled the milk; it was fresh. She took a deep breath. "Bob. Very good," she said. A smile spread across his face.

Ella closed the refrigerator; she felt out of place. Lena picked up a ball of pale orange cat fur from the carpet and presented it to Ella. The fur smelled dank and soulful. "This is from her tail," Lena said.

"Where is this animal?" asked Ella.

"She went to work," said Bob.

The two of them had an earnest look as they held out the ball of orange fur. "We wanted to show it to you," Lena said.

Vivien moved quietly into the curve of her own life. She and Mel bought a home in Palms. Mel got his first job, as an assistant rabbi at a Reform temple. Ella wasn't sure what his day-to-day duties were, but she enjoyed announcing her son-in-law's position to friends or customers at Lou's Shoes, as though it gave her access to a holy place. Vivien was, for a short time, a regular on the West Coast ballroom dance contest circuit, and then found a job teaching the waltz at a Hollywood dance studio. Vivien had become a capable adult — and this made Ella both exuberant and a little lonely.

Ella visited Vivien and Mel's new white-carpeted home cautiously. It was set in a large pattern of green yards and tract homes. Vivien had planted in front a row of stubby palms, round as gangsters, that were lit at night by small blue lights in the lawn. While Lena accepted any furniture Ella gave her, Vivien took as little as possible, even though her house was largely unfurnished. She apparently had in mind an elaborate decorating scheme. It took her a long time to furnish the living room so that more than two people could sit in it. When Ella walked through Vivien's home, she could envision how nice it would look with some of her furniture. She suspected that Vivien accepted the few items she did only to placate her, and then probably hid them in drawers when Ella wasn't visiting: potholders, a few lace doilies, mother-of-pearl napkin rings.

One day, Vivien offered to take Ella to tea. There was no special occasion for the invitation; it was not Ella's birthday, not Mother's Day. "Why?" Ella asked.

"Does there have to be an occasion?" Vivien

said. "Can't I take my own mother to tea?"

Ella consented and spent the entire morning getting dressed for the date. She tried on and took off a linen suit, a lace blouse, a feathered hat, before she settled on an appropriate outfit. To her surprise, she wanted to impress her daughter.

Vivien drove them to Bullock's, and they took the elevator to the tea room, on the top floor. Ladies in pastel dresses, their hair in neat buns, chatted in quiet voices.

Vivien moved with a lithe step. "Good afternoon, Miss Vivien," the hostess said, and led them to a table by the window.

"Who's Miss Vivien?" asked Ella.

"I've been here with the other dance teachers. This is where we come when we want to treat ourselves," she said. They examined their menus. Ella had had no idea there were so many different kinds of tea. Vivien said, "Oh, let me order." To the waitress, she said, "We would each like the oolong."

Her daughter had brought her to this lovely place; she knew how to order exotic tea. The waitress brought the tea, as well as pastries and tiny, perplexing sandwiches. Ella slowly sipped the strong black tea and warily regarded the little sandwiches on her plate.

"This reminds me of where I met your father," she said. "The Treasure Trove at Johnson Massey."

"I remember that story," said Vivien, eating a

sandwich made only of bread and butter. "You sold *tchotchkes?*"

"Not *tchotchkes*," said Ella. "I sold *objets d'art*, made of jade, gold, silver. To Boston's finest clientele . . ."

It occurred to Ella that her daughter would never have purchased any of the objects in the Treasure Trove. She might even have laughed at them. Vivien found meaning in teas with peculiar names, and the rhumba, and the fact that her husband could address an audience in Hebrew. If Vivien had been a customer at the Treasure Trove, Ella would not have known how to speak to her. Ella carefully picked up a sandwich, but her fingers felt fat and childish, and she laid it back on the plate.

But there was this, too: she had created a daughter who was at ease in this elegant room. Vivien understood that she had every right to be here. It was as though that quiet wish had leaped out of Ella and formed itself into her daughter. She reached forward and touched Vivien's hand.

"Have more," said Vivien. She lifted her china cup. Her face was flushed with eagerness to please her mother. "The cucumber's especially good." Ella picked it up delicately and bit into it. It was a perfectly ordinary sandwich.

"Delicious," she said.

Lena decided to give a dinner party; she announced her plans in stages. First, there was a card. She walked the two blocks from her new apartment to her parents' house and thrust her invitation under the door. It was addressed to them in purple crayon and said: *Dinner. Invited. Please!* There was no date; there was, in the corner, a carefully drawn postage stamp. Ella stood in the doorway, examining the invitation, and then glanced at the empty summer street before her; the green leaves were shuddering all at once.

Next, there was a call. Ella was on the patio with Vivien, whose long legs were stretched out on a chaise longue; she was painting her fingernails bright gold. The phone beside them rang. "I'm having a dinner party," Lena said, and hung up.

"Who was it?" asked Vivien, fluttering her fingers.

"Your sister," said Ella. "Look." She handed the invitation to Vivien and called Lena back. "Honey, a what?"

"Who's this?" Lena asked, primly.

"What's this about a dinner party?" Ella asked.

Lena hung up. Ella dialed the number again. "Lena, what's going —"

"I can only talk to you if you can come."

Carefully: "When is it?"

"Soon."

Lena hung up again; it was her favorite demonstration of her new freedom. She would bang down the phone with a juicy, reckless joy at any point in a conversation — when Ella asked whether she had thrown out the brown bananas or whether she had left the wet towels on the living room floor.

Vivien was reading at the invitation. "Eat before," she said.

"Do you think this was that man's idea?"

" 'That man'?" Vivien laughed. "Bob?"

"He couldn't be" — Ella didn't know what word to use — "social?"

Vivien undid a rhinestone clip from her glossy red hair. "That king of debonaire?"

They looked at each other. Vivien took a deep breath. "Well," she said, "she *should* have a party."

Ella again dialed Lena's number. "Lena, who's coming to this dinner party?"

"You. Daddy. Vivien. Mel. Simone."

"Simone?" Ella said.

Silence. "You know. The cat that I like."

"Uh-huh," said Ella. "Did the cat get an invitation?"

The voice trembled. "No."

"Well," said Ella, annoyed by the burden of the dinner party she was now going to have to finance and arrange, "that was your first mistake."

"But" — Lena's voice became high-pitched, insistent — "she sits on my lap and I pet her. Why can't I have a party —"

Even Vivien could hear the tone of Lena's voice; it made her sit up, sorrowful, alert. "Tell her I'll bring a Jell-O mold," she announced. "Lime and cream cheese. Tell her —"

"Mother!" Lena shrieked. "I'm giving a dinner

party and you have to come!" She hung up.

Vivien was pregnant. Ella found out when she and Vivien were shopping at May Company one afternoon. They were shopping, lazily, for table linens. Vivien was quiet; she picked up napkins and set them down after a cursory glance. Suddenly, she plunked down in a chair and began fingering her stomach.

"Are you okay?" Ella asked.

Vivien put her hand over her mouth, closed her eyes, and swallowed. Then she looked at her mother with a stern expression. Ella placed her palm on Vivien's forehead, and Vivien said, softly, "I'm pregnant."

Ella felt the air rush out of her. She plunked down on a chair beside Vivien. "With a child?"

Vivien looked at her wryly "What else?"

Ella realized that she had not allowed herself to think of a grandchild, the way she had not allowed herself to fantasize about Vivien's future many years before. "Sweetheart, how wonderful! How far along are you?"

"Three months."

Ella got up and hugged her daughter with fervor. "What are you going to name it?"

"I haven't picked a name," Vivien said.

"I can help," said Ella, happily. "What about Loretta? I heard that name in a show recently. Or —"

"I'm afraid to name it."

"Why?"

Ella knew why as soon as she asked the question. Vivien looked at her with pleading eyes and shook her head. A bell rang somewhere in the store.

"I didn't plan it," said Vivien, almost apologetically. "It just happened."

"No time is the right time," said Ella.

"I'm not asking for much," said Vivien. She sat up, suddenly argumentative. "I want it to be okay. Boy or girl. I can't let myself think about anything else. I look at you and I don't know how you did it." She stopped, embarrassed.

"Let me think," said Ella. "Loretta. Or Cherise. Or — William." She was charged up with ideas. "I see this child as a — a great inventor. Or movie star. With you and Mel as her — or his — parents, how could it not be?"

Ella cut the air with her hand like a debater. She found herself in the odd role of trying to convince Vivien that her pregnancy was a wonderful thing. But Vivien was studying the floor, with the tense quiet of a competitor reluctant to reveal an advantage.

Her daughter wanted a child who was smart and beautiful, yet she was afraid to yearn for that. Ella could tell that Vivien's hope for her child was bordered by a distrust that she herself had not had.

Vivien took a lipstick from her purse and applied it with neat strokes. Then she said to Ella, "What do *you* think is going to happen?"

"It will be just wonderful," said Ella, and she

meant it, though she was aware of the tinge of uncertainty in her own voice.

That night, Ella dreamed of Vivien's child. She dreamed that it was born from herself. It was a girl, and at birth she was clothed in a lace pink dress; an hour later, she was walking around, speaking in elaborate sentences. The little girl regarded them all with a haughty expression, as though she could not quite believe she was one of them; she swiftly rejected any name that they offered her. Ella awoke violently from this dream. It took some time for her heart rate to return to normal. For a moment, she tasted the sour nausea of pregnancy; then she knew she was imagining it.

Ella did not talk much to Lena about Vivien's pregnancy. What few facts she did mention, Lena tucked away and asked about them again and again. As Vivien grew closer to her due date, Lena talked more about her dinner party, which was taking months to plan. And Vivien talked more about helping her. She repeated her offer of the Jell-O mold and asked whether she could bring a gift for Simone. Lena said no; she simply wanted everyone to meet the cat.

Finally, a date was set. The day before the party, Ella took Lena to the supermarket and guided the cart through the luminous aisles while Lena plucked items from the shelves. "I want to have my favorite foods. Chips. Licorice." Her eyes got dreamy. She chose a polka-dot paper tablecloth and matching napkins and plates. They had arranged the transfer of money in advance. Beside a massive display of Hostess Ho-Hos, ten feet from the cash register, Ella passed Lena a few fives, then leafed through a magazine, as commanded, while Lena handed the bills to the cashier. Ella stopped at a glossy photo spread: "The New Young Americans," featuring pictures of handsome people — actors, writers, artists — laughing, clutching cocktails at a New York garden party. One caption said: *Constance, despite her delicate features, hunts big game.* Another said: *The Young Americans — in touch, outgoing, far out, way in — jumping nimbly from subject to subject. What do they talk about? The Common Market, the artichoke's place in gourmet cooking, Greece.*

"Here," Lena said proudly to the cashier as she placed her items on the counter. Ella watched the young girl, regal with boredom, ring up Lena's purchases. And she saw the happiness fill her daughter's face.

As a final preparation for Lena's dinner party, Ella made a casserole to make sure there would be something everyone could eat. At seven o'clock, Ella, Lou, Vivien, and Mel poured down the walkway toward 237 La Casita. The four of them sparkled tenderly in the warm blue night. Vivien wore a silver metallic sheath that draped over her large stomach; her Spanish red pocketbook matched her shoes. Mel wore the cotton navy blazer he used when conducting services —

284

like a magician's, it had a faint sheen. Ella wore a sleeveless sequin-covered top and pearl earrings; Lou carried his dinner jacket over his arm, because the temperature was 90 degrees. Lena and her husband were giving a dinner party. This filled them with strange wishes, for it was an event none of them had dared to imagine. It was as though a rare and wonderful present was being placed in their hands, and they did not quite know how to hold it. All they knew absolutely was that it was important to dress up.

Lena was waiting on the terrace. "Hi!" she called. "I thought you'd forget it was here."

"Look at our hostess!" said Ella. Lena's face was burnished with powder and her hair was neatly combed. Vivien held forth the Jell-O mold. "I made it especially for you —"

Lena took the plate. "Thank you," she said, politely, "but I've decided that we can only eat foods made by me."

Vivien looked taken aback. They followed Lena into the apartment. Propped on the couch, like a group of guests who had come early and formed their own clique, were several bosomy bags of potato chips. The tablecloth had been spread across the carpet. All the lamps had been dragged into the living room, which was as white and bright as a movie set. Bob was picking up something from the rug.

"Bob!" Lena said. "Don't eat that chip!"

Bob quickly dropped the broken potato chip. He was wearing a rumpled pair of black tuxedo pants and a shiny sharkskin shirt; Lena wore a sleeveless, lime-green beaded dress with a large ink mark on the back. They had pulled this finery from the Goodwill employees' bin; earlier in the week, Ella had sewn up the holes. Bob held out his right hand and damply shook each of theirs.

"How about a blessing, Mel?" said Lou. "Show us those rabbi tricks."

"Well," said Mel, with a hollow laugh. They looked at him, expectant.

"A housewarming prayer," said Vivien, eagerly.

"A housewarming prayer?" Mel asked, bemused. "I'll improvise."

Standing in the middle of the living room, he lifted his arms and let forth a torrent of Hebrew. The others stood around, not understanding the words, but grateful for them.

"Well, that was very nice," said Ella when he finished; he seemed to need affirmation.

"What happens?" Lena asked, bouncing up and down.

"Now it's official," said Lou. "It's a Jewish house."

This was the first time so many people had been in the apartment. Lena and Bob watched, mesmerized, as Ella set cut roses into a vase. Then Bob whispered something to Lena. "Everyone!" Lena called. "We would like everyone to meet Simone."

Lena set the Jell-O mold beside the tubby cat

that was sleeping on the couch — a primitive, thuggish beast snoring loudly, with abandon. At the presentation of the Jell-O, the cat opened its large eyes, stretched, and slowly rose. Its fur stuck up on one side, as though the creature was coming off a three-day drunk. It delicately licked the Jell-O with its rosy tongue.

"It is *not* cat food," said Vivien.

"She's not just a cat," Lena said.

The cat shook itself further awake, rolled over on its back, and made a rumbling noise. Lena rubbed its belly, and the cat's stubby legs wilted with pleasure.

"That cat has had a hard life," Ella said, eyeing it.

"This cat is ours," said Lena. She picked up the cat, a tad roughly, and clutched it to her chest. Simone stared at them with a trapped, irate expression, as though she understood, quite clearly, that she had just missed being a person. Lena kissed the cat's head and Bob stroked its coat. The rest of the guests stood around, left out.

"I've heard that orange cats have the best temperament," tried Vivien.

"It has nice fur," offered Lou.

"You can each have a piece of fur to take home," Lena said.

The guests were silenced by this.

"The party has started. Please sit." And she delicately placed Simone on the couch. The cat gazed at them with a sort of longing, as though it yearned to jump out of its parallel universe.

Bob brought out paper plates piled with potato chips, set one in front of each guest, and stood back, trying to smile. Ella noticed that he had adopted Lou's posture — shoulders forward slightly, hands on his hips. On Bob, Lou's stance was too large.

"And what is this?" asked Lou, looking at the plate.

"Salad," said Lena, eyes narrowing as though daring him to disagree.

"Why don't you sit down and eat with us?" asked Ella.

"Okay," Lena said, although she clearly wanted only to watch them eat. She and Bob sat cross-legged on the tablecloth. "Is everyone having a good time?" Lena asked.

"Of course," said Vivien. "This is a delicious chip." She looked suddenly intent. "I was reading in *Vogue* last week," she said, "how to make original dinner conversation. You're supposed to try never to say something you've said before."

"Then what do you say?" asked Ella.

"You want to avoid questions like 'Have you read the best seller?' Or 'Who is the most influential columnist?' Or 'Where is the real money located today — in the banks, the insurance companies, or elsewhere?' "

"I like *that* question," said Lou. "Where?"

Vivien ate another chip. "The article said you should respond to a question like the one about the best seller by saying, 'Of course, but have you read the worst seller?' "

"Why would you want to read the worst seller?" asked Lou.

Lena and Bob tried to follow the conversation; they appeared jumpy. "How's your salad?" Lena asked.

"Wonderful," Ella said.

"Where is the real money?" asked Lou, dreamily. "Not in shoes."

Mel had been pondering Vivien's question; he looked up. "How about, 'What is your stand on God?' "

"Now *that's* a conversation stopper," said Lou.

"Well," said Mel, taken aback, "everyone has a point of view."

"You, you're a professional in the religious field," Lou said. "What is your stand?"

Mel seemed pleased to have been asked. "In my studies," he said, sweeping his lush hair back with his hand, "I've decided that God is an open term, subject to an evolving definition. In fact, the question is perhaps less important than the work we do to help solve the problems of our local and global communities —"

"*I* think it's when everyone in the temple stands up as you take out the Torah," Vivien said.

"What do you mean?" asked Ella.

"Or when everyone stands up at a dance contest to give a standing ovation." Vivien squinted thoughtfully into her plate. "You know . . . those moments when everyone's united." She paused. "The same."

"I have my own stand," Lou said.

"And what's that?" asked Ella.

"The more customers who buy, someone's on my side. The less customers, someone's not. Sometimes it's the right advertising. Other times you can't explain it." Lou leaned back, obviously surprised at himself.

"Is there any kind of customer who makes you think someone's on your side?" asked Mel.

"Ones who spend a lot," said Lou. "Ones who don't take too much time deciding what they want."

Mel laughed. "I'll agree with that," he said.

Lena, her face red with her desire to contribute, said, "I think whatever Simone thinks. That's my stand."

"That's nice, honey," said Ella. She did not know her own stand on God. Taking a deep breath, she examined the animal, and was disturbed by its long, rabbit-like feet, its thin black lips, and its pointed teeth.

Vivien was struggling to sit in a more comfortable position. "It is just impossible to *move*," she said. She rocked side to side on her hips for a moment and then was still.

"Can I get you a chair?" Lou asked.

"No, I'm fine." The conversation came to a halt as everyone stared at Vivien's stomach.

"What's its name?" asked Lena, sweetly.

Ella, suddenly chilled, said, "Lena, that's

Vivien's business —"

"I was just asking," said Lena. Her tone became bossy. "It needs a nice name."

Vivien looked intently at her sister, trying to see her through the fog of her own thoughts. "We . . . honey, I don't think we've come up yet with a name we love."

"I think you should name it Doily," said Lena, picking one off the tablecloth and holding it up.

"Why?"

"Because it's pretty!"

Lena's voice was too loud, as though she had an innate sense that her suggestion would be ignored. For a long moment, Vivien didn't speak. Then, resolved not to deny her sister her contribution, she said, "We'll think about it. Doily." And quickly added, "Lena? You want to feel? Sometimes you can feel the baby kicking."

Lena scooted forward on all fours; Vivien's eyes followed her palm as she placed it on her sister's stomach. Lena's face was filled with awe. Vivien held perfectly still and put her hand on top of Lena's, as though to comfort her. It also appeared that she was holding Lena's hand to one designated place.

After a few moments, Lena lifted her hand. "I don't feel anything," she said in a haughty tone. Vivien gently rubbed her stomach.

Simone leaped nimbly from the couch, walked into the middle of the circle, and nibbled one long claw. Lena brightened up. "She likes to wave her tail so we can kiss it. Watch."

Lena stroked the cat's brown tail, and it floated up like a plant waving in the sea. Simone trotted around, oblivious, while Lena lunged at her, trying to kiss her tail. Bob joined in. Their faces glowed with pleasure as the air hummed with kissing sounds. The two of them seemed giddy, grateful for the pure act of loving Simone, and when they stopped, they were limp, breathing hard. Lena looked around at her guests, her face organized around one thought. "Now, everyone kiss her tail."

The guests were silent. The cat's tail was frazzled; Ella wondered where the animal had been. "Honey, we're eating your dinner now," said Ella.

Vivien touched Lena's shoulder. "I'll kiss her tail," she said, struggling to sit up in the appropriate position.

Lena sensed resistance. "I want everyone to do it!" She stamped her foot. "You don't want to," she said to Ella.

"No," said Ella, "it's just —"

"Why not?" Lena asked.

"Well," said Ella, "does the cat really want all of us —"

"I *want* you to!" Lena said, and angrily ran into the kitchen. Ella began to rise to comfort her, but Bob got to Lena first.

From the living room, Ella could see Bob and Lena standing together in the cramped kitchen, Bob's hands on Lena's shoulders, he was whispering to her. His shoelaces were untied, and his hair was sticky with marshmallows, but his forehead touched her daughter's as though he were about to tumble into her. Ella watched them speak to each other in voices so intimate that no one could hear.

Ella rubbed her arms; she was trying to think. If Lena was not a child, she did not know what she herself could be. She let out a long breath and looked around the apartment. Lou, Vivien, and Mel were now involved in their own private conversation.

Through the windows, the night appeared a deep and wistful blue, the balcony lights casting misty beams on the swimming pool below. The world was so awkward in its beauty, Ella thought. She wondered how long it would take for Vivien and her to clean up the kitchen; she wondered how long Lena and Bob would be able to live in this apartment.

Lena and Bob came back, holding fresh paper plates: one was piled with red licorice sticks, another with pieces of toast, a third with pastel-colored marshmallows adorned with chocolate chips. Simone padded lightly into the circle again and gazed at Ella with its clear yellow eyes. Tentatively, Ella reached toward it. The cat allowed Ella to touch its ears; they felt like flower petals, exquisitely soft.

Ella asked Lena, "What other things does Simone like to do?"

Lena rocked forward, thrilled to have been asked the question. "She likes string."

Bob took a piece of string from under the couch, and Lena dangled it in front of Simone's face.

Ella watched her daughter and her new son carefully run around the living room while the cat chased them. Simone's yellow eyes were jewels; the cat trotted after the couple, its ears flattened coolly against its head. Bob and Lena stepped lightly, as though they had done this many times. Ella could see that the three of them belonged to one another; she did not know how she would remain part of them. Simone leaped forward with a scream. The cat's eyes were set on the little prize as though it held everything necessary in the world. Whipping her body through the air, the cat brought the string down with her. Lena and Bob knelt by Simone, their faces tender. "Shh," Lena said, cradling Simone's tiny head in her hands while the cat silently thrashed her body around the bit of string.

Fourteen

When Lena and Bob moved into their apartment, Ella had — carefully — taught Lena how to cook. She went through each dish a few times, making sure that Lena understood every step. And Lena watched, mouth open, sampling each item as though she had never before tasted it. Ella demonstrated the Tuna Fish Sandwich, the Peanut Butter and Jelly Sandwich, and Baloney on a Plate by Itself. There was to be no frying in their household, because she did not trust Lena with hot oil, and no baking unless Ella was there to turn off the stove. Lena learned to add lettuce to her tuna fish sandwich, to place slices of Swiss cheese on her baloney plate.

After a few months, Lena told Ella that she did not like to cook anymore.

"Tuna," Ella suggested, over the phone. "It's easy. You just spread it on bread."

"I hate it."

"Peanut butter and jelly," said Ella.

"Bob doesn't like it," said Lena, sounding proud.

"He can manage it one night a week," said Ella.

"No," said Lena. "My husband deserves the best."

"Lena," said Ella, "stop being a coffee commercial."

Lena was quiet. Then she said, "Mother, I want to be a good wife. He hates peanut butter. Don't make me make peanut butter . . ."

Ella headed over with a pound of chopped meat and showed Lena how to mix it in a bowl with onions and bread crumbs. They sat in the living room and waited while the meatloaf baked; Lena wandered from room to room, sniffing the familiar smell. Ella took the finished meatloaf from the oven, sliced it, and put the slices on a platter.

When she got home, she called Lena. "I forgot. Cover it with foil to keep it warm."

"I can't," said Lena.

"Why not?"

"It's gone," Lena said.

"What, it's gone?"

"I ate it," said Lena.

"All of it?"

There was silence. "All of it," said Lena, in a quiet, guilty voice.

By their eighth month in the apartment, Lena and Bob were going out to dinner every night. When Ella was preparing dinner for Lou, she sometimes looked out the window and saw them hurrying through the cool dusk. They were off to Denny's or the House of Pancakes, and they walked a little faster when they passed her house. The cost added up; Ella had told them not to spend more than three dollars on dinner. "Tell your waitress," she said. "Remember. Show her your money and tell her that's what you can spend." For three dollars, they could buy two hamburgers with fries and cole slaw, two Cokes, and one order of Jell-O to split.

A couple weeks later, Lena ran home to Ella's from House of Pancakes, leaving Bob in the House of Pancakes.

"We need MONEY," Lena said, flushed, slapping the bill on the kitchen table. "Now." She was almost sobbing; her fist unfurled, and coins and crumpled dollars fell out of her sticky hand. The bill said $4.07; Lena had $3.75.

Lou leaned back in his seat. "Well," he said. "Almost."

"What happened?" Ella asked.

Lena paced back and forth. "She was mean. Bob wanted red Jell-O. That's what he likes. She wanted us to hurry up."

Ella went with Lena to settle the bill. Bob huddled in his booth like a small animal. When he saw Lena rush toward him, he stood up.

"Where did you go?" he shouted.

"I said I'd be back."

"You took forever!"

"You don't talk!" said Lena. "*I* talk!"

He bit his lip and plunked, distraught, into his seat.

Lena slid in beside him and slapped her hands on the table. Bob's hands covered his face. Ella said, "Let's all calm down."

She had never seen them argue. She began,

without thinking, to stack the dirty dishes, place crumpled napkins on the plates, collect the silverware. Bob turned away from Lena, and his eyes searched mournfully for comfort in the arched ceiling, the hanging orange lamps. Lena massaged her hands, squeezing one thumb as though trying to pull it off.

Suddenly, Bob whipped around and said, "You told me to get it."

"I did not."

"I was scared."

"Me, too."

Lena picked up a cold french fry and ate it. He was staring at her with a defeated expression. Lena ate another fry, then reached up and stroked Bob's ear. "Shh. Mother's here. Shh."

Ella went in search of the mean waitress. She was a big ship of a woman with a name tag saying *Florence*. To Ella, she seemed merely harried. Ella heard her own voice assume a rhythm, a smoothness. "I'm sorry," she said. "This was an accident. They just made a mistake."

"Look," Florence said, "you have to understand. I'm not here to babysit. I've got to keep everything moving."

"Of course," said Ella.

"I need my tips," said Florence. "That's it."

She was clearly embarrassed by the incident as she accepted Ella's money and went off to the register. Ella collected Lena and Bob from the table's wreckage and left without waiting for her change.

Simone continued to be an important presence in Lena and Bob's household. Each morning they set her food in a plastic soup bowl, folding slices of baloney, as a special treat, beside lumps of tuna, a few grapes. There was always a sheen of orange fur on their loveseat, as though it were covered by soft, ethereal mist.

A month after the incident at the House of Pancakes, Ella and Lou took them to Santa Barbara. When they returned, Lena rushed upstairs to greet the cat.

"Where's Simone?" she cried.

She and Bob looked at each other. They had forgotten to leave food for Simone.

"Just put out some tuna," said Ella. "Simone'll be back tomorrow."

They left a large bowl of tuna on the terrace outside their door, but the next morning the food was untouched. Nor did the cat return the next day. Ella woke to a frantic call at dawn. "She's always here," Lena said. "We have to find her now."

For the whole day, Ella and Lena and Bob drove around the neighborhood, looking for Simone. It was a scorching day in the Valley, and they kept stopping at gas stations to buy icy bottles of soda and rub them along their arms. Whenever Ella stopped the car, Lena and Bob spilled into the street, chiming the cat's name into the still air. Their sweaty backs left dark smears on the blue vinyl car seats. Holding plastic containers filled with tuna, they tossed little chunks of it into the street, and their voices became hoarse, calling into storm drains, back-yards, dried-out lots.

Ella waited in the car while Lena and Bob walked through the streets calling for the cat. She turned on the radio when she could not bear to listen anymore. Late that evening, they gave up. On the way home, Ella stopped at a drug-store and bought them sundaes in rippled plastic cups. She wanted so much to comfort them. "Simone's probably all right," she tried. "You don't have to worry. Cats sometimes like to ex-plore. They like to visit other cat friends."

Lena and Bob stared at her, moist-eyed. "No," said Lena. "She needs us." She began to jab at her ice cream with her spoon; then, frustrated, she threw the cup into the parking lot. "We love her. *We* do, we!" she yelled.

After Simone disappeared, Lena and Bob be-came more careless with themselves and the apartment. They left their refrigerator door open one morning, and when Ella stopped by later that afternoon, the kitchen was ripe with a sour stench. Another day, Bob tripped over the phone line and disconnected the phone; when Ella rushed over after trying to get through for almost an hour, they seemed strangely emotionless. "No one calls us but you," Lena said.

It became difficult for Ella to sleep. She woke from violent dreams in which she had to perform actions of great importance, though she had no hands or mouth. In one dream, she looked out the window toward Lena's apartment and saw nothing on the street but empty, grass-filled lots under a vibrant red sky.

One afternoon when Ella picked up Lena and Bob to go grocery shopping, she found them stretched out on chairs by the pool, smoking, their eyes shaded by sunglasses, their faces tipped to the sun, almost like sultry movie stars. At the sound of Ella's heels on the concrete patio, Lena removed her sunglasses, her eyes naked in the bright light.

"Time to go to the supermarket," said Ella. Lena and Bob tossed down their cigarettes and headed out with her.

When they returned, each carrying a brown bag filled with groceries, they encountered a foul smell near the pool, and the air was hazy with smoke. One of the lawn chairs had burned. It looked like a thin, skeletal being, the rubber slats scorched black, dangling. Someone had hosed it down; water dripped from the twisted plastic, and the concrete around it was wet.

All of them understood, immediately, that Lena and Bob had accidentally set the chair on fire. Lena dropped her bag of groceries; a can of tomato sauce rolled across the concrete. Bob set down his bag, covered his mouth with his hand, and began to cough.

"That was yours," he said to Lena.

"Yours."

"It smells," said Lena accusingly. She kicked the chair. "Stop!"

The rest of the patio was undisturbed. The aqua pool gurgled; a tangerine rubber raft drifted across it. Al was coiling the hose in a corner of the patio. Ella went to him.

"They burned up one of my chairs," he said.

"Are you sure," she began, "that it was them?"

He looked at her silently.

"I'll pay for it. How much do you think —"

But Al was shaking his head. "No." He did not look at her. "They're . . ." He stopped.

She waited.

"They're dangerous," he said.

Lena and Bob moved back to Lena's bedroom. Ella and Lou packed up the apartment themselves, because Lena and Bob were anxious and arguing, and it was simpler to just send them home. When Ella and Lou returned home with the loaded truck, they found Lena and Bob at the kitchen table. Lena was scraping some meat off a roast chicken, and Bob was picking through cherry Jell-O. They were quiet, and they were weeping, their faces shiny with tears.

Dolores at Goodwill thought they'd do better in a group home. She was firm with Ella. "You don't want to hate them," she said, "and you don't want them to hate you."

She gave Ella a list of group homes where other employees had lived. The names mingled Spanish and English in curious ways: Casa de

Flowers, Van Nuys Villa, Sunset Vista. The list was marked with Dolores's annotations. *Boring. Only field trip: Zoo*, she wrote beside one. *Poor use of meat in entrees*, she wrote near another. Dolores was focused on the quality of the food, activities, the landscaping of gardens: *Needs more benches in the shade.* Ella found her list oddly comforting, but it sparked in her a whole list of her own requirements. Dolores fixed Ella a cup of coffee and listened to her enumerate them.

"Number one, I want it to be nearby," said Ella. "Fifteen minutes away by car at most. They must have a nice room. It has to smell fresh, not that Lysol smell."

Dolores nodded.

"I don't want everyone living there to be handicapped," Ella went on, a little embarrassed to say this. She continued, "Lena can get along well with all types. The staff must be pleasant and nicely groomed and they have to be — high school graduates. At least."

By this time, Dolores looked worn out. "Look," she said, "the other residents are their peers. Not you." Her expression was one of understanding. Ella took a deep breath. She was only this: a mother who did not know what to do.

Vivien had her baby, a girl, and she and Mel gave her a Hebrew name: Shira. Ella had never heard of this name, but Vivien had selected it carefully. "It means 'song,' " she said proudly.

They would call the child Shelley in her everyday life.

When the baby was four months old, Vivien brought her along when she and Ella took Lena and Bob to lunch. They chose a round restaurant table and placed the infant seat in the center. The baby's simple happiness was stunning, and they sat in its glow like flowers being nourished by its light. Shelley lay captive in her seat; like all babies, she seemed to find the astonishing fact of her existence perfectly natural. Bob did not take much interest in Shelley, but Lena drank in the sight of the baby. With her left hand, Lena clutched the girl's miniature foot, captivated by the tiny toes; she ate her sandwich carefully with her other hand.

While Lena was content to watch the baby and hold her foot, Vivien observed her daughter with a more critical eye. The baby looked mischievous, withholding her future from them.

"She's a born actress," said her grandmother, lightly. "Look at those expressions!"

Vivien didn't laugh. "Do you think so?" she asked. "How do you know?"

Vivien seemed barely able to wait, a mute audience, for the baby to reveal who she was. She carried around a paperback book on child development and knew exactly where her daughter was on the curve. "Four months, and she's rolling over. Both ways," said Vivien. "She's very advanced." She laughed as though this did not matter, but she stroked the child's head with a sweetness that reminded Ella of the way she used to hold Lena's hand when they were little girls.

Like a student, Lena listened to everything Vivien said. She asked questions over and over. "What does she eat?"

"Just milk. Applesauce. She's starting on bananas."

"I want to give her lettuce." Lena held up a tiny shred.

"Not yet. When she gets teeth."

"Pickle."

"Soon."

After Vivien turned down all her offerings, Lena pushed back her chair and sulked. Then she burst out with news about the vanished cat. "Simone is on a trip around the world. She is now having a nice time in Paris." Holding up her purse, she said, with menace, "I have a postcard." Bob looked at her. "Do you want to see?"

Ella didn't know how to respond. But she said, "Honey, I'm sure it's personal and Simone wouldn't want us reading it." Lena shrugged.

With the baby, Vivien was barely able to contain her joy; pride poured off her abundantly, in clear sheets. After a while, though, the pleasure was mixed with concern. Her desire for the child's well-being was so intense that she feared it. She would touch the baby with delicacy, as if barely believing her good fortune.

When Shelley started teething, Vivien allowed Lena to feed her. Lena would lean over, cupping fragments of banana in her palm. She would grandly bring each piece to Shelley's mouth as though no one could do this as well as she did; Lena wanted everyone to watch her. The child's dark eyes were set on her. With each piece of food the baby took, Lena would kiss her on the forehead. "Good," she'd say, and Shelley would gaze at Lena with a sweet, quizzical faith.

Vivien went with Ella to visit the homes on Dolores's list. She took the baby with her as a lucky charm.

The general coordinators were salespeople, shaking hands with a professional warmth and launching into their enthusiastic drone. Ella saw bulletin boards with displays: RESIDENT OF THE WEEK, a blurry photo glued to a gold paper crown: *We salute Regina Somers. Regina has lived here for 2 years and 2 months. She enjoys cartoons, Creamsicles, and brushing Pepper, our dog.* There were displays of arts and crafts: pink grapefruits stuck with toothpicks, marshmallows, and gum-drops; Styrofoam egg containers made to look like farm animals. Some residences were large and expensive, others shoddy, others poorly maintained.

Vivien and Ella barraged the coordinators with questions: How many Jews lived in the home? Why didn't they offer more dessert choices? How was the security? How often did they clean the rooms? Ella could tell halfway through a tour what Vivien thought, because she made no attempt to hide her disregard.

Ella understood that Vivien was evaluating each place as if she were the one who would be living here. This was the way Vivien used to scan the world when she was a child, standing with Lena at the gate of her elementary school and watching her sister trundle off to class. She tried to absorb Lena's experience as a way to repay the distributor of good fortune for her luck in being herself. Lena somehow understood Vivien's message of empathy to her and became extremely bossy. That was when Ella had got Vivien her job at Lou's Shoes.

Vivien's standards were higher, more exact, than Ella's. She walked into bathrooms, peered into the bathtubs for grit. She insisted on tasting the suspicious-looking lunch being prepared in the cafeteria. "When you have weekly entertainment," she asked, skimming the brochures, "what do you mean? Guitar players? Jugglers? Baton twirlers? What?" She left the coordinators a little bit afraid.

By the time Ella and Vivien spilled out of a residence into the aching sun, Vivien had made her decision. It was always no. She was more distressed than Ella at Lena and Bob's inability to live in their own apartment. She was forming her own ideas about what Lena needed, though Ella knew that she would have to compromise; the answer could not always be no. Time was stretching on, and Lena and Bob grew fatter and sadder in Ella's kitchen. Ella and Vivien stumbled across the parking lot. The two of them were becoming bound up in determining Lena's future. It seemed shameful to reveal any elegance in themselves.

Finally, they agreed on Panorama Village. Secretly, Ella liked it because of the name. The residence was a straight twenty-minute shot from Ella and Lou's house; a large basket of fruit sat on each table at every meal; the residents, a mixture of the elderly and the handicapped, spoke amiably to each other; some of the rooms looked out on a tiny plot of agapanthus. Ella thought Lena and Bob could imagine it was their private yard.

Ella signed up Lena and Bob for an interview. Her visits to the residences with Vivien had, until then, been secret; she dreaded telling Lena and Bob about their new home. After dinner, she took them out to get ice cream cones, and on the way home she burst out with "Would you like to live in another place?"

They clutched their cones as if they were tiny, pale torches in the dusk. "It's a house," Ella said. "You'll live with other adults." They looked puzzled. "You will be living on your own again," she said, trying to make it sound like an achievement. "But they'll cook your food. And there's bingo. And arts and crafts."

Bob slurped down the whole scoop. "Where?" he blurted.

"It's just twenty minutes away," Ella answered. The specificity made them more alert.

"Where?" Lena asked.

"Straight down Van Nuys Boulevard. A left and then a right on Mango Boulevard."

Bob dropped the empty cone on the ground and put his hand on his stomach. Lena put her hand over his.

"What about you?" asked Bob.

"I'll come by all the time," Ella answered, feeling helpless. "You can play games. You'll have your own room"— a produce truck rumbled by, and they all jumped.

"Why?" Lena asked.

On the day of the interview, Ella dressed them up. She was the nervous one. She wanted them to look nice — too nice to belong at Panorama Village, even if it was the best choice they had. Bob clapped Lou's aftershave on his neck and smelled his palms; Ella dabbed her perfume behind Lena's ears. They bowed their heads before her, and she combed their hair so that their parts were straight.

"What do we say?" Lena asked.

"Just be your regular self."

"What's that?"

"Joyful and sweet."

Horace Cohen, the manager who preceded Mrs. Lowenstein, took them on a tour. A booming, enthusiastic man, he shook hands with Bob and Lena as if he had just learned he was related to them. He had mastered the art of interviewing vulnerable people. "Do you two enjoy playing bingo?" he asked. "We have a game every Thursday night."

They were distracted, looking around. "I like potato chips," offered Bob.

Horace took them into a sample room, which, though newly painted, had the same shabby tone as the apartment on La Casita. All the rooms were furnished identically, with a dresser and lamps bearing tangerine lampshades. Lena and Bob wanted to touch everything; they pressed their palms to the closet doors, the walls. They pulled open the shower curtain and turned the bathtub faucet on and off.

Ella spoke privately to Horace while Lena and Bob sat in the lobby, examining a yellow yo-yo Horace had given them as a welcome gift.

"What do you think?" she asked him.

"They'll fit right in," he said, as though he had just chatted with them at a party. "Lovely couple. A pleasure to see."

As she walked back into the lobby, for a moment she didn't recognize Lena and Bob. They were hunched forward in their chairs, watching a tiny, pink-haired woman in a wheelchair show them how to use the yo-yo. They seemed very interested in the woman's instructions. Ella noticed only that the woman wore a nubby bathrobe and red pumps. Ella's heart jumped, for she hadn't expected her reaction: Lena and Bob looked as if they belonged.

Ella tried to make their moving day a kind of

celebration. Again, she and Lou put Lena and Bob's clothing in grocery bags; again Ella bought some cellophane-wrapped red roses. Lou offered Lena and Bob his naked ladies snowdome as the beginning of their personal snowdome collection. Ella wasn't sure the gift was in the best taste, but Lena and Bob were touched. Bob clasped the snowdome protectively in his hands during the drive over, shaking it and watching the ladies lose their bikinis again and again.

The electric doors zapped open at Panorama Village, and they all went inside and carried the brown bags of clothes down the hall to Lena and Bob's room, on the first floor.

Ella had expected some fear and struggle, but Lena and Bob walked ahead, as though on a conveyor belt. Lena read aloud the residents' names on the doors: "Helen Horwitz. Abe Hirsch. Betty Winters." Lena paused as she said each name, listening intently to the sound it made.

Ella immediately set the roses in a vase to add a festive touch. "Where would you like me to put it?" she asked Lena.

Lena surveyed the empty room. She ran her hand across the dresser. "Here," she said.

Ella let Lena boss her around. Lena designated the drawers for socks and underwear and shirts, and she was very strict. "That's wrong!" she screeched when Ella put something in a place Lena hadn't designated.

Bob circled the bedroom and darted in and out of the bathroom on a private but significant mission. Finally, he stopped and sat beside Lena on the bed.

"Do you remember where the cafeteria is?" asked Ella.

"Yes," Lena answered. She bent down and tied Bob's shoelace.

Lou was edging toward the doorway. Ella watched Lena hunched over Bob's sneaker and knew that this was where they would live for the rest of their lives.

"We'll call you when we get home."

"I'm going to water our flower," Lena announced, pointing to a bird of paradise growing just outside the window. She filled a drinking glass in the bathroom and dumped the water out the window on the plant. Then she looked back at her mother.

"Bye," she said.

As Ella walked through the hall to the entrance, her heart was beating so hard that she thought she could feel its shape. The electric doors parted; the passing cars seemed remote, unreal. In the parking lot, Lou unlocked the car door and held it open for her, a quaint, gentlemanly gesture.

"Let's go," he said.

She sat down beside him because she did not know what else to do. Her husband started the car. They traveled over the dark asphalt street, which crackled like paper, through the Valley's hazy light. It only took twenty minutes, and then they were home.

Fifteen

Shelley stared at the matted bottom of the pier, trying to see through the cracks to the rest of the day. The late afternoon sun came through the pier, clear and amber. Hundreds of footbeats thundered through the wood as beachgoers made their way to their destinations; she wanted to call out and see who would answer her.

She had stopped moving from boulder to boulder, for one did not feel better than the other. None took her from this terrible, private thought: that she was the only grownup here. To convince herself of this, she tried to think thoughts that a grown person might have. Two kept coming to mind: *What's going on?* and *The rest of the day, I'm a human being.* These were statements the man who had spoken to her had made. Now Shelley wanted to find him. He had understood something valuable about her. She wanted to find him because he had known without even hearing a word from her.

Lena was sitting quietly, clutching her ankles. They had not spoken for some time. A few times, Shelley exclaimed, "It's hot!" just to remember her own voice; Lena nodded. The silence between them made the air seem stale. But she had been afraid to ask Lena any more questions after

Lena said Bob would come to visit them.

Their plans for the day had scattered into pieces, and they were dozens of miles from anyone they knew. This made it difficult for her to think clearly. Tracing three squares in the sand over and over, she wondered what would happen to them when the sun went down. The phrase "lost at sea" went through her mind over and over. Every few minutes, she took a sharp, deep breath to try to keep calm. She hated the sound of that sigh. They had only a couple dollars between them, and the taste of her cherry Life-savers had faded in her mouth.

She stood up. "I have to go out for a second," she said.

Lena's eyes widened. "Where?"

Shelley paused. "I have to do an errand," she said. It was another statement she believed an adult might make.

"I have to do an errand, too."

"I have to go by myself," the girl said.

Her aunt scrambled to her feet. "You have to buy strawberries," she burst out. "Napkins. Hors d'oeuvres. We need food for the party." Lena stood tall. "Remember, Sequin. For our guests."

Shelley wanted to grip Lena's hand and talk on and on about the party. But now she knew there would be no party. She imagined ghostly guests with their sweet cake-breath and their party hats and rubber bands under their chins, but now she could not hear their secrets, because they were voiceless and unreal.

She took a deep, swooping breath and said, "Just wait here. I'll be right back."

Lena rubbed her palms across her stomach and settled down on a boulder. "Go. I dare you," she said.

Shelley scrambled out from under the pier. The afternoon light had deepened, and everything looked as though it were reflected in a golden bowl. The seagulls made great, crying circles of sound above the blue water. She waited for a second to see whether Lena would follow her. When she peeked back in, she saw Lena sitting cross-legged on the rock, grimly patting the sand into the shape of a cake.

Shelley began to head across the beach. She believed she had forgotten how to walk or speak, for her arms and legs were as disjointed as a puppet's. She had to slow herself down, as she was walking faster than she intended, and this made her out of breath. The two of them had run away together, but now, for the first time that day, she existed on the beach alone.

She was sensitive to all the sounds of the world. Her arms trembled; the gulls' cries scraped against her skin. The sand made sugary sounds under her feet. She stopped and surveyed the beach. The world seemed loosened from its rules. She imagined the beach buckling, palm trees jutting up like flowers into the air; she saw the ocean twist into the sky like a glittering blue scarf.

She thought of the different ways she had been alone. She had waited on the front lawn on Saturdays while her former friends had fun without her; she had remained in bed that morning while her family talked in the other room. This was a different kind of alone; it was alone with a purpose.

She didn't know how to go about looking for that man. She wandered past the fortune tellers, the psychics, the guitar players sitting in the hot sun. The sunbathers were a wavy mirage. They looked not like people, but like beautiful, alien beings. She made a large circle around them slowly, so that her footsteps made no sound. She would find the man so that he could again see this knowledge in her, and she wanted to tell him her name.

The beach was bordered by a dry park, and she headed there to get a wider view. The blue shade of the palm trees was cool on her hair. She waited beside a concrete wall, quietly clicking threes behind her teeth.

It felt as if she'd been there a long time, but it was only a few minutes before she saw him. He was beside a boom box, about a hundred feet away. He kept walking forward and back and opening his arms, as though introducing himself to the air. She watched for a while; then her curiosity moved her closer. He was listening intently to the disco coming softly from his boom box; he took a couple of steps, raised his weighty arms, snapped his fingers.

"Who's feeling fat today?" he asked the air with great feeling. He snapped off the tape recorder, rewound it, played it again. She seated herself near the concrete wall, her hands on her knees.

"Hey, there," he said to her. His voice sounded unused. "Are you feeling fat today?"

Her heart jumped sideways when he spoke to her. His question was somewhat odd, but she felt herself answer. "Not really."

"Not really," he said. He picked up his boom box and walked toward her. He walked with the slight bounce of a carefree person, but she could see that the bounce was a little off. "Hey," he said. "I saw you before. What's happening?"

"Nothing," she said.

"Nothing?" he said. "On this beautiful day? Nothing?" He shifted back and forth on his sneakers. "What do you think of my opening line?"

"For what?" she asked.

"For Ambrosio's Aerobics," he said. "So anyone can look like a star."

"Oh," she said.

"Look," he said, putting down the boom box. "I'm practicing for an audition later this afternoon. The Seaside Studios, in San Pedro. Tell me what you think. Imagine the audience here." He drew an invisible line in front of him. "The camera is there." He pointed to the sky. He took a few steps back, closed his eyes, then marched forward, passionately threw out his arms to the invisible audience, and exclaimed, "Who's feeling fat today!"

His huge arms remained open, outstretched, as though he were trying to hold the earth; Shelley found the gesture beautiful.

"Most people think they're fat," she said.

"Exactly!" he said, clapping his hands. "That's part of my theory. That'll hook them. Then I'll show them the way."

She was aware, suddenly, that he was a stranger, but she could not stop staring at him. She believed that a picture of him in a magazine would show him to be a handsome man. And he was asking for her opinion. She waited to be smarter than she felt.

"What's your name again?" he asked.

"It's Sequina," she said, twisting the bottom of her shirt.

The name lilted naked in the air. He smiled a large, sparkling smile. "Sequina!" he said. "Glad to meet you. I'm Ambrosio." He thrust out his hand. After a moment, she understood she was supposed to shake it; his palm was large and rough. His eyes were bright and small and rarely blinked. "Hey, you busy right now?"

She tried not to think about Lena sitting beneath the pier, waiting.

"Why?"

"You want to give me a hand?"

She did not know how to respond, so she followed him.

They were a kind of pair, walking in the same direction across the parking lot. She felt a bit superior to everyone else around them, for her world was different now, bent; it seemed that the light had been folded so that the cars and palm trees were magnified, bigger. He walked so fast that she wondered if he had forgotten she was with him; she hurried to keep up with him.

His car was a battered Volkswagen parked at the far end of the lot. Ambrosio opened the door, took a comb off the dashboard, sat down on the edge of the beige seat and began to comb his hair. Shelley could see an old hair dryer, plastic combs, some free weights, neon Lycra unitards, socks. In the back seat was a rumpled yellow pillow without a pillowcase, a blue sheet, a towel that said *Enjoy Coca-Cola*. Wrinkled copies of *Muscle and Fitness* magazine and a yellow legal pad filled with scrawls, a box of Frosted Flakes, a bag of Doritos, a deodorant stick, and a toothbrush and toothpaste tube were scattered throughout the car. She wanted to see everything inside. The car smelled of wet sand and of male body odor. He seemed to want her both to see everything and to look away.

"Care for a Dorito?" he asked.

"Yes," she said.

He held out the bag, and she grabbed a huge handful of chips and ate them quickly. She was grateful in a way she hadn't expected to be. "Have more," he said, apparently pleased to help her. She ate the next handful more slowly, relishing the spicy taste. He tapped the comb against his palm. "Help me out," he said. "Center or side part?"

"How do you want to look?" she asked, wiping her palms on her shorts. She was proud to be asked.

"Stylish," he said, "but not prissy."

"I think side," she said.

She watched him comb his hair forward and back. His hair was slightly oily, and he seemed embarrassed by that as he tried to smooth it into shape. He picked up a small container of baby shampoo from the floor. "I used this," he said. "I thought it was supposed to be good shampoo —"

"You don't have anything at home?" she asked.

He paused. "This is my home," he said.

"You live *here?*" she asked.

"It's not a bad place to live," he said, a higher pitch to his voice. "I can shower in the beach bathrooms. Nobody bothers me when they see my arms." He looked at his arms as though he could not quite believe they were his. "I don't have to do any of that life-draining shit like wash dishes or empty trash cans or anything like that. I have no goddamn distractions bringing me down." His expression was fierce. "I have two hundred dollars. Here, I can live on five bucks a day. Less, if I have to." She heard the desperation in his voice, his wish to convince her. He waved at the red-roofed condominiums across the highway. "Those idiots; they pay a fortune for their views. I get it for free."

She noticed the harsh, lacy red pattern of sun-burn on his neck, the black curves of dirt under his fingernails. "Don't you get scared?" she asked.

"I'm making sacrifices," he said. "I came here all the way from Wichita. I parked here" — he looked at his legal pad — "sixty-seven days ago. This seemed like a good enough spot. It's quiet at night. I can listen to the ocean. I can plan." He gestured to his paper. "I will first present my class at talent auditions. Spread word of mouth about my unique approach. Then to the stars. I will shape them according to my philosophy." He looked at her. Then, with an innocent expression, he reached forward and grabbed her wrist. Her heart jumped.

"Hey!" she said.

He quickly released her. "Why don't you sit with me?" he said. "Just for a sec."

She remembered standing with Lena and Bob during the dares when they looked through apartment windows into other peoples' lives. It was sometimes unbearable, wondering how the person who sat in those living room chairs was different from her. She was wary of Ambrosio's car, yet she wanted to sit in it.

Gingerly, she lowered herself onto the driver's seat and lightly touched the steering wheel. It was rubbery and cracked with dirt. The sun illuminated the car seat in hot strips.

Ambrosio straightened up his car. He neatly set a small package of Sunmaid raisins, a can of

Pepsi, and box of Frosted Flakes above the glove compartment. He tossed some gum wrappers out the window. He smelled sharply male; it was a thrilling smell, of underarm hair and Aqua Velva and sweat.

He smiled, and his eyes crinkled; he looked old. "So," he said. He looked at a watch stuck in the stick shift and rubbed his palms against his knees very fast. "You look good, sitting there. You like sitting there?"

She held the dirty steering wheel as though she were driving the car. She thought she liked him; that was the thrumming, the feeling of a hundred butterflies in her throat. His forearm was brown and strong, and she had an overwhelming urge to kiss it. "Sure," she said.

"Tell me." He turned and faced her. "Do you think I'm the kind of person who could make a success of myself?"

"Sure," she said.

"Why?"

She was stumped. She looked at the food arranged over the glove compartment. "Why not?" she tried.

"She thought I was stupid," he said. "Dot. My ex. She thought I should just be happy doing that insurance shit. Like I should be grateful. Here's the life I far prefer." He rubbed his face with his hands. "This used to be her car. Ha! She's probably driving around Kansas now, looking for it. But she'd see this car, and all she'd see would be trash. She'd say, What a loser." He rubbed his thighs. "She wouldn't see" — he gestured to the copies of *Muscle and Fitness* — "my library of magazines. My notes."

She had no idea why he was telling her all this. She wondered whether this was what men and women talked about when they sat in each other's car. He had an odd, new expression on his face. He patted back his wispy hair; his forehead looked large. "You're a real special person," he said in a soft voice. "I can tell." He paused. "Could I ask you a favor?"

"What?"

"Could you give me a back rub? Loosen up the old arms."

She was suddenly alert. "Why?" she asked.

"Don't be scared," he said. "You'll be good at it." He turned around and she was looking at his peeling brown shoulders and the curling golden hairs on the back of his neck.

She was sitting in a car with a man who wanted her to rub his shoulders. The world had become a crazy place. There was a black birthmark on his neck.

"What are you scared of?" he asked.

"Nothing," she said. She was just waiting. The world was brimming. It seemed that the trash cans might take off, like rockets, from the beach. She rose up on her knees and placed her hands on his shoulders. They felt like large avocados.

"Good girl," he said.

She did not like the way he said that. She

thought it might be a good idea to get out of the car.

"The Golden Door," he murmured. "That spa where stars go. They're supposed to give great backrubs there."

The beach seemed remote and silent. It was as though she and the man were inside a great, dusty aquarium, separated from everyone else. She squeezed his shoulders once, lifted her hands, and examined them. She was positive there was dirt on them that she couldn't see.

"Keep going," he said.

There was something new in his voice, an urgency. She looked at the food over the glove compartment and wanted to rearrange it, to put the cereal in front of the raisins and then back again.

"Talk to me," he said, in a dreamy voice.

"Why?" she asked.

He was almost weeping. "Please," he said.

She raised her hands an inch off his shoulders. There was only one way to speak to him. "Ambrosio," she said, "what are your secrets? Tell me your fear."

The car was silent. She sensed that this wasn't what he'd expected her to say.

"Well," he said, and stopped.

"Tell me," she said.

"Um," he said. "My wife."

"Go on," she said.

"Mmm," he said. "Cold. I hate the cold."

The yellowed stucco snack stand glared in the dusk.

"You will succeed," she said. "I, Sequina, tell you to relinquish your fear. Throw away your sorrow and bring out your secrets. The world awaits your success." Her voice rang, thin and sweet, in the silence.

Ambrosio turned to her. There were tears in his eyes. She saw a hard swelling, like a tiny, up-raised elephant trunk, under his unitard. He began to stroke her arm with a peculiar kind of tenderness. Her throat ached; no one had ever touched her this way before.

Suddenly, there was no sense in the world. His face was dazed, like a baby's. He clearly had not been listening to her.

"Wait," she said.

He sat, mute, stroking her wrist. She jerked her arm away, grabbed the door handle, and pushed open the door.

"Don't go!" he said. He reached for her bare leg, but she swatted his hand away, got out, and slammed the door. She had just given him a back rub, and what happened! He'd become another animal, and she wondered now what would grow out of her.

The clouds were sinking, brilliant and gold; soon they would blanket the beach in white fog, and everyone would wander through it, calling for someone to love. She was running across the parking lot, running back to Lena, holding out her arms.

Her aunt wasn't under the pier; she was standing beside it, her arms crossed over her chest, her housecoat fluttering in the low wind. When she saw Shelley, she dropped her arms but she did not move.

Shelley ran across the soft sand. Now her hands were curled into hard little balls, and she was knocking threes ferociously against her hips. When she reached her aunt, she was breathing so hard that she couldn't speak.

"Sequina," Lena said, grabbing her arms. "I waited and waited and waited! You took a long time."

She let Lena hold her up, because she was so tired. Her aunt was like an island she had paddled to for a long time. She felt Lena's hands, her shoulders.

"Something happened," Shelley said.

"What?"

"I was" — she held her hands out for Lena to see — "I was in a car with a man. Look." Her palms were pink and trembling and deceitful. She did not know what to tell Lena, but she remembered how the sun lit the lines of dirt on the Volkswagen's windows, making them a dull silver, how the man's shoulders felt soft, how the whole car seemed to wake up when he turned to her. There had been a strange feeling of closeness and a dinginess in the air. All of this pointed to one thing. "I think," she said slowly, "I had a kind of sex. I don't know what kind, but definitely sex."

Lena stepped back. "You did not," she said.

"I think I did."

"Did he kiss you?"

"No."

"Did he touch this?" Lena pointed to her breast.

"No."

"Did he go in and out?"

"No!"

"Then you didn't," Lena decided.

"It was," protested Shelley. It had to be. That was the only explanation for the way the air in the car became glassy, for the way the tiger on the cereal box seemed about to speak. "He was going to cry," she said with wonder. "All I did was give him a backrub, and he was going to cry."

"You didn't do it," Lena said. "*I* did, but you didn't." Lena twisted her fine hair. "It felt good. Nobody cried." She squinted. "Where are the hors d'oeuvres?" she asked.

Shelley sank to her knees, trying to stop the trembling. "I didn't get any," she said.

Lena knelt beside her and smoothed the girl's hair out of her face. "Why not?"

"I couldn't."

Lena stared at her. "You can do everything," she said.

"I cannot," said Shelley.

"I think so," said Lena. She sat back on her heels.

Shelley pressed her hands to her thighs, trying to stop herself from doing the threes. Her heart was beating hard in her forehead, her hands. Finally, she pushed her fists into the sand and held them there.

Ambrosio had not been who she had expected, and she could not keep herself from thinking about her uncle anymore. The beach held an unearthly quiet, as though someone had screamed once and stopped. Someone was missing from the world. The absence was behind the teenagers throwing Frisbees and beneath the water and below the sand and above the sheer gold clouds. Bob was gone; he had left her and Lena ragged children on the hot sand. She jumped up, but the hurt was both inside and out; she had no place to go to escape it.

Lena stood up, too, and efficiently brushed off Shelley's arms. "Are you okay?" she asked.

Shelley couldn't answer. Lena patted her head. "Now I want to walk on the pier," she said.

She pointed to the top of the pier, which stretched into the shining water. The pink and green lights were coming on in the game booths, food stands, the Ferris wheel. Dark waves crashed around the thick log supports that held it up and spray shimmered into the air.

The pier looked like a very beautiful place. But Shelley felt all its loveliness denied her. Her uncle was missing from the world. She wished the gulls would slice holes in the sky, holes that would suck up everything on the beach, towels and cars and sunbathers and umbrellas. And herself. She wanted to disappear, because she did not know how to live here now.

"I want you to go to the pier with me," murmured Lena. She took Shelley's hand, and the two of them walked down the beach.

Shelley, Lena, and Bob had last been together on a beautiful day in March. Riding the RTD bus down to Panorama Village that morning, Shelley felt the cool spring air blow through the window, a sweet and sour combination of lilac and gasoline. It was a happy, optimistic smell. This day, Shelley was wearing all the parts of her new outfit at the same time. The aqua satin miniskirt was one she'd found on a bench at the playground of her junior high school. Her small feet were loose in a pair of pumps with two-inch heels. On her hair was a red sequined headband from one of her mother's dance costumes. To this, she had attached a rhinestone tiara from last year's Miss America Halloween costume, creating what she thought was an unusual, stunning crown.

The RTD bus groaned down Mango Boulevard deeper into the San Fernando Valley. When she saw Lena and Bob, Shelley pulled the cord, skittered to the front of the bus, and carefully made her way down the steps in her high heels.

As always, it took her a moment to get used to the fact that she was there. The world in the Valley was so different; it was hotter, the streets were wider, and her skin was more tender in the dry air. She was often surprised by the relief that embraced her here.

"Hey!" Lena exclaimed. "You're here."

Lena and Bob reached for her, and she hugged them back, holding her head steady because of the tiara. Bob wore a lime-colored T-shirt, Lena wore her yellow apple-dotted Lane Bryant dress. Their hugs were muscular, enthusiastic. Something about the insistence of their arms made Shelley so grateful that her throat tightened. She waited until the bus roared away before she spoke.

"I am just charmed to see you," she said. She kissed her aunt on the cheek and grandly extended her hand to Bob. He looked at it, puzzled.

"You're supposed to kiss it," she informed him.

He did, wetly. She wiped the kissed hand on her skirt.

"You're here," said Lena.

"You thought I wouldn't be?"

Lena shrugged. "You're twenty minutes late."

"Twenty-two," said Bob, pointing to his watch.

"Both of you look grand today," Shelley said. She touched her aunt's hair. "That is a very distinguished barrette."

Lena lifted her hand to feel her plastic barrette, which featured a smiling cow. "I know what I'm doing for the game today," said Lena.

"Me, too," said Bob.

"Mine is better," said Lena.

"Everyone is equally good," said Shelley. Seeing that they did not believe this any more than she did, she added, "You guys. Guess what I am." She propped her hand against the trunk of a jacaranda tree, adjusted her shirt so that it fell off one shoulder, and shot out her hip.

They looked at her, puzzled but interested. "You can guess now."

"A girl," said Bob.

"No."

She strolled carefully down a strip of lawn, a movement she had picked up from a model in a commercial. Her smile was so open-mouthed that it resembled a frozen scream. She took off her tiara and twirled, holding it out.

"Here I am with my hat!"

"A girl with her mouth open," tried Bob.

"No, Bob," she said. He looked discouraged. "Today, as Sequina, I am a fashion star for 1978."

The words echoed, loud and ridiculous, down the street. Lena was biting her thumbnail.

"What do you do?" asked Lena.

"I'm not sure. I walk around, and people copy me." She thought for a minute. "People want to wear my headband."

"You need to put on a sweater!" Lena crowed.

"Excuse me, but it's eighty degrees," Shelley said.

"You're a child," said Lena haughtily. "You need a sweater and socks."

She could feel them pressing toward her, wanting.

"I want to play now," Bob said.

Shelley felt them hover as though she were a celebrity and they wanted to touch anything that belonged to her. Lena asked Shelley to let her smell the strawberry lip gloss that Shelley wore on a string around her neck; then she had Shelley press the lip gloss to her own lips. Bob, who wanted to be included, requested that a waxy spot be rubbed on his hand. Then the three of them shot down the street. Lena and Bob both wanted to carry Shelley's backpack; Lena enthusiastically plowed it along the sidewalk. Bob picked it up and slung it over his shoulder and stroked it as though it were a luxurious fur. Their attention made her heart feel like a humming-bird, fluttering, suspended. There may have been no reason for her importance, but they believed in it, and she decided that there was no reason for them to be dishonest with her.

Their warmth touched her. It felt good to pour love onto them, which they drank in like thirsty flowers.

"Me first," said Bob. His blue jeans were a bit large for him, and he kept yanking them up. "Everyone stop."

They did. They were in front of the Hacienda, a gold stucco apartment building. By the lobby was a bush riotous with red flowers, the color almost obscene. Bob bounced on the balls of his feet, excited. "I dare you to go look in the window of that apartment," he said, pointing to a glass door that was half open. "Step in it for one second and say hello. Then step out. Me first."

Bob crossed the patio outside the apartment with as much stealth as his blue sneakers would allow. He touched his fingertips to the glass, then stepped onto the flat beige carpet. "Hello," he said quietly, his arms dangling by his sides, his palms open as though in supplication; then he ducked out. Shelley and Lena were right behind him. The apartment smelled unused, like a new car.

Shelley stood behind Lena. She wanted to get this dare over with, but she also wanted to know how it felt to stand, uninvited, in a stranger's living room. When Lena was done, Shelley stepped inside. "Hello," she said. The soles of her feet felt raw. Some bananas in a bowl were still a little green. One leg of the coffee table was bandaged to the top with white medical tape. She felt the urge to rush through the place and grab everything. Then she thought she heard footsteps, and she jumped out.

They bounded to the sidewalk and ran to the end of the street. When they stopped, breathless, Bob shoved his hands into his pockets and grinned.

"It was a nice apartment," he said.

"Do you think they heard our hellos?" Lena asked.

"Maybe," Bob said.

They were pleased with themselves. It was as though, through their transgression, they all owned the apartment a little bit now.

"Okay," said Lena, "now me."

She plucked a cigarette from a pocket; from another she took a plastic red lighter. She pressed the button, and up flipped a golden flame; she leaned over and lit the cigarette.

"I dare you to smoke it," she said, handing it to Shelley.

Shelley gripped the cigarette with her entire hand, like a murderer clutching a knife.

"No," said Lena, grinning. She arranged Shelley's fingers so that she held the cigarette between her second and third fingers. "Watch me," said Lena, proudly. She took it back and inhaled.

"Tell her to go *phhhh*," Bob said.

Shelley tried. The cigarette tasted bland, like wet paper; then she tasted ash.

Lena guided her hand to her mouth again. Shelley put her lips to the end and delicately exhaled some smokeless air.

"Look at her, Bob."

Lena and Bob lit cigarettes for themselves, and the three of them walked along the sidewalk, smoking. The smoke rose from their mouths as though it were one gray word spoken by the same person.

"Look how she holds it. Like me! Bob. Doesn't she?"

He stopped and regarded Shelley. He dropped

his cigarette and ground it, primly, into the side-walk.

"I think she holds it like me," he said.

Mango Boulevard was lined with gigantic superstores, splayed out, with bulky grandeur, behind their big parking lots. Beyond them, the street melted quickly to empty lots, tufts of silver-green scrub grass, and a deep concrete drainage basin, which held only a thin brown stream. There was a heavy, clear silence here, cut only by the occasional rush of cars.

At the end of the boulevard, a thick, muscular overpass stretched across the southbound freeway. There were two lanes for cars crossing the overpass, and a four-foot concrete wall rose on either side. Generally, at this point, Shelley, Lena, and Bob turned around.

"Let's go have a snack," said Lena, standing with Bob at the end of the sidewalk.

"I want to walk on it," said Bob.

He stepped onto the overpass; Lena and Shelley followed. Shelley put her hands on one low concrete wall and peered down at the freeway, a long stretch of empty asphalt, shallow pools of oil glimmering with rainbow colors in the light. Every few moments a car zoomed by.

Lena and Bob were uncertain about what to do. "It's a fashion shoot," said Shelley. "What to wear when you're walking by cars." They stared at her. "You are Maribelle and Jacques, and you are my stylists." She set them on either side of her and took their wrists. "I dare you . . . to fix my hair now."

They turned around attentively, and she answered questions that they were not capable of asking. "Yes, Jacques, I think my hair could benefit from more nutrients." Or, "Maribelle, darling, do you really think I should go blond?" They patted her hair with their hands. Below was the whish of cars. "Thank you, Jacques and Maribelle," she said. "Let's go back."

Lena and Bob looked over the concrete wall at the ribbon of freeway, and their faces grew pensive.

"Stand on it," said Lena.

Shelley touched the wall. "This?"

Bob's hands covered his face; he was giggling, almost weeping. "Stand up!"

"Why?"

"I want to see you," said Lena.

"Dare you," said Bob. "Dare you, dare you —"

They grabbed her hands.

Because she wanted to please them, she carefully placed one foot and then the other on top of the wall; it was about a foot thick. She gripped their hands so tightly that she could feel their pulses inside their palms.

A cold thrill of panic passed through her. The wind, tasting of honeysuckle, came as a shock against her face. Her body was fragile in the wind; her satin miniskirt blew flat against her thighs.

The world was completely different. Up here,

she could see some cars rising over the horizon, one, then another, as though they had seen her and were swiftly coming toward her. They were small and bright in the distance, silver fish — and then they grew bigger, and became station wagons and compacts and vans. She thought she would shriek as they came closer, but she didn't; they and their drivers passed under the bridge to the rest of their lives. Then the new cars made a fresh and deafening roar.

Something like joy cracked open, wide and huge, in her chest. She lifted her face.

The sky was so juicy and blue that she wanted to bite it. Her lips, in the dry wind, felt full and hot. It was as if she had never really looked at the sky before, and she wanted to jump up and float in it, surrounded by the buoyant, peaceful blue. Lena's fingers and Bob's were knit hard in hers, and they were pulling, as though holding on to a kite that, if released, would shoot up and disappear. She was certain that as long as she stood here, they would hold her. She knew that if she stood here forever, they would never let her go.

"Okay," she whispered and leaned back, breathless. They caught her in their arms and helped her stand on the overpass.

"Was it fun?" asked Lena.

"It was like an earthquake." Her heart banged away in her chest. "You were good holders." Her fear registered in her legs, all at once; they trembled, filled with air. She started to walk back to the sidewalk, and Lena followed. Bob did not.

"I'm trying now," said Bob.

He was shyly backing away. Shelley reached for his hand, but he stepped back.

"Bob, you already had your turn," Lena told him.

"But I want to stand there, too," he said.

He rushed across the overpass to the other wall, his jeans slipping down as he ran. His arms reached forward, embracing the air.

He turned once to look at them. His forehead was lined with wrinkles, but his blue eyes were merry as a child's. His eyebrows were raised, as though he had just had a marvelous idea.

"Watch!" he said.

Bob leaped onto the wall. And then he sailed over it, in a calm and normal movement, his body falling forward toward the ground.

There was no slowing of the world. Shelley saw the white glare of a gull landing on the overpass, a beer bottle rolling down the right lane, the shudder of a sycamore across the freeway. She tried to run across the overpass, but her legs were uncontrollable, as though she was being kicked from all directions and was trying to kick back.

Now the sky was hard, a blue shell encasing them. There was the wail of swerving cars, the crack of cars against each other. Shelley put her hands on the slab of concrete.

The cars weren't going straight anymore. They were crooked, as though they'd just been dropped there, pointing in all directions. Their horns rose in a chorus, sounding in waves, like a great sobbing; one was a long, flat bleat across the sky.

And there was her uncle, lying very still on the freeway. Shelley's breath went faster and faster. She could not slow down her breath. She began to drum a rhythm on her thighs, *onetwothree, onetwothree.* She was humming *Yankee Doodle* in her head, *onetwothree.* Lena was beside her, making a hoarse, sobbing sound, tiny and high, the type of sound Shelley had heard only in dreams. The two of them stretched their arms into the air, trying to reach Bob.

Sixteen

They had been traveling, Ella thought, for miles. The day was stale and sticky against her skin. She and Vivien had driven slowly all through the streets around Panorama Village, but still they did not see Shelley or Lena. The suburban streets were syrupy with sounds of a Saturday afternoon, the hum of a dozen pools, the slap of a basketball against a sidewalk, the cough of a car engine.

Whenever they turned a corner, Ella thought she saw Lena. The day had played tricks on her from the start: the fire that had swept through Lena's room, the way that Lena and Shelley vanished so completely. It did not seem at all strange to her that she believed that she saw her daughter, in a variety of outfits, walking the street. Once, she thought she saw Lena in a smart navy pantsuit with a matching hat; once, in a flowered muumuu, carrying a shopping bag; once, in a slick black bathing suit, stretched out in the sun. She even thought she saw Lena in a gray suit, gripping a briefcase, as though going to an office job. Each time, Ella's heart picked up. At last she couldn't remain silent. "There," she said to Vivien, as they approached a woman in red shorts watering her front lawn. "Faster. That's her."

Vivien squinted skeptically, but sped up until the car was beside her. The woman turned around and was a stranger. Annoyed, Vivien put her foot to the gas and zoomed off.

Ella was embarrassed. "From a distance it looked like her," she tried.

The red vinyl seats gleamed with the Valley's heat. Vivien sat forward, her shoulders taut, her fingers drumming on the steering wheel. The more fiercely she drummed, the calmer Ella became. It was a flimsy calm and made the car thin as an eggshell.

"Maybe," Ella said, gazing at the houses, "she's fallen in with a bad crowd."

Vivien laughed. "A bad crowd of what? Ninety-year-olds?"

Ella felt foolish. "I'm just guessing," she said. "Lena is a peaceful girl."

"Let's try again," said Vivien. "Where did they say they were going?"

"I believe they went out for a soda," said Ella carefully. "Or perhaps for some helpful cleaning materials for the room."

"What kind of cleaning materials?" asked Vivien.

"Well," said Ella, "some room freshener, maybe, or Handiwipes —"

"When has Lena ever cleaned up her room?"

"She tries," Ella answered. "In small ways. I've even seen her try to make her bed."

"Maybe they went to set more fires," said

Vivien. "Or maybe they went to steal something."

Something toppled in Ella's chest. "How did you know she steals?"

Vivien pulled over to the curb, reached inside the glove compartment, pulled out a container of Tic Tacs, and placed one on her tongue with the care of a gourmet tasting a fine delicacy. She rolled it around in her mouth for a moment before answering.

"Mrs. Lowenstein called me."

"About that, too?"

There was a troubled silence between them. "Maybe you weren't home," said Vivien quickly.

"Where would I be?" asked Ella. "I'm always home."

"All right, all *right*," said Vivien. The car filled with the scent of mint. "One. Let's try to think logically. Where would you go if you'd burned something up? Maybe they got thirsty. They did get a soda. What then? Maybe they went to buy more matches. Or to a movie. Or the cemetery, to visit Bob. Maybe they've been kidnapped." Vivien made a fist with one hand and released it. "Dammit! I have no idea what my daughter might do."

Her voice was shaky but low, as though she were talking only to herself. "I think we should call the police," she said more loudly. "Not tell them about the fire, but I think they could qualify now as missing persons."

Ella cringed at the idea; it suggested that a crime had been committed. "Any minute," said

Ella, "we're going to see them."

Vivien didn't start the car. "Mother," she said, and with that word she brought back everything that happened the last time Shelley and Lena had left Panorama Village. "They were probably walking along the street, thinking it would be a regular day."

Vivien drove a little farther and stopped at a corner that sloped down to the freeway. The cars flowed ahead soundlessly and in unison, as though inhaled by a single breath. One after another, they headed south — toward Santa Barbara, San Diego, Mexico — or north to San Francisco, Seattle, Canada. Now Ella remembered what happened that morning.

Tears of shame sprang to her eyes; her hands were open, grasping nothing. She had let her daughter and granddaughter leave Panorama Village. Ella remembered Shelley and Lena running lightly down the hallway that morning. After they turned the corner, the carpet showed no trace of their footsteps, and the blue walls shone with a bland light.

Now, watching the cruel, glittering cars, Ella remembered everything about the day of the accident. The call from Shelley, her voice so cracked and high that she sounded like a young child. The long walk through the hospital corridors, past sick and injured people. The moment she saw Bob in the morgue, still and white on a steel table, the towel over his hair dark with blood. When she saw him, the shock went through her like a great, consuming pain. That pain helped her, quickly, make a decision; Lena could not see him like this.

Ella was allowed to stay with Bob for a little while. This man had effected such a curious magic: he had made her daughter into a wife. Ella had never thanked him. She did not want to leave him — even though he was not living, she believed he could still be afraid. For the fourteen years that Lena and Bob had been married, she had, in most ways, been his mother. This made her oddly shy; she did not know what to say to him now. Gently, she touched his hand. She had never looked closely at any part of him. His hands were small and somewhat dainty, and his fingertips were callused from driving. Perhaps they concealed a great, unknown talent. They inspired a strange respect.

Ella had so many questions. What was it about Lena that he had loved? What happiness had Lena brought him? What did they whisper to each other at night?

It took a long time for her to leave. She felt protective of him. It seemed that they were getting to know each other then — his hand was limp but seemed somehow attentive. Both of them had been devoted to Lena. She believed he was trying to comfort her.

Vivien swerved into a parking lot; the tires

screeched. They were beside a bright orange brick building. Ella gripped the door handle and looked out. They had arrived at the International House of Pancakes.

"They're here?" asked Ella.

Vivien was half out of the car. "I don't know. Maybe. Let's run in and check."

The two of them flew across the parking lot, buoyed by Vivien's idea. Inside was the dizzy bustle, the smell of maple syrup and fried eggs; there were waitresses and plastic menus with photos of greasy, abundant breakfasts. Metal lamps, shaped like silver trumpets, hung over the grill. Vivien strode quickly to the back of the restaurant, peered at the customers in their booths, turned a corner, disappeared.

Ella walked in the other direction. Ceiling fans turned slowly above her head like propellers. She had last been at an IHOP with Bob and Lena about seven months ago. She could see the three of them in their favorite booth in the corner. Lena always ordered a cheeseburger and Bob a turkey club deluxe. Ella reminded the waitress that Lena did not want lettuce or tomato with her burger and that Bob preferred his sandwich on rye toast. She cut Bob's sandwich into pieces for him and wiped away the ketchup that ended up in Lena's hair.

Lena and Bob ate in the same painstaking way. They had a private ritual involving their french fries and a shared pool of ketchup. Lena would dip her fry thoroughly and Bob would dip his

daintily. As they shared the ketchup, they sometimes whispered secrets into each other's ear.

That day, when they rose to leave, Lena
touched the orange booth, the dirty plates, as
though saying goodbye. Then she clasped her
mother's hand, like a small girl. "That was a
good lunch," she said, and her hard grip made
Ella feel appreciated, good. They walked out in a
crooked chain, Lena clutching Ella's hand and
Bob holding Lena's.

Now Ella turned around in the crowded shop,
acutely aware that she was alone. She almost
bumped into Vivien as she returned to the door.
Vivien was moving in the breathless way one
runs to catch a plane.

"You see them?" Vivien asked.

Ella shook her head.

"Dammit!" said Vivien. "I thought for sure
they'd be here." She paused. "Are you all right?"
she asked her mother.

"I'm fine," Ella said.

Vivien pushed open the glass door. "Let's go."
Vivien's voice sounded strained, a tone that Ella
had never heard. "Let's get back to Lena's room.
We've got to call the police."

Ella followed Vivien across the parking lot,
watching her daughter's hair flutter in the warm,
blue wind. "Mrs. Lowenstein can help us," said
Ella. "She'll have some leads. Just give me a few
minutes. I can talk to her."

Vivien suddenly stopped; she looked stricken.

"Mother, hold on a second. We have to talk."

She rubbed her hands over her face; they were trembling. Ella tried to put her arm around her shoulders, but Vivien did not lean into her, as she usually did. She quickly wriggled to a straighter position and looked at her mother intently, like a lawyer about to take on a difficult case.

"Mrs. Lowenstein called me about something else," she said.

"Yes?" asked Ella.

"We talked about how much she admires you. She went on and on. You know you make a great impression on people. She also says she loves your taste in shoes."

Ella's heart began to march, for these were the kind of words that could only precede some awful statement. The cars in the parking lot were moving into the street with great ceremony.

"People see your appearance first," Ella said. "Then they get to know the real you."

"She asked where Lena's September rent was," said Vivien, "and I said I was sure you'd paid it, but then I thought, well." She was speaking quickly, not looking at Ella. It occurred to her that Vivien was the sort of person who believed that not looking someone in the eye might fool one into thinking she was not delivering bad news.

"Wouldn't it be easier if you just let, well, me pay it and you could pay me back?"

"*You* pay it?" said Ella.

Vivien smoothed her hair behind her ear and, as if she had rehearsed the lines, said, "I can help out, Mother. You can pay me back whenever you want."

"I like paying Lena's rent," said Ella, which was not entirely true. "Mrs. Lowenstein is accustomed to my checks. They're yellow. It would confuse her if she didn't see mine; she might lose it, and then where would Lena be?"

"I know you have a lot on your mind these days," Vivien went on. "Maybe you'd like to relax —"

The fact that Vivien was picking her words with such care made Ella want to scream. "Relax? I'm always relaxing!" said Ella. "I like to do things! I love to pay Lena's rent!"

She remembered, suddenly, watching from her doorway when Vivien walked with Lena to school; occasionally, Vivien would lift a hand to touch Lena's back. Bits of the world rushed in on them — the magnolia trees, the wispy clouds. They seemed almost inhuman in their vulnerability, frail purple shadows, and Ella stood, rapt, until they rounded the corner and disappeared.

"I know you do," Vivien said quietly.

"What's next?" Ella asked. "You want my bank account? To kick me out of my apartment?"

"No!" said Vivien. "Mother! Come on! You have to let me help you! She asked me to do it." The words sat between them, cold as ice. "Just for a while," Vivien added, but both of them knew this was not true.

The noise from the restaurant and street melted together. Mrs. Lowenstein did not want her to write the checks anymore. It was an impossible request. What was she if she could not take care of Lena?

Vivien opened the car door for Ella and walked to her side of the car and they both sat down in it. Vivien's red hair was beautiful, gilded by the afternoon light. She twisted it and then let it fall over her shoulders. It was as though she was trying to prove that she was the child, but it was too late; she had said what she had said.

Ella looked out the window and tried to imagine a future without herself. The world would not need her any more than it had needed her before she was born.

She saw Vivien sitting with Lena and Shelley in an orange booth, the three of them having lunch without her. They would be in their favorite booth, in the corner, and would have many things to discuss. The waitresses would have new uniforms, perhaps with shorter skirts, and their hairdos would float, creamily, in an unimaginable style. Vivien would preside over the table, captivating Lena and Shelley with stories and jokes. Lena would be wearing a silk T-shirt Vivien had bought her, lovely but impractical; Lena's hair would even be dyed a lustrous red. Shelley would lean back in the booth, luxuriously, stretch her camisole over her new breasts.

There would be a more delicious chocolate cake on the menu, and a four-layer coconut cake and other new, inventive desserts. Vivien would order fried appetizers and pies with whipped cream, and they would all eat everything with relish, without making a mess.

She wondered how, then, she would belong to them. It was such a hopeful act, bearing and raising a child. She remembered how Lena and Vivien, as infants, were almost the same, olive eyes gazing up at her with a pure and profound trust. She remembered standing in the dark bedroom when they were infants. She was moved by their position as they slept, small arms thrown over their heads, as though they were dangling from a branch, or one tiny hand on a stomach and one upraised, as though carrying a flag. They slept with utter faith in her perfection. She would stand for a long time in the violet twilight of the bedroom, simply feeling this understanding between them, even more powerful, more hopeful, than love.

Now it was different. It was aggressive; Vivien and Lena were stealing their lives beyond her. She wanted to sit with them; she wanted to come along, too. A storm of greed gathered in her.

"I want to take care of Lena," she said. Her voice was thin and ragged.

Vivien grabbed her hand; Ella assumed that the gesture was meant to comfort her, but its abruptness spoke of Vivien's fear.

Vivien gently moved her thumb back and forth on Ella's wrist. Ella did not know how to respond. She understood, fully, for the first time, that someday she would be dependent on Vivien. It was as though they had just met in this car, two strangers, and she looked at Vivien critically, as she would a stranger, noticing that the part in her hair was uneven, that her lipstick was slightly smudged. She tried to imagine Vivien bringing her groceries and paying Lena's rent. Ella trembled at this outrage, and her body filled with a sick, wild feeling. To be dependent was to be invisible, and her mind shut at this idea. She released her hand from her daughter's, sat straight against the seat, and firmly clasped her hands, like a person who was strong and independent. She sat like this for a few moments, but her assertive posture told her nothing about how to release herself. Then she looked at Vivien, her daughter who was now almost forty, and experienced a wave of sympathy for her, for she did not know how Vivien could prepare herself for this. Carefully, Ella reached over and smoothed Vivien's hair off her face; Ella needed to feel what about them had remained the same.

Ella looked through the window at the customers in the restaurant. They were doing such simple and lovely things: lifting forks to their mouths or bending over their hamburgers or laughing or drinking Coca-Cola. They were moving together in a timeless way, and their

351

casual happiness made the restaurant seem a safe place. Ella sat with Vivien in the car, watching the customers, and wished she were with them. On the thick boulevard, cars streaked by, silent, swift comets, soft blurs.

Seventeen

The pier stretched, shining, into the sea. It smelled like the stale end of a celebration — the pink sweetness of cotton candy and the gasoline engine of the merry-go-round. It was late afternoon sliding into dusk, and the air above the pier shimmered, radiant, under the purpling sky. Pink and orange horses rose and fell on the merry-go-round, their manes blazing. A great, glowing disk spun at shocking speed; it held people strapped to its sides like ants stuck against a dish. There was tinkly music and a delicious, roasting smell and voices shouting, "Two out of three wins top shelf!" Whistles screeched, bells rang. At the end of the pier, Shelley could see the silent, turning Ferris wheel.

"Sequin," Lena murmured, looking up at it. She gripped Shelley's hand. "We can go on a ride."

The name sounded ridiculous to her now — like the name of a baby, a child whose head was packed with nonsensical dreams. Now Sequina was the name of a girl who had terrible pictures going through her mind. She made herself imagine worse and worse things, almost as a dare. Shelley forced herself to imagine how Bob felt, falling from the overpass. She pictured him lying on the freeway, staring up at the empty sky, searching for them.

She could not bear to think of him as lonely. Her thoughts turned the pier and its lights into someone's bad joke. And Lena still regarded it all with an untroubled innocence. "Look," she exclaimed as they walked by the cotton candy man, who was putting a paper cone into the whirling metal bowl filled with what seemed like pink hair. They passed another man who resembled a molecule, for he was covered, head to foot, with brilliant blue balloons. Then came the game booths — slanted Skee ball boards and a table with a honeycomb of drink glasses in which you tossed pennies. There were tiny basketball hoops and boards painted with clown faces whose mouths were jagged holes. Cut-glass dolphins sat beside plush blue penguins and bears with glossy fur. Lena stared at all of them. With her hands balled in her pockets, she asked, "Which would he like?"

Shelley shrugged. "I don't know."

She rushed ahead of Lena, trying to disappear into the crowds on the pier. She wanted to hurt the world. Here, the games were crowded and violent. Boys aimed plastic olive-green rifles at wooden monkeys that popped up from behind jungle scenes. Her ears filled with the rattle of fake artillery. She kept walking forward; she wanted to hurt the world. She began pushing roughly through the crowd, impaling strangers with mean stares. She did not apologize when she bumped into them. She grabbed handfuls of napkins off the snack stand counters and dropped them on the pier. The sleazy music wheezed around her. Every person there would one day be dead, and she would one day be dead, and the pier seemed to be made of paper. No one spoke to her. Amid all the crazy lights and sounds of the pier, there was an overreaching quiet. The continents of her heart had broken apart, and she wanted to hurt something, the world or herself.

At the end of the pier, where the stands cleared, there was the railing and the ocean, a huge, glimmering piece of foil. She went to the railing and held it. Some part of her understood people who hurled themselves into oceans, who wanted to stop thinking.

Perhaps she should be dead. It was a shameful thought — that she was nothing more than a piece of trash. She tightened her grip on the railing and squeezed her eyes shut and tried to imagine falling into the sea. It would be frightening, and the water would be cold. It would hurt, not being able to breathe and sinking quickly into the salty water.

She stood there, eyes closed, standing in front of the Pacific. Her face relaxed, as she thought a dead person's would. She tried to still herself, but her mind flooded with fantasies. Her grand funeral, with lines of mourners snaking out into the parking lot, enormous piles of roses, and a special song created just for her. Her former friends opening the doors to their homes and walking into the street, calling her name. Her family gathered around the table on her birthday, lighting another candle and singing *Happy Birthday*. Each year, the cake would grow more radiant and she would become dimmer in their minds.

The last thought made her choke. It was a sound like a bark, not a sob, but more primitive. Her feeling was not simply sorrow; it was a hot, shameful hope. She opened her eyes and put her hands on her throat and felt the muscles quivering. She listened to her cough as though she was trying to interpret it. Gradually, it stopped. The sea spray rose up in her face; thousands of floating droplets glittered in the air.

She was aware of her aunt leaning on the railing about ten yards away; Lena was trying to copy her. Lena stood with her hands holding the railing, her eyes squeezed shut. After a while, she opened her eyes.

"I found you," Lena said. She reached out, trying to catch the luminous spray. "Will you go with me on a ride?" she asked.

The waves pushed toward the shore, making a long brilliant swell along the length of the beach. Shelley nodded; there was nothing else to do but go on a ride with Lena.

The Ferris wheel man cranked a wooden lever, and the wheel turned. A seat rose before them, and they slid into it. He buckled them in with cloth buckles so frayed that they looked of little use. The seat was blue metal, with blue nails in the sides; the metal had the thinness of a Tonka truck. Tiny rosebuds of dried gum were clustered in one corner. The man swung a wooden bar in toward them, and it snapped into place.

There was a clanking and whir, and the seat began to rise. Shelley gripped the wooden bar and felt the air rush against her face, and the ground fell away, and they were rising quickly, up and up. Lena made a sound like *eeee* and she was laughing, and the chair swung with the wheel's motion so that it looked as if they might tumble from the chair. Shelley wanted to scream. Then the chair swung back, and her stomach filled with air and fell back in place, and she did scream. She was grateful for the motion of the Ferris wheel, for the simple terror it created, for the solidity of the wooden bar. The wheel turned and their little bench kept rising, and then falling. After a few revolutions, the chair crested the top and then stopped.

The chair squeaked as it gently bobbed back and forth. It was as if they were hovering in clear water. Shelley carefully lifted her hands from the bar; her palms were damp.

"Look," said Lena.

It was quieter here, a thousand miles above everything. Below them was the world Shelley wanted to hurt. Each game booth was a tiny box of white light, and there were the players, small as dolls, leaning hard into their guns. From here, she could see the shabby, splintered backs of the game booths and the workers on their breaks, smoking or talking. North, the coast faded into silent hills, and to the south she saw airplanes lifting, wings glowing, into the sky.

The last time she had felt suspended, this high up, was on the overpass. How wonderful that had been! Bob and Lena had gripped her with devoted hands; they looked at her as if she were a beautiful kite. They knew that she belonged to them in a way that she belonged to no one else. They held her up above the freeway, and they knew — with a kind of genius — that she would not fall.

Lena did not seem frightened up here; unlike Shelley, she didn't hold the wooden bar. "Look," she said, "I can see so far. There's the water. There's the sand. There's the parking lot." She sat forward. "I don't want him to be all alone," she said. "I think he'll be sad."

How serious Lena's face was. She rocked back and forth on the seat, staring at the water and sand; she scrubbed her knees with her palms.

"Do you understand?" Lena asked, wanting an answer.

"I think so."

She said it just to say it, for she did not understand. The metal chair floated in the blue air. She did not understand, because he was gone.

Shelley suddenly needed to do perverse, impossible threes. There were two clouds above the right side of the pier, and she wanted to grab the third to join them. Or reach inside herself and yank out a third arm, quivering, bloodied. Everything needed to be fixed.

"I need to go down," she said.

Now she was half-standing, holding the wooden bar. She looked through dozens of empty, bobbing seats to the black rubber mat below. Lena's hand was pulling her arm.

"Why?"

"I can't say."

"Why?"

Lena's face was so sweet. Everything needed to be fixed. There was nothing above them but sky.

"You want to know?" she said. "Fine. Look at me."

Holding her hands above the wooden bar, she tapped it three times — three times with her thumb, then with her middle finger, then with her pinkie. Because her pinkie brushed the bar a fourth time, she had to start over. To six. Then nine. It was such an innocent action. But the sound of each tap was terrible.

Lena watched.

"I'm a crazy person. I can't stop."

Lena reached forward and put her hands on Shelley's. The girl's hands twitched beneath them. Lena squeezed her fingers very hard.

"I'm crazy."

Lena was gazing at her. "Is this a secret?" Lena asked.

"It doesn't matter."

"*Is* it?"

"I guess so, yes."

Lena sat up straight with excitement. Her lips were trembling. "What's wrong?" Shelley asked.

"Nothing!"

Shelley stared at her. Lena slapped the metal seat.

"You told me a secret!" said Lena. *"Me."*

That trust filled her aunt with a joy so enormous, she could barely sit still. She made a gleeful sound, banged her heels against the metal floor, and lifted Shelley's hand to kiss the small knuckles. Her eyes were bright with gratitude. "You said a secret to me."

They sat in the Ferris wheel seat and looked out at the beach. Shelley's pulse slowed until it was almost regular. When she touched the back of her neck, she found that it was damp. There was one breath, then two, then seven — each breath marked one more second since her secret had been released. She had not planned to tell anyone in this world about her threes; now she waited for something to happen. The beach was almost empty. The people seemed to have taken the light with them, and the clouds were rimmed with gold. The hollows in the sand were purple; the sand was like a cloth rumpled over a globe of glass.

Nothing happened; she was surprised, buoyed by relief. Shelley glanced at her aunt; there was one more thing she wanted to ask.

"Lena," she said, slowly. "I have a question.

Do you think you could have stopped him?"

Lena regarded her with a puzzled expression.

"On the overpass. I wish I could have run and jumped on Bob and made him stop." She leaned forward, needing to explain and explain. "I wanted to jump on him and pull him back."

"He wanted to stand on the wall," said Lena. "It was a dare. He wanted to stand up."

"But I want to make him not want to," said Shelley. "I want to go back and freeze the air." Gently, their seat rocked back and forth.

"You're a nice and smart girl," said her aunt, patting Shelley's leg, "but you can't freeze the air."

"Why not?"

Lena shrugged. "*I* don't know. Because you can't."

"Oh," Shelley said. She had handed her burning, flawed heart to Lena, and her aunt had held it and then handed it safely back to her.

Lena held Shelley's right hand in her lap, holding it as an item of immense value. With her left, Shelley kept tapping threes, softly. She touched her throat, the muscles that had quivered with the sound she'd made. There was much she did not understand. Bob's absence was heavy and everywhere, but inside her was a new lightness. She couldn't have frozen the air because. The seat creaked in the quiet, and floated back down to the pier.

The Ferris wheel man snapped open the wooden bar and held it aside, like a chauffeur holding open a car door. In the air was the sorrowful feeling that the day had ended.

Stepping out of the metal chair, Shelley felt chilled; it was as though she was just being born. Trucks drove around the beach, raking the sand and leaving it in ripples, like a shag rug. The pier was filling up with people on dates — college kids, their laughter cawing, impressing one another with their noise. There was a visible police presence — officers in black uniforms, leaning against the pier's railing or walking in that confident, cruel way. Shelley was aware that she and Lena, the retarded woman and the adolescent girl, looked out of place, that others were watching them. Her stomach was enormous and empty, and she wanted somebody to give her dinner.

As they headed toward the entrance of the pier, Lena slowed down. "Stop," she said.

They did. She fixed worried brown eyes on Shelley.

"Is the day over?" Lena asked.

"Almost."

Lena turned her hands over and over each other, as though she were trying to warm herself, and she stared at Shelley as if the girl knew something that she did not.

"What's wrong?"

"I have to say something," Lena said. People poured around them, their voices a rising din, and Shelley stood on her tiptoes to hear.

"Tell me."

"I don't think he loves me anymore."

"Who?"

"It's our anniversary, and he didn't want to see *me*."

"What do you mean?"

"My husband didn't *come*," said Lena. She looked straight at Shelley. "Maybe he doesn't love me anymore."

Shelley was shocked by this wrong, terribly wrong, explanation. "No," said Shelley. "Oh, no." She touched Lena with helpless gestures, as though patting down a huge piece of clay. "That's not true."

"Are you sure?" Lena asked.

"Yes."

"Why didn't he come?"

"He can't anymore." Shelley made these words as soft as she could. "He wanted to, but he can't."

Lena's chest was rising and falling fast, like that of a little bird.

Shelley worried that her words, flying out of her, sounded silly. Yet she needed to speak. "He wanted to," she marched on. "How could he not want to see you? How? In your new top." Her voice sounded like another person's voice — too loud and insistent —as if she expected to be stopped. But she knew that Lena longed for her to be convincing. "And your presents," Shelley tried. "I just — know it. He wanted to come."

Her words trailed off. The lights from the rides bounced gaily in the dark. The other people moved in one direction, as though hypnotized by the dancing lights. She and Lena, in their revelations to each other, had become naked. And this gave way to an indescribable tenderness. Her hands felt small and useless, and she wished they would swell to a great size, like baseball mitts or palm fronds, so that she could hold them over Lena, shield her with them. She had never felt like this before. She stood on her tiptoes again and smoothed down Lena's collar. Then she said, "Let's go."

Lena walked toward the entrance, looking down at the damp wooden beams. She seemed not to notice the people around her, but she did not bump into them the way Shelley had. A sound boiled up from the very center of Lena, a sound like a bright balloon punctured, collapsing. It was instantly familiar to Shelley, even though she had never heard it before. Very quietly, Lena was crying.

Lena went slowly, making her soft sorrowful sounds, and then she stopped. They were standing in front of the Wonders O' the World Miniature Golf Course. The golf course resembled a small, ruined city. Apparently, it had not been used for some time. The green tarp was torn, lit by pale circles from tiny spotlights. Each hole featured a replica of a famous landmark. There was an Eiffel Tower, an Empire State Building, an Egyptian pyramid. Crumbled plaster revealed webbed chicken wire sticking out of the Notre Dame; the White House had only one pillar. There was a cracked, pink castle, swirling up like a strawberry Softee, and a perfect, tarnished Taj Mahal.

Lena stood by the little gate for a few moments, mesmerized; then she stepped over the low gate. Lena was as tall as most of the buildings, and she moved among them like a respectful giant. She touched the peeling gold dome of the Taj Mahal.

"Lena," said Shelley, standing by the gate. A few orange cones had been set outside the golf course, in an attempt to keep people out. "Come out of there."

"Who lives here?" Lena asked.

"Nobody," said Shelley. "It's a miniature golf course."

Lena took a Kleenex out from her pocket and rubbed it all over the gold dome. The tissue tore with her enthusiasm.

"We have to go."

Lena ignored her. "Come here," she said. "You have to come here."

Shelley stepped over the little gate and went to her.

"Is this the best one?" Lena asked.

"What do you mean?"

"We have to clean it up."

Crouching, Lena began to pick bits of wet paper from the white plastic gutter around the hole. Shelley knelt beside her. The wet tarp had a bitter smell. Beneath it, through the wooden cracks, came the roar of the sea.

A red rubber flap covered a little door that led inside the Taj Mahal; before Shelley could stop her, Lena crawled through it. "What are you doing?" called Shelley. "It's a hole." But she too wanted to see the inside, and she followed her aunt. The space was not really a room; they could not stand up straight. A little rise in the middle of the space held a plastic white cup where the ball could fall. Shelley wondered whether any human being had ever been here. The floor, a skein of black rubber, was torn, and the plaster walls were soft and veined with blue-green.

It was strangely peaceful inside the flimsy Taj Mahal. Below the floor cracks, Shelley could hear the hiss and spit of the ocean. "Bob would like this," Lena said.

Squatting, she leaned forward, grabbed hold of the rubber, and ripped it off the bolts; droplets of water sprayed around it. A salty smell rose from the crumbling floorboards.

"Help me make it nice," Lena said, "for Bob." Her words were so firm, Shelley nodded.

They crawled out, looking for a bit of Astro-Turf to install as a carpet. Lena sent Shelley to four different spots around the golf course to find the best and greenest piece. Shelley measured the ancient AstroTurf against her outstretched arm and tore off a ragged square. The two of them shook off the water and spread it over the boards inside. Shelley wasn't sure the room looked any better, but Lena beamed with approval. The room now had a bright green rug. Lena looked expectantly at Shelley.

Shelley, sitting on her heels, surveyed the room. An idea came to her. She would give Lena a party. She would celebrate her aunt's anniversary with her.

"I'll get more stuff," she said. She crawled out, hopped over the gate, and pushed through the crowd. The crowd's hectic energy was irrelevant; she moved through it with a fresh purpose.

At a sausage stand that offered free samples, she took a few pieces and some napkins and put them in her pocket. She asked for two plastic beverage cups, which she filled with tap water; they could pretend it was soda or wine. She went into the foul public restroom and unwound long pieces of toilet paper to hang as streamers. At another stand, she asked for a cup of crushed ice, because parties always required ice. Carefully, she made her way through the crowd, holding the cups of water and ice and the toilet paper.

As she stepped over the gate and past the little monuments, Shelley felt she was walking across the entire world — there was the Empire State Building, the Egyptian pyramids, the Eiffel Tower, and Notre Dame.

Lena was waiting eagerly. Shelley crept inside. She then set one cup of water in front of Lena and one in front of herself. She took the sausage pieces from her pocket and arranged them on a napkin. They shone deliciously with grease. The ice cup she set in the corner. She wedged one end of a toilet paper strip on the ceiling and stretched it, artfully, to the other side. The gold scarf hanging around her shoulders she also took off and tied to a loose nail. Lena watched all of this with a suspicious expression.

"What's this?" she asked, touching the streamer.

"It's a party," said Shelley. "For your anniversary. It can be just us."

Lena stared at the sausages and squeezed her feet. "We have to invite him," she said firmly. "Even if he can't come."

Lena looked at the ceiling as she said this. From the pier came many sounds — the thump of rock music and the whap of Skeeballs and screams of thrilled people on rides. Lena hugged her knees to her chest.

"So," Shelley said. "He's invited."

Lena's face blossomed into pleasure. Her eyes settled on Shelley like headlights, trying to illuminate the girl's real meaning, until she was satisfied that Shelley meant what she said. "Okay," said Lena. She sighed, a long, mournful sigh, and gently lay the present for Bob — the snowdome from Sav-on — in the corner. "Okay."

They had their party. They sat on the small AstroTurf rug, and Shelley put three sausage pieces on one napkin for Lena and three on another for herself. "The sausages," she informed Lena, "are filet mignon, and the tap water is champagne. It is an extremely fine brand, without bubbles."

Lena gave Shelley a cigarette and lit one herself. They ate their sausages slowly, savoring each fatty bite; salty brown juice ran off their chins. The waves under the pier were becoming more aggressive. When they crashed against the beams, a fine spray rose through cracks in the green carpet.

"I would like some ice, please," said Lena, and Shelley pinched up some and dropped a bit into each cup of water. They drank it; it was delicious. They were both quiet, contemplative, like two businessmen sitting at a club, smoking, considering their day. Napkin curtains fluttered, sheer against the colored lights. It seemed as though they were the only people in the world. Each was grateful for the presence of the other.

Shelley remembered that she had Lena's teeth in her pocket; she took them out, and Lena carefully set them in the corner. Lena loosely wrapped her gold scarf over the snowdome and the teeth. They looked more festive.

"Why would he like a snowdome?" asked Shelley.

Lena thought about this. "He likes to shake and see the snow."

Shelley nodded. She hoped her aunt would keep talking. Lena seemed to understand, so she told Shelley more about Bob. "We went shopping together," she said, her voice hushed and reverent. "We put tuna in a little cart." The words continued, each a hard, bright diamond in the darkening room. "I'm called Mrs.," Lena whispered.

They sat like this, the spray below them sending a topaz mist into the room. They rested their arms on the windows, and the smoke from their cigarettes rose into the cooling air.

Shelley thought, briefly, of the world they had left that morning. Her mother would not believe that she and Lena had set up this little party. She remembered how she had been afraid to join her family that morning at breakfast, how her mother had been so worried about her.

For the first time since they had left Panorama Village, she wondered what her mother's day had been like, or her father's, or her grandmother's. This day on the beach had been her own sweet belonging, a secret between herself and Lena. It occurred to her that her family might be worried about them.

But for now, they were at the party. It was important to remember everything. They had put together a small party for Lena's anniversary; they had done this all by themselves. She wanted to remember the blue-veined walls, the rug of plastic, the way Lena drank her champagne, one sip at a time, to savor the taste. It was important to remember how they crumpled up the napkins, translucent with grease, and put them in a corner; the tenderness with which they dipped their fingers in the melted ice.

Footsteps sounded across the tarp. Someone knocked on the plaster walls, and a sunburned face appeared at the window. It was one of the policemen from the pier. Only his uniform made him resemble a policeman; his face was rosy and young. "Hey," he said, "you can't sit there. Property's off limits. Come out."

He declined the last piece of sausage, which Shelley offered him; he just wanted to get them out. The policeman was huge and his wooden club wicked and his gun an innocent, violent item lodged in his belt. Shelley crawled out of the Taj Mahal and held out her hand to Lena.

They stood before the policeman, sneakers damp, their hair tangled; they were exhausted. Shelley felt her shoulders droop with an unexpected obedience. The policeman observed them with a gentle expression. It surprised her; it made her understand that no one else had truly looked at them all day.

"You two lost? What happened?"

Shelley shrugged.

He took a walkie-talkie from his pocket and muttered into it. On the other end, a man's voice spoke in a flat, inhuman way. "Let's go, ladies," the policeman said. "Let's get you home."

They followed him to his squad car in the beach parking lot. His black shoes crunched across the sand. The beach was like the surface of the moon, a barren place. The trash cans were stinking and overflowing, and the sand had become blue-white. Shelley and Lena followed the policeman across the beach. Shelley hurried with the brisk, hopping steps of a little girl, as though she had been waiting to revert to this. Lena loped beside her, fists hard, steps enormous, as though she were climbing a towering hill.

Shelley looked back at the pier just once. The rides, loops of candy-pink and green, turned in silence; the Pacific Ocean surrounded the pier like an infinite sheet of black glass. The lights on the Ferris wheel blinked every few seconds, like a heartbeat. She wondered about the people now on the pier; what would they remember of this night and where would they go. She wondered what would happen to the moments she'd spent with Lena and Bob at Panorama Village. She wanted to keep them safe in her mind. She remembered one afternoon as the three of them walked together. Lena's housecoat was vibrant with flowers. Bob's T-shirt clung to his chest. Shelley was wearing a pair of dangling turquoise earrings with a darling purple beret. While Lena and Bob slowly ate a package of Jujubes, Shelley skipped ahead and then ran back to them. The sky above them was cloudless. Their shadows stretched long against the sidewalk as they headed toward all the brave acts they would do that day.

Eighteen

Ella sat on Lena's bed and watched the day change. She saw the air deepen under the glare of the sky. Ella had never been so aware of the precise movements of a day, the way it shimmered from clear blue to pale orange. She sat, a quiet audience, observing this, and she wanted to tell Vivien how compelling the light was, but it occurred to her that Vivien might not be interested at all.

They had returned to Panorama Village from the House of Pancakes. Vivien called Mel, checked with neighbors, Shelley's friends; then she put in a call to the police, reporting that Shelley and Lena were missing. Vivien wanted to drive again to look for them, but she was advised to wait in Lena's bedroom in case Lena and Shelley called in. This was all right with Ella; after her conversation with Vivien, Ella had developed a low, dull headache, and she did not feel like going anywhere. The day had stretched on for countless hours. She was so tired, she found it difficult to speak. It was enough to sit on Lena's bed and watch the deepening of the light.

She and Vivien discussed the fire with Mrs. Lowenstein, but, in Ella's view, only Vivien and the director were in attendance at the meeting.

Mrs. Lowenstein's face was hard with complaints. In a slow, caramel voice, Vivien told her of Lena's many friends at Panorama Village, her good behavior over the last twelve years. All the arguments seemed obvious, and Ella had thought of them all before, but Vivien spoke clearly, with her own conviction; this made her arguments entirely new. Occasionally, Vivien asked Ella her opinion in a voice that sounded tender, yet insincere; and Ella pretended to listen to Vivien's questions so that her daughter would not feel hurt. After a while, Mrs. Lowenstein began to grow weary under Vivien's insistence; Lena would be able to stay. Ella let Vivien negotiate the cost of damages she would pay.

At 7:05, the phone rang, and Ella answered. She heard a male voice, its soothing authority; it was coming from far away. Then Shelley's voice came on the line. "We're okay," she said. "We went on a trip."

"We're all the way at the beach!" Here was Lena. The sounds of their voices were calming; her ear felt warm. Ella carefully wrote down their location and looked at Vivien.

"I found them," Ella said.

Vivien drove to Lahambra Beach, to the parking lot beside Lifeguard Station 23. By the time they arrived, it was after eight. The day was worn out; the battered snack stands were shut for the night.

A car marked Beach Patrol was sitting at the

far edge of the large parking lot. The lot was slowly emptying out. It was dark, except for some broken, skeletal streetlights; the police car was a lone beacon of yellow light. As Vivien's station wagon drew closer, Ella could see Lena and Shelley in the back seat. They were eating doughnuts and talking animatedly.

Cars streaked down the highway beside the lot, making pale bands of brightness. The asphalt rumbled, loose, under the tires. Vivien parked a few yards from the police car, and Shelley and Lena jumped out and ran toward them. Shelley made excited leaps, as though she could barely stand to remain on the asphalt, and Lena bounded along beside her, in a crooked path.

Vivien flicked off the ignition and jumped out of the car, leaving Ella to open her door. Heavily, Ella hoisted herself up, gripping the door, and then shut it, without much force; the door made a delicate, metallic slap. She began to hurry toward them. She could not distinguish one of them from the others — Vivien, Lena, and Shelley were faceless, purple figures in the darkness, a dozen yards away. "Girls?" called Ella. "How are you?" Her words vanished into the dim air.

Suddenly, there was no reason to rush. Shelley, Lena, and Vivien were a group, complete. The few yards between her and her family were a vast distance. Her mouth was dry; she slowed down.

It was apparent that Lena and Shelley had been in the sun all day. Their faces were sunburned and their hair coarse from the sea air. Shelley wore that tank top; Lena, in her housecoat, looked not quite dressed. They were not wearing sweaters. The three of them were talking, their voices overlapping. Ella felt herself thinning from Lena, from all of them, in a way that only now was perceptible to her.

Here was Vivien, handing Lena and Shelley cartons of orange juice. Her daughter was forty years old. She was talking fast, asking questions, trying to learn everything about their day all at once. The way Vivien stood looked unfamiliar to Ella. Vivien was not standing like a performer; she seemed not to care whether anyone was looking at her. A sheen of sweat glowed on her forehead, and her hair stuck to her cheek. It was as if she wanted to take up a great deal of space, to distribute herself generously to both Shelley and Lena; she was listening intently to her sister and to her daughter. And there was more. Vivien was wearing makeup that Ella had never noticed before — a little pale concealer under her eyes. Vivien was preparing to be older. She had done this quietly, without telling Ella.

Shelley, her hand firm on her aunt's back, guided Lena forward. Gold glitter twinkled mysteriously above her right brow. Vivien had spoken of her daughter with fear, but to Ella the girl was taller than she had been that morning. She walked as if thrusting herself, like a knife, into the air. Her answers to Vivien's questions burst out in a tremendous rush; she herself could not wait to hear what they had done this day. Lena whispered in Shelley's ear, and the girl knelt and tied Lena's shoe. Ella saw how Shelley squeezed Lena's foot and stood up, how Vivien wrapped a sweater around Lena's arms.

And here was Lena. The sand and sky behind her looked like a painting so new that it would smear if touched. Yet Lena looked the same as always. She smoothed down her housecoat and kicked at the asphalt with her red sneakers. Lena did not change, yet the world changed, stubbornly, around her. Lena stood on the cracked asphalt, and the cold night spread itself above her. She rubbed her arms and shivered, but looked at her surroundings with a surprising calm. Lena had been all right during this long day. Ella released her breath. All during Lena's life, Ella had worried about how the world could harm her. But the world could love her as well.

Ella suddenly needed to sit down. Her head felt empty and light and she was, all at once, extremely tired. She walked about twenty feet away from them and grasped the back of a bench. She was sweating, her face and armpits damp. Her knees gave way, gently, and Ella was hanging on to the bench, an act that required great strength. It was important not to fall. She pulled herself over and sat on the bench; the wood felt solid and comforting. Ella listened to her breath, so loud in her ears, and wondered why she was tired. Everything had slowed down.

For a moment, sitting on the bench, she believed she had disappeared. She knew her name: Ella. That was all she knew about herself. The world before her presented itself with great clarity. There was nothing but the beach, the sky, the sounds of the street. She was someone, in a silk dress, sitting by Lahambra Beach. Her hands were those of an old woman, tender and bluish, though she believed perhaps she was also a young woman, because her legs were thin and fine. From the certain bitterness in her mouth, she knew she had recently had a cup of coffee. And she knew from the beautiful rings on her fingers that she was married to a loving man.

She sat on the bench. There was no one to claim her. Her blouse was wet with sweat, and she fingered it with curiosity, not fear; she felt wholly free of fear. The cars flashed by, harshly, and when they were gone, the street was wide and quiet. The beach around the lot spread out, a cool, deserted plain of black. The dark air astonished her, for she had never precisely seen it before. It was the color of deep sapphire, and beneath it, the sand and water and trash cans were radiant and pure. The visible colors were so vivid that she could almost smell them: the red of a beach sign delicious as a strawberry, the flashing green signal on a distant boat fresh as mint. All the plants around her were full of immense energy. Elephant palms surged up, trembling, from squares of dirt. It was as though everything on the earth was rising into this light and darkness, all with the same awkward desire.

She took another large breath, sat perfectly still. Her heart beat fully and too fast. Whom did she love? Who loved her? It could be anyone passing in those cars. The faces of the drivers were indistinct but peaceful, and she saw some of them glance at her with a curious expression. No one claimed her. The beach was exceedingly quiet, the business of other people unimportant and far away. In the air was the tart smell of dried salt, of sour fumes from the cars. There was dark and pale light flowing from the streetlights, which illuminated the purple bougainvillea petals clustered in a damp gutter and lit up the silver of abandoned aluminum cans. Everything was so beautiful, it brought her a sharp joy and sorrow at the same time.

A large gray cat was coming across the parking lot, approaching her with an elegant stride. It stopped, its dark eyes gazing at her. Then it settled down on its haunches, its back feet long and slim as a rabbit's. She and the cat stared at each other. The animal, which had a pale, hairless scar traveling down one side, was still, unblinking. Its tail gracefully flicked up.

She wondered what its name was, what it had eaten that morning. She wondered what a cat saw in its dreams. The cars rushed by. She wanted to know what the cat saw in her, whether it found her beautiful or worthy or sad.

They looked at each other. *"Myaw,"* said the cat. It stepped over to her pumps. Its walk was delicate but determined. Its tiny nose sniffed her feet. Her pumps were falling off her feet slightly. It was too difficult to reach down and put them on properly. The cat knew this about her, too, and looked at her, its face fine-boned and sorrowful. It seemed to want to kiss her. It yawned, and she looked into its wet mouth, its tiny teeth like a sharp white fringe.

Everyone else had faded away; she and the cat looked out at the beach. It stepped closer and butted its face against her arm, as if trying to express itself, and she heard a guttural, savage noise. Then the cat stepped back and licked her wrist, still scented with hand cream, with its dry pink tongue. She watched the cat lick her upturned wrist, its small head bobbing with effort. The cat seemed pleased with her taste and hungered for it.

Ella sat very still as the cat licked her. Her heart was thrumming, fast, in her chest. She stroked the cat's thick body, and the cat vibrated with pleasure; easily, without reservation, it accepted her. There was a feeling rising now from the deepest part of her, inside her heart. The cat's back pressed up, with yearning, into her hand. It wore a dirty clear collar circled with grimy rhinestones. She ran her finger along the cat's thin scar, which felt smooth as glass. The feeling she now had was to surround the cat. It was a very powerful and tender feeling, coming

from the center of her heart; she wanted to surround the cat and protect it from harm. The cat
stared at her with its enormous eyes, and Ella believed that it wanted to protect her as well.

She and the cat sat beside each other for a little
while. Silver clouds floated across the night sky,
and on the beach, teenagers flapped their towels
out on the white, velvety sand. Ella touched the
base of her neck with her fingertips. Her heart
rate had returned to normal. How had she come
to live in such a beautiful place? How had she
such luck to belong to the world? How had she
come to feel such tenderness?

She knew that she was old. She knew that her
name was Ella. A chill went through her, and she
held her breath; she waited.

"Mother," a voice said.

There was a woman walking quickly across the
parking lot. Ella recognized her. It was Vivien,
her daughter. Here was a person who loved her.
Ella's mind felt gluey, as though it were shifting
around. Vivien looked concerned. Ella wondered how she had come to sit on this bench.
Something was wrong with her, and she was
ashamed.

Vivien put her hand on her shoulder. "Why are
you sitting there?"

"There is this nice cat," Ella said, very softly.
She raised her hands to her face. Her hairline was
damp. She did not know what had just happened.
"I got tired," she said, feeling the words form
themselves, like large bubbles, in her throat.

Vivien's hand rubbed her shoulder, and Ella started; her shoulder was sensitive, delicate as paper. She felt the exquisite pressure of Vivien's fingers. It was an astounding thing, to be touched by a person who loved you, to hear the sweetness in another's voice. She looked up at her daughter.

The day had come to an end. Ella felt the heat melting from the air. She looked out toward the Pacific, wondering how the dawn would look to-morrow, flushing orange across the sea. One day the morning would begin without her.

What would she feel, then, while the day spread itself in all its glorious tastes and colors and sounds? Perhaps Lou would drive up in the worn-out Ford they had driven to California, wearing a garish red suit she had never seen. "Hello, my love," he would say, gripping her wrist. His chin would be blue with stubble, and his cologne would smell like an enormous party, tawdry but sweet.

She did not know where he would take her. Ella could only imagine that he would grasp her hand, squeezing it twice gently, the same assured way he had squeezed her hand on their first date. The door of the Ford would swing open. And before she got into the car, she would look back at what she was leaving.

How she would miss the world she had lived in: the way her lemon trees stood, fragrant in the morning mist; the way the warm wind whispered through the magnolia trees; the way the San

Fernando Valley spread out before her as she drove over the 405 freeway, the valley hazy and wide and rimmed with golden hills. And Ella would deeply miss, too, the world she herself had constructed, the world she had made out of love.

This was the world that contained Vivien's exuberant lope toward her, her lipstick shining and her arms outstretched, and also the way Vivien looked away, hesitating when Ella brought her a new decoration for her home. It held the way Lena bent over her snowdomes, organizing them into neat, luminous rows, and also how she had stormed through the backyard as a teenager, when she did not know where she could go. It harbored the way Shelley blushed when she was about to do something exciting and the fact that her hair was an absurd tangle that always needed to be brushed. This world held every single feeling she had had about every person she had loved; it was what she had created: unique.

Ella wanted to be able to comfort Vivien and Lena and Shelley on the day of her death. She imagined them waking up, hollowed, the sun and shadows perplexing them — but they had been shaped by her presence and her feelings.

Vivien helped Ella stand. Ella leaned against her daughter a little, and felt her adjust her stride to accommodate her mother's weight; slowly they began to walk to the car. Thin palm trees swung up, with a kind of joy, into the darkness.

The sky swept toward morning, toward light.

Ella felt the rise and fall of her daughter's breath against her arm. Lena and Shelley were slouched in the back seat of the car, drinking their orange juice. They looked up, their faces alert, as though they had just heard a sudden, startling word. They would ride home, the four of them, together. The car door swung open, and, very gently, Ella took Vivien's hand.